Cate Quinn was a travel and lifestyle journalist for *The Times*, the *Guardian* and the *Daily Telegraph*, alongside many magazines. Prior to this, Quinn's background in historical research won her prestigious postgraduate funding from the British Arts Council.

Quinn is the author of the bestselling Thief Taker series. *Blood Sisters* is her second modern thriller.

🐦 @CathWritesStuff

Also by Cate Quinn

The Thief Taker
Fire Catcher
Dark Stars
The Changeling Murders
The Bastille Spy
The Scarlet Code
Black Widows

BLOOD SISTERS

CATE QUINN

ORION

An Orion paperback

First published in Great Britain in 2022
by Orion Fiction,
This paperback edition published in 2023
by Orion Fiction,
an imprint of The Orion Publishing Group Ltd.,
Carmelite House, 50 Victoria Embankment
London EC4Y 0DZ

An Hachette UK Company

1 3 5 7 9 10 8 6 4 2

A CIP catalogue record for this book is
available from the British Library.

ISBN (Paperback) 978 1 4091 9702 7

Typeset by Input Data Services Ltd, Somerset

Printed and bound in Great Britain by Clays Ltd, Elcograf S.p.A.

MIX
Paper from
responsible sources
FSC   FSC® C104740
www.fsc.org

www.orionbooks.co.uk

To Ben and Natalie

I

Beth

When Lauren found me, I was sitting on the sticky floor, flicking the plug-socket-switch that powered the lights on and off. Staring straight into space.

Click. Off. Click. On.

The bar was empty at that point. There was the smell you get in bars after closing time, when everyone has gone home. Yeast and sour fruit, cut at the edges with a little stale tobacco. I remember looking at my hand, and noticing I was holding a half-drunk bottle of beer. At some stage, the sun came up. Harsh dawn rays began shining through the cracks in the heavy curtains, the blinding yellow hue of outback Australia.

That's when it suddenly felt real.

Click. On. Click. Off.

The yellowed socket was overloaded with multiple plugs from a cowboy lighting rig that should have been ripped out in the Sixties. Back then the building was a prospector's big house, during a short-lived gold rush, when this little nowhere town had money. When that changed, there were more mining men needing beer than ladies wanting fancy houses.

I wonder how long after it was, when someone decided that

backpackers – girls like me and Lauren – made the perfect bar-maids. My understanding was expendable females were a long tradition.

Click. On. Click. Off.

There was a blood spatter on my ankle. It was shaped a little like a bird with one wing. I was still wearing the short-shorts they made us wear to our bar shifts. Not a good look with bony legs and prominent knees.

The outfit worked on Lauren, though. Obviously.

Click. On. Click. Off.

The teacher who used to visit disadvantaged kids in the trailer parks, told us there was something like five litres of blood inside a human being. You don't really appreciate how much that is, until a man's heart has stopped pumping.

Lauren

I mean, I was *hysterical*. That was what Beth said.

'*You were hysterical.*'

I was. Of course I was. Some guy was dead.

Well, yeah, OK. He wasn't just *some guy*. I mean, we knew him.

Some guy is, like, *a turn of phrase*. Beth and I worked in the bar every night. He was *there* every night. We knew him.

No, I would not say we were friends.

No. It is not accurate to say I was his *girlfriend*.

Not at all.

Like. *Ew.*

I'll bet that guy Dillon – the one with all the sketchy tattoos – has been saying stuff. He didn't like me from my first shift, when I got his drink order wrong.

Anyway, it's true, I didn't feel exactly right about it, getting on the bus out of town. But we had missed it once already. It didn't come for a straight week. So yeah, we grabbed our bags and left in the morning. And I appreciate, that makes us look bad.

Dillon

Most of us blokes who drink in The Gold Rush are mine workers. Single and in our prime, if you know what I mean. The pub gets new barmaids every three months. Fresh meat. Keeps things interesting. But I always knew something was wrong with these two. None of the others are gonna tell you like it is, but I will. Blondie-Lauren was a fucking prick tease, plain and simple. She liked all the attention. And the dark-haired one? Fuck me dead. What's *with* that? Like you send a girl who's flat as a board to work in a *bar*?

I didn't understand why they were friends at first. Like, you'd think Lauren would have another good-looking girl. Then I worked it out. I'm smart that way, right? Smart with people. Lauren isn't all that up close. She's boring too. One of them who loves the sound of her own voice. Tried to talk her through all my tatts one time, and she cut me dead before I'd even explained the spider on my neck. Beth was more like us guys from around here. Had a similar upbringing, moving around all the time. She's had some hardships, you know? Lauren was on another planet. Like, after *two months* she still couldn't figure out where to get the cold beer from the cooler. And she acted like it was funny. You can imagine what old landlord Pete made of *that*.

Anyway, I reckon Lauren kept Beth around to make her look

better. I told Lauren that too. That's when she started getting mean. Giving me the old brush-off. Well, maybe just after that. Few days before the camping trip.

2

As the familiar police station comes into view, I'm fighting a pop of anxiety. I take out my ID. The picture shows a young woman with scruffy blonde hair, making fierce eye contact with the camera. Tara Harrison. Probationary Constable.

The metal-clad box of a building with its Australian flag hasn't changed at all in six years. As I press my palm on the heavy door, bad memories filter up of my time here as a civilian.

Inside, the small waiting area has three metal chairs bolted to the green lino floor. A woolly-hatted Aboriginal woman is watching a vending machine where a pack of Cheetos has only partially fallen, caught suspended in its coil.

She makes a slow double-take of my blue eyes and tanned skin against the navy box-fresh police uniform as I enter.

'Tara?' She's staring in disbelief. 'You in fancy dress or something?'

'Hello, Aileen.' I look down self-consciously at my clothes. 'I'm a probationer cop now.'

She returns my uncertain smile. 'Heard you moved to the city.'

'Yeah, I got sick of equality and good coffee. Thought I'd come back here for some bad treatment.' I grin. She smiles back.

'I'm only in Dead Tree Creek until I earn my stripes,' I explain.

I glance at the vending machine, walk to the side, and slam it with my shoulder. Her snack drops free.

'Rough town for a trainee cop,' says Aileen.

'So people keep warning me.' I'm trying to keep a light tone, because the shock in her face at seeing me dressed for work hasn't gone away. 'What brings you here?' I ask. 'Someone in trouble?' I jerk my head in the direction of the secure door whilst stooping to retrieve her food.

'Misunderstanding with one of Mirri's kids,' she says, her eyes flashing thanks as she takes the Cheetos from my hand. 'I'm here to pick him up.'

We exchange an uneasy glance. 'Misunderstandings' between police and the Black community are why I joined the force.

'Is someone coming to give you a ride home?' I ask.

'Nah. Them with cars, they're all working today.'

I reach into my pocket and pass her my keys. 'Red car out front,' I tell her. 'Pump the gas pedal hard or she won't start.'

'Appreciate it, Tara. I'll get one of the boys to drop your car back later.'

I shrug. 'You've done me heaps. I'd better get inside.' I head towards the interior security door and fit my key.

On the other side is a familiar space. An unmanned desk. Rooms beyond, two with safety glass windows. An ancient fan grinding away. Out of view, a snoring sound suggests someone is sleeping in one of the two cells. The station is eerily empty. The complete opposite to the madhouse of Perth.

My eyes glide to a large map of Australia on the wall, its corners peeling away. Left-centre, is a jagged red-marker outline of the station's jurisdiction.

Three thousand square kilometers of red dirt.

In the centre is the tiny speck of Dead Tree Creek – now just a grid of streets, the old river having long since been run dry by the mining industry. The smaller Aboriginal Moodjana community sits north, a few kilometres out of town. I stare at it for a moment. As a kid I lived in the suburbs with my foster sister, but as soon as we got old enough, we spent most of our time with her mob in their place. I've not been back for years.

Taking a breath, I head for the open door marked, SERGEANT ANDERSON.

He's at his desk reading some papers, exposing the thinning parts of his white-streaked strawberry blond hair. He looks up to reveal the genetics of a man who doesn't belong in outback Australia. Heavily freckled skin, and a nose knobbled by relentless sun damage. He might have been a constable when I was last here. Like me. The weirdness of that throws me, and he starts speaking before I can announce myself.

'Harrison. I've been trying to get hold of you all bloody morning,' he says, without preamble. 'Something's come up.'

Before I can ask what, Anderson reaches across to grab a sheet of paper from the far edge of the desk. I catch my name at the top. 'So you're making a go of the police now, eh?'

'Yes, sir.'

'Good. When I knew you, you were just a scruffy young girl giving us coppers grief.' His washed-out blue eyes are on mine, piercing for all their lack of colour. 'You could still do with dragging a comb through that bloody bird's nest,' he adds. 'Police set an example to the community.'

'Wishful thinking, in this town I think, sir.'

His eyes flicker amusement. 'Maybe, Harrison, but that doesn't stop us trying.'

He looks like he's about to say something more, then changes his mind, dropping his eyes back to my file.

'I imagine Perth have already told you. This beat is a tough learning curve for rookies. You qualify at my discretion, and I don't do any female-quota-filling bollocks. It's merit or not at all.'

'Quite right, sir,' I tell him. 'Why bow to progress?'

He eyes me for a moment. 'Let's see how you go,' he says finally. 'I know we're all supposed to be right-on nowadays, but I'll tell it to you straight. This is a mining town. Little thing like you is not going to be much help to their partner if they get into strife.' He shakes his head. 'When I joined the force, there was a minimum height.' He looks me up and down sadly. 'People don't realise what police out here are up against.'

'I might be small, but I'm strong and I keep going. Like the Duracell bunny.' The joke falls flat. 'And maybe my partner won't get into so much strife with me around. Female cops are more likely to have a conversation before getting heavy.'

Anderson gives a dry laugh. 'Spoken like a true city copper,' he says. 'Last policeman round here who tried to talk down a fracas wound up with a pool cue as a facial piercing.'

He claps his hands together.

'Well, like I say, I was trying to get you in early. Something big's gone down, and we need all hands on.'

My heartbeat picks up. I wasn't expecting a chance to prove myself so soon.

'What happened?'

He looks me dead in the eye. 'A murder in the local pub, Harrison. Bloody bad one. Horrific, to tell you the truth.'

3

Dillon

You want to know about that last lock-in? It got really messy, really fast. Us mining blokes who drink in the bar had never seen anything like it. It was like a dick-swinging contest, only with girls. And fuck me dead. Girls can be fucking evil.

I reckon they got carried away, eh? Sense of power and all that. You could see it in their eyes. Lauren had this mad look to her.

Everyone's saying she killed Paul. Seeing her that night, I can believe it. One of the fellas cracked a tooth and Skinny Dave says it still hurts when he uses the toilet.

Sex game gone wrong is what all the blokes reckon. 'Cause Lauren was into that stuff, wasn't she? Bondage or whatever you call it. I know I like getting inked-up and all, but she was into pain in a serious way. It's not only me that says it. Paul had pictures. And you only had to be there that night. The things she made us do, you know? What they get up to in American colleges, they got no business complaining about a bit of banter.

Lauren

We wanted to get our own back. That's the whole point of hazing, isn't it? We paid our dues. You get your own back in the end.

Beth

When I think back, I guess it all started in Thailand. We got scammed. Lost all our money, besides some cash in our pockets.

After that it was only a matter of time before we needed to find work. Or rather, *I* needed to find work. I'm fairly certain that Lauren could have called home at any point. She was maybe playing along, being a good friend. I don't know. We've been buddies since college, so I know how wealthy her family are.

I said to Lauren we should go to Australia next, because we had these open-jaw tickets. We had been planning on Venezuela, but we could pick fruit or work on farms. Save up.

I don't know what got into Lauren in the recruitment place. Maybe she was hungover. In college, I always looked to Lauren to know what to do. Out in the real world, though, it was definitely the other way around.

The agency lady took an instant dislike to Lauren. Some people do. Personally, I think her lack of inhibitions is completely refreshing. And what people don't get, is Lauren might look in her pocket mirror and say out loud how gorgeous she is or something, but it is a total outer shell. Underneath she is not confident at all.

The lady had a phone call come through. I remember her saying: 'I don't hire anyone who lies on their CV. If they lie, they'll cheat. And if they cheat, they steal.'

I had this nasty feeling she was talking about me, but of course she wasn't. But coming from poverty, you're used to people forming a bad impression of you, not based in fact.

Halfway through the call, Lauren gets up, helps herself to some water. Then starts, kind of, *moseying* around the office, lifting papers and things. The recruitment lady's face was hilarious. She flapped her hand at Lauren, like, *sit down!* And Lauren comes and sits down all puzzled, like she can't figure out what she did wrong.

The agency lady got off the phone. The files in front of her she moved to one side. Like, *not for you!*

She looked at us carefully, tapping her nails.

'Not much work about,' she says. 'Banana picking season is basically over and capsicums won't start for another month. I do have some bar positions.'

We sat up a little in our seats.

'A place on the outskirts of town,' she says. 'Technically a strip joint but you'd be waitresses, wearing the teeniest tiniest little uniforms. Crop top and hot pants. Means you get a lot of tips.' She was looking at Lauren.

Lauren glanced at me. 'What do you think?'

'Sounds OK,' I said uncertainly. 'I mean,' I tried to sit up straighter, 'if you think they'd want me.'

We both knew they'd want Lauren.

The woman looked me briskly up and down.

'You'd do fine,' she said, picking up the phone. 'I'll give 'em a call.'

She made another lengthy call. I was praying Lauren didn't go for another look around. Eventually the lady put the receiver down.

'Good news and bad news,' she said. 'They've just been raided. They're not so keen to take on foreigners without visas for waitressing. What they do have is a slot for a couple of dancers.'

There was a pause.

'Like . . . lapdancers?' said Lauren finally.

'It's all very classy,' said the woman. 'You'd be on stage, using a pole. Technically you're freelance, so no visa problems. You don't have to interact with the audience. Not if you don't want to, anyway. And you keep your knickers on.' She meant panties. 'Again, if you want to. Your call.'

'We're not that desperate,' said Lauren, with this dismissive snorting sound.

The lady made a big deal of pausing. I was anxious now. I had fifty bucks to my name and it looked like there were no jobs.

'That leaves . . .' She picked up a piece of paper. 'There is a place, but it's in the outback,' she said. 'I mean real outback. Not Alice Springs.'

'Well . . . OK,' replied Lauren. 'Part of our itinerary was to make a trip to The Outback.'

Lauren said it with capital letters, like it was the Taj Mahal, or Hollywood Hills, and you could tell the lady couldn't imagine anything more stupid, than going out into the middle of Dirts-ville just to take a look. Coming from Dirtsville, Nowhere, USA myself, I couldn't help but take her point.

'There's a pub,' she explained, speaking slow like we might be hard of hearing. 'Real local place. Best meat pie for two hundred kilometres.'

We only figured out that joke later. Best meat pie. Only meat pie. Ha ha.

It's funny until you actually have to *eat* that meat pie.

'We'd love that,' interjected Lauren. 'Local culture.'

'Ri-ght,' said the woman. 'Well, there's a lotta that, to be sure. I won't lie to you, girls, the landlord out there has had some problems in the past. He's an old-fashioned type. Used to work the place with his wife, but she died five years ago and things have gone a bit downhill since. He likes things done a particular way. Been there a gazillion years. Lives in his own little bubble, if you know what I mean.'

We didn't.

'Hashtag-Me-Too has skipped him by, put it that way,' she said, framing quotes with her hands and taking in our confused expression. 'Ordinarily we send girls somewhere else. Lotta nice pubs between here and Alice. Family run places. But since fruit-picking season is coming to a close, all the other jobs are booked.'

'It's just bar work, right?' said Lauren uncertainly. 'No . . . table dancing?' She glanced at me. 'It sounds good, right?'

'You need a sunny disposition,' said the lady, staring hard at me.

'Oh, that is me, totally,' said Lauren. 'I am *always* sunny. It's a life skill I have.'

It was true but the lady looked annoyed.

'I like bar work,' I said.

She looked at us some more.

'We-ell,' she said. 'It's free accommodation, free food. The girlies who work hard, they leave with good money.'

'What about the ones who don't work hard?' I asked.

'Well. They tend to just . . . y'know, leave.' Her fingers danced around the desk. 'But you look like good workers. I can make a call, getcha a ride this afternoon.'

Relief was flooding through me.

'Sign us up,' I told her, looking at Lauren, who shrugged.

The lady reached for her phone. Before she dialled the number, she looked at us both again.

'You sure you girls don't want to be dancers?'

4

In Sergeant Anderson's office, his words hang in the air.

Murder. A bloody horrific one.

I stare back at him. His beat is in a wild town of miners and prostitutes. Anderson isn't a man to use phrases lightly.

'Victim is a white male, aged twenty-nine. One of the mining regulars who drank in the pub. General opinion is the murder was carried out by two backpacker girls who worked behind the bar for a couple of months or so.' He pauses. 'There was a lock-in. Drinks after hours. Dead bloke is Paul Hunter,' he adds, as though this explains it all. 'He was the same age as you, so you must have gone to high school together.'

'I remember the name,' I say, dredging details. He was in with the crowd of popular kids. A football player.

'You can understand why a young woman might take against him?'

'I haven't seen him in nine years,' I say. 'And I didn't know him very well then. Different mobs, you know.'

'But?'

I shrug. 'I thought he was a prize dickhead, who fancied himself a ladies' man.'

I expect him to remind me to use impartial facts. But he nods.

'Paul can't-keep-his-hands-to-himself Hunter,' continues Anderson. 'Two pretty Americans. Locked in a pub together with a lot of strong grog. It was a bloody recipe for disaster.' Anderson clears his throat. 'Not the kind of thing I'd put a new recruit on if I could help it. *But*. I'm a man down, because Craig is out on the road. And some kids have already managed to get into the crime scene through a *window*, or cellar door or something; took pictures of the body. Uploaded on bloody-Insta-whatsit. Townfolk are getting hysterical. We need to police the area, keep people away, alright? Until the clean-up people arrive from Perth.'

'You're bringing in outside clean-up?'

'Blood splatter experts, the works. Like I said, it's a bloody shocker in there. Word on the street is the blokes in the pub gave those girls a standard Gold Rush welcome, if you know what I mean. No joke too blue. Looks like these backpackers blew up over it.'

'You wonder what made them do it,' I say.

'Americans are more sensitive, maybe,' opines Anderson.

'I meant the blokes, sir. Why treat the barmaids so badly?'

Anderson looks confused.

'The other officers are out on the road?' I ask, deciding to change topic.

'Officer,' he corrects. 'Singular. He's tracking down the suspects. Lauren Davis and Darla-Beth Jackson jumped on a bus out of town first thing this morning.'

He pauses. Takes a breath.

'If they did it, it's a bloody terrible thing, what those girls were capable of,' he said. 'You're in at the deep end, Harrison, no doubt about that.' He throws his freckled hands apart in a gesture of uncertainty. 'Like I say, I got no choice. In a couple of days, Perth will send their boys, and commandeer the case for themselves. Until then it's all on us. I need you to secure the door or window, or however those kids got in. And get some plastic sheeting over the corpse before the flies get it.'

'Isn't that contaminating the crime scene, sir?' I'm wondering why the sheeting wasn't put down right away.

'Yes, it is, Harrison, but if the alternative is to let the town's population of teenagers sneak in for a selfie with the body, whilst two thousand bluebottles chew on the victim, I reckon it comes down to lesser of two evils. So I'm expecting you to be bloody careful and keep this between us. Wear gloves. Refrain from pouring yourself a pint and using the bathroom.'

I nod, the logic of it weighing heavily against my training. 'I won't let you down, sir.'

'See that you don't.' He locks eyes with me. 'I've read your file,' he says. 'Top marks on all your written tests. But as far as I'm concerned, your firearms scores are a fail. You'll need to get those up.'

'I got the highest mark for fitness,' I point out. 'My superior officer in Perth said that could count towards firearms . . .'

'Not on my beat,' says Anderson, firmly. 'You got blokes in this town who bench a hundred kilos for fun.' He eyes my arms pityingly. 'I need you with good weapon skills for your own safety. I don't hold with sitting a few exams and fast-tracking to a senior role. In my day you learned on the job.'

'Yes, sir.'

'Alright, get going, Harrison. You know the pub, right? Gold Rush Hotel.'

'You sure they'll let a woman inside, sir?'

'Very funny, Harrison. It's not as bad as it was. One of the young blokes from the Aboriginal reserve will be waiting to let you in.'

'Reserve, sir?'

He picks up on my tone. 'Isn't that what we're supposed to call it nowadays?'

I wrinkle my nose. 'I guess it just sounds a bit . . . I dunno, like you're protecting wild tigers or something. The Moodjana people call it the mission.'

'I thought "mission" was offensive. Enforced Christianity and all that.'

'The Moodjana never converted, just kind of absorbed the bits of Christianity they agreed with. So I guess they've taken that word's power, you know?'

Anderson shakes his head. 'I can't keep up with this stuff. Reserve. Mission. Whatever you want to call it. The local fella is called Jarrah. Sometimes helps unload their beer barrels now the landlord's past it. You know him, right?'

'Yes.' I've been trying to forget all about him.

'Not seen him for a bit?' suggests Anderson.

'I haven't been back to the Moodjana community since my sister's funeral.'

Anderson frowns. 'Your foster sister, you mean? The Aboriginal girl who died?'

'Died in police custody in this station, yes, sir.' I keep unwavering eye contact. 'And we were both fostered, which makes us sisters in my book.'

Anderson looks as though he is considering saying more on the subject but changes his mind. 'We're still waiting on another vehicle,' he says. 'But you've got your own car, right?'

'Yeah. Not right at the moment,' I qualify. 'Someone's borrowing it.'

Anderson's brows move together. 'And when will you get your car back?'

'Probably tomorrow.'

Anderson makes an exasperated noise. 'Well, you can walk to The Gold Rush but it's bloody hot out there. Use my car for the time being.' He slides the key over the desk. 'Don't run it flat out,' he adds. 'She's got a two-hundred-horsepower engine and one hundred and ninety-nine of them are dead.'

'Thank you, sir,' I say with feeling, as my hand closes on the key. 'For giving me the chance.'

'No need to thank me, Harrison,' he says gruffly. 'I've only got you and Craig to police three thousand kilometres and he's got a better car.'

5

The Gold Rush Hotel is a big building, taking up an entire corner of a block. A wrought-iron veranda in pale green creates a shaded walkway on the street below. The sign above the entrance where the two streets meet is recently painted but completely outdated.

Like Anderson said, Jarrah is outside waiting in the beating mid-morning heat. It's a strange feeling, seeing him again. Annoyingly, he's even more good-looking now. Broad shoulders prominent beneath his red T-shirt, and a few extra centimetres on his softly waving dark hair. He looks older than the laidback musician I remember. The brown eyes I've been trying not to think about since I left still have that unusual golden hue.

'Tara!' I wasn't sure how he'd greet me, but his smile is totally disarming. 'Welcome home.'

I smile back, struggling to make eye contact. 'Hi.'

Perfect. I've regressed to the ten-year-old girl with a massive crush on Yindi's older cousin.

His eyes track to my uniform and his happy expression falters. 'Not sure I'll ever get used to seeing you dressed that way,' he says wincing. 'Prefer you in T-shirt and boardies, eh?' He winks.

Is he flirting with me? Jarrah is my shortest and longest

relationship to date. Friends for eight years, two more to realise how we felt about each other. Then . . . I don't like to remember how quickly it all fell apart.

I look at my shirt self-consciously, then force myself to look into his eyes.

'After Yindi,' I say, 'I had this idea I could get justice, you know? Do something from the inside.'

Jarrah's face takes on a mischievous smile. 'You thought you'd come in with your white skin and save all us poor blackfellas?'

I laugh. 'Maybe a bit in the beginning. I was so angry. But . . . when I started learning all the police stuff, it became more than just about doing something for Yindi, you know?'

Jarrah raises an eyebrow. 'True?'

'Yeah. It's the first thing I've been good at. Even made me care enough to get my head around the books.'

Jarrah absorbs this. It's funny how easy he is to be around, after so long apart. Some people are like that, I guess. You feel like yourself with them. I find my mind drifting to whether he has a girlfriend now, and I pull it back.

'I've got a bit of purpose too,' he says. 'I'm studying to be a human rights lawyer. And I'm involved in a lot of community projects now. Helped build the new school. We're fixing the meeting hall roof now.' He pushes a hand through his wavy hair, like he's proud but doesn't want to admit it. When I knew Jarrah, he played music when he wasn't singing and wrote songs with any leftover time. I guess Yindi's death affected both of us differently.

'You still play guitar?' I ask.

'Yeah. 'Course I do. You still speaking some of our lingo?' He has switched to the Moodjana language.

I shake my head, keeping doggedly to English. 'I don't have any connection to the community anymore.'

Our eyes meet for a moment. It's impossible to read his expression.

'Shame,' he says finally. 'Your Moodjana wasn't bad. You'll come down and see Mirri, though; your honorary mum?'

He's joking about Mirri. She's everyone's mother, who'll let her. House full of kids, and I was always welcome there. Mirri is all soft curves and smiling eyes – the exact opposite of the foster mother who added me and Yindi to her house of neglected kids.

Jarrah is waiting for an answer.

'Um.' I rub behind my ear, where sweat is stinging from the sun. 'Yeah, probably after I've got settled.'

He looks annoyed. I'd forgotten how he could always read me.

The pause widens. I glance over to The Gold Rush, and suddenly we're both very aware of why I'm here.

'Lot of our mob reckon Paul Hunter caused trouble in the community, you know?' he says finally.

'What kind of trouble?'

'There was a big fight. One of the Elders, Uncle Jimmy, accused him of arranging parties with our girls. The young pretty ones.'

I feel the hairs on the back of my neck stand on end. 'Has it been reported?'

'Probably not. You know how things are. People are afraid. Report a problem and the welfare come and take our little kids away, eh? Like what happened with Yindi.' Jarrah jangles the keys. 'Given to some weird white foster farm. No offence.'

I shrug. 'They weren't my family either. I was just lucky Yindi was there. Don't know how I would have survived without her.'

We exchange a look.

'I'm proud of you, turning copper,' says Jarrah, finally. 'Make something good come of it, I say.'

He turns to the door and fits the large key.

'You ready?'

It's all happening too fast. 'Have you seen it?' I'm stalling. Suddenly the last thing I want to do is go inside.

Jarrah's eyes cloud. 'No, but I saw the other copper when he came out. Want me to go in with you?'

'I'm OK.'

'Sure? It's no bother . . .'

'I'm sure. It's a crime scene.'

He unlocks the door and pulls it open, unleashing a waft of pub fumes.

'Take care in there,' adds Jarrah, stepping back to let me go past.

I barely hear him. The fear is hitting me.

Inside is dark, with chinks of bright light shining through gaps in the heavy curtains. Dust and a few fat blowflies turn circles in the slices of sunshine. The wood-panelled bar is up ahead. Almost immediately as I step further in, the boozy tang takes on the metallic edge of blood. The flies are already settling in one area. Only a handful, but by midday, this will be a black hump of wings and eyes.

Heart thudding, I unroll the plastic sheeting given to me by Anderson.

The dark mass beneath the flies has a shape now. One I can't quite identify as human. I force myself to put one foot in front of the other.

When I'm a few metres away, I make out a hand, bloodied, curled up. Muddied fingernails. The wrists are secured behind the back with . . . handcuffs. Blood and dirt-spattered fluffy pink handcuffs.

Shade by shade, other details reveal themselves. Bruises. Blood clots. What's left of Paul Hunter is unrecognisable. Was he beaten? Tortured? There's a ragged dirty opening where a mouth once was.

A pulse surges in my throat, and I swallow hard. But now my stomach is heaving. I throw the sheet wildly at the body and it lands only partway on the remains, sending blowflies winging away in all directions.

Shit. Shit.

I hold my breath, step forwards, and tug a corner of sheeting to fully cover the corpse. I want to straighten the plastic, respectfully right-angled, but nausea wins the fight. I lurch for the door, hand tight over my mouth and race out on the blistering street.

Trust my luck, Jarrah is still out there. In two staggering steps I pitch forward and only just manage to chuck my guts up into the nearest drain. Jarrah takes a quick step to my side, and sweeps two falling strands of blonde hair back from my face.

Great start to the new job, Tara. You've lost your breakfast in front of your high school crush.

'That bad, eh?' Jarrah says, sympathetically, still holding my hair. I only manage a half nod, before a second wave hunches me back over the drain cover.

I straighten, wondering where the hell I'm going to clean myself up. I've never been the kind of girl who carries Kleenex.

'Here.' Jarrah notices me patting my pockets, takes his T-shirt off in a single-handed easy movement and passes it to me.

'I can't use your shirt.' I'm looking everywhere but his chest.

Jarrah presses it firmly into my hand.

'Crikey,' says a high-pitched male voice from somewhere near my shoulder. 'Female coppers, eh? No stomach for it, I reckon.'

I straighten up and turn, trying to pull together the remains of my dignity, grateful for the T-shirt to hold to my mouth.

The speaker is a wrinkled old man in an outsized black cowboy hat. He eyes Jarrah, now dressed only in jeans and sneakers. 'I see you wasted no time getting undressed for the pretty police lady,' he observes.

A flicker of annoyance flares on Jarrah's face. I catch his eye and it melts away.

'I'm Pete, the landlord,' the little man says. 'I won't shake your hand.' He tilts his head, looking angry. 'Best come upstairs,' he decides, indicating the first floor of the pub with his head, 'I'll show you what those girls have done to the place.'

6

Lauren

Beth and I became besties at our college sorority. For two years, we did a bunch of stuff that was *supposed* to be charitable works but was just a donation tacked to an excuse for a foam party, or an all-night pancake house. I felt protective towards Beth from the get-go. Not everyone is neurotypical. Not everyone makes a lot of eye contact. People are different. But college girls can be very judgemental. Like, I've heard people say Beth looks shady. She has a cunning face or untrustworthy eyes or something.

I guess it's easier to blame someone for their difficulties than accept life deals some people a shitty hand.

Anyway, Beth and I always said when we graduated, we'd travel the world and volunteer. Like *really* help people. Not wash Thai elephants and all those backpacker clichés.

However. If I'm being honest, up until Perth, that was what we had been doing.

So Beth took us to this recruitment agency place to get a job. I had never considered real life actual work before. It all sounded totally fun. An outback bar. At the time, I didn't think about what sort of place would send someone on a ten-hour round trip to Perth to pick up a couple of barmaids with no notice.

Beth

When I started college, I had a plan. I wasn't going to be the nerdy girl anymore. I was going to be the *kooky* girl. Subtle but important distinction.

College-girl-kooky means you can like books; *so long as* you also wear red lipstick, quote arthouse movies, and dress in creatively mismatched items obtained from thrift stores. This was way out of my skill set, but I was determined to get into the best sorority house, Alpha Sigma Psi, where all the politicians and senators' wives and lawyers went. There were sponsored places for dirt-poor applicants like me, I just had to get selected.

My name wasn't going to work, so I shortened it. Darla-Beth to just-Beth. Knowing nothing about sororities I did a lot of research. At the start of college there's a process called rushing, where the houses are supposed to fawn all over you to get you to sign up. Then the tables flip and they select who they want.

First day of rush week, and things were not going so hot. My plan *not* to let my voice get all reedy and strange in group situations had tanked. Plus, I was fairly certain my new style wasn't working.

Two perfect-looking girls had approached me about joining Alpha Sigma Psi, and I'd talked fast about how the right houses can set you up for life. I was trying for animated but I think I came off as intense.

You could tell they were already dismissing me. 'Sororities aren't about getting into a "social elite",' said one, miming quotation marks, 'or setting you up with employment prospects.'

'Oh.' I was totally confused. The girls exchanged glances.

'They're about *philanthropy*,' said the second girl in a patronising tone. 'Charitable acts, you know? Doing good?'

'Um, can you tell me anything about the admissions process?' I managed lamely.

They looked shocked like I'd breached another protocol. Or maybe it was fear because they knew what girls were put through to get in Alpha Sigma Psi. I sometimes find those expressions hard to distinguish.

The first girl grinned. 'Let's just say, only the strongest make it,' she said, her face suggesting this didn't include me.

I frowned. 'Like . . . hazing?' I thought dangerous initiations were only in movies.

'Oh *no*,' said the first girl, winking at her friend. 'Hazing totally isn't allowed anymore.'

'Uh-uh.' Her friend shook her head smiling. 'Hazing is illegal now.'

'OK.' I swallowed. 'So . . . how do girls pass the admissions?'

'Well, we could tell you,' said the first girl. 'But then we'd have to kill you.'

I must have looked terrified, because she put both hands on my shoulders in a way that made me jerk in shock, and peeled out this totally over-the-top laugh. The other girl dutifully joined in.

'I'm *kidding*,' shrieked the first girl. 'Oh my gosh. It's just, you know. Our house slogan or something. We're all sworn to secrecy, so don't ask, OK?'

I nodded.

She pressed a form into my unresisting hand. 'So come by the house maybe,' she said. 'See what's up.'

'Sure,' I said. 'What's the address?'

But they were already walking away.

Good job, Beth. You're the only girl on campus who didn't even get rushed.

I was leaving when this lone blonde girl came up to me.

Effortlessly beautiful in this effortless way, clothes thrown on in a way that just happened to perfectly complement her honey skin, and light blue eyes. Her hair was streaky highlights, artfully tousled as if she'd just rolled out of bed. I figured she must be pretty dizzy if she didn't notice I had been rejected by two of her sisters.

'*Hey*, girl!' She had this totally fake tone to her voice. That undulating LA thing. She paused. 'Did you sign up to Alpha Sigma Psi yet?' She looked me up and down. 'We could use some more interesting girls around.'

That was how I met Lauren. I've been looking out for her ever since. Especially where men are concerned.

Mike

The mine is an all-male environment, fellas in their mid-twenties to late-thirties. One or two a bit more cuddly like me, but most of the blokes are muscular build from the work. We earn good money, but you're underground, long hours. So there's a lotta men who sorta lie in wait for the new barmaids. There's not much else to do in this town. When the girls arrive, I try to make sure no one's giving them a hard time. And yeah, of course, after a few drinks you can think silly stuff. Marrying one of them, or whatever. But it's not like they're ever gonna look at me. Backpackers have everyone cracking on to them in Dead Tree Creek.

It's weird to think . . . I just can't get my head around Paul being gone. Doesn't seem real, you know? We grew up together. Paul was the life and soul. This place won't be the same. Won't be the same at all.

Dillon

Pete the landlord, he always sends old Bluey out to pick up new barmaids. Talk about a trial by fire. Some of them girls never seen an honest-to-God workin' man before, in all their lives. This big, bearded . . . this great galah . . . two teeth in his whole damn head . . . drivin' up in his stinkin' old ute, that he lets his dogs sleep in . . .

Pete reckons some of those backpackers don't even get in. Anyway, first night, we like to scope 'em out. See what they're like. What they might be up for. A girl's gotta be pretty stupid to go actin' like Lauren did the first night, though. 'Cause the contract is for three months. And you'll be having all the fellas not takin' no for an answer, if word gets around you're easy.

Lauren

So. Beth and I were in Perth, outside the recruitment office, 2 p.m., like they said. This vehicle pulls up. I thought it was an extra for a movie or something. I'm from LA, right?

It was like this broken-down truck thing, and all the paint had peeled off. And it had been sprayed. Like *graffitied*, in this jerky writing, like a crazy person had done it. It had 'Merry Christmas' in red on one side, all dripped and dried like the car was bleeding.

And this guy gets out . . . I was like, *holy shit*.

7

Pete leads me up a broken staircase to a back part of the pub.

'You got your notepad?' he barks over his shoulder. 'Because there's damage I want you to take down, right?'

Notepad. I can picture it, left ready on my kitchen counter this morning. Growing up in a chaotic foster home where the policy was 'more kids equals higher profits' didn't give me the best start in organisation.

Distracted, I fish around and manage to find a folded-up takeaway flyer in my pocket. I click my pen, ready.

'Mr Neville . . .'

'How d'ya know my surname?' he demands as we climb the staircase. 'You cops been checking up on me?'

'I saw your name on the licensing sign,' I tell him.

'Oh, right. You're observant at least. They teach that, do they?' He doesn't wait for an answer. 'You're a little thing for a copper, aren't you? What are you? Five three?'

'Five five,' I reply, gritting my teeth. 'Not that it's—'

'Small-boned is your problem,' decides Pete. 'Makes you look little even under that big vest they make you wear. You can tell Sergeant Anderson, I was asleep,' continues Pete. 'Didn't see nothing. Didn't hear nothing.' He stops as we reach a mould-ering hallway carpet and taps his right ear. 'Deaf as a post in this side. Mining accident. Always lie on my left side, that way I don't get woken up by that rabble downstairs after I've gone to bed.'

'You go to bed with people still in the bar?'

'On their first and last Friday the barmaids do a lock-in. I'm too old for 3 a.m. finishes nowadays.'

'You sleep here?' I peer into the dark rooms beyond.

'Fuck me dead, woman, don't you listen? This is the barmaid quarters. I'm on the other side.' He waves a hand.

'Just to welcome you to the twenty-first century, Mr Nev-ille, they let us women officers arrest people for bad language nowadays.'

He eyes me. 'This way.' He throws an exaggerated arm and signals I follow him past peeling wallpaper through a door at the end.

It opens into a good-sized room, with basic furniture and kitchen facilities. There's a flabby brown leatherette sofa, sagging in all directions, as though heaving its last sigh, and a bulky TV several years shy of the invention of plasma screens. The cooking area is marked by a stripe of lino glued to the wall.

The whole place has a morning-after-party feel. Old beer tins populate a chipped glass coffee table, empty bags of Cheetos strew the floor, and multiple ashtrays are flowering with brown-tinged dog-ends.

'You only have to look to see the mess they left it in,' says Pete, jabbing a gnarled finger in random directions. 'There's more. This way. It's a nice place. Or least it was.'

I follow him, glancing back to note a broken slide lock, hang-ing by a single nail on the door behind me.

'What's the reason for the lock on the door?' I call to him, pausing to take a better look. Pete turns, seeming gratified I'm taking his complaint seriously.

'Security. Like I say, it's good quarters they get.'

'You thought they'd need something besides the mortice lock on the door leading to the street?' I'm remembering the way the door outside was secured.

'There's another door on ground level, links to the pub,' he says. 'Good for the girls, 'cause they can roll out of bed and start their shift. But we've had problems in the past. Locals getting confused after a few too many. Wandering up here, and scaring the life out of some poor girl in her bath towel.'

The small lock suddenly seems completely inadequate.

'Do you know how it got broken?'

Pete shakes his head savagely. 'I only know it'll cost to fix it. There's more,' he says. 'This way.'

I move across the carpet which is spongy underfoot.

'You got your kitchen here, kitchenette,' says Pete, proudly, as if I'm an interested rentee. 'You can see they done some damage to the microwave. Must have turned the stove on when they were drunk, or something. Melted the bottom. See?'

I'm wondering why a microwave would be perched on a working stove.

'Sixty dollars if you were to buy it new,' continues Pete. '*Sixty dollars.*' He glares at me, looking for a reaction. Finding none, he beckons me to another open door.

'Come look at the bathroom.' He points inside a tiny windowless room, where the oldest bathtub I've ever seen has been stuck down with a rim of toothpaste-thick calking. My tanned face is reflected back at me in a brown-spotted mirror. The heat has added a halo of frizz to my streaky blonde hair.

'They made their own shower without asking.' Pete jabs an accusing finger. 'Reckon they're plumbers or something.'

A plastic pipe, held in place with duct tape, runs from the bath up the wall, where it connects to a basic bathroom tap. I'm quietly impressed by their innovation but think it best not to mention that either.

'They damaged the paintwork,' explains Pete, pointing. 'And left a big mess besides. Don't they teach young ladies to clean up after themselves nowadays?'

I take in the collection of expensive-looking shower gels and shampoos littering the floor. Designer branding and graphics. They look so out of place it makes me feel sad.

'I haven't shown you the worst part yet,' says Pete, interpreting my silence as quiet disgust. 'This way. The bedroom.'

'There's only one?' I confirm.

'Only one bed, love. Usually one barmaid takes the bed, one has the sofa. These two, they liked to share.' Pete makes a face as though this is somehow unhygienic.

He covers the short distance to a closed door and pulls it open. Across the doorway is a ragged line of string, and a handwritten sign that reads: DO NOT ENTER.

I take in the bedroom beyond. When I do, a thousand micro-observations explode in my brain at once.

Blood splatters on the bed.

Broken glass.

My eyes flit over all the devastation.

'Mr Neville,' I say, swallowing hard. 'What in hell happened here?'

8

Beth

When Bluey pulled up outside the recruitment place, I didn't even want to get in the car.

Bluey's not a real big guy, but that great beard makes him seem enormous. Plus, he's all gummy and gross, where most of his teeth have fallen out. Wife-beater shirt, bleached-out tattoos. And he stinks. Like, no offence to Bluey, 'cause we know him now, and he's a good person and all. But he smelled like he'd been drinking for a straight week.

Lauren, however, is never fazed by people. Her default is to like everyone until they prove her wrong. The opposite of me. So faced with this great lumbering alcoholic, she starts out all friendly, shaking his hand, which shocked him a little. You could see he looked pleased, like a little kid. Lauren made some joke about the fact his car said 'Merry Christmas' on the side in spray paint, and he gave this grisly wheezing laugh. Like for real, I expected him to cough up a lung.

He goes: 'Yeah, 'cause I'm like Santa Claus, right, delivering new toys to all the good little boys down in Dead Tree Creek.'

I nearly said to Lauren, right then, 'Maybe this isn't such a good idea.'

Lauren

Bluey reminded me of one of the prospectors from those old cartoons, you know? Big ginger beard and eyebrows, and little twinkling light blue eyes underneath. True, he could have used a shower. But after my time at rehab I have learned never to judge on appearances. The sweetest, nicest people can let themselves fall into bad condition in certain circumstances. They're still human beings, under dirty clothes or unwashed hair. Just sad ones.

But inside that truck. OMG.

Keep in mind Beth and I were both hungover. At the start we were being polite, but after a few hours we gave up and had our sleeves over our mouths. Bluey rolled down the window but somehow the smell didn't get better.

I got talking to Bluey, asking him stuff. He admitted the real reason his truck had 'Merry Christmas' on it was an attempt to win back his ex-wife who, several decades ago, had thrown battery acid over his ute around December time, before leaving with the children. Back then he'd thought it was a good idea to paint over the wreckage, and drive over to the women's refuge, but they wouldn't let him in.

'What kind of place won't let a man see his wife and kids at Christmas?' he said.

I asked him how his children were now.

He said: 'Ah, they're all grown up. Don't see 'em much. On me birthday, I sometimes get a call.' He went quiet.

I asked him about the guy who ran the bar, and he looked confused. Then the question kinda worked its way through his brain.

'You mean the pub? The landlord? That's Pete. Yeah, since his old lady died, he's a real old bastard. Don't worry, love. As soon as the girls can tell one fridge from the other, he stops givin' 'em hell.'

I wasn't worried. Even crammed in Bluey's stinking car, the red-rimmed highway felt open and exciting. This great grey line stretching flat, with the sun setting on the orange-gold sand.

Beth

First time we saw Dead Tree Creek it was getting dark. We'd passed straight up nothing for what felt like forever. Not a gas station. Nothing. I kept thinking what would happen if the car broke down, since there was no cell phone signal. I asked Bluey, and tried not to sound nervous. He said: 'Beak down? I've got enough supplies in the back to last us a few days, 'til someone finds us.'

Dusk was falling and the first sign of civilisation was this twinkling town in the distance.

'The gold mine,' Bluey told us. 'Most of the blokes round here work underground.'

I realised the lights were moving. It was big diggers or trucks or something.

Dead Tree Creek finally came into view. Two blocks of these pretty brick houses with iron balconies out in the middle of no-where. The phrase that came to my mind was 'faded grandeur'.

Lauren clapped her hands together and was like, 'Oh, *cute!*' Then she remembered the smell, and put her sleeve back over her nose.

There was another block lined with a bunch of stores, with names like the Golden Nugget, the Lucky Prospector, the Gold Mine, that sold trinkets, and nice old municipal buildings that suggested someone expected this place to do big things back in the day. That was it. The whole town was barely larger than three blocks, plus a convenience store on the outer limits, and a red-light district street we later accidentally walked down.

Bluey explained you couldn't see a lot of the homes, because miners had blasted out subterranean domiciles with dynamite. This was cheap and kept a constant temperature in the desert extremes.

'You got the Aboriginal place a few kilometres out,' said Bluey, gesturing a ways off with his hand. 'Government houses and that. Got their own community. Everything they need.' He looked sad. 'Lot of bad feeling between the townspeople and the Indigenous folks at the moment. 'Cause of what the mining corporation are doing to Aboriginal land.'

The Gold Rush Hotel was right on the main truck highway out of town. Bluey dropped us on the step with our backpacks and drove away.

The pub looked . . . unique. There were signs pasted every-where. The bumper-stickers-humour you get in novelty shops. Like: FREE BEER YESTERDAY!, and SOUP OF THE DAY: BEER. Not exactly funny, but . . . eclectic. It was a theme that continued as we moved inside, where the air switched from hot and dry to hot and moist, with a distinct boozy odour. Homemade signage on every wall. Beer mats, postcards, and pinned-up currency bills from all over the world. Like a junkshop or something. Cork hats, strings of crocodile teeth, and a bunch more signs. The largest one read: BAR RULES: MEN, NO SHIRT, NO SERVICE. WOMEN, NO SHIRT, FREE BEER.

I glanced at Lauren. She was taking it all in like it was the greatest thing ever. There was a big smile on her face.

Lauren

The Gold Rush Hotel was *so exciting*. From the outside it reminded me of an old movie theatre. Inside everything was really old. There was a bar made of real carved wood, with a ton of colourful bottles and local paraphernalia stacked behind. I was totally thrilled at the idea we would actually work here.

At that point the place was empty besides this little guy. Kind of shrunken. With this strange mismatch of a white shirt, shorts, knee-socks, and a big black cowboy hat.

He pushed the brim up to get a good look at us, flashing a red sweaty line where he wore it too tight. 'You the new girls?'

I didn't know what to say, but luckily Beth was there, and she has worked jobs before. So she said: 'We're here to work. Are you Pete?'

He gave this grudging little nod, like maybe he was, but he wasn't ready to tell us just yet.

Beth

Landlord Pete was a small, perpetually angry man, wizened up with his own rage. The first thing he said was: 'Do you girls know what a lock-in is?'

9

I'm staring into Lauren and Beth's bloodstained bedroom, wondering where to start.

'God only knows what they got up to last night,' says Pete, his lip curling in disgust.

'You taped up your own crime scene?' I manage, eyeing his makeshift barricade and signage. My heart is sinking, running through all the contamination that has already happened.

'Not for the first time,' Pete confirms proudly. 'In a small town like this, sometimes you gotta help the coppers out.'

'Has this been reported to the police?'

'I'm reporting it to you now, aren't I? And make sure you take down all the particulars, because there's a chance the insurance will cover it. The mirror. Smashed all over the bed. Write that down.'

My eyes track to the wall. Scrawled large in deep red lipstick is 'Alpha Sigma Psi'.

Alpha Sigma Psi?

'Mr Neville,' I begin firmly, 'have you moved anything from this room?'

'I've only got started,' says Pete, apparently disappointed with

39

his own idleness. 'Any personal bits, I chucked 'em all in there.' He gestures to a cardboard box outside the door. It contains an assortment of worn cosmetic tubes and pots, a lonely stub of Chanel lipstick with the lid missing, and a notebook journal. 'But the girls at the launderette already told me they won't do bloodstains. So sheets, pillows cases, all need replacing. Gonna cost me twenty bucks a piece.'

'It's important you don't touch anything else,' I tell him. 'We'll need to take a statement of what you've moved or cleaned.' I'm jotting furiously on my makeshift notepad.

'Police don't clean anything other than body parts, that right?' Pete is saying,

'Yes, but . . .'

'I've already lost today's trade. Now you're telling me my Saturday night's gone, over a pair of murdering mongrels?' he demands.

'You're very certain the backpackers are murderers, considering you didn't hear anything,' I say pointedly.

Pete shakes his head in disgust. 'They were bad news from the start. Very first shift, the blonde one, Lauren, reckons she's scared of the dark or something. Won't get the beer from the cellar. I knew then they would never keep that cooler stocked.'

'Lauren didn't like to go into the cellar?' This strikes me as unusual.

Pete adjusts his cowboy hat, exasperated. 'Oh, *neither* of 'em wanted to go down there. Too good to climb down a ladder, eh?'

Possible entry scenarios are flitting through my head. 'Your cellar has a hatch onto the street, right?' I say, remembering it. 'Could someone have gotten up into the pub that way?'

Pete's brows draw down deeply. 'No, love. It's locked. Bluey's got a set of keys but before you ask, he was halfway to Port

Hedland making a delivery that night, so you think twice before accusing the poor bloke.'

'I'm not, I . . .'

Before I can stop him, Pete scoops the journal from the odds and ends box and presses it into my luckily-still-gloved hands.

'Read that and tell me those girls didn't do it,' he says, opening it so the pages face out. 'That's evidence.'

It's a flimsy softback journal. I flick through to see it's written in two sets of handwriting. One unmistakably girlish, the other crabbed and square. 'BEGGING FOR MERCY' stands out in craggy capitalisation halfway down the page.

I blink. It reads like a bucket-list of violent acts.

My eyes focus on a cluster of short statements.

'MAKE THEM DRINK PEPPER SAUCE!!'

'MAKE THEM EAT MUD PIES!!'

'MAKE THEM EAT THEIR OWN PUKE!!'

My mind skids back to the ragged-dirty-mouth of the victim.

'Found it under the bed,' says Pete with relish. 'Looks like they've been planning it for a while, I reckon.'

'Mr Neville, are you telling me your barmaids wrote this? And you took it from under their bed?'

I'm trying for a stern tone, but my heart's not in it. And it rolls off Pete in any case. He glares at me, stabbing a finger to make his point. 'Still think they didn't do it? All girls together, is that it?'

'We'll be taking careful stock of the evidence and interviewing relevant people,' I say.

My eyes settle on a glistening tangle of used condoms, wedged down the side of the bed.

'Has anyone else been in here since last night?'

'Half the guys in the pub by the looks of it,' says Pete in disgust.

'Did you see something to suggest that was the case?'

Pete glowers. 'I just know the type of girls they were.'

'We need to leave,' I tell him, putting out a restraining arm. 'This could be evidence we're walking all over. I don't want you coming back in here until the police say you can.'

I steer him none-too-gently from the apartment. We're back on the landing now, heading down the stairs. I have no idea how I'm going to explain this to Sergeant Anderson.

My radio buzzes unexpectedly. I press the button to receive. It's Anderson.

'Harrison? Craig's picked up the two backpacker girls.'

Too late, I realise I've got my volume turned up too high and Pete can hear everything.

'He's driving them back now. I need you in,' Anderson booms, as I fiddle desperately with the radio.

'Yes, sir.' I glance at Pete, who's not even pretending he isn't listening in.

'Must be your lucky day, Harrison,' Anderson deadpans as I switch the dial up, down, then finally to correct levels, so only I can hear. 'They're saying they'll only speak to a woman, and you're the only one we've got.'

'Copy that, sir. On my way.' Nervous excitement bounces through me. I turn back to Pete.

'I don't want you or anyone else going back inside,' I tell him sternly. 'Someone will be back to tape it off properly.'

'They arrested the killers?' asks Pete, oblivious to the rebuke.

'We don't know they're killers.'

Pete blows air like a horse. 'Everyone round here knows it. Not just me.' He pauses for effect. 'Those girls killed him, because they couldn't take a joke.'

IO

Sergeant Anderson is staring at the backpacker girls' journal. His gloved hands shut the book and drop it back in the evidence bag, his head shaking slowly. 'You read this?'

'I saw a couple of sentences. It's like a list of ways to torture people.'

'Bloody horrible stuff. Goes on for pages. Those are some very disturbed young ladies.' Anderson drags his eyes from the evidence bag. 'So, Harrison, how did you get on with the body?'

'I put the sheet over the remains.'

'Well done. I heard you puked your guts up?'

'In the drain on the street,' I admit, wondering how the word got back so fast.

'You wouldn't be human if you didn't,' he says. 'Good you made it outside. My first fatality was a road traffic. Fella sliced in two. I nearly up-chucked on what was left of him.'

I try and fail to push away the image.

Anderson holds up the leaflet I used to make notes. 'Forget your notepad?' he says dryly.

'I didn't realise I was going to need it . . .'

'You always need your notepad. Never know what you might find, and writing it down makes it official.' He squints at my efforts, trying to read the scrawling script.

'Is that an "H" or . . .?' Anderson holds the paper at a distance. 'Never mind.' He looks away, giving up. 'What did you make of it?'

I'm not sure what he's asking me.

'The body, Harrison. Your assessment. Before you lost your lunch down the nearest drain, what did you observe?'

'The flies weren't circling right for a body four hours old,' I tell him, without hesitation.

Anderson rolls his eyes. 'You're a police officer, Harrison, not a bush-tracker.'

'I did a bit of bush stuff as a kid,' I counter.

'Forensics will tell you how long the body was there. Leave that to them, right?'

'Right.' It was a constant of my training. Logical methodology. Only facts that can be presented in a court.

'So,' he says patiently. 'Describe the victim.'

'Battered.' My heart speeds up. 'His lips were all torn up, and his face was covered in mud. Completely covered. Especially around and in his mouth. Smeared all over his teeth. Like someone had repeatedly smashed dirt into his face.'

My mind flashes back to the girl's journal. The references to force feeding.

'What else?'

'His hands were cuffed behind his back and the body was badly injured,' I manage, juggling awful pictures in my head.

'He'd been roughed up?' asks Anderson, quietly. 'Take your time.'

I shake my head. 'No. Maybe. He had lots of little injuries . . . Not like the kind you get in a punch-up.'

Anderson lifts his pen. 'What sort of injuries, Harrison? You'll need to be specific.'

'Cuts and scrapes, and puncture marks. Bruising. Little bruises everywhere. All over.' The nausea from earlier threatens to flood back. 'Like he'd been tortured,' I conclude. 'A lot of dirt on his skin too.'

Anderson's expression tightens fractionally. 'So he was naked?'

'Yes.' I realise my rookie error. 'Yes. Yes, sir, he was naked.'

'First detail to observe,' says Anderson, helpfully. 'State of undress. Removing clothes is a form of assault, so you log it if observed. Right?'

'Right.'

He looks up at me. 'You sure you're OK, Harrison?'

'I'm fine.' I close my eyes.

'What about cause of death? Anything obvious jump out?'

'None of the injuries seemed serious,' I say. 'Suffocation maybe? From the mud.'

'Anything else?'

I shake my head slowly, unwilling to spend any more time with memories of the awful corpse.

'Come on, Harrison, you can do better than that,' admonishes Anderson.

The damaged body shimmers horribly in my mind. I drag my memory along the body, remembering the hands curled palm up with dirty fingernails. 'Multiple injuries suggest a sustained attack. No obvious defensive wounds.'

'Very good,' says Anderson approvingly.

I think some more. 'The handcuffs,' I say, picturing the pink fluffy restraints. 'They were flimsy. Hunter was a strong guy. He could easily have broken free if he wanted.'

Anderson looks thoughtful. 'Suggests a bit of hanky-panky that Hunter started out complicit with.'

'Certainly didn't end that way.'

'No.' Anderson nods firmly. 'Good weighing up of the facts, Harrison. Bloody shame,' he mutters, his eyes flicking to the family photo by his computer. 'I've known Paul Hunter since he was a little kid.' Anderson's mouth is a flat tight line. 'He was a bit of a ratbag, but he didn't deserve this.' He breaks from his thoughts. 'Well, Craig's driving the suspects back to the station.'

He lifts a folder of papers from the top of a tidy stack on his desk and passes it to me.

'This is what we have on them so far. Police files we pulled from the United States.'

'That was fast. The girls have a record?'

'They were both arrested in college for the same misdemeanour. Funny thing is, the records have been redacted. We don't know what they were accused of.'

II

Lauren

There was, like, zero decompression between arriving and getting to work. We were literally standing in the bar with our backpacks. Hadn't unpacked. Hadn't showered from the five-hour ride. Pete starts telling us all this information super fast.

Apparently, on the first Friday new barmaids start, and on the day they leave, the pub did something called a 'lock-in'. The only part I understood was that today was Friday.

Beth

The deal was, we locked the doors and no one else was allowed in. Some of the customers stayed on, and they bought us drinks, kind of like their fee for staying. That way, we weren't breaking any laws by opening late. Pete was hazy about how long a lock-in could go on for. It seemed to depend on when the last customer wanted to leave. This sounded sketchy to me. We would basically be trapped inside the pub with a bunch of guys we didn't know, for an indeterminate period of time. And I thought that before we met Paul Hunter.

April

Paul Hunter and I were childhood sweethearts, you know? I always liked him, but I never thought he noticed me. He was the footy king; the guy all the girls tried to get with. Always scoring goals, getting into fights, an' winning 'em, all that. He won everything. It was the happiest time of my life, when we got together. He was four years older, used to pick me up from school in his car. Yeah, we were on-again-off-again. But we always got back on track in the end. I'm twenty-six now, so what does that make it? Ten years? Ten years and the cops treat it like nothing. I wasn't even asked to identify the body.

Oh, I know who killed him, alright. It was that fucking little blondie. If I could get my hands on her now, I'd rip her head off . . . Fucking *Lauren*. Lot of family men stopped bein' family men when she started in the pub. Wasn't only Paul she cracked onto.

It's all round town that those girls put on a sex show. On the bar, you know. *Totally* starkers. Apparently, Lauren has a piercing. *Down there*. What's that, if not asking for it?

Dillon

Not many blokes remember this, but April was mine first. She was the first girl I ever got with at school, and the tattoo with her name, on my bicep – that was my first one too. April was even with me in the fella's living room when I got it done. Anyway, then Paul swept in, and he was a few years older. Got the car, all that, you know? I used to think about . . . well, best not get into that. I got that 'April' tattoo covered up with an eagle now, anyway. When Lauren showed up, it crossed my mind maybe

Paul would ditch April. But he loved the drama too much. They both did.

Now Paul's gone ... He could be a bit of a dickhead. Up himself, all that. But it's made me realise, he was like a brother to me, that guy. Always had my back, looked out for me at the mine, where things can get aggro with so many blokes. I can't imagine Dead Tree Creek without him. All of us blokes from the pub are chipping in for a tribute. Proper send-off. Least he deserves.

Lauren

After the lock-in debrief, Pete showed us the pub kitchen. It was super interesting to find out what goes on backstage. The menu had something called a jaffle, which was like a grilled cheese sandwich. I noticed Beth looked totally stressed, like she was trying to memorise everything he was telling us. Then it kind of dawned on me. Like, *oh*, we're expected to *do* this? Because the agency never mentioned anything about cooking.

Beth

The kitchen equipment consisted of a large freezer and an industrial deep-fat fryer.

'A decent feed and cold beer, since we can't guarantee 'em good company.' Pete barked a short laugh. 'These men work hard for a living. You gotta always remember that.'

Lauren and I were nodding so quickly my head had started to hurt.

'You serve 'em fast. Don't piss 'em around, eh?'

Now we were shaking our heads.

''Cause, fuck me dead, some of these girls the agency sends don't know a cold beer from a warm arsehole, you know what I mean?'

Lauren was completely pale now. She slid me a stricken look, like: *Did he just say that?*

Pete patted the mammoth freezer with something approaching affection, and used both hands to snap up the massive locking handle. There was an audible sound of the rubber seal unsticking itself. Inside, in no apparent order, was a jumbled mass of miscellaneous catering-size food bags.

Pete grabbed one and hefted it.

'You gotcha oven chips here. Anything white, probably chips. Fries, you call 'em. Don't say that to the customer, mind,' he added, fixing us with a beady eye. 'They wouldn't like it. An Aussie bloke eats hot chips.'

My eyes drifted to the seven-pound bag, which had FRIES written on the side.

Pete ripped open the pack in a single practised movement we would later find to be extremely difficult, then threw the whole batch right into the smoking fryer. He switched back before the explosion of bubbling fat could spray him.

'Them hungry men out there won't thank you for going slow, when you've got four orders rolling,' he explained.

I fully expected Lauren to pitch in, and explain we weren't planning on burning ourselves for $10 an hour, but she didn't. It was only later she told me she was too busy wondering what she was going to do if someone ordered something other than fries.

After our nano-training to be chefs, Pete took us upstairs to see our 'living quarters'. Our apartment was right above the pub.

Pete started explaining things to us, at double-speed. Like all the work arounds. Don't push this, in case you cause a fire, and don't lock that, you'll get trapped inside.

'I used to have more kitchen equipment in here,' Pete told us. 'But you're not going to be doing much cooking anyway; you get your feed downstairs in the pub.'

We found out later that Pete only had one meal a day, and considered anyone who ate breakfast to be extravagant.

He showed us the bedroom. I had a kind of sick feeling looking at the double bed. I was remembering Lauren's wash bag, filled with condoms. When Lauren gets stressed she can get . . . needy.

'I've got you a couple of tight T-shirts with GOLD RUSH on them,' said Pete. 'You can wear the short-shorts you've got on already,' he added generously. 'Uniform is denim cut-offs and you supply your own.'

Lauren

The apartment was super cool. It had these big wooden window shutters. Pete talked for a long time about the microwave. He seemed extremely proud of it. Like it was a rare classic item. Later I accidentally melted the plastic feet by turning the stovetop on, and it became one of our jokes, the way it lurched to one side. Like everything in this place is drunk – even the microwave.

I'll admit I did have a minor freak-out when I saw there was no shower – just a grungy old bathtub. But as Pete was yakking away, Beth took my hand and sort of squeezed it. Like, *We got this.*

I started planning to get some throws for the couch and stuff.

Make it nice. New sheets, coverlets for the bed we'd be sharing. Since college, I don't like to sleep alone. Beth is cool about it. Says that's what best friends are for.

After he toured us around, Pete eyed his watch. 'Pub opens in twenty minutes. Let's show you how to work the till.' We found out later he meant cash register.

Beth

When Pete took us back down to the bar I noticed he'd put up a sign in our honour. Handwritten, but badly. Like, a lot of the letters were wrong.

NEW GIRRLS TONITE!

The first thought that came to me was Lauren. I remember thinking: *She is not going to be able to handle this.*

Bluey

Can't make sense of what happened to Paul. Just can't make sense of it. Young guy like that. Whole life ahead of him. Breaks my heart. He'd tell me about his plans, you know. Stuff he didn't share with the younger guys. Paul had dreams of making something of himself. There was more to him than the macho banter in front of his mining mates.

And I know there's talk about the backpackers, but Lauren is a lot better than what people said. She cared for people, you know? I was proper crook one time; I mean, real unwell, like, and Lauren was the only person come knock on my door, check I was OK. Brought me some food. Only veggies and crap I don't eat, but her heart was in the right place. Both alright in my book. Nice girls until this place got to 'em. Not like what the people in town make them out to be.

And I don't believe that dirty stuff. What everyone's talking about.

12

Sergeant Anderson is frowning over the international police report.

'Never seen that before,' he tells me. 'We know the backpacker girls were accused of a crime, but we don't know what. Only that some charges were dropped. They were both eventually convicted of disturbing the peace and supplying alcohol to a minor.'

I frown down at the front page, seeing long strips of black where descriptions of arrest and reasons should be. Only names, ages and college location are intact.

'Alpha Sigma Psi,' I read the address. 'It was scrawled on the wall of the girls' apartment. In red lipstick.' Things come together. 'Greek alphabet letters are used by college sorority houses,' I say. 'Lot of bad behaviour in those places.'

'Is that like a fraternity?'

'Yeah, a female version,' I say. 'We have them here too. But . . . I think in the US it's more of a big deal. The right sorority will give you advantages for life, friends in high places. But you have to be accepted by members and pass initiations. That's how they keep wealth and privilege in the same families for generations.'

'Any reason to scrawl your college sorority on a wall?' asks Anderson.

'I guess there's a kind of . . . tribal mentality to sororities and fraternities,' I say slowly. 'Like a football team. Wear the T-shirt, chant the name.'

'Graffiti your rented apartment?'

I shrug.

'I'll look into why they blacked out the charges on the rap sheet,' says Anderson. 'I'm not an expert in how they do things in America. Maybe they hold the records centrally. We won't find out until tomorrow at the earliest now,' he adds. 'Different time zones.' Anderson sighs. 'At least we know something more about the body. Forensics are moving Hunter as we speak.'

'We have a forensics department?'

'It's a loose term,' concedes Anderson. 'We're waiting on the city boys. In the meantime, there's old Danno. Danno Death, we call him. Tags toes at the hospital. Completed a forensics course last year, steps in if we need him, and we use his morgue.'

'What about assessing the scene?' I'd been hoping I might be allowed to watch.

'Danno did that too. Put tape up and all that.'

'Aren't they supposed to be separate people? To avoid subjectivity?'

'That'd be lovely, Harrison, and I'm sure over in Perth, you have a forensic, a crime scene analyst, a toxicologist, and a fella to spritz your face with water when you feel hot. Down here we got Danno with a roll of stripy tape and a bare pass in night-school forensics and we count ourselves lucky to have that.' He claps his palms together, glances at his computer screen. 'Righty-ho. Story so far from Danno. This was no calculated kill. It was a violent and frenzied attack.'

I wince.

'He'll give us more on that in the report,' says Anderson, catching my eye. 'His early supposition is death was most likely by asphyxiation. Poor bloke's throat was stuffed so full of dirt, he couldn't breathe.' Anderson's face contracts. My mind skids back to the torn-up mouth of the body, mud crusted thickly around the lips. I feel my stomach lurch and realise that Anderson is still talking.

'No clothes, so no wallet, no phone with the body,' he's saying. 'Priority to find those,' Anderson says. 'Danno found a card for a knocking shop on York Street on the floor, but nothing to suggest it belonged to Hunter.' He takes a breath. 'Well, no point in hanging around. We've got cause to charge the backpackers.'

'What with?' Things feel like they're running fast.

Anderson looks at me for a long moment. 'Murder.'

'Murder? Not . . . manslaughter?'

Anderson frowns deeply. 'Where are you getting that from?'

I clear my throat uncertainly. 'The apartment lock was broken. Maybe the girls felt threatened. In fear of their lives even. Might have been self-defence.'

'Self-defence has to be proportional, Harrison.'

'Understood. But a woman in danger might need stronger violence to defend herself than looks reasonable to a bloke. Especially if she knows her attacker to be violent. You'd have to be sure he doesn't get up again.'

'I don't think it follows,' says Anderson mildly, still frowning. 'Paul Hunter looks to have been suffocated with mud, for chrissakes. There's not a judge in the land would agree that is proportional.'

'Maybe,' I concede. 'What about provocation?'

'We don't want to get into victim blaming, Harrison.'

'That's my point,' I say frustrated. 'If the victims are Beth and Lauren, we're blaming them for someone else's behaviour. They worked in that pub for months, right? We both know the culture in The Gold Rush. What if they snapped?'

Anderson shrugs. 'Well, this is for the court to decide, not us. Look. We either charge them within twenty-four hours or let them go. Doesn't mean we don't look into other avenues. But if we discharge them they could do a runner.'

I can't argue with his logic, and I feel defeated. Like I should have made a better case, but I don't know enough.

'It just seems like the girls would have to be really stupid,' I say, making one last stab at putting my thoughts into words. 'To write out a murder plan, act it out, leave the evidence lying around.'

Anderson shrugs. 'People do stupider stuff every day, take my word for it.'

We're interrupted by the rumble of a car pulling up outside the flimsy walls of the station.

'Sounds like Craig's back with the suspects,' says Anderson.

We move to his window. Craig leads out two girls in handcuffs. They both wear denim shorts and tight T-shirts.

One is blonde, with golden skin and a slight frame, like a wispy little fairy. She looks the typical beautiful beach-dwelling traveller chick, with stacks of artfully eclectic bangles on her tanned wrists, dangling earrings and a silver toe-ring. She has a confused expression, like she's waiting to be told this is all a mistake.

The second girl is dark-haired and plainer, less well suited to her short-shorts. Like it's a uniform she's copied but doesn't understand. My initial impression is . . . oddball. She has dark hair that hangs straight and limp, slightly lower than her pointed chin and broad jaw. Her light brown eyes are set far apart in a heart-shaped face, unusually small, neat, and upturned at the corners, like a fox.

'Well, Harrison,' says Anderson, following my gaze. 'You ready to meet them?'

13

Lauren

After the lightning apartment tour, Pete took us downstairs to 'show us the ropes'. At this point I was still confused. It only just was dawning on me that we were expected to work *that night*.

Beth

Pete gave us about ten seconds of 'training' – essentially naming the location of everything at high speed and having us repeat it all back. His educational style comprised of making eye contact in brief, infrequent, terrifying bursts, accompanied by a question we couldn't answer.

'So,' he'd say, eyes fixed on us, furiously. 'Where'd I say the cooler was?'

'Um, over there?' Lauren pointed to a likely looking piece of equipment, labelled 'cooler'.

'I didn't say anything about a cooler,' he said, the glare intensifying. 'If you'd been fucking *listening*, you'd know that, eh? Pay attention, girls. Fuck me dead, it's not a lot to ask. All you gotta do is hand beers out.'

He clapped his hands together. 'Righty-ho. I'll go open the doors. You girls ready for your first shift?'

It was ironic. I have often wondered why Lauren worked so hard to get me into Alpha Sigma Psi. I figured she must be thinking the same thing about me now. Like, why had I persuaded her to come out here, to put up with this abuse?

Lauren

'Training' is a loaded term to Alpha Sigma Psi girls. And totally, Pete's aggression was somewhat déjà vu. The first part of the college pledging process, freshmen girls are basically screamed at to complete impossible tasks by seniors. I noticed Beth had that same distant expression during Pete's training that she wore during the hazing. Defence mechanism, I guess.

Beth

Pete took us into the bar and opened the trapdoor leading to the cellar. I knew right then, Lauren was never going down that ladder. From how Pete explained it, at least twice a night I'd be descending into the dark. My palms were sweaty at the thought of regularly dropping into that bad dream. But I also knew I would never put that on Lauren. She didn't even need this job.

Weirdly, as I followed Pete down into the boozy blackness, I had this very intense memory, not of the pledge night cellar, but a few days before the ceremony, when our whole bright futures were still ahead of us. Lauren had invited me back to her college room and had heaped a towering mound of expensive clothes on the bed.

I was perched nervously on the edge of her designer coverlet.

'I didn't think sororities were about what you looked like,' I said, as she sorted garments.

Lauren grabbed a dress and held it up with an appraising eye. I caught the word 'Prada' on the label. 'Well, I wanna say it's not,' she tossed the dress down, and plucked up something in blue satin, 'because it kind of isn't. I mean, you are totally hot enough to get in. It's your style. You have this thrift store vibe going on,' she continued. 'I get it. But Alpha Sigma Psi is, like, bohemian.'

She might as well have said their look was Martian.

Lauren absorbed my confusion, holding bunched-up fabric to my face. 'Too light,' she tutted, flinging it down. 'OK, so, Beta Sigma are the sporty ones,' she intoned, presenting a manicured finger, 'Zeta Pi Deltas are super slutty; crop tops, lots of skin. Gamma Rho Omegas are classy. And we're, like boho.' She gestured to her own outfit. 'See?'

'The sororities have personalities and matching looks. Like Barbie or something?'

She laughed. 'We don't say it out loud. But . . . totally.'

'It's the easiest code on the planet.' I was actually somewhat disappointed. 'Doesn't that mean really dumb people can get selected?'

She laughed again. 'Word of advice. Only nerds call people dumb. And it's more like a language than a code. OK,' she held up a skirt and nodded emphatically, '*this* would look *so* cute on you. You'll need accessories . . .' She pivoted and opened a drawer stuffed to bursting with jewellery. 'Plus, I have a bunch of lipsticks that are, like, super-duper-perfect for your colouring.'

'You don't like my lipstick?'

'It's not your shade, OK? I can tell you won't be offended by that.' She was right, I wasn't. 'Revlon, right?' She narrowed her eyes at my lips, assessing.

I nodded, transfixed by how she could tell a brand of lipstick by looking.

'It's a nice colour, if you were, like, blonde,' she said. 'But you have this dark hair.' She reached out and fluffed it. No one had ever touched me like that before; with such entitled confidence. It made my scalp tingle. 'So striking. I'm mousey, so, you know,' she sighed dramatically, 'only option is highlights. But for you,' she winked and twirled a pink-nailed finger, 'dark hair, red lips. *Love* it. I totally get the shade you're going for, but . . . *Revlon don't use carmine*.' She delivered this in a stage whisper, with her hand cupped at her mouth, as though divulging the most shocking scandal.

I shrugged. 'I picked it because it's what Amelie wears. In the movie.'

Lauren looked confused, then clarity dawned. 'Oh,' she said. 'You're doing kooky. Styled right that could totally work. I could *for sure* make a case for a kooky girl.'

'You really think I could get in?' A heady excitement was building. Could this come down to the right lipstick?

There's a whole process to get through,' said Lauren. 'But . . . you seem tough. I'm sure you'll make it.'

'What kind of process?'

'I could tell you, but I'd have to kill you.'

Lauren

Hell week? It was fun, it was a bonding experience. I mean, don't get me wrong, it is the most fun I never want to have again. But when you're all down in that cellar together, you wind up tight with the other girls. The thing about trauma. It makes you close. Obviously, you forgive them afterwards, and you all go on to party. Everything we do is in the name of friendship and sisterhood. Because when you graduate, these are the people who are going to open doors for you.

Sometimes I think Beth struggled with that. She's from a different background, where if someone is mean to you, you hold a grudge, like forever.

First time I met Beth I knew that not everyone would *get* her. Some people have a very two-dimensional view of personality. My dad always says I attract lame ducks, but he doesn't understand that there is more to life than alpha-types. Some people just need a chance.

And I *knew* Beth was cool. So I argued a lot for her to get a spot. I was totally proven right after initiation too. I did apologise to her afterwards for . . . you know . . . what happens to the girls.

Beth

Lauren *did* apologise. When I brought it up later, she rolled her eyes, and was like: 'I told you I was sorry about the pledge party. Can't we forget about it? People do stupid stuff when they're drunk.'

I didn't see it that way. I mean, sure, people do stupid stuff when they drink. But it's never exactly out of character, if you ask me. It's always in the context of who they really are. It doesn't matter how much alcohol I drank, I would never have done what Lauren did at my initiation.

14

Police Constable Dooligan's arrival makes Anderson's office feel a lot smaller. He looks like your classic muscle-head. Gym-ripped, with a bull-neck and tanned forearms bursting from his short-sleeved blue shirt.

He has designer wraparound sunglasses and the reddest hair imaginable, boyband-sculpted, like he's auditioning to be a police pin-up.

I guess him at around my age, and he reminds me of the popular kids at school, of which I definitely wasn't one.

'This is Constable Craig Dooligan,' says Sergeant Anderson. 'He's the drongo who pissed his pants, and left the body uncovered.'

'Yeah, I thought Pete had got me down there to show me a broken window, or something,' says Craig, removing his shades and looking harrowed, but completely unoffended.

He looks different without his sunglasses. The bridge of his nose is freckled, and his eyes are a very distinctive green under chaotic dark brows.

'Ran out there, screaming like a little girl, I don't mind telling you.' His eyes meet mine. 'You saw it, right?'

I nod tightly and we share a look – two people who have seen the unspeakable.

'Bloody relieved when Anderson told me girls had gone on the run and I had to drive after them,' he adds. 'I'll be having nightmares about the state of that poor bloke, I reckon.'

'Tara here managed to get a sheet over the body,' says Anderson, proudly. '*And* secured the premises. Better watch out, Craig, she'll be after your badge.'

'Good on ya, Tara,' says Craig, with absolute sincerity. 'Wild horses couldn't have got me back in that pub.' He shakes his head in horror. 'You're a fair dinkum copper, I reckon. First shift. Trial by fire, eh?'

I manage a weak smile. Anderson addresses Craig.

'You used your car time to speak with the fellas at The Gold Rush that night?'

Craig nods. 'They all said more or less the same thing.'

'Which was?'

'Everyone was totally shit-faced. Couple of blokes remember an Aboriginal girl showed up at the pub.'

We all exchange glances. Moodjana people never *ever* frequent The Gold Rush.

'Any idea was she doing there?' asks Anderson.

'Few of the blokes assumed she was there to make trouble. Lot of grief between the Moodjana people and the miners at the moment, you know?'

'Anyone get her name?' asks Anderson.

Craig shakes his head. 'At some point Paul's sometime-girlfriend April Dean arrived, wanting a blue with him.'

Anderson visibly shudders. I remember red-headed April from school. She started punch-ups for fun. From Anderson's reaction, she hasn't changed.

'April's got a motive,' says Anderson. 'Let's check out her movements.'

'The fellas reckon they managed to get April out again without too much drama,' says Craig. 'It's all a bit hazy, 'cause they were feeling no pain at this point. Wasted. But all the drinkers swear blind neither Paul nor the Aboriginal girl were there when the pub emptied around 3 a.m.'

We all consider this. 'So the other drinkers reckon Paul left early. But somehow his body got back in the pub?' I conclude.

Anderson frowns. 'The Gold Rush has security cameras on the front door. Pull the footage, Craig. Let's see if Paul left the pub like the blokes say. See if we can ID this Black girl who showed up too. Check if anyone else enters after the blokes staggered out at 3 a.m.'

Craig nods.

'Anything else?' asks Anderson.

'Yeah, one of the blokes, Mike. He says when they spilled out into the street, there might have been an Aboriginal bloke parked up opposite, watching The Gold Rush.'

Anderson considers this. 'Might have?'

'He was blind drunk, sir. Says he wouldn't swear to it.'

'Maybe the driver was there to drop the Aboriginal girl off,' says Anderson. 'Or pick her up. Could help us ID her.'

'It was pitch black at 3 a.m.,' I say. 'How could he have known the bloke in the car was Aboriginal?'

'He reckoned it was one of the cars you get on the mission,' says Craig, uneasily. 'Old, battered, dusty.'

I shrug. 'My car looks like that.'

'Well, do the department a favour and give it a wash.' Anderson thinks. 'That said, I agree with Tara, ethnicity is a leap. Make or model?'

'Reckons an old Holden.'

66

Anderson rolls his eyes. 'Fair few of them round here. Any of the other blokes see this bashed-up car and driver?'

'Nope.'

Anderson nods thoughtfully. 'Alright, let's do what we can on the mystery car. Craig, get back to your witness and quiz him on who was sat in the driver's seat. OK. What about the actual lock-in?'

'Things got pretty extreme,' says Craig. 'By all accounts clothing got removed, including Lauren's. What a couple of blokes *do* remember, is Lauren and Beth went up to the apartment at some point. Customers were serving their own drinks for a bit.'

'The girls' apartment was above the pub,' says Anderson. 'Paul Hunter could have gone up there. Hidden out until everyone else left.'

'The apartment lock was broken,' I agree. 'There were signs of what could have been a struggle in the bedroom.' It does all seem to fit. I remember the pile of used contraceptives down the side of the bed, and unpleasant scenarios cycle through my head.

We're all quiet, contemplating when Anderson breaks the silence. 'Are your suspects still insisting on a female police constable?'

Craig looks sympathetically in my direction. 'Yep.' He crosses his arms at his chest and I wonder if he finds it difficult, with all the muscle in the way.

'Best get on with it, eh, Harrison?' opines Anderson. 'Murder charge.'

I manage a nod.

Craig's eyes widen. 'We're charging the backpackers with murder?' he asks Anderson.

'Bloody hell, I don't need two of you questioning my judgement,' grumbles Anderson.

'No, sir,' frowns Craig. 'It's just . . . Paul Hunter . . . He was one of those bully-blokes you know? Even his so-called mates hated him. And how many domestics have we been called to for Hunter and April Dean? She's dodged serious assault charges a couple of times. April goes troppo if she gets a sniff of tequila.'

'True,' agrees Anderson. 'But she couldn't have beaten Paul Hunter half to death and asphyxiated him in the ten minutes she was in the pub.' He fans his hands wide. 'We work on the evidence we have. If we don't charge those backpackers we're not doing our job. Plain and simple.'

Craig nods, his mouth twisting as if he wants to say more. He turns to me.

'So, you gonna take a crack at 'em?' asks Craig, nodding to the back of the station, where I assume he has secured the girls in a cell. 'Hell of a first interview. We usually give the newbies a shoplifter.'

The possibilities are unravelling frighteningly before me. What am I going to do if they start confessing? I've only got basic interview techniques down and this is most definitely advanced.

'Chances are you'll only get their name and address,' says Anderson, seeing my nervousness. 'Don't get smart, alright? No playing TV detective. Last thing we need is them to get released on some technicality, because some idiot didn't follow procedure. Right? Stick to the rules *exactly*.'

'Yes, sir.' There's real fear now, cold and thick. I take a steadying breath, trying to run through what I was taught about interviewing.

'And for chrissakes,' adds Anderson, 'double check you turn the recorder on and the red light is flashing.'

68

15

We're in a little side room for conducting interviews. My interviewee is staring into space, like she's deep in thought. Anderson has briefed me to spend no more than ten minutes – in theory, not enough time for me to seriously stuff up.

The first thing I notice is how completely vacant she looks. There is no expression in her eyes, which are a pretty pale blue. The rest of her is pretty too. Not beautiful, but she has this . . . shimmer to her. Her skin is golden. She has brown eyebrows plucked into slim arcs, and her top lip, slightly too large in relation to the bottom, has a pronounced cupid's bow that is almost indecently pouty.

There are signs she hasn't been taking care of herself. Dirt under her chipped turquoise-polished fingernails and crustings in the corner of her eyes. A matted clump at the back of her bleached-blonde hair, and a single angry pimple on her chin.

I unwrap the shiny CD and push it into the machine trying to stop my hands from shaking. The recording device is so old I've never used one like it before. For a terrible moment I think I won't be able to work it. I find the button to start, and a red light glows.

I clear my throat. 'I'm probationary constable Harrison.' She raises a single unimpressed eyebrow. 'Darla-Beth Jackson, you are being charged with the murder of Paul Hunter.' My voice sounds pleasingly official. She flinches at the word 'murder'. 'Do you have anything you want to say about that?'

She takes me in, a ghost of a smile on her lips. I feel conscious of my unstyled hair.

'My name isn't Beth,' she says.

'Oh.' The interview room feels suddenly very small and hot. My cheeks burn. 'You're Lauren? Lauren Davis?'

She nods, watching my face.

'Right. OK. Sorry about that.' I frown, leafing through papers as if they're going to help me. I can imagine Anderson and Craig outside, shaking their heads in horror.

'You're Lauren,' I confirm. 'Well, Lauren, you're being charged with murder.' I sound weirdly like a game-show host, congratulating a guest on being selected. I'm inwardly cringing at who might hear the replay.

She turns her eyes full on me, looking slightly puzzled. Her fingers creep over her bare arm and pluck at the skin. 'He's dead?' she asks. 'For sure?'

'You'll have to tell me who you're referring to.' I know it's a wrong move as I say it. I'm asking pedantic questions when I should be trying to be her friend.

Just as I expect, she smiles a little smile and turns away, dismissive.

'Do you mind telling me what happened last night?' I try.

Too soon, Tara. You're supposed to establish rapport.

'Um,' she looks up at the ceiling. 'Is the air con broken? It is so hot in here.'

'I'm not sure,' I admit. 'Would you like a drink, or anything?' It's occurred to me I should have asked this before starting the recording. And now it's on tape that she wasn't offered refreshments. A sweat breaks out on my forehead, as I try to remember if this is an infringement of her rights.

Lauren shakes her head slowly. Relief. That makes my mistake less bad, maybe.

'So last night . . .' I begin.

She cuts me off.

'You said you were a probationary constable, right?' she observes. 'Does that mean you're starting out?'

'First year on the job. I did two years training,' I add, consciously sitting up straighter in an effort to look more authoritative. Does this count as building rapport? I get the distinct impression Lauren is experienced in this kind of question-and-answer scenario, and she's running rings around me.

She turns away, and as her profile switches, I catch sight of a livid oval bruise, like a bite mark, below her ear. Lauren notices me staring. A muscle twitches in her jaw, and she unhooks a loop of pale hair, letting it fall to conceal her neck.

Don't go playing detective, I remind myself. *Stick to the script.*

'Could you answer the question, please?' I say. 'What happened in the pub last night?'

'Which pub?' she asks innocently.

'The Gold Rush. Where you work.' I feel my hands curling into fists.

'I don't work there,' says Lauren, leaning back in her seat. 'I got fired. Sleeping with the customers.'

I fall on this gratefully. 'You had a relationship with some of the men there?'

She sits up a little, alert now. 'Define relationship.' She repeats the skin-plucking gesture, and scratches at her forearm.

'Were you having sex with Paul Hunter?'

It's too abrupt, but surprisingly, she nods. Her eyes range around the room.

71

'Regularly?' I realise too late I should have asked her to confirm verbally for the recording.

'Well, it was kind of casual. Not like every night or anything.' Did I mistake it? A flash of pain in her eyes when she described their relationship as casual.

'What about last night?' There's a faux uninterested note to my voice that I hate the sound of.

'I think . . . Yeah, it was pretty wild.' Her eyes are on the ceiling now and her voice is strange. Strung out. 'He made me come, like, three times.'

Her eyes dance on mine, and I have the disturbing sensation she sees right through me. Maybe she's been playing me.

'To be clear, you are referring to Paul Hunter? Who was found dead in The Gold Rush pub in the early part of this morning?'

Her eyes widen suddenly as if something awful has occurred to her. 'Did Bluey find him?' she asks in a quiet voice. 'Was it Bluey?'

My eyes flit to the door, maybe hoping someone will burst through and rescue me. I swallow. 'I can't tell you details about the crime,' I say, trying to sound official. 'I'm here to ask you questions in connection with the death.'

She falls against the back of her chair, with a blank expression. I fill the silence with information from her file.

'You volunteered out on the Moodjana mission, right?' I say. 'Did that cause tension with the mine workers you were serving drinks to?'

Lauren sits bolt upright. 'What's that got to do with *anything*?'

I'm taken back by the ferocity of her reaction. Should I risk pushing further?

'Why don't you tell me what happened at the pub last night?' I suggest.

She looks thoughtful. 'Well, *probationer* Harrison,' says

Lauren. 'I *could* tell you. But then I'd have to kill you.'

I swallow and my eyes flick to the clock. Time has run away with me.

'Interview terminated at 1600 hours,' I say, fighting to regain the last semblance of competence. Lauren looks almost disappointed, like a cat whose mouse unexpectedly escapes.

16

Lauren

That first shift. Honestly, I have no idea how we got through it. It was full on. The regulars were super friendly. But they kept distracting us, wanting to talk, and Pete would lose it and start shouting that someone didn't have a drink or whatever.

If a customer crunched the can in his hand, that meant he was ready for another drink. Like, no one raised a billfold, or their hand, or made eye contact or anything. Just pulverised the beer can and expected you to see it, dotted amongst all the men sitting at the bar.

The locals had a good vibe to them. They defended us from Pete, calling him a grumpy old bastard. It was funny.

Pete said we were allowed to drink on shift so long as we paid for it ourselves, but the last thing we needed was alcohol. Plus there was a stapled-up wall of photos of all the girls who had previously worked at The Gold Rush, and . . . I don't like to sound judgemental or anything . . . but they looked so drunk. I couldn't believe they had allowed themselves to be photographed in that state.

Though the work was hard, it was exhilarating. It was like the time we did the twenty-four-hour pancake cook for the Kappa

Rho fraternity boys, only this was real. Real life. We were earning actual money. It was super cool.

Pete

There's always a full house the night the new girls arrive.

Beth

When the doors opened and the men rolled in . . . I mean, these men literally had their mouths hanging open. And the problem with Lauren is when she starts flicking her hair, doing this sort of pouty thing, that can totally be misinterpreted. When you know her, you understand it. But it can look a little . . . vain or something, when you first meet her.

The men were all heavy-set. Big arms and bodies. The older ones had fat bellies. They wore dusty pants and steel-capped boots etched with red dirt. Most of them had high-vis jackets, emblazoned with MINING CORPORATION in big letters, like they were all in the same beer-swilling tribe.

In our short-shorts uniform, Lauren and I might as well have been wearing bikinis. I'm used to not fitting in – try being the smart kid in the trailer park, or the poor scholarship girl in a college sorority house. But here I felt like we were another species.

The first drink I sold would have been to Mike, I think. Swan beer. Obviously. They all drank Swan.

Despite Pete's massive selection of weird liqueur drinks, and two beer taps, the customers knocked back these little tin cans at breakneck speed. Keeping the bar-top cooler stocked was a permanent problem.

'That cooler is thirty years old,' Pete told us proudly. 'Started life as a little ice freezer but she gave up on that ten years ago, so now she cools the beer down.' He tapped his head to signal the dizzying intellect of this decision. 'But on cold days, the old girl can pop back to life,' he continued. 'If you hear a buzzing sound get all the tinnies out real quick or they'll blow their ring pulls and all be fucked, right? You got that, girls? 'Cause if you let my beers freeze it comes out of your wages.'

Lauren had laughed. She thought he was joking.

'People come here for a cold one,' Pete said, like a million times. 'They don't get cold beer here, they might as well go to the convenience store.'

Only twenty beers could be decanted into the cooler. You had to take the cans from a particular spot, else they wouldn't be fully cold. Only the cold spot changed, depending on stock rotation, time of day and possibly phase of the moon.

Lauren

I had cooler trauma, by the end of that first shift. I swear. It gave me nightmares. I still don't have the least idea how that thing worked. Every time it ran out, poor Beth had to go into the cellar. I felt super guilty, because I know she did that for me. I did try to help, but even standing close to the open trapdoor, my legs started shaking so bad I couldn't get down the ladder.

But . . . before we knew it Pete called last orders, and we were doing our very first lock-in. We had the whole place to ourselves and the guys were buying us all kinds of drinks. I remember thinking that part was fun. I mean, they had kind of an eccentric sense of humour and all. There were some jokes about LA that I didn't understand. A bit of hazing the new girls, like college. Same the world over, right? Groups like to test out the newbies, give them hell.

And seriously, though I am sworn to secrecy, you would *not believe* the things you have to do to get into a sorority house.

Beth

The tension. The tension behind that bar.

It was only about three of the younger ones who stayed. Mike, who was stocky with brown hair and teddy-bearish dark eyes to match. Paul, who seemed to think he was God's gift to women, blond with very deep blue eyes. Handsome, but with a seedy edge. Then there was this weaselly little guy with a goatee called Dillon who was completely covered in amateur tattoos. Macho-type emblems, predatory animals and naked girls, all over his arms and back, and right up to his chest. He sucked up to Paul and was always the butt of his jokes. Dillon was one those guys who actually said, 'I'm not racist, but . . .'

As soon as I went to close up, the atmosphere shifted. There was a distinct sense that now they thought they had a chance with us.

'You're from California?' said Dillon, openly staring at my butt as I locked the door. 'Isn't that where they make all the pornos?'

I think I mumbled something like I didn't know. And Lauren, of course, she was chattering away the whole time, and not getting that some of these guys were now seriously thinking to try it on.

That was the first lock-in and I thought it was bad then. We had three months until we had to do another one. It didn't occur to me the men were biding their time.

Lauren

We goofed around, making cocktails out of all the weird sugar-liqueurs. Mike was this big guy who you could tell was a total softie at heart. Paul didn't say a whole lot, but you got the impression he was the boss. Dillon was quick with the jokes. Not the nicest jokes, but I figured he was on edge and trying to impress.

I remember being totally shocked at how much they drank. I had never, in my whole life, seen men so drunk. Like, it was a badge of honour they were all staggering around and slurring. I have no idea how they got home. I think they *drove*.

Dillon

We were always having a laugh and a joke with them in the beginning. They loved it. Loved the banter.

Beth

I barely noticed Paul at first. He looked like all the others. Thick-set from working. A little better-looking, maybe. Chisel-jawed with a chip in his front tooth. That first lock-in, he hung back, watching Lauren. The other guys were trying their luck. He was forming a battle plan.

Dillon

Paul always got a girl when he put his mind to it. And he put his mind to Lauren.

17

I leave the interview room with the beginnings of a headache throbbing at my temples. Anderson is waiting outside with a deeply sympathetic expression, which tells me how badly I did.

'Well, Harrison, you fucked that up good and proper.' Anderson isn't one to mince his words. 'Hell of a first interview, though. Things can only get better, eh?'

'Yes, sir,' I agree miserably.

'The good news is the guys from Perth will be here tomorrow morning. They'll have a female with them, so you won't have to do round two with the second girl.'

I want another shot. I felt like I was getting somewhere with Lauren. When she asked about Bluey finding Paul's remains . . . I should have pushed that more.

Anderson glares over my shoulder. 'What is it, Dooligan? Spit it out?'

I turn to see Craig hovering uncertainly, obviously uncomfortable to witness my crash and burn.

'I viewed The Gold Rush camera footage,' says Craig.

'And?' barks Anderson.

'Gold Rush cameras only run between 11 p.m. and 2 a.m.,'

says Craig. 'Landlord Pete reckons nothing ever kicks off outside those times so he doesn't want to spend the extra few cents on electricity.'

Anderson rolls his eyes. 'So what have we got?'

'April Dean staggers in at 1.19 a.m., leaves at 1.28 a.m.'

'Fits with what the blokes have already told us,' says Anderson. 'Anyone else leave?'

'Not between 11 p.m. and 2 a.m.,' says Craig.

'Any way to leave the pub avoiding the cameras?' Anderson looks at me. 'Entry or exit points, Harrison?'

'There's a street-level beer hatch, leading to the cellar, and up to the pub,' I say. 'But Pete keeps it bolted from the outside.'

'OK. Good work. What do we have left to do?'

'Still trying to ID the Aboriginal girl,' says Craig.

'What about the mystery Holden?' I suggest. 'I could check car records.'

'Dooligan's checking out Holdens registered in the locality. But . . . if the driver *was* from the mission, it's unlikely to be documented to the current owner.'

'Moodjana culture is communal,' I say. 'People share things. Hard to fit that to the Western way, you know? That's mine, this is yours.'

'Alright, Harrison, I know you've got friends on the mission. Just stating fact.' Anderson checks his watch. 'I make it half hour 'til end of shift. How about you knock off early? Start fresh tomorrow, eh? We've got another eighteen hours to charge Darla-Beth Jackson.'

'I'd rather stay and finish the day, sir.'

Anderson's face does something like he's reassessing me.

'Very good, Harrison,' he says. 'Not much to do, though.'

I consider. 'I could look into the brothel card found on the pub floor,' I suggest.

Anderson looks confused, then clarity dawns. 'Magic Molly's,' he says. 'Not really a lead, Harrison. Half the blokes in town visit York Street.'

I glance at Craig for confirmation and am taken aback to see he looks deeply uncomfortable. Can't imagine him as a customer. He's more the sort of strait-laced bloke who gets up at 5 a.m. for a protein smoothie and cold shower.

'I've got nothing better to do,' I tell Anderson. 'Might as well eliminate it. Best practice and all that.'

'Very good, Harrison. Why not? Check it out.'

'Is Craig coming with me?'

Anderson coughs into his hand like he's disguising a laugh. 'Mucky Mol's is not our Craigo's kind of place.'

I look back and forth between them, noting Craig's mortified expression, and wonder what I'm missing. Is he gay? Whatever it is confirms one thing. Anderson doesn't regard this as anything more than a dead end to be closed off.

Twenty minutes later I'm alone outside Magic Molly's, having walked the length of Dead Tree Creek's infamous red-light street. The buildings have low frontages of corrugated iron, with multiple doors set facing the road. This design is a throwback to the town's heyday when prostitutes would be arranged like horses in stables, to meet endless demand from gold prospectors. *Starting stalls.* A term from my school days floats back to me. Boys like Paul Hunter would brag about visiting York Street. It looked very different back then. A legal red-light district, so long as the girls stayed in the houses. Nowadays it still has a sleazy air, but most doors are closed, over half of the brothels are boarded, and the rest look deserted or falling apart.

Magic Molly's looks like the last one to be doing any meaningful trade, with its trademark lurid pink neon boasting twenty-four-hour opening. As I approach, I notice a newer sign offering tourist entry to the 'historic building' daily at 4 p.m. I guess they've been forced to diversify.

Leaning in the doorway is a raven-haired woman with a ravaged face on the wrong side of thirty for the night trade, dressed in a short dress, long gloves and vertiginous heels.

She takes in my police uniform and her face shifts to wary.

I fall back on my training; engage first. Question later.

'Quiet shift?' I observe.

'Yeah,' she agrees with feeling. A smouldering cigarette magically emerges from behind her back. 'On a smoko.' She draws heavily then looks up and down the street. 'It's been dead for months. Bloody Asians, isn't it?' She notices my expression. 'I don't mean ... I'm not being racist,' she says unconvincingly. 'Only those Asian girls will do anything for $80, you know? I tell my fellas, you're paying a hundred and thirty bucks for a good clean Aussie girl. Those Asians, they don't do health checks, nothing. Probably been sex trafficked, most of 'em.' She gives a weary shrug. 'Men will be men, I s'pose.' She sucks three times deeply on the cigarette, in the way of someone who's been told not to let customers see her smoke on the door, and palms it, a dragon-like cloud streaming from her nostrils.

'I'm here about a murder at The Gold Rush,' I tell her.

'Don't know nothing about it,' she says, instantly defensive. 'I was here all night. The boss, she'll tell you.'

'No one's accusing you,' I reassure her. 'I wondered if you recognised the bloke who was killed.'

I scroll on my phone, trying to find the picture of Paul Hunter.

'I see so many blokes, love, they all merge into one. Perks of a mining town.'

'Would you mind having a look anyway?'

She rolls her eyes and moves forward, a denial already on her lips. But as she sees Paul Hunter's face her eyes widen and she takes in a quick breath. Her face hardens.

'Yeah, I remember him,' she says, taking a shaky puff of her cigarette with narrowed eyes. 'He hasn't been here for a long time anyway. Boss kicked him out.'

'For what?' I can't imagine what would get you ejected from a rickety whorehouse on a dead-end street.

Her face closes down. 'You'll have to ask the boss. He's the one who died, is he?' she adds in a hard tone. 'Dead bloke whose picture got shared on social media, right? The backpacker girls killed him.'

'What makes you think that?'

'Just what everyone's saying.'

The palmed cigarette slides up to her mouth again, and she repeats her check of the empty street.

'Like I said,' she says, firmly, 'you gotta ask her indoors.' She jerks a thumb towards an unseen owner. 'Right now, I'm working, you'll get me into trouble.' She takes one last giant pull on the now-spent cigarette, and grinds it under her spindly heel with impressive accuracy.

'Your boss,' I try, 'she inside?'

'She's busy. Doing one of the tours.' She looks over my shoulder at some invisible approaching trade. 'Come back tomorrow. Afternoon's a good time to catch her.'

18

When I arrive back at the station, Craig is waiting for me outside, leaning up against the steel exterior of the building, bulging arms crossed at his chest. He's wearing his sunglasses and looks like he's posing for a calendar shoot; styled hair, booted foot pressed up to the cladding.

'Hi, Craig.'

'Good first day?' He pushes himself away from the wall and takes off his shades, morphing from gym freak to college boy.

I smile. 'Good and bad,' I admit. 'In at the deep end, for sure.' I wonder how someone with red hair and light eyes can have such dark brows.

'Anderson asked me to do some firearms training with you,' he says, pushing his hands in his pockets and rocking slightly on the balls of his feet. 'Town can get rough at night. Squaring up to some big drunk fellas is all part of the beat.'

'Isn't it brain over brawn nowadays?' I try for an engaging tone. 'My training was all about thinking your way out of possible altercations.'

Craig's brow furrows.

'Maybe in the city,' he says, echoing Anderson. 'Mining town like this, you need to be able to hold your own, take a man down if need be. Show the rest not to mess with you.'

I want to tell him that times are changing. Policing should be about communication, not intimidation. But it's a bit soon on the job to throw my opinions around.

'Guess I should accept your offer of help then,' I say, aiming for a smile.

'I've got time now if you like?'

'Sure. Thanks.' Craig seems like the kind of bloke who'd bore you to sleep talking about fitness routines and bullet calibers. But if I want to pass, I need to train.

'Follow me. The firing range is a few blocks away.'

'The station has its own firing range?'

'Not officially. We've repurposed an old building. I can tell you all the stuff I mucked up as a probationary constable in Dead Tree Creek on the way,' he adds with a sideways grin. Maybe there's more to Craig than waxed hair and muscles.

We set off at a slow walk. 'You find anything about the mystery Holden?' I ask.

Craig shakes his head slowly. 'Not yet. Few hundred in the area. I'm working through. So far a couple of the owners have a record for minor stuff. Drunk and disorderly. Traffic offences. Nothing to link them to The Gold Rush.'

We cross over the road. 'So, pretty big case,' I say as we reach the other side.

Craig blows out air. 'Tell me about it. Biggest thing to happen to this town in a long while.'

His eyes skid to my face and back again, as if he's wondering whether to mention Yindi.

'You'll have reporters in by tomorrow,' I tell him. 'Might even make the nationals.'

He nods, slowly. 'It will be out of our hands by then,' he says.

'Perth will take the whole thing. We'll be the bogans who get in the way. Be lucky if they let us bring them coffee.'

I nod sadly at his assessment. It dawns on me that for all my nerves, it's a thrill to be part of a real-life murder investigation.

We pass The Gold Rush, its doors and windows now professionally sealed with tape. Forensics must have gone for the day.

'Was that your local?' I ask, glancing towards it.

'I wouldn't drink in that place if I was dying of thirst,' Craig replies, going immediately up in my estimation. 'Right load of drongo pissheads in there.' His green eyes slide to the pub and away again.

My eyes catch something on the corner of the pavement by The Gold Rush. A trail of ants, each bearing a perfect pale larva.

'What is it?' asks Craig.

'Oh, nothing.' I've slowed down without noticing. 'You don't often see that,' I explain.

The flies in the pub. They weren't circling right either. The two facts are connected. More than that. Important somehow. What was it Yindi's uncle used to tell me about how flies circled?

Craig is looking at me quizzically.

'Those ants are moving blow-fly larvae.'

'Oh, right,' Craig sounds politely uninterested. 'You into all that stuff? Bushcraft and that?'

'Not really. But my older sister – foster sister – was Aboriginal,' I explain as we walk on, leaving the ants to their hoard. 'State regulations meant my foster parents had to honour her heritage. Let her people take her for visits, and bush trips. She let me tag along.' I point at the ants. 'We did a lot of watching out for stuff like that. Things out of balance.'

'Sounds like police work.'

'Maybe.'

Craig considers for a moment. 'You and your sister were both fostered? Black and a white kid together?'

'Yeah. She always said they stuffed up taking her from her family. Shouldn't have been allowed to give her to a white foster home. I was eight, she was ten. When I was little, I basically wanted to be her. She had this mega extended family, and I didn't even know my dad's name.'

'You guys always acted like sisters at school,' says Craig. 'Even though . . . different appearances, you know? There was something the same.'

I'm confused. 'You remember us from school?'

'Yeah.' He snatches a glance at my face. 'You don't remember me?'

The mist clears, and a younger, fatter Craig steps forward. 'You've changed,' I manage, trying to fit the sweaty, buck-toothed, round-faced boy from the past with gym-honed Craig.

'Right little chunker I was,' agrees Craig easily. 'I got an inheritance from my nana. Decided to make the best of it. Fixed my teeth, got in shape, you know? Went to college. Took me a few attempts to pass the fitness to join the police, but once I got into it, it became like a habit. Feel better for it too,' he concludes. 'Well, here we are.'

We've arrived at an abandoned-looking industrial building now. Single level, fibro construction. Several official-looking signs declare it to be property of Dead Tree Creek police.

Craig unlocks the thick security door.

'Ladies first,' he says, holding it open for me. 'Actually, I think you're the first woman to have ever seen it.'

19

Lauren

Waking up in Dead Tree Creek that first time was totally surreal. In the context of the men in the bar, it hadn't seemed we were drinking so much. But the next morning. Ugh. I remember the sound of Bluey's road train pulling up, like *right outside* our window. A road train, FYI is an Australian invention. Five of the largest freight trucks you can imagine, coupled together, so a single driver could make the same amount of noise as an entire truck stop. This was at what felt like 7 a.m. We'd only gotten to bed, maybe a few hours before. I rolled over and looked at Beth. She was like: 'Guess we're getting up.'

Despite the hangover, it was an adventure. Like, we were real working girls with our own place, not depending on anyone. Using all these rickety old kitchen appliances. Opening hundred-year-old window shutters. I was determined to see it through.

Beth

We trooped out into the hot sun, which was blasting down at this point, giving our hangovers this extra shade of wrong.

The town had lots of little gem stores that I guess were aimed at whatever trickle of tourists passed through. They had big vaudeville-type signs, but original, not for show, and shopfronts loaded with trays of colourful jewellery – tiny gold nuggets and semi-precious stones set into necklaces and rings. Then, the flip side, pawn shops, trading more or less the exact same stuff.

We passed the coach station, which was basically a Greyhound sign and a timetable showing one bus a week out of Dead Tree Creek.

Tomorrow. Seven a.m. And not for seven days after that.

Lauren wanted to get some things to pretty up the apartment, so we found a dollar store. I hugely admire that about Lauren, because I would never have the energy to make a temporary accommodation look nice. She did the same with our room at college. We always had the nicest place.

After buying a bunch of throws and cushions, we walked a few blocks and found this little café on the edge of town. All boho signage and mismatched chairs – like something you might expect to see in Europe. It was super cute and didn't seem to fit the place at all. There was a refrigerator stocked with bright bottles of cold-pressed juice.

At this point Dead Tree Creek was growing on me. It seemed very liveable. Plus it helped we didn't have to do another lock-in for two more months.

We ordered smoothies and chilli dogs, since that seemed to be the speciality, and Lauren noticed me looking at the prices and said, 'You don't have to worry about money, Beth. I can always loan you. Doesn't even have to be a loan.'

I was plodding my straw into the soupy depths of my smoothie, trying figure how to explain how I didn't accept friendly handouts. Never had, never would.

We heard this voice behind us. French accent.

'Are you girls out on the next bus?'

We both turned around. The speaker had used the plural but was only addressing Lauren. He was curly-haired and tall, with a faded band T-shirt, battered Levi cut-offs and a guitar slung over his back. His face was beautiful. That's the only word for it. Elf-like with perfect light blue eyes.

Lauren batted her lashes very fast.

'Why?' she replied. 'Are you?'

He gave this kind of lazy smile, and shook his head.

'I work here,' he said. 'Across the street.' He indicated with his head, towards what appeared to be a ramshackle building of co-working and indie office space. 'Protecting the rights of the Indigenous people.'

I was mesmerised by his arrogance. Like he thought he was some great saviour or something. But Lauren's smile grew wide.

'*Cool*,' she said. 'We work here too. At a bar in town. But we totally want to see the outback and stuff,' she added quickly.

'You should come out to the reservation,' he said, his square jaw dimpling. 'Aboriginal culture understands things that we don't get, with our fast cars and glass buildings. We've lost the flow of nature, and they're like, *connected*. But they need our help,' he concluded, earnestly.

I remember rolling my eyes.

He introduced himself as Marc, then sat himself down at our table without asking. 'You must have seen on the news, the Mining Corporation has committed an atrocity on Aboriginal land.'

I glanced at Lauren. 'I heard about that,' I said, knowing she wouldn't. 'It was a big story. A sacred Aboriginal site got destroyed, right? There were some ugly protests. I didn't realise it was *here*.'

Reporters had filmed a sobbing Aboriginal Elder, blood streaming down his face as he was roughly manhandled by mine security, broken placard trailing in the red dirt.

Mike

OK, so right before Lauren and Beth arrived, our mining company went and blew up the wrong bit of rock. Honest mistake. But we got blackfellas showing up, shouting. You felt bad every day you got to work. Some of the blokes protesting were my friends, and there they were, waving signs in my face. Security got heavy. Too heavy, I'll admit. Dragged Black people off for a kicking. An old man ended up with a broken nose. Everyone was stressed.

It was already starting to get really hot too. You had the flies and all that. Bosses, cracking the whip, wanting more gold per tonne. Beth and Lauren should never have gotten involved.

Beth

Marc got very animated about the mining company, but it all seemed acted to me.

'That site was *thousands* of years old,' he told Lauren, melodramatically pounding his fist on the table. 'Now the mining company's security are attacking peaceful protestors.'

'That's *awful*,' said Lauren, her eyes shining with tears.

'We're helping to get the people's voices heard,' continued Marc. 'You'd look good with a banner,' he added, winking. This wasn't directed at me. Obviously.

I glanced at Lauren, like, *Should we tell him we work in a mining pub?* We were basically serving drinks to the enemy. And I had no idea what the men in The Gold Rush would think of us protesting against their employer.

Lauren's hand curled softly around my forearm. 'We'd like to help,' she said.

I should mention at this point, that Lauren has a tendency to see the absolute best in people, which means she falls in love incredibly easily. And, because she has been into human rights since forever, she more or less fell in love on the spot. Around the exact same time I decided I hated him.

Lauren

Beth never seems to enjoy male attention. Now I come to think of it . . . I don't actually *know* if Beth is into guys at all. Or maybe she's not into sex. Not sure. I've never seen her make out with a girl or anything, but then again there was pressure at our sorority house to be quote-unquote 'straight'. Which I don't even believe in, by the way, because I think everyone is on this *scale*, which is incredibly non-binary, and everybody *could* be gay or homosexual or whatever you want to call it, with the right person.

I didn't see Beth with a lot of guys, is what I'm trying to say.

Beth

It's pretty hard to get with men, with Lauren around. I don't blame her for that at all, by the way. She's told me a few things that happened to her growing up, and those events have wired her to see her value in a certain light. Could have gone in the opposite direction. She could have gained a GC ton of weight and dressed in shapeless clothes. Lauren turned a vulnerability to her advantage. The people who hate her for that, just don't get it.

In any case, I did once remind her of our night in Thailand, a little after we arrived in Perth. She acted like she'd forgotten. Then she slapped her hand to her forehead, in this fake way, and was like: 'Oh my God, we did, didn't we? We totally made out.'

Only I remember we did quite a bit more than that.

Lauren threw her head back in this weird false laugh. Like a hyena. She bent forward at the hips like she couldn't contain it. By the time she straightened up, I was regretting mentioning it at all.

'Oh my God,' repeated Lauren, panting with laughter. 'That is soooo funny!'

I knew right then what she meant. We should never talk about it ever again. Never. But I don't think that influenced my feelings towards Marc. Pretty sure not.

Mike

Oh, *Marc*. Yeah, I remember that guy. Total prick.

93

20

Inside the shooting range is a basic set-up. A line of targets, sandbags and insulation to prevent ricochet, taped lines on the ground to signal distances.

It's hot, even for early evening, with a dry timber smell to the air. The building is essentially a corrugated iron shell and the only cooling facility is a yellowed ceiling fan. As Craig switches it to life, flies wheel out from their resting places. He crosses the room and fires up a grungy wall-mounted commercial bug killer, its neon tubes caked in charred insects and upturned black legs.

Craig busies himself retrieving bullets from a locked cabinet, and hands me a pair of ear defenders and safety goggles.

'We use our own guns here,' he says. 'Keeps it simple.'

'OK.' I'm growing more nervous by the second. 'I just point and shoot?' I wave a fly away from my face.

'That's the idea.' He smiles at my question.

I ready myself, putting on the protective gear, loading my gun. It's hard to stop my hand shaking as I take aim. I've got muscle memory from all the painful recoil of past practice.

I line up the sights, the target, let out a steadying breath and smoothly squeeze the trigger. The gun goes off, reverberating back into my palm.

'Fuck!' It's out of my mouth before I can catch it. I stand wincing, shaking my fingers. 'Sorry,' I tell Craig, rubbing my ringing hand. 'I haven't learned to stop the recoil yet.'

Craig frowns and moves towards me. 'Show me that again?' he says.

I take aim.

'Do you mind if I . . .?' Craig steps behind me. 'Can I adjust your arm?'

'Sure. Yeah, OK.' Craig's large frame is so close I can feel his body heat. He positions my elbow and slides his hand over mine on the gun.

'You're strong,' he says, sounding surprised as I set myself to shoot.

'I hide it well.'

'OK,' he says. 'Don't worry about aiming this time. Just squeeze and pull.'

This time the recoil is absorbed by Craig's thick palm.

He steps back, frowning, looking at my grip.

'What?' I follow his gaze.

'Yeah. I thought so,' says Craig. 'Because you're stretching for the trigger, you're not catching the recoil. That's why it slams you every time.'

'What does that mean?' I holster my gun.

Craig's frown deepens. 'Get bigger hands? You're shooting a standard police issue . . . so . . .'

I glare at my weapon, dejected.

'It happens to guys with small hands too,' he assures me. We both stare a fraction too long at Craig's large hands.

'Do any small-handed people pass firearms?' I ask, looking away.

'Um. Yeah. One or two, maybe . . . Let's take a break, grab a cold one,' suggests Craig. 'Might help to have a beer in you, eh?'

'There's a bar here?' I'm looking around.

'There's a fridge.' Craig lopes over to the edge of the room, where a tiny bar-fridge is whirring. He opens the door and pulls out two cans of Swan. 'Here.' He tosses me one. I catch it.

'Thanks.' There's no seating, so we slide to the ground, backs against the slow heat of the corrugated iron wall.

I take a long sip of beer. 'So, what do you think happened in that pub?'

He frowns in thought.

'Well, Paul Hunter is a real prick, isn't he? He's probably in there, doing things he shouldn't. Goes too far. One of the girls loses it.'

'I can imagine all that,' I counter, 'but handcuffing him and torturing him? Stuffing mud in his mouth until he suffocates?'

'Yeah,' he agrees thoughtfully. 'One thing I learned as a copper. People never fail to surprise you.'

I swallow the rest of my beer in one gulp, and stand, readying my gun. 'Can I go again?'

'Sure.' Craig stands, and ambles behind me, back over to the taped spot on the floor.

Ten metres. To pass I need to hit the target three times from ten metres. Easy, I tell myself.

Craig peers into his beer can as I take aim. 'So what brings you back? You got a fella here?'

'No.' It comes out too quickly, because I'm shocked at how my thoughts flash to Jarrah. How I broke things off before they started. More than that, I just miss him, I realise with a jolt. I miss my old friend.

Craig is speaking. 'Why the police?'

'As in . . . why'd I join?' I keep my eyes on the target. 'Seemed like a steady job.'

He frowns. 'But something happened with your foster sister, a few years back, didn't it? There was all that stuff in town. Riots and that. Wasn't there a campaign by the Aboriginal community?'

My arm lines up the gun. 'A law. It was a law got passed.'

'Right,' says Craig. 'Police brutality. Yindi's Law.'

I take aim and fire. A family of flies scatter as the bullet thuds harmlessly into a sandbag.

'You're a little battler, I reckon,' Craig says, eyes flashing under his thick brows, 'to come through all that and join the force. Good on ya.'

'Thanks.' I shoot again, and tuck my palm into my armpit, trying not to swear.

'That was closer,' says Craig. 'You nearly hit it that time.'

My eyes drift with the regrouping blowflies. And now it comes back to me – the answer I was missing earlier. If flies smell meat, they zigzag, not circle like these are doing.

But not all the flies in The Gold Rush were moving how you'd expect by a dead body. It was like . . . they were distracted.

Craig turns to me. 'You OK there, Tara?' He puts a light hand on my arm. 'We can stop if you want.'

The ants. The ants near The Gold Rush were carrying blowfly larvae. They were in the wrong place too.

'I think there could be a second body.' As soon as I say it, I know it's true.

'You've been through a lot today, Tara,' says Craig, sounding concerned. 'Are you sure . . .'

'Under the pub,' I say. 'We should call Anderson.' I pull out my phone.

'Well, this is a first,' he says. 'Never had a girl bail on me before her second beer.'

I glance over at him, not sure if he's joking. Because this is hardly a date.

'Craig, I'm serious,' I say. 'Forensics took the body, but those ants were moving blowfly larvae. And the flies were zigzagging all over, like they could smell another food source.' I take a breath. 'The only thing big enough to attract a fly away from a dead body, is another dead body.'

Craig appears uncertain. 'You're sure?'

I nod. 'I'm sure. I need to call Anderson.'

'Here, let me,' he sighs. 'But you'd better be right, Tara. Because if you're not, Anderson won't thank you for ringing him at dinner.'

21

Beth

Marc drove us out to the Aboriginal reserve two hours after we met him at The Green Table. Lauren can have that effect on men.

On the journey Marc yapped away about how great his charity was for helping the Indigenous people be part of the political system. He started on how Dreamtime was the dawn of creation, when the earth was soft and huge creatures made tracks on the landscape. Lauren was all misty-eyed. Marc seemed like exactly the type of egotistical moron I try to keep her away from. His weird deifying of the local customs was covert racism in my opinion. As a kid, I remember a similar brand of head-patting bullshit from Christian volunteers on the trailer park.

'To the native people the site the Mining Corporation destroyed, was touched by a God,' he concluded. 'There were thousand-year-old rock paintings smashed. In our culture it would be like swinging a wrecking ball at Notre Dame.' He turned to look at Lauren instead of the road, which stressed me out. 'When will man realise you cannot eat gold?' Marc asked with total sincerity.

Lauren gazed at him. 'Oh my gosh,' she said. 'That is so *profound.*'

I noticed I had little half-moon indentations in my palm, where I'd been digging my fingernails.

At this point it was clear to me, we couldn't get drawn into volunteering, and also work at The Gold Rush. Based on how the miners spoke about the Aboriginal community, relations were not good. Joining Marc's cause seemed like asking for trouble.

Lauren

The reserve wasn't how I expected at all. From how Marc spoke, I thought it would be little huts or yurts. Instead, it was like a town. There were these super-basic houses with corrugated roofs all in rows and bleached-out straw-grass for a yard. Kids were running about unsupervised, shouting and laughing. Adults were wandering around at a slower pace. Dogs ran at our truck as we drove by. I was a little intimidated but Beth seemed chilled.

Marc explained the Indigenous way of raising children is a community effort. Aunties and uncles are like extra moms and dads, cousins are brothers and sisters, and everyone else in the group is a cousin. This totally resonated with me. There is so much wrong with the isolating home I grew up in. If *I'd* have had back-up parents, my childhood wouldn't have been so messed up. It was fascinating, but . . . I sensed a little tension between Beth and Marc.

'You are very quiet,' observed Marc, looking at Beth. 'I guess this must be different to anything you've ever seen before.'

'Not so much,' said Beth, smiling. She was watching a little girl dancing in the road with a hula hoop.

'Well,' frowned Marc, looking straight ahead, 'we're not just helping the protestors. Our organisation is also about making sure these kids attend school. Giving them a proper education.'

'Because you know what's best for them, right?' Beth hadn't taken her eyes off the child with the hoop.

Beth

Marc was a total douche. All I asked him was this: if his charity thought Aboriginal culture was so great, why did a lot of their set-up revolve around forcing it into Western educational norms? We'd had the same flavour of do-gooders show up on the trailer park and treat us like we were in-breds for wearing white after Labour Day.

It was a genuine question, but Marc took it badly. Lauren had to explain I was an analytical kind of person.

After that Marc seemed to be trying to prove to Lauren he was smarter than me. Which seemed a silly thing for him to compete over. Intelligence isn't everything, and he had looks.

Lauren

Marc's charity had their own building on the reserve, where all their projects took place. It was like the hub of community volunteering. Marc wanted us making placards for the protest against the Mining Corporation. But Beth found this opportunity for female-only mentoring work, supporting Indigenous girls who had been in trouble with the police. Empowering them to have a voice in the political system. Perfect for two Alpha Sigma Psi graduates, who had majored in politics and sociology. Getting women into high places is basically our mantra.

Dillon

Lauren studied politics? *What . . . ?*

Beth

I acted on impulse, which is not like me at all. I was planning on making a couple of placards and leaving before someone snapped our picture for social media or something. But the way Marc was steering Lauren around with his hand on the small of her back really bothered me. And all the close family connections of the local people was impacting in a way I can't explain. There were similarities with the trailer park. And – in a twisted fairground mirror kind of way – with the sorority house. It made my college years feel ugly and distorted, like we'd lost something important.

Added to this, I *knew* I could give those Indigenous girls a voice. Their *own* voice. Not just how guys like Marc thought they should be.

When I signed us up for the mentoring project I didn't fully appreciate we were double agents now. Good guys by day, villains by night.

Lauren

Beth can be very dramatic. I do remember her talking about, like, *Don't mention to the guys in the bar where we volunteer.* I didn't really get the issue.

Anyway, Beth and I were directed to this old cinderblock building, where twenty or so teenage girls were lounging on fold-out metal chairs. I went in high energy. They basically ignored me, scrolled on their phones, or talked to one another in their own language. Complete bust. I crashed and burned. I'm not ashamed to admit it. The only thing I got was from this girl called Charlee, with bleached-blonde tips to her curly dark hair. Apparently, everyone was super mad about the sacred site.

Charlee

This girl, Lauren, was cr-azy, eh? We were there to learn about politics, and she was asking us where we bought our jeans. I just tuned her out. Everyone was dealing with this raw grief. The Mining Corporation . . . They didn't even *know* the pain they'd caused. Like, oh, what? We killed your mother? There's heaps of those around here, just find another one.

Dillon

There's always tension between these communities, right? The miners, and the Indigenous people. Who owns what. The Blacks reckon they own the whole country. That's why I never bought a house, 'cause they'll try to claim your backyard. True. Happened to a bloke who knew my mate's auntie.

Anyway, now the blackfellas are whinging over a heap of rocks. Saying it was some ancient land going back generations. Pick another heap of rocks, eh? Move on. And now it's all so much drama, blokes at the mine are losing their jobs for racist language, all that stuff.

So us miners get off shift, head to the pub for a bit of light relief. No one's going to take it well if two little *barmaids*, who know nothing about nothing, are fraternising with the enemy, are they?

They're supposed to be on our side.

22

It's dark by the time Anderson joins us outside The Gold Rush. One by one we slip under the crime scene tape.

'You'd better pray you're right, Harrison,' Anderson says, handing me a heavy flashlight that was outdated police issue about ten years ago.

'We're actually going to take a look?' I thought he'd refer things directly to the Perth team.

'I'm not risking making an idiot of myself without checking it out. Craig tells me you're basing this theory on some kind of bushcraft you learned off your sister?'

I explain about the blowflies.

'Sounds like a load of bloody voodoo if you ask me,' says Anderson. 'And if you've got me all the way down here for nothing, it's a black mark for you. The wife made pot roast. It'll be cold by the time I get back and she'll be spitting nails.'

'I think it's worth a look, sir.'

'Alright. Any idea where this second body might be?'

'Underground,' I say. 'Explains why the ants could get to it in the heat of the day.'

'We can get into the cellar without going through the pub,' says Craig helpfully. 'Just through there.' He points to a large wooden hatch set low down against the wall of The Gold

Rush. 'Pete unlocked it for the forensics' visit.'

I eye the chunky padlock hanging loose. Anderson rolls his eyes, taking in the small entrance.

'Sir, look.' I point at the hatch. 'The hasp for that lock is screwed into the wood.'

'And?'

'It would be easy enough to unscrew it and screw it back without anyone noticing.'

Craig shines his flashlight. 'She's right, sir. All you'd need is a screwdriver.'

Anderson waves his light, and nods thoughtfully.

'That means, *anyone* could have gotten in that night,' I say. 'April could have doubled back. One or more of the blokes. Or a different person entirely.'

I'm thinking of the hard look on the face of the Magic Molly's woman, when Paul Hunter was mentioned. Someone from the mission, too, could have easily driven into town, and back. They could rely on a massive raft of relatives to automatically give them an alibi if police made accusations.

That thought makes me so uncomfortable I push it back. What would I do if I had to arrest someone from the Black community? My stomach tightens at the thought of Jarrah's face.

Anderson peers. 'Alright, good spot, Harrison. Let's kit up. We can dust it for prints later.'

He waves a bag of disposable clothing.

We pull on gloves, suits and overshoes, and Craig opens the heavy hatch which creaks loudly. I shine my flashlight to reveal a wooden chute for beer barrels to roll down, and a padded mat at the bottom to break their fall.

I slide down first, eager to prove myself. Craig lands behind me. Anderson takes up the rear, making an ungainly crawl on all fours, complaining loudly about his knees.

'Slow down, Harrison!' he calls as I step ahead into the dark, flashing light around the cellar. 'Remember your training. Secure the scene. Assess risk. Check your sergeant isn't going to fracture his neck on the way in.'

'Sorry, sir. It's just, I'm sure there's something here.'

'We all want to do the exciting bits. Good police work is first and foremost keeping you and your colleagues safe, right?'

'Right.'

As soon as Craig's strong torchlight sweeps the cellar, I see the disappointment on his face.

'Nothing here,' he says, shining his light around to show shiny beer barrels, stacked up.

Anderson curses, coming in close behind me. 'Forensics have already looked it over.' He points to tape, sealing an open doorway back up to the main pub. 'They'd hardly have missed another corpse.'

I sniff the air. 'Can't you smell it?'

'I can smell beer and a load of bullshit,' says Anderson. 'Cut your losses, Harrison. Admit when you're wrong.'

'Like a . . . toilet smell,' I insist.

'Give me bloody strength.' Anderson is turning to leave.

I walk forward and stop by a rusted old metal cable leading right through the floor above.

'Part of the mine shaft from the prospecting days,' says Craig, helpfully. 'There's a few around town. Premises have to keep them for historical preservation.'

'What's underneath it?' I ask.

'An old mine, of course, you bloody drongo!' shouts Anderson, already heading back in the direction of the hatch to the street. 'No one's been down there since the 1800s.'

My eyes drop to what would have been the entrance. A kind of trapdoor, with a big round handle.

'Look,' I say, pointing to where the dirt is disturbed. 'Someone has opened it recently. Forensics?'

'No forensic tape to seal the scene,' says Craig. We exchange glances. Wordlessly, he kneels down and closes his gloved fingers around a heavy old ring pull. With one yank of his thick arm, he brings it upwards, exposing an ancient shaft dropping two metres below.

The smell tells us everything we need to know. Craig recoils, and shines his flashlight down, covering his mouth.

'Sir!' Craig's voice has a strange wavering pitch. 'I think you should get over here.'

There's a crash of Anderson colliding with a beer barrel and swearing.

'*Fuck*.' Craig exhales the word, turning his body full away from the opening. 'Fuck.'

'What is it, Dooligan?' demands Anderson.

'Not what, sir. Who. There's a dead girl down here. She's . . . It's bad.' His voice catches.

Anderson places a paternal hand on his shoulder. 'Alright, Dooligan. It's alright.'

Craig points the flashlight back down for Anderson, then looks past me, straining his neck not to make eye contact. 'It's an Aboriginal girl, sir,' he says, sounding choked up. 'Look at the bloody state of her.'

23

Lauren

I am an extremely open person. It's just the way I process life, you know? So, for sure I felt uncomfortable not mentioning our volunteering project in that bar. I didn't even see why that was necessary. That need for secrecy . . . I think it did make me a little crazy.

Beth

The thing with Lauren is she has no mental filter. She will tell people anything. Literally. At college she would walk into a house meeting and be like: 'Oh my gosh. Does it smell of vagina in here? It totally smells of vagina.'

That persona, in an outback pub, causes problems. But, even by her standards, Lauren seemed . . . I don't know . . . hyped up. By our second shift, Lauren was telling the drinkers that she dates both men and women. How she was in rehab for the longest time. You could tell the men were interested for all the wrong reasons, but Lauren doesn't pick up on any of that. It's not in her nature to hear those degrees of inference.

Lauren tosses her hair, and says: 'Oh yeah, well. I kind of fell in with a bad crowd as a teenager. LA scene, all that, you know? I got into some unhealthy habits. But I was one of the lucky ones. My dad got me into the best rehab in the state.'

When Lauren talks this way, you can basically hear her dad's words. I can imagine him sat in some country club, sipping a martini, and bragging about how his money has solved all his daughter's problems.

Lauren's dad has no clue that she is in actual fact on a boat-load of non-prescribed medications, and she regularly skips her bipolar meds because they make her feel emotionally dead inside and kill her sex drive. (Lauren didn't phrase it like that. What she actually said was: 'Can you imagine someone with *this* body, who is not having regular situationships? Oh my gosh. Like. *No* way.')

I have never met Lauren's dad personally, only spoken with him one time on the phone right before we left, when he warned me not to let his daughter get stressed ('because we all know what she's capable of when she's stressed'). But I think he has a lot to answer for. After Lauren's mom died, he outsourced his problematic daughter to therapists and nannies, replacing them as and when they couldn't cope with her mood disorders.

He has no idea that one of those highly paid nannies did stuff to Lauren that wouldn't be polite conversation in his fancy country club. And he wound up eventually medicating Lauren for ADHD. Which, the way she tells it, was basically sedation.

Anyway. None of that therapy ever taught Lauren that there are times *not* to spill your personal details. So Lauren would go into each and every shift at The Gold Rush in a sleeveless singlet and short-shorts, and gab about her clit piercing and bisexuality. Or sound off about the destruction of Aboriginal land, or how Indigenous people were pushed out of the political system.

Never once noticing it was like a pressure cooker, building and building and building. Something had to blow.

And Paul . . . He used to stare at Lauren, when he thought no one was looking. Like he was taking mental notes. I saw something shift in his face, too, when the Indigenous reserve got mentioned. Paul knew we were hiding something.

24

Most of the night I lie awake, alone in my small rental, images of battered dead girls and police cells flashing through my mind. My thoughts keep flowing to Yindi, and the way she died, like water pooling downstream.

At dawn, rather than spend any more time with my dark imaginings, I decide to go in early, determined to improve my interview techniques. I shower, pull on black pants and grab a blue police shirt from a clothing hanger suspended on the door – a little trick I perfected to avoid ironing. Not perfect but most of the creases drop out.

I button it on and take in my basic kitchen-living area. There are still boxes from where I haven't unpacked. So far only my chin-up bar and a few free weights have made it out and I'm dressing in the kitchen where my clothes are.

Groceries are still in their bags on the countertop. I rustle through them, looking for something to eat at work, and settle on a plastic-wrapped chocolate muffin, and a share pack of M&Ms. As an afterthought I grab a mini box of breakfast cereal. Not a great lunch. Probably should have written a list.

I walk to the police station in the dawn light. Parked outside is my battered old Peugeot. I smile. Someone from the Moodjana community must have dropped her back last night.

I let myself in to the metallic baked-air smell. There's an old drip coffee maker which I turn on, after which I locate a small bookcase with a bunch of training manuals. I dump them on my desk and I flip pages at random, frowning with effort.

'Come in, Harrison!' bellows Anderson, leaning unexpectedly into view to shout through his open doorway.

I start, almost dropping the manual I'm holding, before composing myself to stand. Crossing the room, I see Anderson's office is in its usual simplistic state. A single picture of his bottle-blonde wife and grown-up sons sits beside his computer along with some neatly stacked files. On his desk is the pink notepad I found in the backpacker girls' bedroom.

'Rough night?' he asks as I enter the stagnant eddy of his labouring air con. 'You look bloody terrible.'

'You don't look so hot yourself,' I reply, noting his red eyes, underscored by bags bunched into his thinning skin.

'Yeah. Lot to sort out. The pot roast didn't get eaten, put it that way.' He casts an apologetic look towards the framed shot of his wife. 'Bloody horrible business you've walked into, Harrison. Even without your family history, no one would blame you for putting in for a transfer.'

'It's all part of the job.' Even to my own ears I sound fake.

His mouth twists as if he'd like to say more, but decides against it.

'I knew when I joined the force there'd be some demons to face,' I add, seeing he isn't convinced by my show of indifference.

'Well, if you're sure,' he says finally. 'Because I was there long enough to see the girl pulled out, and I'm warning you, in all my thirty years I've never come across anything like this case.'

The caution settles like physical ice in my bones.

'Right,' he says, when I make no answer. 'You're here early, working through the bad stuff.' He takes another glance at his family photo. 'Not everyone will thank you for it, but it's a good sign. Means you're already getting some coping mechanisms. Right?'

I nod.

'Good. We've got some more info on how Paul and maybe the girl died. I'll come to that. First, we've fingerprinted the cellar hatch.'

'Oh?'

'It's a bust, I'm afraid. Just Pete's and Bluey's prints.'

'Could someone have worn gloves?'

'Could have. But that would involve a fair bit of intelligent thought.'

We're both picturing the men who drink at The Gold Rush. April Hunter. None of these people seem like the type for careful plans.

'OK, so if someone did come through the cellar hatch, it would have been premeditated,' I summarise.

'I think it's fair to assume that. But it's probably more likely no one came through that way.'

I absorb this.

'Let's get on to this dead girl.' He's not quite looking at me, and a pulse of cold adrenalin fires through my chest.

'Did she have the same kind of injuries as Paul?' There's a tremble in my voice, and it feels like forever when Anderson finally answers.

'Sadly so. We've got photos already. Fast-tracked 'em overnight.' Anderson's hand lands on a stack of upturned pictures on his desk. He hesitates in the act of revealing them. I nod tightly.

Even though I'm expecting the worst, seeing her takes my breath away.

Her face is covered in dirt and mud, the lips deeply cut and torn. A dusty tideline of earth on her teeth. I am in momentary powerless pain, imagining her last moments.

There are about ten images in all. Different shots of her dirty bruised back, arms, legs.

'Do we think she was the Indigenous girl who was in the pub that night?' I ask.

'Most likely. But she had no ID. I've put feelers out to the Moodjana community, but meeting with the usual stonewall.'

'What's there?' I point to a close-up of her ankle. 'A tattoo?'

'Maybe,' agrees Anderson. 'A lizard or goanna or something?'

'Could be a totem animal,' I observe.

'Might be a way to identify her,' says Anderson. 'We've no clue why she was with Paul Hunter.' He shakes his head. 'OK, preliminary theories from forensics. See all these little marks? It looks like one or more people threw rocks and stones at the victims. From the similarity of the injuries, Hunter and the girl were probably killed at the same time in the same way.'

It's a horrible thought.

'Cause of death for both looks like obstruction of the airways with soil,' he adds. 'Danno's running some tests to clarify.'

'So someone moved the girl's body, and left Hunter's? That doesn't fit with two girls in a drunken frenzy.'

'Maybe they panicked, tried to hide the bodies and got disturbed.'

'No chance Hunter murdered the girl, and the backpackers attacked him out of revenge?' I suggest.

'I was thinking that, too, but it doesn't look like it stacks up. There are differences between the two victims, though. The girl has no sign of restraint like Hunter.'

'And she's clothed, more or less,' I say, pointing to a mud-streaked midriff string vest, and tiny jersey shorts. 'Hunter wasn't.'

'Well observed,' says Anderson sounding pleased.

My eyes slide to a prone picture of the girl, her mouth filled with mud, her body peppered with deep bleeding marks.

'Fuck,' I manage.

'Yeah. If those American girls did this, we're gonna make sure they're put away,' says Anderson, shutting the pink notepad determinedly, dark anger clouding his features.

'Did we find out anything more on the mystery car parked over the road?' I ask.

'Craig's got nothing so far,' says Anderson.

'Does he still think the car was owned by someone from the Moodjana community?'

'It's an open theory,' says Anderson diplomatically.

'Sir, if the Holden was driven to The Gold Rush from the mission, it would have passed by the roadhouse.'

'Right,' Anderson nods.

'Don't we have a traffic camera right by the roadhouse?'

Anderson frowns. 'How in hell do you know that? On second thoughts I don't want to know about your youth gone wild.' He gives me a half smile. 'The traffic camera is good thinking, Harrison. I'll tell Craig to check the cars that passed through.' He nods. 'OK, let's get back to this dead girl. And since you're on the case, and willing to learn, we should discuss your car crash of an interview.'

'Sorry, sir.' Gloomy defeat rolls through me.

'Don't be sorry,' says Anderson. 'Take the lesson.' He sighs. 'Unfortunately, it's a hard one. Your interview is inadmissible. All of it.'

25

Lauren

A few weeks in, we had sort of slipped into this routine. Drink at night. Sleep until noon. Head out to the reserve to work. Come back. Put up with a load of shit from the regulars. Rinse and repeat.

Three times a week, in the early hours of the morning, Bluey's massive road train truck would park outside our bedroom window with the engine rumbling at ear-bleed levels. At dawn, these loud native birds set off. I have never slept so badly, which made everything kind of surreal.

We'd worked on making the apartment nice, with a few throws and things from the dollar store in town. It looked totally cute by the time we were done. Like a San Francisco loft. So Beth and I had this happy daytime world, where we'd get breakfast at The Green Table. Sometimes call on Bluey and hear his old stories about mining for gold and stuff, then head out for our volunteering project. It was like we were two different personas. Only the working-in-the-bar-persona had a weirdly dreamlike feel. As though nothing you did had *really* happened.

Beth

You know if you put a frog on a hot plate, and turn up the heat, he doesn't realise his feet are burning? That was us. The comments and atmosphere in the bar started building. But . . . slowly. Like I couldn't tell you the point at which it became normal for me to have a guy show me pornography on his phone. Or to drink so much I couldn't remember going to bed. It was a slow progression.

Mike

I didn't tell anyone this, but I had some feelings for Beth. I didn't like the blokes showing her naughty pictures and all that. But you start playing the bleeding heart in The Gold Rush and you get it in the neck from Paul.

Beth

Most days, Lauren insisted we went to see Bluey. 'Let's go check on the old guy,' she'd say. It wasn't exactly fun because Bluey's house stank, and reminded me way too much of some of the trailers I grew up near. But Lauren does that sometimes. She gets it into her head that someone needs help, and she gives it whether they like it or not. She did the same with me when we started college. Lauren will give this impression of being a space cadet, but she has this sixth sense for vulnerable people. When someone *needs* help, she's there. Always.

So Lauren would chatter away to Bluey, tidying away his beer cans or whatever. I would quietly clean things whilst he wasn't looking. Once we'd succeeded in improving Bluey's home, we'd head to the reserve.

Lauren

The girls were still not buying my mentoring skills. They acted super close to one another, like a family. Similar clothes; jeans and T-shirts. There wasn't an obvious clique to break into. I focused on three girls who seemed like a unit. Charlee, whose bleached hair tips changed colour every week, and were now pink, and two quieter girls she called her cousins. Medika and Keira.

Medika

Lauren seemed to think we'd want to be like them. But her life sounded pretty sad and lonely. No family and a long way from home.

Keira

There was stuff I wanted to ask. About applying for scholarships. Lauren made me feel shy. I liked Beth, though.

Lauren

Marc's organisation had given us this pamphlet, which read like legal small print, telling us confusing things, like we shouldn't necessarily talk too much or expect immediate answers to questions. I had decided to be myself, which was *not* working. Beth, however, was totally connecting. I couldn't believe it. *Beth*.

Beth

Usually, Lauren knows how to behave and I watch her for clues. But here it was like she couldn't follow the most basic rules. Which was weird, because we had a very useful pamphlet.

I view all social manners as equally illogical and silly, so it was nothing new to me to scope a new group's codes. These girls weren't into loud talking and lots of eye contact. Big deal. There's no *reason* to stare at someone's face or talk non-stop when you meet them. Also, none of the girls had grown up around political conversations. I totally related. You can be really, really smart, and not know what a senator is. Specialised vocabulary is just another sorority house system. Mean gatekeepers that only let one kind of person in.

So there we were. Roles reversed. Maybe I could have helped Lauren more, but part of me still remembered pledge night. I didn't *hate* she was struggling, put it that way.

Then this girl shows up. Tula.

Lauren

When Tula walked in, I swear to God, the whole room fell silent. She had this total supermodel *presence*. Striking blue-green eyes, golden-brown skin, and an upturned nose that made her look mischievous, but somehow glamorous too. Like, an Audrey Hepburn vibe. She wore these oversized heart earrings and gold necklaces just the right side of bling. Same tight jeans and a loose-fit slogan shirt as the others, but they looked different on her. Maybe because Tula was closer to our age. Also, OMG, her *body*. That just shouldn't even have been legal. I was completely drawn to her.

Beth

Tula strode in and draped herself on a chair, long legs splayed, looking around with this knowing smile. Didn't acknowledge Lauren and I were there. She waited until all eyes were on her and said to the girls: 'So this is where you've all been hiding, eh?'

The atmosphere totally changed. I got the impression a few girls were scared, or maybe something else. Lines were being drawn, for sure. I thought there might be an actual fight. Keep in mind most who showed up at our mentoring project had prior convictions and were trying to stay out of trouble. Lauren noticed none of this, of course. I should have known Tula would be her downfall.

26

My whole interview was inadmissible?

My brain is making a white noise and I have a completely un-expected urge to cry. Lack of sleep, I tell myself, pulling it back.

'Don't take it to heart,' Anderson says, 'she was strung out, Harrison. Not your fault and heck of bad luck for your first time. Suspect needs to be in a state to understand the questions, right?'

'She's got withdrawal?' The worst thing is, I *did* notice. Pinned eyes. Scratching. All the signs of someone coming off opiates. Empty packages of medication in the apartment.

Anderson nods sharply. 'Some smart lawyer will wipe the floor with us if it turns out we interviewed her in that state. A right load of drongos we're going to look to Perth. Strewth.' He runs a hand through thinning hair.

'You got some bloody good stuff too,' he says. 'She admitted to a sexual relationship with the deceased and that could be gold dust.'

'Yes, sir,' I say miserably. 'What about assigning an urgent interview status?' I ask, hopefully. 'If you determine an interview urgent, it can be legal?'

'Only if you've recorded the decision in your pocket notepad or journal beforehand, and justified it on the recording,' he says.

There's a long pause.

'Write it down in your daybook, bloody quick,' he says under his breath. 'Maybe it will be enough. Far as I'm concerned, we discussed it prior, but you forgot to mention it on tape, right? Considering you're only a probationary, they might be lenient on allowing it as evidence.'

'Thank you, sir.'

'And don't tell bloody Craig. I never gave him any leeway as a rookie. He'll be spitting.'

'No, sir.' I pat down my pockets for a pen and don't find one. Sighing, Anderson hands me his.

'Alright, well. What have we learned, Harrison?'

'Don't interview people under the influence, sir?'

'Everything, and I mean *everything* has to be recorded. More criminals get away because some snaky lawyer has pulled apart our paperwork than from lack of evidence. Got it? Oh, and carry a bloody pen.'

I nod again.

'Good. Looked like a fair bit of swotting up you were doing before I called you in,' says Anderson, eyeing my loaded desk through his doorway. 'Looks like a bloody mess to me. Unless you tighten that up, you won't last here. Good policing starts with paperwork. You stuff that up you drop us all in the shit.'

'Yes, sir.' I add it to my list of 'must-do-betters'.

'Well, you can take a break from the book mountain. You're on towing duty. Some mongrel dumped a wrecked car outside. Not our mysterious Holden either.' He pulls a half smile.

'Is it a red Peugeot?'

Anderson squints in thought. 'Might have been red once,' he acknowledges.

'That's my car, sir.'

'*Your* car? That thing's a bloody write-off!'

'She's a little battler,' I say, proudly. 'Two hundred thousand kilometres, and still going strong. Few bumps and scrapes but it's all surface wounds.'

Anderson's bushy brows jerk up then down again. 'Well, park it round the side, would you? Don't want people mistaking us for a junkyard.'

To my relief his computer beeps and he eyes the screen.

'Here we go,' he says. 'Email from Danno Death in the morgue.' I flinch at the nickname. 'Forensics on Paul Hunter are back.'

'So fast?'

'Yeah, what old Danno lacks in quality he makes up for in speed.' Anderson's face is deadpan and it's hard to tell if he's serious or not. 'People give a shit down here. We can all pull together when we need to.' Anderson's voice betrays pride. He pauses. 'Since you're in so early, how about I print it out, let you take a look?'

27

Beth

It was embarrassingly obvious how attracted Lauren was to Tula. She more or less climbed into her lap the moment she arrived.

Lauren

Finally someone I could relate to. Tula had this cool lizard tattoo and I asked her about it, since I remembered Marc explaining the Aboriginal culture had totem animals. He launched into this long explanation I didn't follow, but I took that they could represent family and spirit. I asked Tula what her tattoo meant.

'Tricky,' she said, locking eyes with one of the girls until they looked away. 'Tricky and deadly.'

Beth

I had grown attached to my mentoring group. My favourite, Charlee, was a natural leader, who was super smart and totally got the idea of political campaigning from the inside. She styled herself like teenagers I knew back home, with bright clothes and sneakers. Her closest cousins, Medika and Keira, started out pretending they didn't care, but you could tell they were just used to being knocked back. In contrast to Charlee, they both wore their wavy brown hair tied back in ponytails, along with baggy T-shirts and the same tight jeans they all seemed to wear.

Charlee

How Lauren got let out on her own I'll never know. I watched her try to butter a piece of bread once. This dizzy moll is supposed to be teaching *us* stuff. Beth . . . her view was outsiders like us should get on the inside, that was how change really happens. She made a lot of sense, and I did admire how Beth had actually gone and done it herself. But she'd given up so much to get there.

Beth

It made me reflect. A good deal more than I'd been prepared for. I was never going to get all gooey over sacred land, and trees with souls. Obviously. But the girls' reaction to how I'd ditched my whole family – my brother, cousins – to get ahead at college . . . Yeah, that total disbelief got me. Like, suddenly, it didn't make sense to me either. For the first time I wondered if the cost had been worth it. I felt closer to the girls, and I felt like I'd just started earning their trust, when Tula shook the whole thing up.

Obviously, she had an ulterior motive for attending and Tula was clearly the kind of person who uses people. Initially I assumed she was targeting Lauren. I was both completely right and completely wrong about that.

Lauren

Tula had been scouted for model work, but had turned it down, because she wanted to start her own business. Cosmetics made from native ingredients. I thought that sounded totally cool. I asked her if she was here to apply for government funding. Her aquamarine eyes skidded about the girls. This little smile came on her lips, and she said: 'Yeah. Something like that.' She took off her sneakers and crossed her bare feet into her lap on the chair. 'Bank won't give blackfellas business loans,' she said, stretching her lean arms towards the ceiling like a cat, without taking her eyes off the other attendees. 'Reckon I'm high risk.' She raised her voice. 'But this mob know all about that, don't you, girls?'

At this point, Charlee, with her exploding ponytail of pink-tipped curls, swung around and put her hands on her hips.

'Why are you here, Tula?' she demanded.

Tula's smile broadened, revealing dazzling white teeth. 'Why do you think, Charlee?' Tula said something in her native language, slowly, like she was sounding the words out for impact. The other girl, Charlee, turned away looking angry and confused.

Beth

It bugged me, how Lauren mistook her attraction to Tula's looks with some deep connection. I had more in common with Tula than she did. You could tell Tula was tolerating Lauren's incessant talking in case Lauren might be useful to her. That kind of polite uninterest always pushes Lauren to work harder. It was sad to watch.

I tried to ask Charlee what the deal was with Tula, but she completely closed down. Later I overheard her say something to another girl about Tula and recruiting. Like 'don't let her recruit you'. They kept saying this Indigenous word that when I asked didn't seem to have a direct translation. Something about 'bad for the soul'.

Lauren

Beth was completely down on Tula. Imagining she had nefarious reasons for joining the group or something. I remember thinking that Beth was being . . . like, possessive? Around Tula. That was the vibe I got. She wanted Tula for herself.

28

I'm settled over a thick stack of paper headed 'Coroner's Report', chugged out in bleached ink, on Anderson's old printer. It's a long list of injuries, running to many pages, written in complicated scientific language which is hard to decipher, even for someone who has seen the body.

I'm wondering if Anderson has over-estimated my abilities, since I'm struggling. It's a relief when Craig enters the office, stuffing the last part of an energy bar in his mouth, wraparound dark glasses perched on the waxed tips of his red hair. He makes straight for the table I'm working at, then hesitates.

'One way to research, I guess.' He eyes my piles of books, then his gaze slides to my open packet of M&Ms. 'You work out?' he asks, frowning.

I wonder if he's being cheeky and decide he probably isn't.

'Yeah. I've got a chin-up bar and weights and stuff,' I say. 'Haven't joined the gym here yet.'

'Well, you'll undo all your efforts if you eat junk,' he says briskly, drawing nearer to my desk. 'Anyway. Guess what I've got?' he asks, eyes shining beneath his dark brows.

'Doughnuts?' I smile.

'Ha ha. I only carb-load on Fridays.' He pats his solid abdomen and dangles a cluster of plastic bags from his free hand. 'I got evidence from the mineshaft.'

'No way!' I stand fast, a few of my badly stacked papers fluttering to the ground. 'You got evidence processed already?' I stoop to pick up pages. 'It's OK, I've got them,' I say as Craig bends to help.

He straightens. 'I was down at the mortuary bright and early bagging and tagging. He waves the bags. 'Want to take a look?'

'Am I allowed to?' I glance towards Anderson's office.

Craig looks surprised. 'We're not formal like in the city. Down here you learn on the job, eh?' He sits on the corner of my desk, and it creaks under the weight of his muscles.

'Aren't Perth sending a team this morning?' I ask.

His face falls fractionally. 'Yeah. Well. They're not here yet,' he says. 'And until then we need all the help we can get.' He flashes me a disarming smile and sets the evidence bags down, one by one, on a nearby table.

He pauses for effect. 'In no particular order, ladies and gentlemen, this was found in the mineshaft with the girl's body. We have Paul Hunter's clothes. Paul Hunter's phone. Paul Hunter's wallet.'

'*Whoa.*' This seems huge.

'The clothes aren't muddied or bloodstained. Suggests they were taken off before Paul Hunter was murdered.' His green eyes flicker. Craig lifts a bag. 'Here's something interesting. His wallet was stuffed with cash. And I mean *stuffed*.' He turns the bag to show a dog-eared leather wallet in profile, literally bulging at the seams with canary-yellow fifties and sunny-red twenties.

He waves it, letting it sink in.

'OK. Next up,' says Craig. 'Mobile phone. Screen cracked. Still works, though. Passcode, 000000.'

'For real? He never changed the default?'

'Yep. Basic kind of guy. I get the fun job of uploading it all later. Hard to read texts and call logs with the glass so badly splintered, but I took a quick scroll through pictures and videos. Not nice viewing, and that's only what I could see through the broken glass.'

'Oh?'

'There's an expanded memory with about two hundred gigs of porn on there. Real hardcore. Looks as though the fellas down the mine have some macho thing. Who can share the most shocking stuff.' He shifts slightly on the desk.

I wrinkle my nose.

'There's nudey pics of Lauren getting shared too.'

'Paul shared pictures of Lauren?'

'Hard to know for sure if the pictures came from Paul or somewhere else,' says Craig. 'But they were all sharing passing them around. Mining culture,' he adds disdainfully, 'who can be the biggest dick-swinging prick.'

'Lauren must have felt completely humiliated,' I say.

Craig hesitates. 'What I don't understand, is why didn't the backpackers leave?' he says finally.

I think about my own early training in the police. 'Maybe they assumed the guys' behaviour was normal, and their reaction was the problem. Women are more likely to adapt themselves to fit a social situation, and they're often taught to be people pleasers, you know? Don't cause a scene.'

'So they just internalise stuff until they blow?' Craig looks unconvinced.

'That's what's messed-up about this whole thing,' I say. 'Everyone's talking about Lauren and Beth. No one's asking why a pub full of big muscle-bound guys would get their kicks harassing two vulnerable girls who were isolated and unprotected.'

Craig considers this. 'Jealousy, maybe? Backpackers tend to be educated. Going places.' He shrugs. 'Anyway,' he says, 'pornography wasn't the only thing in Paul's vids.'

He removes the cracked phone.

'Shit.' I peer closer. 'It's her, isn't it? The dead girl?'

'Reckon so. Strictly PG,' he adds. 'She's talking, or singing actually, I think in the Indigenous language. You know the lingo, right?'

'There's more than one lingo.'

'Take a look.' He heaves himself up off the desk, leaving the phone in front of me. 'I'm gonna grab a mega-meat sanger from the van. Want me to get you something?'

I glance at the clock. 'It's not lunchtime.'

'Yeah, I like to keep the protein count up. Back in a sec.' He winks. 'If Anderson asks, tell him I'm out back with the evidence.'

29

Beth

I have thought a lot. A *lot* about what happened during the time leading up to that lock-in. How and why it happened. The multiple overlaps with our college pledge week. How Lauren felt about Paul. How I felt about Tula by the end. It was as though we were doomed to live out the same stuff again like a weird Greek myth.

There's a psychological theory, that when hazing goes wrong, it's because something called 'group think' has happened. 'Group think' is when regular people do terrible things in a group scenario, which they would never do individually. There are several factors that increase the likelihood of this phenomena. Stress. That's a big one. A bunch of people who don't know each other well, or have a reason to want to impress other members. Helps, too, if the majority are none too smart.

But the main thing is, someone crosses a line and nothing is done about it. Once something dangerous or damaging has been carried out unchallenged, it opens the door for worse things to happen. Like a tacit permission has been granted.

Initially, I thought that line was crossed when Lauren started sleeping with Paul. Now I realise it was way too late by then.

When I think about it, I can pinpoint the line-crossing much earlier.

It was the night Lauren friended all the men in the bar on her Facebook.

Lauren

When you leave rehab they tell you not to have secrets. At this point my whole personality was a secret. I was keeping my bar work from the people on the reserve. Lying to the miners about what we spent our days doing. It was exhausting. Plus a completely shitty feeling, being so unpopular with those girls. The only person who had any time for me was Tula, and Beth seemed to be inventing issues around her. At least the guys in the bar wanted to be my friend, right?

Beth

I noticed Tula was singling out people for private conversations. She would speak to them in their language, and some of them would be shaking their heads really hard. Like, *no, no way*.

It didn't shock me too greatly what Tula went on to do, put it that way. But Lauren will always see the good, right up until her heart gets snapped in two.

Lauren

There was this loud exchange with Tula and two of the other girls, which Beth made a total big deal of. I didn't understand the fight because they spoke in a different language. But Tula explained afterwards it was a cultural thing, like her people were high energy. Some girls were jealous of her boyfriend. But Beth wouldn't stop saying how shady it all was.

Beth

Charlee told me that Tula was using some sketchy dating app. Sugar daddies looking for sugar babies, or something. I tried to suggest to Lauren that Tula might be trying to sign girls up for sex work or something, but she went completely nuts, and said I was totally paranoid, and this wasn't the trailer park. Lauren comes from a little bubble where stuff like that doesn't happen. But you could tell it was on her mind when we got on shift at the bar later.

Dillon

Like I said, Lauren was a prick tease, wasn't she? She wanted it, but pretended she didn't. Friended us all on Facebook to show us her dirty pictures. Then acted like she didn't want the attention.

Mike

I friended Lauren, and she friended me back right away. Yeah, I was stoked about that. Suddenly, all the guys were sending her requests. I felt bad, because I know what Paul uses Facebook for. I almost warned her, but Paul looked at me like he was gonna thump me.

Beth

Naturally, Lauren is not the kind of girl to put security on *any* of her accounts. If you're her friend, you see everything. Unfortunately, there were old shots from college. Like fundraisers with some of the fraternities where they would do wet T-shirt competitions, and foam parties, and dumb stuff like that. Essentially, a whole bunch of ways to get the sorority girls to take their clothes off. I was in them too.

And there were others, taken from Lauren's pledge night. Lauren had forgotten those. Obviously.

Lauren

I had never even seen those pictures. Apparently, on Facebook there's a separate section for images you've been tagged in. In any case I totally didn't expect the guys, to like, scroll through my entire account. Who does that?

Mike

I didn't like those pictures of Lauren. I thought she looked scared. They'd been taken down in some cellar or basement or something, and it didn't look like she wanted to be there.

Lauren

All of us who were at that pledge night have, like, camera trauma. Even now, if I see someone flashing a phone at me, it brings me out in a cold sweat. Also a particular novelty ringtone. I will literally get palpitations if I hear that ringtone.

Beth

When you are restrained, with a lot of your clothes missing, and someone starts filming what's being done to you . . . there's a feeling of violation that cuts very deep. Humiliation, I'm told, is the hardest emotion for human beings to process. And those sorority girls took our humiliation for keeps. Those pledge videos got passed around the fraternity . . . I can't even finish that thought. It didn't surprise me, that when the defence lawyer showed footage of that night in the courtroom, three of the girls on tape had panic attacks.

Dillon

Paul wanted *that* Lauren. With the handcuffs and that. Exactly like she was in the photos. That was when Paul started talking about a camping trip.

Beth

Keep in mind, the culture of pornography in the bar was completely entrenched. The guys acted like it was regular TV or something. Now they had access to Lauren's Facebook photos the two things seemed to . . . merge, maybe, is the best word. Like they couldn't tell one from the other.

Paul made a lot of comments about videoing Lauren. She would laugh it off, but I thought it was totally creepy. Like he wanted to own her, or something.

30

Craig returns faster than I expected, holding a sub roll stuffed with three kinds of concertina folded meat. He hovers over my desk, where I've been watching the video of the dead girl, not cold and muddied on a slab, but alive and vibrant. She has the charisma of a pop singer. A fluid assurance, like she knows all eyes will be on her.

'So?' Craig takes a man-size bite of filling and bread. 'Anything?'

'She's singing a song,' I say. 'I think a traditional one.' I press play. The girl is swaying. Her legs are bare and the lizard tattoo is clear in shot.

'The words are about loving your country,' I say, my lips moving. 'About a special place.' I blink for a moment, processing the translation. '*Let me take you to my precious land, where the rocks run orange red*,' I say. 'There's more, but . . . I can't remember the rest.'

I can remember the feeling, though, back when Yindi would take me out to the mission with her. Warmth. A campfire.

'The song probably means something more to a Moodjana person,' I say quietly.

His eyes slide thoughtfully to me. 'Do you think someone on the mission might know anything about her?'

'If they did, they wouldn't tell the police.'

'Not even you?' Craig suggests hopefully.

I shake my head. 'I used to run around there with Yindi as a kid. I don't have any connection anymore.'

He looks at me for a second, then lets it drop.

'Did you watch any of the other videos?' he asks.

'No.'

Craig leans over and takes the phone in his sandwich-free hand.

'OK. There's a couple of sexy home vids, too,' says Craig, scrolling. 'Pretty amateur recording, and you can't see a lot . . . but . . . you get the impression it's not a relationship built on mutual trust and respect.' He looks deeply depressed and holds up the phone.

'Jesus Christ!' I catch a flash through the cracked screen and look away reflexively. 'Was that Lauren?'

'With Paul. Sorry, should have warned you,' says Craig. 'Pretty extreme, right?'

'Yeah. I mean, depending on consent, I guess . . .'

Craig nods. 'Paints a certain picture? Lauren and Paul are into some out-there sex.'

'I don't think she realises he's filming her.' I point. 'Look at the angle.'

Craig's face twists. 'You think he was making secret vids of them in action?'

'Hey! Dooligan!' Anderson's voice reverberates around the office.

'Yeah?' Craig turns, looking unconcerned given Anderson's tone.

Anderson closes in, a wedge of newspapers in his hands. He stops at the sight of Craig's mid-morning snack, momentarily distracted. 'Blimey, Dooligan, do you ever stop eating?' he demands.

'Not if I can help it.' Craig grins disarmingly.

Anderson glowers. 'You picked up the morning papers, right?'

'Um. Yeah. I stuck 'em in your in-tray.' Craig lowers his sandwich defensively.

'You didn't read the headline?'

Craig's forehead crinkles good-naturedly. Anderson slaps down the newspapers.

Splashed over the front pages are images of Lauren and Beth.

'Those mongrels in the press have done our job for us.' Anderson waves a newspaper. 'The backpackers were already involved in a murder. Three years ago, at college.'

31

Beth

When I was a kid, I figured out how to do this neat thing. Like, I basically learned to disappear. I was nine when my dad finally took off permanently, with the peanut butter jar of rent money for good measure. My mom dealt with it badly, somehow decided it was my fault. After two or three days, I realised I could sort of . . . go out of myself. I remember thinking how cool it was. I could literally decide not to feel.

Only since the sorority pledge, it sometimes happens without me doing it on purpose. Like my mind has learned the reaction, you know? Bad situation. Leave.

Lauren

Beth was acting a little strange in the bar. Maybe a couple of times in a shift she'd kind of zone out. I tried to help out more. Take more of the load. I still couldn't do the cellar, though. I felt bad about that.

Beth

After they found Lauren's Facebook pictures, there was a total change in atmosphere. Entitled, is the word I'd use. Like we had made ourselves their property to jerk off to. The jokes got worse. You'd get suckered into a normal conversation, then it would suddenly take on this nasty edge. I had assumed I'd developed a permanent thick skin after the hazing at college. But here I was, exposed, like a crab out of its shell.

Lauren

One of the reasons Beth and I are such good friends is because we were both so traumatised by what happened on that pledge night. Like, some girls didn't care about anything apart from not being convicted. I'm a big believer in karma, and the wheel of life, and stuff like that, and there were so many bizarre similarities between that initiation, and the final lock-in.

Dutch door action, right? It gets done to you. No one talks about it. You just pass it forward. Goes on for generations. Like what happened to Tula.

Beth

The Aboriginal reserve increasingly felt like our safe haven. I was even letting my guard down somewhat, with Tula. Sometimes you'd get snatches of this little-girl-lost underneath the bravado. Like she was scared about the situations her body could get her into. I also could identify with a lot of Tula's childhood; growing up in poverty with an addict who should be caring for you, but is emotionally damaged. Tula and I shared a bond, in that respect. But because Lauren struggled to connect with any of the other girls, it was like she thought she should get Tula all to herself.

Lauren

Tula and I had this important connection, which Beth didn't understand. Like me, Tula was the product of a holocaust. Hers was the Stolen Generation, where thousands of lighter-skinned Aboriginal children were torn from loving families and forcibly adopted to whites. Tula's mom was literally ripped from her mother's arms and put in a children's home. I could not stop crying when Tula told me that story. I felt this absolute synchronicity between our lives.

Beth

Kids were taken from 1910 right up until the 1970s and beyond. The idea was to breed them out. Annihilate Aboriginal culture. I understood how this was a devastating, far-reaching crime that didn't just affect the stolen children, but everyone who came after. Like, when Tula was small, her mom would hide her in the garbage if she heard police sirens. Really sad. But I didn't understand why Lauren thought this gave her something in common with Tula.

Lauren

Tula's mom turned to drugs and alcohol to numb her pain, just like my mom. And whilst my grandpappy on Dad's side never spoke about escaping the Nazis, he always carried a picture of his sister and her children who died in a concentration camp.

I swear Tula would even get this facial expression that reminded me of my dad. Like, I was asking her, why start her own company? And she was like: 'So I call the shots, and no one can take it away from me.' *Exact* same tough-guy jawline. She had that survivor's drive. Succeed or die. I completely understood where that came from.

Thanks to Tula, I was understanding the other girls better now too. When they found out I had been in trouble with the police, a lot of barriers dropped. And once I started listening to their devastation at the sacred site destruction, I finally got it. Aboriginal people have this incredible connection to the land. They view it like . . . a person. More than that. A beloved family member. Someone they take full responsibility for.

Dillon

When Wooloonga Ridge got smashed up it was like anyone in a high-vis was open to getting shit. After the TV crews left, we had these young Black girls show up at the gates, the drama queen ones, saying they got 'trans-generational trauma'. *Trans-generational trauma.* Like according to them, some whitefella did something to their great-grandmother back in olden times, they feel that in their blood now, or something. I mean, you gotta get over it, don't you? If something happened a hundred years ago, doesn't give you an excuse to kick a police officer in the nuts *now*.

Lauren

Aboriginal people don't see time in the Western way. It's fluid. So pains of past ancestors can visit with young people and cause trauma. It's a beautiful culture, where plants and even inanimate objects have souls and everything is connected.

Beth

I don't think you need to believe in Dreamtime or animism to understand that the attempted extermination of a race of people will have emotional ramifications for generations to come. Bad stuff comes around. Look at Paul. And Tula. At some point the past always arrives back to haunt you.

Lauren

Because of what happened to her mom, Tula's thing was taking the power back. Not accepting the Western invader's attempt to force its laws and culture on the native people. At the time this all made sense to me. But when Tula did what she did a few days later . . . it's hard to describe the feeling of betrayal. It went very, very deep. And . . . I don't know. Maybe I wanted to hurt her back.

Charlee

Tula has this way of getting under everyone's skin. It was like having an angel and a demon on my shoulder. Tula was all about staying pure. Not bowing down to the system and betraying your people. But now Lauren had finally started listening, she wasn't as establishment as she first seemed. Her and Beth were teaching us how to use the system to our advantage.

Beth

For sure, I don't feel the way I used to. I don't *care* about people the way I used to. It's like I'm behind a glass wall, looking in at all the feelings. Or looking down at myself from the ceiling or something.

When that happens, the stuff I remember comes in pieces. Not joined up. But maybe one single image will keep blazing back into my mind when I least expect it. Often, I don't understand it. Like, I didn't *consciously* feel mad at Tula. So why do I keep picturing that last lock-in, Tula crawling on that bar, giving a blowjob to a bottle, whilst all the men jeered at her and Lauren filmed it?

32

Anderson glowers at the newspapers and I inwardly sigh. Looks like some smart journo hacked Lauren and Beth's social media.

The newspaper images are low quality and show the girls in fancy dress. Beth is clothed as a Chucky doll, in gore-spattered short-cut overalls, and Converse sneakers. She holds a long-handled axe and her face is menacing, as though she's about to bring the weapon down on the photographer.

Lauren is dressed as Carrie; white dress, so much blood on her face, only her blue eyes are visible.

Craig and I stare at the headlines.

They're variations of the same thing. MURDER SORORITY SISTERS, SORORITY KILLERS, HAZED TO DEATH.

'Fuck.' I look up at Anderson.

'Lauren and Beth were both implicated in the death of a girl at college,' Anderson explains. 'Severe hazing. She suffocated.' He looks at us meaningfully.

'Are you serious?' Says Craig.

'Oh, it gets better,' says Anderson grimly. 'Or worse, rather. Seems part of the initiation is new recruits get locked in a cellar together and are not allowed to leave until a certain amount of food and alcohol has been consumed between them. Like *Lord of the Flies* with vodka. That's a best guess, because none of the girls would disclose the exact process. The girl who died was fed a variety of things, besides vodka. There was pepper sauce, cocoa powder, worms in her stomach. High levels of salt in her blood. A few witnesses admitted the victim was blindfolded and vomited several times through the ordeal. She was left unconscious, but alive, and when they found her the next morning, she was unresponsive. Ambulance took her in, but she died a few hours later. Cause of death was a blood alcohol of 0.5% and asphyxiation from her own vomit. But a murder charge was brought.'

'And Lauren and Beth were in the frame?' I ask.

'Them and ten other girls. All claimed the sorority had some blindfold system where no one knew who was doing what to who. At least that's what they told the cops.'

'Was anyone held to account?' I know the answer already.

'Nope. Parents sued the college for a couple of million. But the girls themselves were acquitted in court. Judge ruled death by alcohol poisoning, not by hazing. There were appeals but none stuck. If they'd gone with manslaughter, maybe there would have been prosecutions.'

I'm so incensed on behalf of the dead girl, I could punch something. 'Why was this redacted from their police report?'

'That's what I'm trying to find out,' says Anderson. His eyes drift to the newspapers. 'EVIL SEXY GIRL KILLERS is a good story. A bloody *great* story with the pictures. Must have been in the American news at the time it happened. Somehow it was covered up. Maybe it's a powerful sorority, and someone high-up pulled some strings. We're waiting on Perth to arrive with the big guns on that. Get international clearance on the old reports.'

'Shouldn't they be here soon?'

'Nah, there's a flood out on the main road, and the girls' blouses can't drive through a bit of water.' He shakes his head. 'Dooligan here drives through worse on his way to *work* during rainy season. Bloody city slickers.'

'So you want me to interview the other girl? Beth?' I'm more excited than I thought I would be.

His eyes slide to mine and away. 'We might give her the morning to stew a little, eh? There's enough to charge her with and we've a couple of hours yet. Another half day in the cell and I reckon she'll change her mind about needing a female copper.'

'Yeah. OK.'

'Don't take it to heart, Harrison. It's what being a rookie is about. Only way to learn. No one makes it through their first interview with textbook delivery and a full confession. Anyway, Dooligan's following up a lead today if you want to go with him.' He pauses. 'We actually managed to get something the newspapers didn't,' he adds dryly.

'What?' I ask.

'Lead on the mystery car.'

'Oh?'

'Yeah. Your theory checked out, Harrison. Kind of. No number plate matches for the night of the lock-in. But you got me thinking, so I ran checks on all the crime reports from the roadhouse in the last year. Turned out a few months back, someone reported an Aboriginal girl causing trouble. And guess what she was driving?'

'Tell me it was a bashed-up Holden.'

'Got it in one,' says Anderson, sounding pleased. I breathe out.

'So the car parked outside The Gold Rush probably belonged to the dead girl,' I say.

'There's more. The caller described a loud altercation between a local girl and one of the women from the long grasses. The ones who sleep with the truckies for grog. And the girl in question had a lizard tattoo.'

33

Beth

Seemed like the nights were getting worse and the days were getting better. But it wasn't long before Tula showed her true colours. One day we arrived at the reserve to be told Tula was gone. Driven away, taking three of the girls from the mentoring project with her. Not just any three. *My* three. Charlee, Medika and Keira. I couldn't help thinking she'd done that on purpose to get to me. I was ... maybe mad. Disappointed.

Lauren took it really bad. She basically wears a button that reads ABANDONMENT ISSUES, and Tula had just pressed it.

Lauren

I was remembering things, like, how Tula got weird when I asked about her boyfriend. How she was always jumpy when messages came through on her phone. I felt totally stupid. Beth was right. She'd been playing us all along.

Even at this point, I was still a little in love with Tula. It's strange to admit that. Because of how much she disgusted me, later on. Or maybe *I* disgusted me. Whatever.

Beth

Unfortunately, the day Tula left was the exact same day the guys in the bar found the picture of Lauren's mom.

Lauren

Last year on my birthday, when I was feeling super low, I'd put up this glamorous shot of my mom from her Actor's Equity card. It's my favourite image of her. Hair swept up, and this cool mysterious expression.

Dillon

The comment about Lauren's mum was a *compliment*. That was when we all started thinking Lauren was a livewire, you know? Prone to flying off the handle.

Mike

I don't know why Lauren got so upset. I felt bad for the girl. Wanted to go see if she was OK, but she was in the ladies' bathroom.

Beth

Mike was concerned for Lauren. Paul was calling him a big girl's blouse, if that's even a saying. You could kind of see the cogs turning in Paul's mind. Like how he could turn the situation to his advantage by pretending to be a nice guy like Mike.

Lauren

Paul found me crying. I remember thinking at the time how typical that was. Nowhere was safe. Not even in the goddamn women's bathroom.

Paul did offer to help, though. Said he'd keep the guys in line. Told me something had happened to his mom too. I saw this different side to him. Like he wasn't just this square-jawed cowboy type. He was vulnerable. But he kept it hidden.

Beth

Not a lot of people know this about Lauren, but the only thing she isn't forthcoming about is how her mom passed. Like she will tell you literally anything else. She'll tell you her mom's dead, but she won't tell you *how* her mom died, and people basically never ask, because that would be such a morbid question. But her mom was this big party girl in LA. Sometime actress, big-time substance user, and prone to flashes of brilliance, despair and mania, in fairly equal measure.

Lauren says she was too young to remember much. But when she talks about her mom, she uses words like 'luminous' and 'iridescent spirit' and says how she would sing and dance with her.

She has one black memory of her mom not getting out of bed, which she says she feels like was almost another person entirely. Then her mom wasn't there anymore.

Her dad's accounts are mixed. Like more how Lauren's mom would lose it sometimes and start throwing shit. Or wake them up at 6 a.m., singing and dancing and wanting them to join in.

Anyway. Point being, when your mom commits suicide, you don't want a bunch of leering men eyeing her up. Obviously.

Now we had a bigger problem, in my opinion. Lauren would never have seen the subtlety of this. She was used to people helping her. But as far as Paul was concerned, now she owed him and he was calling it in. Just as we shouted last orders, he leaned across, and said to me, real quiet: 'Hey. I thought I saw two girls who looked like you hanging around the Aboriginal place. You wouldn't want the fellas round here knowing that.'

I just looked at him. He grinned like a shark and tapped his nose.

'Don't worry, love,' he said, winking. 'I'll keep it under my hat.'

I had this bad feeling, like he was getting ready to ask for something I didn't want to give him.

It never occurred to me to ask what Paul was doing on the reserve.

Lauren

That was the first shift when I told Beth I wanted to leave. The bus was three days away. I just wanted to go.

Beth

I know what people will be blaming us for not leaving. It was the same out in the trailer park, where people would trash the women worst of all. If you blame the victims, you don't have to accept it could happen to you.

We had about a month and a half left, but we were waiting for some delivery or something for Pete to hand us our first paycheck. We'd been surviving off tips which weren't so good as the agency lady suggested. I needed the money, and convinced Lauren to stay another week, just until the cash arrived. I regret that now. Obviously.

Anyway, it was around that time we started the journal. Lauren had this travelogue notepad diary thing which she'd never got around to filling out, and we repurposed it.

Lauren

There is an idea in rehab, about avoiding situations where you feel powerless. I had this cool idea, like to take the power back, based on something a therapist showed me once. A diary, writing out your fantasies of what you'd do if you were in charge.

Beth saw it more as vengeance, but when she started on that road, it was funny. Something took hold of us both. Like, it didn't seem to be *entirely* about the guys in the bar somehow. A lot of pledge night scenarios made it into the book.

But yeah, we'd be giggling. Talking about how we'd get our own back. Started out pretty tame, but . . . it got funnier the more extreme we went.

Beth

I couldn't say for sure who began the conversation, but Lauren and I would go back to that gross apartment and drink, and kind of discuss getting our own back.

34

The long grasses. I haven't heard that phrase for such a long time.

As a girl, I knew the long grasses as a bad place. With adult eyes, I see the overgrown bush on the dusty highway where homeless women camp. The nearby roadhouse has historically had problems with truck drivers approaching young girls.

I drag my mind back to the situation.

'If the Holden parked outside The Gold Rush belonged to the dead girl,' Craig is saying, 'maybe our witness was mistaken about someone in the driver's seat?'

'We don't know for sure it belonged to her,' I point out. 'Only she drove it to the roadhouse that time.'

'Well, this is what you're going to the long grasses to find out,' says Anderson. 'Harrison, I thought you might be able to help Craig, what with your Indigenous connections and all.'

Craig catches my expression and clears his throat. 'I'll go drive the car around front,' he says, slipping away. 'See you outside.'

'Sir, I have no more connection than you do,' I protest to Anderson.

'Yeah, but . . . you used to knock around the mission, right?' His brow crinkles.

'Yes, with Yindi and her mob, but there's more than one tribe in this area. They all got forced onto the same land back in the Sixties.'

'Ah right,' I can tell my explanation is completely lost on him, 'but you speak some of their language.'

'I only speak a bit of Moodjana. There are hundreds.'

'Well,' he steeples his hands at his mouth, 'do your best, eh? It's not a nice place, if you catch my drift. We get a lot of missing girls washing through that area.'

'What's being done about them?' I enquire pointedly. 'Do we just write them off?'

'Don't get political on me, Harrison. It's not racism. It's pragmatism. Missing persons from the homeless fringes don't count as high priority, black or white.' He looks at the towering stacks of forensics papers. 'Old Danno's Latin not making much sense?'

'No,' I admit with relief.

'It takes a while to understand medical jargon. The blokes in the hospital never miss a chance to remind us coppers how clever they are. Try reading them out to Craig in the car,' he suggests. He turns towards his office, pausing to spin on his heel. 'Oh, and you might want to swing by Target at some point today.'

'Another lead?' He never mentioned it.

'They sell these things called hairbrushes, Harrison. Also steam irons. For those occasions when hanging your shirt up and hoping for the best doesn't work. Like every day you've been on shift, for example.'

'Ha ha. Remember, I don't have a wife to iron my shirts, sir.'

Anderson makes a noise like he's exhaling hot coffee.

'I should be so bloody lucky, Harrison. A good police officer irons his own shirts. Or hers. And don't forget your notepad!' he concludes at volume as I head for the door.

I swing back to grab it and exit before he can give me any more grief.

The station felt hot, but outside I'm slammed by the wall of heat. Craig is on the pavement trying to lead a shrieking woman away.

It's April Dean. I recognise her from school. Her red hair swings in solid corkscrew curls at shoulder height, and her white skin is hidden under fake tan and thick make-up. She wears a pale pink playsuit and sways on cork wedge heels.

'She's in there!' April yells. 'I'm gonna cunting *kill* her. Bring her out.' She waves a newspaper with a blown-up image of Paul looking handsome but worse for wear. The headline reads: TORTURED TO DEATH. She cups her hands and shouts. 'I know you're in there, Lauren! You fucking *bitch*! Come out and face me!'

'Calm down, April,' says Craig, sternly, one hand on his gun. 'And I'd ask you to keep a lid on the bad language.'

'Fuck you, Craig!' rages April. 'Send her out.'

I can see things escalating so I take a quick step forward.

'I'm so sorry for your loss, April,' I tell her. Her pale green eyes flicker uncertainly across my face. 'You must be so cut up about Paul,' I add.

Her face crumples, a sniff shakes her small shoulders. 'Yeah.' Her lip wobbles. She takes in a deep breath of air and lets it out. Then dissolves into tears, body shaking, eyes streaming.

'He was the love of my life,' she gasps between sobs. I pat her shoulder.

'We're doing all we can,' I tell her.

There's a sudden blast of loud music from her phone. A novelty ringtone every teenager downloaded about five years ago. April's hand reaches to pull it out, then stops. Her eyes flick back and forth, stricken.

'New fella?' I suggest. I'm fishing, but she bites.

'Dillon's been looking out for me, is all,' she says defensively. 'It's not what people are saying.'

I leave a pointed silence and her expression turns to panic. 'We were all drunk at that lock-in. Paul's only got himself to blame for what Dillon did . . .' she gabbles. Craig's eyes widen and April's narrow. 'You can't speak to me without a lawyer,' she hisses. Then totters off at speed, lurching briefly on her wedge sandals.

'Blimey.' Craig watches her go. 'How did you do that?'

'Do what?'

'April Dean has a pop at six-foot blokes for serving her the wrong drink. When she gets going there's no stopping her. I was getting my handcuffs ready, and you step in and get her admitting to a relationship with one of the men in The Gold Rush. Least I think that's what happened.'

I shrug. 'Talk before you arrest, right?'

Craig looks towards April. 'Guess I gotta learn that one.' He takes out his phone. 'Better text Anderson about bringing her in, eh?'

35

Mike

April was a lovely little thing back in school. Smart too. But there's nothin' to do round here, but drink, eh?

I'm terrified of her, and that's a full-grown Aussie male speaking. You never know how she'll react, and if she's had a tequila, fuck me dead, you'd better look out. We were all relieved when Pete stopped letting her in the pub. Even Paul, I reckon. It was always some fucked-up drama with Paul, but April brought it to the next level. She snuck in The Gold Rush sometimes if she knew Pete was out. There were rumours about her and Dillon, 'cause she'd do anything to stir the pot. What I don't know is how she got into the lock-in.

Beth

April came in the bar one night, a few days after Tula had taken off, blind drunk with a friend, and started bad-mouthing Lauren and me when our backs were turned. Mean stuff about our figures. I think she must have known we could hear her. A couple of the blokes got her in a taxi when she couldn't stand, which was about 8 p.m. I was so glad when she left. She had that ringtone on her phone. Same as one of the older girls at our sorority. I could see Lauren jump half out of her skin every time it went off.

Lauren

For some reason April completely reminded me of someone at college. One girl in particular. I still have nightmares about that sophomore – her voice. Telling us what we had to do to the new girls. That night April was there it was so bizarre. I had this insane compulsion to pick up her drink and pour it down her throat. It came from nowhere, this animal urge. Totally weird.

Beth

I don't blame Lauren. Studies show that torturers are often more traumatised than the people they torture. Rats actually get more stressed when they're forced to watch other rats being electro-cuted, than when they're subject to shocks themselves. I'd like to explain that to Lauren. But we don't talk about what happened, because that night all us girls invoked the oath. Alpha Sigma Psi. Keep our secrets or you die.

Lauren and I said it after the last lock-in too.

Lauren

Beth definitely gets flashbacks. I'm more like . . . I don't know. Chill, I guess. Like it does *bother* me. A lot. I wish we hadn't done what we did at college. But somehow, I don't let it get under my skin the same way it does with Beth.

OK, so, true. The image of that girl tied to the chair on pledge night never goes away. And now, I also have nightmares about Tula, and the things that happened at that lock-in.

I totally believe in all the higher power stuff they teach you in rehab. But sometimes, I'm hit by the scary possibility that things really are random. What if I'd reacted differently when April punched Beth at that lock-in? Would Mike have done what he did?

I don't know.

I keep reminding myself that Beth will never tell. She's just *like* that. About rules and stuff. But now I'm wondering. Like, is that right?

36

The squad car coasts along the dust road, with Craig at the wheel. Inside is pin-neat and clean, smelling strongly of the deodorant Craig probably covers himself with when he leaves the gym. He's a good driver, and is also proving extremely helpful at interpreting the forensic report.

'Likely cause of death,' I read aloud. 'Asphyxiation by blockage of trachea by substrate.'

'Death by choking on dirt,' returns Craig.

It's such a horrible thought, I can't stand it. The victims' last hours alive must have been unimaginable suffering.

I swallow. 'There's something on gastric contents. Dirt. Capsaicin extract ... this is actually translated.' I look at Craig. 'Pepper sauce. Paul Hunter had pepper sauce in his stomach. Not the girl, though,' I leaf over and back, 'only him.'

'Same thing happened at the girls' college sorority, right?' says Craig. 'The dead girl was made to drink pepper sauce?'

'Yeah.' There's a loaded pause.

The wide roadhouse is on the horizon. The only man-made thing for kilometres. And beyond it, the long grasses.

'What do you think about April and Dillon?' I ask Craig.

'I'm not surprised they were getting it on,' I say. 'It's probably got nothing to do with why Paul died, but ... I think you're right to ask Anderson to get her in. She might be keeping something from us.'

Craig nods. 'Hopefully we'll find out something about our female victim from the women in the long grasses.' He glances at me. 'But . . . There's a lot of anger about the Mining Corporation digging up land owned by the Moodjana.'

'The Moodjana don't *own* the land,' I explain. 'They take care of it.'

'That isn't the same thing?'

'When you marry someone, do you own them?'

'Maybe if you're a bloke like Paul Hunter.' Craig looks across to share the joke.

'Love, honour and obey,' I say, ignoring him. 'That's basically the arrangement First Nations people have with the land.'

'Oh.' Craig sounds thoughtful. 'The dead girl's tattoo. Anderson says you think it's a totem animal. Isn't that her tribe or something?'

'I'm not an expert,' I say. 'So far as I understand it, you get a totem for your skin name. From your mother's side. From your father or your grandfather, you get your country totem. It can be a plant or an animal, I think.'

Craig's face shows naked confusion.

'Basically, it's a good system for protecting the environment, and making sure no one marries anyone of a similar gene pool. You've got a duty to protect your totems, including their land. Binggadji, they can usually eat emu, but they never eat honey ants which Moodjana can eat. It's supposed to be all in balance. So no one's hungry and nothing runs out, right?'

'I sort of remember that from school,' says Craig. 'I didn't realise anyone actually did it.'

'It only works right if no one chucks you off your land,' I say, realising I sound exactly like Yindi. 'You also get your own personal totem that gets decided for you at birth. Or maybe you grow into it. It's more, like, your personality. So a kookaburra is symbolic that you're a happy person, someone who works for the community and sees the bright side and . . .' There's a lump in my throat that won't go down. 'Sorry,' I gulp. 'Give me a minute.'

Craig pauses. 'That was your sister's totem?'

'Yeah.' I stare straight ahead. 'Anyway. Could be the lizard wasn't a totem. Maybe she liked that tattoo.' My voice is steadying as I talk. 'But . . . if it was her personal totem, lizards are born survivors. They adapt to their circumstances. They're also smart, fast and tricky.'

Craig looks thoughtful and we drive on in silence for a while.

'You forgot to scan down to the conclusion of the report,' he says, eventually.

I flip pages. 'OK . . .' My eyes settle with relief on a few paragraphs that pass closely for English. 'Estimated time of death for both victims. Between 1 a.m. and 5 a.m. Trajectory and depth of injuries suggest the likelihood of more than one attacker.'

'I think that means—' begins Craig.

'At least two people of different strengths threw stones.'

'Different strengths,' agrees Craig. 'Or different intentions.'

We're both quiet.

'What if the backpackers did it, but it wasn't their fault?' I suggest. 'Like, what if the sorority hazing made them vulnerable, traumatised. PTSD flashback or something.'

'I don't know if PTSD works that way,' says Craig. 'A flashback long enough to stuff dirt into two people's mouths, whilst they choked and probably screamed the place down.'

I flinch at the uncomfortable image.

'And both of the girls would have to experience the same reaction at the same time,' continues Craig. 'Doesn't fit, does it?'

I shake my head. 'No,' I admit.

The shaded overhang of the roadhouse is drawing nearer, a cinderblock ark on an asphalt lake.

Rows of petrol bowsers swelter in the relentless sun, and a huge tanker truck is pulled up to refuel.

Behind the filling station is the main body of the large fibro building, stuck with a jangle of Coca-Cola and Victoria Bitter signs, along with handmade posters for takeout pies and late-night feeds.

'Difficult to imagine how they got the materials out here to build it, eh?' observes Craig as we close in on the isolated facility.

'Indigenous people used as slave labour,' I reply. 'Same as the airstrips.'

It's bordered by a dense tangle of bush. At first glance you'd never picture a community living deep out of sight in the under-growth. A government sign announcing, PROPERTY OF THE CROWN. NO LOITERING, gives the game away.

'You been out here recently?' Craig tilts his head at the road-house.

'No.'

'We've gotten a lot more trouble out here since the government have banned problem drinkers from buying grog.'

'Same in Perth,' I say, thinking of the forlorn people who lingered round Coles at night-time.

Craig nods. 'Ideal location out here. Grog shop. Steady stream of truckies willing to buy for banned drinkers in exchange for favours.' He sighs. 'What did the government think people were going to do? Just stop buying it?'

I smile, thinking not for the first time that Craig is smarter than his appearance suggests.

'Lot of clever idiots down in Canberra,' he concludes.

37

Beth

It's funny how time passes. Like in the beginning, it was super slow. I can remember almost every moment of when we arrived and the first day. The weeks became a month . . . then it begins to blur. When you're around people who get really, really drunk, it starts out quite shocking. Then it becomes like a shield. Gets easy to drink more than you would usually, and not notice.

Nightly drinking was not doing Lauren any favours. She was starting to look ill, and I suspected she was messing with her medication doses again. I decided we should definitely bail, just as soon as we got our money from Pete. Six weeks backdated wages, which would be enough.

Then Pete suddenly decides to be a total motherfucker. Tells us we won't get our cash for another *month*.

Pete

There was a delivery got missed. It takes those big road trains a straight month to do the round trip. I told 'em, stop bloody whinge-ing. You'll get paid when I get paid. Simple as that. That's how we run things out here. If you don't like it, get a job in the city.

Dillon

Pete does it to all the girls. Make sure they work out the full three months. Always tells them five minutes after the weekly bus has just left. Some barmaids leave anyway. Catch a ride or pay someone to drop 'em at the next town. If they stay, we know they're desperate.

Mike

I came right out and said it to him. I said: 'Pete, you old bastard, you've gotta give those girls their money.' Paul muscles in. Tells me not to be a sticky beak. 'Course all Paul cares about is getting Lauren for his movie collection. Wish I'd done more. Said more. Stopped the girls going on the camping trip.

Beth

The guys knew we were stuck in town. Very quickly it became like this battle to get through the night without anything really bad or offensive happening.

Lauren

I'd literally just have arrived on shift. They'd be like, 'Oi, blondie! Get over here! I'm dry as a nun's nasty!' I mean . . . seriously?

Beth

There was now a running joke comparing us to their favourite porn stars. Because we were from California. Which makes total sense. Obviously.

We both developed this laugh . . .

Lauren

We'd kind of go, 'Ha ha ha,' when they said something inappropriate. It was a defence mechanism. We didn't always stick to our no-drinking-before-10 p.m. rule. Weekends the bar stayed open late, so things got pretty messy. At one point I remember getting clear. It's too much. We're leaving. I debated lying to Beth. Telling her we'd been paid and giving her the cash myself.

But . . . that meant asking my dad for more money.

I got as far as typing that email. Then I read it back, imagining my dad's face.

After that, I put a finger out, and deleted the whole message, one letter at a time.

Beth

Filling out the journal with ways to get our own back became more than a joke. It was like . . . a way of blowing off steam, after spending seven hours fielding questions about how we styled our pubic hair, or whatever. We were writing in it every night. It was the first thing we did when we got back.

Lauren

We *totally* weren't serious. None of it was serious. Silly stuff, you know. There were a lot of suggestions around force feeding or yakking it up. Joining Alpha Sigma Psi basically means you sign up to being bulimic for three years. It was harmless in the beginning. Like a dare to ourselves, almost.

38

Craig pulls into the long slip road that allows the vast vehicles to pull to a stop at the roadhouse.

Bad memories are floating up.

Yindi had just gotten her driver's licence. We stopped here for cold drinks, and a security guard peeled himself off the back wall and began walking within three paces of us.

I was giggling. 'Why's he following us?'

There was a dark look on Yindi's face. 'He's not following you, bub. He's following me.'

I remember the feeling really clearly. Like something had been driven between us.

'You OK, Tara?' Craig is staring at me, concerned. 'Bad memories?'

'Ah, yeah. Last time I was here was right after my foster mum kicked me out.' I opt for a half truth, pushing the memory of Yindi aside.

'How old were you?'

'Sixteen.'

'Harsh.'

'Yeah, well, our foster home was more of a pile-'em-high-feed-'em-cheap model. Mum got paid per kid, and after Yindi died I wasn't very easy to live with. Fell in with the wrong crowd.

Drinking. Final straw, my foster mum caught me up at the hospital pretending to have meth poisoning. She swapped me for a kid that was less hassle.' I give him an embarrassed smile.

'Why would you pretend to have meth poisoning?'

'To get the free grog.'

'The hospital gave out free grog?' He looks genuinely bemused.

'Yeah, until they realised Dead Tree Creek's feral teens were gaming the system. Strong alcohol is, like, an antidote to small doses of meth,' I explain. 'Nukes it. So the hospital gave out half bottles of rum.'

'How did you find that out?' Craig sounds caught right in the middle of horror and admiration.

I shrug. 'Hanging out on the mission, I guess. There were a few cases of bad homebrew rum back then, so the young kids got warned. Meth is a silent killer. Check your bottle seals.'

'I used to make homebrew rum,' says Craig thoughtfully.

'You did?' I can't work out if I'm more surprised by the confessional streak, or the idea of Craig breaking a rule.

'It was strategic,' he quantifies. 'I was pretty good at science and my aunty worked up at the brewery . . . so I figured out how to make super-strong hooch. Sold it to the popular kids to stop from getting my head kicked in, but I can't say I enjoyed their company.'

He flashes me a conspiratorial smile. Two outcasts, trying to live amongst the normal people.

'You're lucky you didn't blind anyone,' I tell him.

'And you're lucky not to have a record for defrauding the hospital.'

'Wouldn't have looked good on our police applications, eh?'

We exchange smiles, and I feel weirdly close to Craig, with our dual murky connection to illicit grog manufacture.

I glance out at the roadhouse. 'Shouldn't we park up a bit

closer to the bush?' The sun is brutal out here, and the idea of walking even a small distance makes me feel hot.

'If we're going to the long grasses,' says Craig, matter-of-factly, 'we're gonna need some grog. Otherwise they won't talk to us.'

I stare at him in disbelief. 'Do you know how patronising you sound? You know that fewer Aboriginal people than white people in this country drink alcohol, right?'

'These are peripheral people, Tara,' says Craig in a tired voice. 'It's . . . how things are.'

'If they're banned drinkers,' I say, 'you're breaking the law.'

He looks at me with a serious expression. 'Tara, every Friday night I arrest ten drunk white dickheads, who get a fifty-dollar fine, and are back in the same pub the following week. Are you telling me you agree with a legislation that essentially applies only to Black people? That bans them buying a beer in their own country?'

'No,' I admit.

'Then why are you on my case?'

Craig parks up. He looks at the roadhouse in his rear-view mirror.

'You know, the last time I saw Paul Hunter was in there,' he tells me. 'Must have been . . . four weeks ago, maybe.' He sounds thoughtful.

'You were mates?' I'm surprised, and wondering where he's going with this.

'No way,' says Craig emphatically. 'I mean, he was one of the jocks who bought my grog sometimes, back when I was a little fat kid. Few months ago I came to the roadhouse for a feed after a night shift,' he continues. 'Hunter's at the counter and I didn't realise it was him until I'd already sat down. It was one of those awkward moments, where you can't leave without seeming obvious.'

'Paul worked nights?'

'That's what I thought at the time,' says Craig. 'But . . . now I'm thinking, maybe he was here for something else. Lot of vulnerable women in the long grasses, right?'

'Maybe Hunter knew the dead girl before she came to the pub?' I suggest.

I let this possibility percolate. It raises more questions.

'Anyway,' Craig focuses on the long grasses up ahead, 'guess we can only ask.'

39

Beth

Right after Pete pulled our wages, Marc started big-time flirting with Lauren over text. From nowhere, fifty messages a day. When a guy does that, it's not a good sign. Ask my mom. Usually means he's been dumped and you're his standby.

But Lauren can fall in love with someone in the time it takes to snap your fingers. Even, actually, *especially*, if it's the *idea* of someone, if you take my point. Plus she'd just been burned by Tula.

The way Marc operated – bombarding her with poems and cut-pasted quote messages from positive-thinking gurus – it was *exactly* the way to reel Lauren in.

She got obsessed with checking her phone, and you could always tell by her face when she had gotten a message from him. That went on about a week. Until right before the camping trip.

It was around this time I began to notice that Lauren couldn't survive as an adult. I guess it never came up before because we'd always had catered accommodation and a cleaner.

It was kind of funny initially, watching her giggle over trying to boil an egg or something. Before long we basically lived off the greasy stuff in the pub. Or my trailer park repertoire, of using hotdogs, peanut butter and Cool Whip in creative ways. For almost two months we were hungover every day, barely sleeping, getting up at noon. Existing on potato chips and canned food. We were not in good health, is what I'm saying.

I don't know at what point we started to drink like The Gold Rush men did. Drinking to get trashed. All I know, is when you descend to that level, you change. Become a bit more hopeless. A bit sadder. The idea of getting back to who you were starts to seem a long way away.

The gap between us and the guys in the bar wasn't so wide anymore.

Lauren

Beth is totally amazing. She can take, like, a package of saltines and a jar of mayonnaise and make a meal. Seriously. Plus she has this super neat trick where she drops a handful of peanuts into a can of soda. It's, like, the perfect snack.

I had this feeling like we were proper travellers, totally living locally, doing everything ourselves. Showering in that weird old shower. Taking our clothes to the laundry place. Eating whenever we felt like it. Letting it all hang out.

Dillon

Lauren had this big crush on a greenie backpacker. Kind of guy who we'd drink under the table if he ever showed his face in The Gold Rush. Me and the fellas were ripping on Paul. Saying Lauren was the one who got away.

He sipped his beer slowly, watching her whilst she was texting.

Turned left and right to make sure we were all listening and said: 'Nah, mate. I checked around. That hippy's not interested. Sees Lauren as a mess around.' I swear I saw his nostrils flare. Like he'd smelled blood.

Mike

Paul always hits on girls when they're vulnerable. It's part of his system. I was worried about Lauren. All us blokes knew about Paul's favourite hobby, and it seemed like he was getting out of hand, you know. He didn't even have space on his phone for all the vids. He'd go off in a corner to check his text messages, so God knows how many women he had on the go.

Dillon

Paul was up to something, and he wasn't letting his so-called mates in on it. Right before the camping trip I overheard him arranging to meet with some girls. Plural.

I came straight out and asked, 'Are you having a party, or what?' He laughed, said he had some business down at the Aboriginal reserve. I asked if we were invited. Paul said, 'Nope.' Bastard.

I reckon he was having sex parties down there and not inviting any of us.

40

We park up in the scrub, the tall grass and bush stretching out ahead of us.

Craig is eyeing a female figure on the horizon, who emerged from the grasses at the sound of our engine. He adjusts his hair in the mirror before opening the car door. I get out the other side, pulling on my police baseball cap against the heat.

'Hey!' The woman in the distance nears. She has curling grey-streaked hair held in a woven headband off the dark skin of her face, and a T-shirt and long skirt that have seen better days. Her feet are bare and I wonder that they're not burning on the dusty ground.

I raise a hand in greeting, smiling, but she addresses Craig.

'Hey,' she says. 'It's pretty-boy come to see me. How's it going, handsome?'

It's impossible to tell if she's ripping him or not.

'Hello, Mary,' says Craig cordially.

'The parole constable tells me I'm not allowed to buy grog,' she returns. 'I'm not allowed to associate with known drinkers.' She sniffs and rubs at her nose. 'I tell them. All police are known drinkers. Tell them to keep away from *me*.'

I get the feeling she shares the same joke anytime a police officer comes out here, but Craig manages a smile even so.

Wordlessly, he holds up the bag with the grog inside. She takes it and folds the top over as though she's uncomfortable with the contents.

'More in the car,' says Craig easily. 'If you don't mind answering a few questions first.'

'You can ask,' she concedes.

Craig reaches into his police vest and just in time I realise he's about to pull out a picture of the dead girl.

'You can't show an Indigenous person images of someone who's died,' I hiss, slapping his hand down.

'Sorry, I forgot.' He turns to the woman, who is looking at us with interest.

'Has anyone from the long grasses had a blue with an Indigenous girl at the roadhouse?' asks Craig. 'Lizard tattoo on her ankle?'

The bag of grog shifts in Mary's arms, and she puts a hand out to stop a bottle sliding free. She looks at us for what feels like a long time.

'Wouldn't know,' she says, finally. 'I gotta share this,' she adds, holding up the bottle, and looking back to the waving grasses.

'Wait. How about I get you some more grog?' suggests Craig. 'It won't make any difference.'

'Hold up.' Craig casts me a 'keep her talking' look and retreats in the direction of the car. Mary shrugs.

'He's alright, that one,' she tells me. 'Polite, you know? Nice bum, eh?' she concludes, nudging me knowingly with her elbow.

I flush, realising I haven't taken my eyes off Craig's retreating figure.

'I wouldn't know. Haven't noticed.' I swing my eyes determinedly on Mary.

'I'm Constable Harrison,' I tell her. 'I'm new.'

'I heard about you,' says Mary. 'Tara Harrison. Jarrah. He talks about you.'

'Yeah?' I try for casual. 'Good stuff, I hope?'

'More than good.'

I find myself blushing bright red. I desperately want to know what Jarrah says, but I'm not about to ask. Mary watches me with amusement.

'On your mind, is he?' she asks.

I shake my head. 'Not really. Maybe a bit,' I concede, since she's obviously not fooled.

There's a long silence. She studies my face.

'Maybe you should go see him. Work things out,' she decides. 'You were the white kid hung around with the kookaburra-totem girl?'

There's a lump in my throat. 'She was my sister. Foster sister.'

Mary smiles. 'She chattered like a kookaburra too. Clever. Good with words. Brave.'

'Yeah.' It's bittersweet to be reminded.

'She got killed by police, eh?' Her eyes don't leave my face.

I nod. 'Injured during an arrest at a protest rally, and the officer on duty didn't believe she was crook. Let her die in a cell.'

Mary stands for a long moment, before coming to a decision. 'You speak the lingo?'

'A bit of Moodjana, yeah. Not the Binggadji language.'

Mary puts a hand on my arm. 'Maybe you can help us,' she says in Moodjana. 'Come with me.' She flips a hand over her shoulder and turns to the bush.

I open my mouth and shut it again, looking towards Craig who is returning from the car, shouldering a slab of grog.

'Don't worry about your boyfriend,' says Mary, already almost out of sight. Casting a quick look back at Craig, I plunge off into the grasses in pursuit.

41

Mary beckons me to follow her into low-lying shrub, and we walk for a long time through the maze of tough-leafed plants. It's hard going and all the bushwalking I did as a kid was back in another life. Tough spinifex spikes my ankles and cobwebs stick to my face.

As soon as low bush closes around us, Mary dumps the grog, pushing it into a nearby fan of grass.

'Saving it for later?' I suggest.

'We're a dry community out here,' says Mary. 'I've not had a sip for two years.'

'Why take the grog from Craig?'

'Don't want to hurt the copper's feelings, eh?' She grins. 'And if the cops think we're drunks, prostituting ourselves to the truckies, they leave us alone.'

Mary darts through the undergrowth. As we get deeper, she begins singing a navigation song, about two eucalyptus holding hands, and a mound curled like a dingo's tail. I remember Yindi telling me about this practice. I didn't see the point when you could use a phone or a map.

Now I see it. I can't image anyone outside the community being able to track through the bush like Mary is doing. The women are completely hidden out here. Untraceable.

A branch twangs dangerously close to my face, and I stumble on an ant hill.

'Spirits not sure about you,' observes Mary as I dodge thorny branches.

'I'm not sure about them,' I admit, disentangling a creeper, and stubbing my foot on a tree root.

'Maybe easier if you take your boots off,' she suggests, nodding to her own bare feet.

'Police issue,' I tell her. 'Have to stay in uniform.'

Mary shakes her head disapprovingly. 'Here.' She takes my hand, wipes beads of moisture from my sweaty forehead and touches my hand to the ground. 'Maybe the snake will smell you now,' she says, without conviction, heading off again at speed.

Another branch whips me in the face as I follow, and something about the way Mary placed her hand on the earth jogs a thought. The way Paul died ... Dirt suffocating him. He worked for the Mining Corporation, didn't he? And they recently destroyed a sacred Aboriginal site.

Dirt. Soil. *Land.*

'Did anyone want payback?' I ask Mary as she flits effortlessly through the wilderness. 'For the damage at Wooloonga Ridge?'

I'm remembering Jimmy, one of the Elders, the footage of him on TV making an impassioned statement against the Mining Corporation.

She shakes her head agitatedly. 'Someone gets cheeky, you put a spear through his leg. Maybe send kurdaitcha man, to point the bone, curse them dead.' She glances at me with a grin to show the unlikeliness of this practice being used. 'Besides, there's no payback on whitefellas. We're just really, really sad buggers,' she adds with a sardonic smile.

We walk some more, desert grass crunching under my heavy police boots, until we finally arrive at the edge of a strange little encampment. There are one or two tents, but mainly blankets.

Through some low bushes I glimpse a cheery fire ornamented with scavenged objects repurposed as cooking facilities. A huddle of girls and women sit cross-legged, talking, preparing bush tucker. One kneads a damper-bread dough in an empty Victoria Bitter box.

'Come around this way,' says Mary. 'Better not let them see police here.'

She leads me to a small tent and kneels.

'What is this?' I'm trying to take it all in. The quiet industry. Laundry drying in the sun.

'It's a safe place for women. They can spend a few nights, or as long as they need,' says Mary, unzipping the tent. 'No men allowed, and we move camp regularly, so only people we want can find us. We get women escaping bad relationships, or getting away from drugs. Runaways too. And recently,' she takes a breath, 'we had three local girls hiding here. 'Medika, Charlee and Keira.'

She pulls back the flap to reveal three folded blankets and some clothes. Bright colours, the kind teenagers wear.

'We think these girls were being sex trafficked,' she says. 'They managed to run away when their van stopped at the roadhouse. Got into the bushes and we hid them.' Her eyes settle on my face, pained.

'They wouldn't say a word about the men they got away from, besides they were whitefellas. I've never seen three girls so scared,' she says with conviction. 'They lived with us for a week. We were trying to work out how to help them. They went crazy at any mention of police. Said the men would hurt their families if they went to the authorities.' She sighs from somewhere deep in her soul. 'Then someone betrayed them.'

My blood turns to ice. 'Who?'

Mary's face is grim. 'The girl who died. Tula Wunjarrah.'

I digest this information. If Mary can say Tula's name aloud so soon after her death, I think it means she doesn't regard their relationship as close. But I'm not sure, and I don't want to risk asking.

'How did she . . . how did Tula know about this place?'

'Few weeks ago, she came to hide out here. Told us some whitefella wanted her dead.' Mary shrugs as if the questionable truth of this is irrelevant now. 'She left and when she came back she was looking at those trafficked girls. Like she *knew* something. That night Tula brought yara-ma-yha-who, they came here,' continues Mary. 'Took the girls.'

'Wait . . . Yara-ma-yha-who took them?' Something has been lost in translation. A yara-ma-yha-who is a mythical monster, but I must have misunderstood.

'Medika, Charlee and Keira,' Mary repeats the names. 'Gone. Taken.' She zips down the tent flap with feeling.

'Have you . . .' My mouth is dry. I clear my throat. 'Have you reported them missing?'

'We tried. Police wouldn't listen.' She looks at me hopefully.

'I'll do everything I can,' I promise her, trying to put the facts in order.

Something occurs to me. 'Did Tula have any reason to be in The Gold Rush pub a few nights ago?'

Mary's forehead crinkles. 'She was seeing a whitefella from the mine who was no good. He drank there.'

'Is this the same whitefella who she said wanted her dead?'

Mary shakes her head. 'No, no. That whitefella chasing her was a business partner, or something. This other one at The Gold Rush pub, he was like . . . a boyfriend. He gave her money. She met him online, one of those sites for rich white men dating pretty girls or something.'

Cogs turn. 'Was this whitefella's name Paul Hunter?'

She nods slowly, 'Think so yeah.'

'What are police doing here?' A flat, angry voice breaks into our conversation. I turn to see a furious-looking woman standing a few metres away.

I hold my hands up in surrender. 'I'm here to help.'

It's the wrong thing to say. The woman picks up a stick. 'None of you police listen to us,' she accuses. 'You don't care what happens to our girls.'

The worst thing is, I have absolutely no defence against what she's saying.

'You'd better go,' Mary decides. 'The way back is easier. Head for the heat haze above the roadhouse.'

'You need to leave,' says the woman.

'I'm going. And thanks,' I tell Mary.

'Don't bother coming back,' returns the other woman. 'We'll be gone.'

I turn away, defeated, with terrible thoughts tumbling through my head.

42

Beth

It seemed like Marc was playing Lauren. I mean, it had been weeks, but he still hadn't asked her on a date. Then he mentions this weird bush phenomenon called Min Min lights. Like, mysterious lights in the desert, basically.

Marc tells Lauren he has always wanted to see this. But he doesn't own a car for environmental reasons. Obviously.

And *Lauren* remembers, like, hey, the guys in the pub have transport. I knew what was coming next.

It kind of became a question of who was using who. You know?

People assume Lauren is dumb. I think that's even what she wants them to believe. But she isn't. She really isn't. She's trusting, which is not the same thing.

Mike

Lauren all over, isn't it? Reckons the world owes her a favour and a free ride, 'cause she looks the way she does. You can imagine how Paul felt about that. Thinks he's finally gonna get his rocks off, then Lauren invites some pretty boy from the greenie hippy place. That bloke didn't buy a single tinny either. Not so much as a pack of potato chips. Long-haired prick.

Dillon

Paul made it clear I wasn't invited. So, of course I knew. He was going to bang Lauren.

Lauren

One of the things the locals often talked about was this thing called Min Min lights.

So, as far as I can make out, this is, like, a mysterious thing that happens out in the desert. Lights. And you, like, do not know where they are coming from. And if you try to find them or go after them, or whatever, they vanish.

Paul had talked about going camping but we'd been putting him off.

Then we were talking to Marc, and he's all like, Min Min lights, and how he's never seen them, yada yada yada. And Beth and I . . . I guess we thought maybe it could be a cool trip.

Beth

We were both waiting outside the pub to go. Our. One. Day. Off.

Pete wanders out and shouts something about us taking his best customers. Like, 'Thanks, Pete! You have a good day too!'

Paul drives up with Mike in this big white truck. Lauren doesn't notice, but it's a flashy car he has, even for a guy with no kids on a mining salary. I have an antenna for this stuff because when people at the trailer park showed up with expensive things you learned to keep out of their way. Few weeks later you could bet the cops would show up, and they'd pull you too if they thought you were an associate.

In the back are these brand-new tents. Two. And two sleeping bags. Paul looks really proud of himself.

He's like, 'I picked these up for you.'

That made me nervous. Because you could tell he'd bought them new.

When Mike arrived, he gave a long look over them, and sort of sniggered.

'You drive all the way to Park Ridge for those?' he asked Paul.

'Might have,' said Paul defensively. 'What's it to you?'

'Nothing,' said Mike, taking another look at the box-fresh tents. 'What they cost you then? Fifty bucks a piece?'

'Something like that,' replied Paul cagily.

'Two of 'em, eh? One of those for me, is it?'

Paul laughed. 'Depends if you play your cards right, Mike-o.'

Naturally, Lauren missed all this. I had a nasty feeling about him spending money on camping equipment and what he was expecting in return. It seemed obvious he imagined him and Lauren in one of those tents and me and Mike in another.

Marc arrived late. And he had this girl with him. A super pretty French girl called Sophie. And he was all like, 'Oh, do you mind if she comes along?' And of course Mike and Paul are fine with it. I didn't turn around to see Lauren's face.

Marc and Sophie brought no tents or anything. They got in the car, but it soon became clear conversation wasn't exactly going to flow in the group.

After about forty minutes we pulled up at a gas station out of town, and Paul sent Mike to load up a whole lot of liquor.

I got out to help Mike, and I overheard Paul on the phone to someone. He was discussing where to deliver the girls.

For a moment I was so sure he was talking about us. I totally freaked out. Like, I could barely stand. It hit me how Paul was driving us into the middle of nowhere. We were completely in his power. It was familiar, that feeling. Cut off, nobody who cared.

Then Mike says to Paul: 'Who were you talking to? Your girlfriend?'

Paul blew it off, like it was work stuff, and people weren't doing what they were supposed to. I should have felt relieved, but that sick sliding fear didn't go away.

I didn't realise until that point how easy it was to send me right back to that sorority night. All the feelings were still there, exactly the same. Like they'd been carefully wrapped in tissue paper, perfectly preserved, waiting for the right reason to spring out.

I chewed my fingernails that whole three-hour drive into the bush.

Mike

I'm the only one who knows this. But Paul had started working with this Aboriginal girl, would have been a month or so back now. Said she'd worked as a model and he could barely talk about her without drooling. Paul tried to play it off to me like it was some business arrangement or something. Yeah, right, mate. Like you meet a red-hot stunning girl to go into business with her.

43

Miraculously I make it back from the long grasses on Mary's scant directions, hugely relieved to see Craig is sitting in the car, sipping an energy drink, his deep red hair visible from a distance.

'Jesus, Tara, don't run off like that!' he says. 'I was worried.'

'Sorry. Wasn't intentional. That lady wanted to show me something in the bush. I didn't want to risk losing her.'

'Look, I'm not going to tell Anderson, alright? But this is exactly the sort of thing he automatically chucks out rookies for. You put yourself in danger. And me. It could have been a set-up.'

'OK. Sorry. And thanks.'

He pauses. 'So . . . what happened?'

I take a breath, and fill him in on what I learned.

'No way!' A number of expressions pass over Craig's face. 'That's mad. Good work.'

'If Paul was Tula's boyfriend, they likely came to the pub together,' I say. 'Probably in her car, since it was parked outside.'

'So our witness got it wrong?' suggests Craig. 'Saw a bashed-up car and leaped to conclusions?'

'Maybe.' My mouth twists. It certainly feels like a dead end for the time being.

Craig nods his head and comes to a decision. 'You look like

you could use a cold drink,' he decides. 'Believe it or not, the roadhouse does a mean iced coffee.'

It's so hot the asphalt is spongey as we cross the roadhouse parking lot, and a sharp tarry scent shimmers in the air.

'They should get some shade on here,' grumbles Craig. 'I melted my boots last year walking in for a midday feed.'

I'm struck by how everything is the same, right down to the smatter of outdated ice cream and pie brand signs taped to the glass.

We walk through the whir of the roadhouse automatic doors, and into the blissful cool of the air con. A middle-aged truck driver sits at the counter, working his way through a meat pie.

'You want a sandwich or something?' asks Craig.

'Just a muffin, thanks.'

'For lunch? What would your mother say?' He waggles a pretend stern finger.

'My foster mum wouldn't have cared if we ate cat food.'

'Sheesh.' Craig's forehead puckers. 'Sorry to hear it. She still fostering kids?'

'I heard she breeds dogs now.'

'I'll get you a sandwich.'

I take a seat at the counter whilst Craig collects us sandwiches and two iced coffees from the self-service machine. My eyes drift to a countertop display of ageing doughnuts. Two wasps have crept underneath the cheap fly cover and are twitching their feelers on the sugary surfaces.

An old TV is secured to the far wall. Beth and Lauren's faces flash behind a network news banner. Smiling close-ups of them both are interspersed with footage of the boarded-up Gold Rush, which out of context makes them appear shockingly callous.

See? the compilation seems to say. *They're laughing about it.*

Craig returns with coffees in one hand and an armful of pre-packed sandwiches. He deposits the food and drinks. Then with difficulty perches his strapping thighs on the raised stool, feet crossed at the ankles.

'Tuna,' he says, sliding my sandwich over, and unwrapping two boxes for himself. 'Protein.'

I eye it suspiciously. 'Thanks.'

Craig glances up at the TV, green eyes thoughtful.

'It's everywhere,' he says shortly. 'Big story. So, tell all.' He sips coffee. 'How come you got to see the camp?'

'Maybe just being a woman, I guess. And speaking a bit of the language.' I frown. 'Wish I spoke more, though. The women out there reckon Tula brought out some . . . yara-ma-yha-who.'

'Like a bad spirit?'

'I don't know,' I consider. 'I felt like she meant something else.'

Medika, Charlee and Keira. Taken in the night.

The TV flickers. Beth and Lauren are lead news. No one noticed the Indigenous girls were gone.

I swallow, my mouthful of sandwich feeling hard in my throat. *I'm going to find those girls.*

As soon as I think it, I feel better. Then I remember the woman on the door of Magic Molly's. She mentioned trafficked prostitutes operating in Dead Tree Creek. Could there be a connection?

'Shall we follow up at Magic Molly's on the way back to the station?' I suggest. 'They told me to come back in the afternoon.'

Craig rubs the back of his thick neck nervously. 'Yeah, so. I've been meaning to talk to you about something.'

'Really?' I reply warily.

'You know you've got a past, with your sister and all that?' he asks. I raise an eyebrow.

'You've heard of Trish, who runs Magic Molly's?' His

confessional tone is starting to unnerve me. Craig sighs deeply. 'She's my mum.'

I was absolutely not expecting that.

His eyes land squarely on my face. 'I mean, I didn't grow up with her or anything,' he says quickly. 'Mostly lived with my aunty. Didn't have much contact with Mum. Anyway, Anderson wouldn't want me at Magic Molly's. Conflict of interest, you know. Sorry.' He flicks his eyes up at me then studies the inside of his coffee cup intently, brow drawn. 'I can drop you off, though,' he adds, still looking down.

I absorb this. 'How do you feel about your mum now?' I ask finally.

'We've patched things up a bit,' he says, risking a glance at me. 'I see her from time to time.'

I think of my own severed relations. Birth mum gone, and my birth dad was never in the picture. Relationship with my foster mum is not worth talking about. The battery-children-farmer, we used to call her. I wonder if she ever cared about any of us, crammed into those bunk beds.

'Big of you,' I say finally.

'It's one of the reasons I became a cop,' he adds. 'Mum hit the bottle pretty bad at one point, when I was still living with her. Meant I wasn't shielded from . . . all that stuff.'

I'm silent, thinking about this.

'So how's it working for you?' I ask. 'Is catching criminals healing old wounds?' The ineffectiveness of his strategy is hitting me in far-too-personal waves.

He makes a small smile and lifts his coffee, rolling the cup between his hands. 'Not. As. Yet.' He hesitates. 'And you?'

I meet his eye for a moment. 'Not as yet.'

We finish our coffees in silence.

44

Lauren

The camping thing was fun, you know? We were out in the wilds. Paul and Mike could do all these practical things. Light fires and stuff. It was totally impressive.

Where we were. Oh my God. *So* beautiful. There was this big lake, and colourful birds took flight as we pulled up. At this point, we realised we didn't have much food. Just a *whole* lotta alcohol.

But, whatever. Beth and I were sorority girls, right? I mean, the pipes in our house got regularly clogged from people barfing up their dessert. So we are *kind of* used to not eating. It wasn't such a big deal for us.

Sophie, the French girl, you could tell she was pissed. Marc came out with something about love and friendship being the only food we needed, and she was like, 'Tell that to the kids in Africa.'

But we totally weren't going to let that spoil our fun.

So. We're waiting for sundown. Min Min lights.

It was super exciting.

Then someone suggested we play a drinking game.

Beth

Paul suggested we play a drinking game. I think he'd had it all planned from the outset.

To set the scene, there was half a bag of potato chips that got silently fought over. Sophie acted super entitled. She was the one who ate all the potato chips. I thought Lauren was pretty gracious about it, because I know for a fact she was starving and they were technically hers. Marc hadn't thought to bring any food, and he didn't buy any drinks either, even though we stopped at the store. He essentially arrived with a half-litre water canteen (bought from some Parisian eco-store, naturally), and a liability, in the form of his French friend. Oh, oh. And a guitar. He brought his guitar. Obviously.

At this point, I assumed Lauren must be losing interest in Marc. Contrasting Marc with the guys from the bar, it was clear who the adults were. For all Marc went on about living off the land and learning from the Aboriginals, he didn't know shit. Whereas Paul and Mike, they quietly got on with stuff. Didn't complain. They set up the whole camp whilst we sat around like babies, and Sophie bitched about the biting insects. I did offer to help, but Mike wouldn't hear of it.

That was when I started seeing him in a different way, I think. Strong and kind, instead of drunk and loud. Plus, when Marc began strumming the guitar and crooning in this high voice, Mike gave him this long head-shaking look, and was like: 'Mate. No.' Which I for one appreciated.

I should have been glad Sophie and Marc were there, but I didn't like how they highlighted how much Lauren and I had upped our drinking. You could tell they were a little disgusted by how drunk we were.

It was weird, suddenly being on the other side of the bar.

We played this game involving a pack of cards. Every time you took a card, you tipped a little of whatever you were drinking into the same plastic cup. So it ended up as this gross mix of like, beer, white wine; Mike and Paul were on whisky, making sure to pour generous measures. Whoever drew a royal card had to drink the cup.

Lauren

It was a fun game. Loosened everybody up.

Before we knew it, we were all actually having a good time.

We started playing 'Never Have I Ever'. Like, never have I ever recorded a sex tape. Never have I ever had a ménage à trois. Never have I ever masturbated in a dorm room full of people.

Mike

Ah, we were living the dream, eh? Out in the bush with these hot girls, telling us all these dirty things they'd done round the campfire. Good times. I remember Paul nudging me. Like, *it doesn't get any better than this*. He knew he was in, for sure.

Seemed clear to us. Sophie was with that weird guitar kid, for whatever reason. Her loss. So that left Lauren and Paul. Beth and me.

Then . . . I don't know what happened. But we ended up playing this game. I dunno. Like something the girls had played at college.

Beth

Those questions were totally for Marc's benefit, but you could kind of see Paul and Mike's jaws hanging open. Mike made this weird noise like a squeak at one point. Lauren suggested you had to kiss the person who'd done it, or maybe they had to kiss you if they had. Something like that. Whatever it was, the questions changed, and suddenly people were trying to come up with things Paul and Mike wouldn't have done.

Lauren

Sophie was the worst. She was like: 'Never have I ever been to Paris.' 'Never have I ever slept on a Thai beach.' Ugh. That is totally not the point of that game.

Beth

Paul kissed me. I kissed Mike. Lauren kissed Sophie, which she played up for everyone present even though Sophie was trying to say that girls kissing girls wasn't allowed.

Marc and Sophie ended up kissing many times because of the questions Sophie chose. It wasn't super racy or anything, but you could tell by the way they looked into each other's eyes, that was only because there were people present. Lauren is suddenly like: 'Let's play something else.' There's a funny look on her face. She starts telling them all about our sorority house, and what girls have to do to get selected. I'm looking at her, like *Lauren*. Because we swore an oath not to tell.

Lauren says it's cool because this is stuff before we pledged.

She doesn't get into what happened after. Obviously.

Paul and Mike are kind of fascinated.

Sophie is all like, 'I've heard about that. Hazing, yeah? It's a French word, actually. You do fucked-up things to people to make them part of the group. It's very stupid.'

Lauren

Sophie declared war. She totally declared war.

45

Craig drops me off at the top of York Street, and this time, there's no one on Magic Molly's open door. I walk right in to find a small reception area looking a lot like a mid-range hotel.

Behind the desk is a middle-aged woman with a blonde bob blow-dried to sleek submission, and movie-star-perfect smoky-eye make-up. I see the similarity to Craig instantly. She has the same unusual eye colour, and high cheekbones.

She holds the receiver of an old-fashioned pink phone and is frowning heavily.

'No, *no*,' she says in a hard local accent that doesn't match her immaculate appearance. 'We don't keep them that young. And you should be bloody ashamed of yourself for asking.'

She ends the call.

'Tours start in twenty minutes, darl,' she says, sliding a leaflet towards me as she makes a note on a pad in front of her. After a moment she looks up, her face questioning. 'Oh.' Her eyes widen, fascinated, taking in my uniform. '*You're* here about Paul Hunter,' she decides triumphantly as if solving some particular-ly taxing riddle. 'Whole town knows,' she adds to my unasked question. 'It was the backpacker girls, right? They'd had enough of being called sheilas or something.'

She considers me carefully.

'Not seen a girl-cop round here before,' she muses. 'Tough job, I reckon. You sure you don't want to work for me? Pretty little blonde like you would make a fortune. You've got that surfer-girl look.'

I clear my throat, trying to sound authoritative. 'You knew Paul Hunter, right?' I say. 'Your girl on the door said you chucked him out.'

'Yeah,' she shrugs. 'Bad behaviour.'

'What kind of bad behaviour?'

'He wanted a lot for his money, put it that way.'

'Could you be more specific?'

Trish looks lazily at her watch. 'We're expecting a tour group in an hour,' she says. 'A way to make ends meet, you know. Like I said, the girlie trade isn't what it used to be.'

I nod uncertainly, not sure what she's getting at.

Trish rolls her eyes, false lashes making contact with her eyebrows.

'You really are new, aren't you?' she says. 'Don't you watch the movies? You *pay* prostitutes for information, darl.'

I take out my wallet and peer inside. 'I'm low on cash,' I admit. 'Would twenty be OK?'

'Haven't you ever bribed anyone before?' she scoffs as I wave the note. She snaps the bill out of my unresisting hand and fashions it into a neat roll. 'Like that, see? And . . . here . . . slide it into my palm.'

I let her move my hand around, bamboozled by it all.

'Twenty is fine,' she tells me, wedging it under her bra strap. 'Ten would be OK for a street walker, even five, maybe, if they were drunk or stoned.'

'Thanks.' I'm wondering if I've just committed a crime.

'Alrighty.' I get the sense I have shifted into Trish's transactional personality and wonder how long I have on the clock. 'To answer your question, Paul Hunter wanted things for his money that our girls weren't willing to do. He was always trying to get more from his time, you know? Didn't like the rules. Our ladies perform a physical inspection on a man before they do business with him.' She lists on her fingers, 'We ask the gentlemen to shower. Protection is compulsory, even for oral services, no exceptions. That's a legal requirement.'

'Paul Hunter didn't like that?'

'Oh, he kept complaining. The Asians this, and the Asians that. I told him. Those girls were trafficked, darl. Illegal. Slave labour.'

'So Paul Hunter frequented the illegal places? With trafficked girls?' I leap on it a bit too eagerly. Trish raises an eyebrow.

'They all do, darl,' says Trish in a bored voice. 'Trust me, men do whatever they can get away with.'

My thoughts flit to Craig. Not a nice expectation to grow up with.

'Do you know anything about Indigenous girls being trafficked as prostitutes in Dead Tree Creek?' I ask.

Her eyes widen. 'As much as you do, I reckon. Feds did a crackdown on the backstreet places. Deported all the illegals months ago. They're gone now. The whole bloody lot, thank God.'

'Immigrants? No Indigenous girls?'

'Strewth, girlie, you could try reading your own reports. Far as I know it was a trafficking ring selling Cambodian teenagers. Nasty men. There was a big swoop to arrest them.' She looks sad. 'Those raids came too late for York Street,' she adds gloomily. 'This part of town used to come alive at 7 p.m. Lights flashing, girls in their undies. We're the last ones left and between you and me we earn more from tourists than sex work.' She shakes her head. 'Way of the world, I guess. The internet has made sex cheap.'

I switch tack.

'Was Paul Hunter angry, to be chucked out?' I ask.

'*Oh* – yeah.' She rolls the sounds around dramatically. 'Made his feelings clear.' She makes a thin victorious smile.

'He threatened you?'

'Reckoned he was going to run me out of business. Start up his own place. I didn't take it seriously, darl. If I had a dollar for every time someone said they'd burn this place down, I wouldn't need to do the tour groups. Ah ha ha.' She gives a strange articulated laugh which doesn't reach her eyes.

'Do you remember what he said? What words he used?'

'He told me York Street was out of date. Men wanted no-holds-barred places – like fight club but with sex – and he was the man to do it.'

'As in . . . no health checks, no protection?' I venture hopefully.

Her narrow eyebrows shoot up. 'And the rest. You wouldn't believe the kind of things men want to do to women. Greek. Watersports. Hardsports. Rough play. I ceased to be surprised twenty years ago.'

'You don't do that stuff here?' I confirm, trying not to let on I have no idea what she means.

'No way, darl. I've got ladies to look after.'

'Did Paul Hunter mention anything about recruiting girls?' I ask.

'Blimey, he wasn't selling me the place, darl. Just sounding off about what a big man he was. Look,' she says, finally. 'You want my opinion, a man like Paul Hunter couldn't have organised a piss-up in a brewery, let alone run a brothel. He wasn't a smart bloke in that way. Not to mention, that man had never washed a towel in his life.' She eyes me for a moment and sighs. 'If you've heard a rumour, that's most likely all it is. There's always talk flying amongst the mine workers about new brothels. Extreme sex, young girls. Mostly they're just exercising their mouths. I try not to pay attention.' She looks at the pink clock. 'If you think Paul actually followed through with his threats, he probably wasn't working alone. My advice is to find his business partner.'

The finality in her tone is astonishingly clear. Decades in the trade, I suppose.

'Nice talking to you, Constable Harrison,' she concludes. 'If you see my boy Craig, say hello from me. And if you ever want a different line of work, give me a call.'

46

Lauren

The camping trip totally escalated because of Sophie. It was her fault. We're all sat around the campfire, and *Sophie* was being all high and mighty about American environmental policy or whatever. As if Beth and I are directly responsible for all the world's problems. I mean, we didn't ask to be born in America. We didn't pass the gun laws. We don't, like, *run cattle farms*. What the f—?

All this after she'd eaten my potato chips and you never heard me say a word about it.

Then we're talking about sorority houses, and she's acting like it's all stupid when in fact it's a very big deal.

Beth and I exchanged a little secret look, and I knew we were totally going to show them.

'Well, you know,' I said to Sophie. 'I don't think a single person here would have got into Alpha Sigma Psi, besides me and Beth. You don't have it in you.'

Beth

Keep in mind, we were all super drunk. Like *so* drunk. The girls had stopped bothering to go into the bush to pee. Even Sophie. We'd yell at everyone not to look, and stagger a few metres from the fire.

Lauren had spent the last half hour spinning the dirtiest 'Never Have I Ever' questions imaginable. Basically, fluffing all the guys to imagine her in various extreme sexual scenarios. There was a lot of tension. At least two people at that fireside had things to prove.

The waxing strips plan was genius. Because if you don't regularly bikini wax, it hurts way more. But Paul and Mike were all trying to be so manly and stuff. We took it too far. I'll admit we took it too far.

Mike

Turns out the girls were, how do you say it? Soyrity girls? It's like a club or something, all the girls want to get into, only you have to do fucking crazy shit to become a member.

Apparently, one of the things was every new girl had to be waxed by someone older. Sounds pretty kinky, if you ask me. And these are the people who are running the country over there. Strewth. Anyway, the girls thought it would be funny to wax everyone.

Lauren pulls out these waxing strips she has in her toilet bag. Like, what kind of girl goes *camping* with no food, and a whole box of strips to wax her pubic hair? They were these sticky strip things you put on the skin. Ripped off. Never known pain like it, I'm telling you.

Lauren

The rule was you kept your underwear on. That meant Beth and I had barely any hair to wax. Both Mike and Paul wore, like, Speedo-style briefs which was super hilarious in itself. Beth totally got blood lust or something. The strips I'd brought along, if you don't smooth them out flat the wax gums up and doesn't pull off cleanly. Combine that with more than a half-inch of hair, and what it does, is basically rip the skin right off.

As you can imagine, those guys were a total hairy mess. Beth had this super evil glint in her eye and you could see her lightly laying strips on the hairiest part.

It was hysterical because you knew how much that would kill. And after the shit they'd put us through, I wasn't crying for them. Only I think Beth did take it too far.

Mike

That was what they did to criminals in olden times, wasn't it? Pulled skin off. It hurt like fuck. We had a new respect for the girls after that. Especially Lauren. She kept going. Don't know how she stood the pain.

Lauren

Sophie totally broke the rules of that game. She was, like, allergic to having any fun. Marc had done one little waxing strip and bailed. It was pretty obvious to me, Sophie was never going to do it. She launched into this big speech about body hair being natural before we started, and kept looking over at Marc for approval.

Beth

You'd think we'd have learned when to stop at college. But we hadn't. Obviously. In fact, it seemed to have made us worse.

Lauren was asking me to do more on her, because that meant the guys had to do more too. It was difficult to see in the campfire, but I was like, 'Lauren, I think it's bruising your skin.' And she was still like, '*Do more, do more.*' She couldn't feel it, was the thing. Those pills she takes. Unlike Paul. He was roaring in agony every time Lauren pulled the strip off. We were all in hysterics.

It was about that point we noticed that Marc and Sophie had walked off.

47

I arrive back at the station to find Craig at his desk ploughing through paperwork.

He raises a hand in greeting as Anderson emerges from his office with a dried-out cheese and pickle sandwich in his hand.

'Well, Tara,' says Anderson, without smiling. 'Looks like you're up.'

I have no idea what he's talking about. He takes a bite of the tired bread and chews with effort.

'Beth hasn't cracked,' he says, through his mouthful. 'Still insisting on a female, and no sign of Perth. We've got another hour, and I don't want to leave it any longer.'

'You want me to interview Beth? Now?'

He swallows, his Adam's apple bobbing. 'No, I just want you to make me bloody repeat myself all day.'

'I spoke to Trish at Magic Molly's . . .'

He looks surprised. 'You get something out of her?'

'Maybe. Yeah.'

'Well, that's a first,' he says. 'All my years of policing, I've never known a prostitute volunteer useful information. Perhaps there's something in this female communication stuff after all. OK, type it up for me later,' he says. 'Beth is in there waiting, so look sharp, Harrison. Let's get this done. In and out, eh? Name, address, charges. Anything else a bonus, right?'

'Yes, sir.' I pause. 'If you don't mind, I'm going to take ten minutes to get my thoughts in order. We got some extra information out in the long grasses and—'

'I do mind, Harrison, we're cutting things fine as it is.'

I stand my ground. 'Ten minutes won't make any difference. I want to be prepared, sir.'

He hesitates. 'Seven minutes.'

'Thank you, sir.'

I sit at my computer and recap my notes. Anderson's right, it is easier from a tidy desk.

I check the time. Tapping a pen to my mouth, I perform a Google search of Alpha Sigma Psi, Beth and Lauren's house.

The sorority has an unnatural fixation with death. Even the motif features a skull and crossbones. It has also been linked with several hazing fatalities over the course of its seventy-year history.

I ponder this, running a few more searches. Looks like all the major sororities in the States have incurred hazing-related deaths, leading to a change in the law to make hazing illegal. All colleges ban hazing, but that hasn't stopped the practice. The vast majority are alcohol poisoning. Several are more disturbing, especially the historic ones. Accidental electrocution, strangulation, and lethal beatings all feature a number of times. I shudder.

I glance at the clock. My seven minutes has gone in a flash.

Even so, I feel a burst of expectation as I head for the interview room and open the door. Everything is more familiar already. The seating arrangements, the recording device. Everything besides the suspect.

Beth sits opposite as I seat myself, twisting her hands nervously. She doesn't look me in the eye.

The initial impression I had of her as an oddball is exacerbated.

Her wide face seems to be missing normal expressions. The wide-apart eyes add to the feeling of emotional distance. Her figure is rail thin and boyish, and her straight dark hair has grown limper in captivity, bordering on greasy.

I read my notes, following my written steps.

'Darla-Beth Jackson?'

She nods.

'For the tape, please.'

'That is correct. But I go by Beth.' Her voice is unnaturally low, the intonation rising as though every statement is a question.

'Based on the evidence, we'll be charging you with murder,' I tell her. She jolts, closes her eyes for a moment. I rattle off the rest of her rights from memory, then check in with my notepad again.

Suspect identified, charged. So far, so good. I take a breath.

'You were very sure about wanting a female constable,' I tell her. 'How can I help you?'

She doesn't answer.

'What about the night of the murder?' I press. 'Do you have anything to say about that? Anything to clear up?'

Silence.

'How about we talk a bit about your college?' I suggest. 'You went to West Coast, right?'

Her eyes widen in surprise. 'Yes.' It sounds as though her throat is tight.

'Expensive place to study,' I observe. 'Expensive sorority house too.'

She coughs into her hand. 'I got a scholarship. And the sorority had subsidies.'

'Yeah, but that doesn't pay for everything, right?' I smile fanning out my hands. She makes the smallest of smiles in return. 'Why not pick a different sorority? One with fewer financial burdens?'

'The cheaper sororities don't get you into high places.'

'You wanted to get into high places?'

Her mouth twists and she shrugs. 'I guess . . .' She lifts her shoulders and drops them, and her face tightens. 'I'd come too far and worked too hard to settle, you know? I'd gotten out of the trailer park. Do you know how few people do that? I wanted to keep going. Make everything I'd left worth it.'

Her eyes meet mine, and I see myself reflected back. For a moment we understand each other.

'How did you afford all those college extras?' It's a risky question and I'm half expecting her to shut down. But she doesn't.

'I gave blood.' She rubs at a fingernail with an unconcerned expression, then looks at me. There's something removed about her face. Something absent. 'If you play the system you can do four different blood banks in a month.'

I calculate. 'You donated blood four times a month?'

'Until I got anaemic. I also fainted a lot. Got a reputation for being somewhat delicate. Of course, no one knew.'

'Not even Lauren?'

'Oh sure.' She corrects herself a shade too quickly, I notice. 'I tell Lauren everything.'

'And what about her? Does she tell you everything?' It's a question to keep the interview flowing. But to my surprise, Beth fades into herself like a wilting flower.

'No,' she says miserably. 'She doesn't tell me everything.'

I fight to keep my voice casual. 'What . . . what kind of things doesn't she tell you?'

'Sexual stuff,' says Beth quietly and with obvious bitterness. 'She has secrets. Things she does that . . .' She scrunches her face slightly as if distracted. Her mouth moves without words coming out.

'Beth?' I ask gently. 'You were saying? Lauren keeps sexual secrets?' There's a silence.

'I don't want to say any more,' she says.

The interview door snaps open and Anderson enters the room. I switch my attention back to Beth, thrown off track.

'For the tape, Sergeant Anderson has entered the room,' I say, stumbling a little on the words.

'Sorry to interrupt you, Tara,' says Anderson. 'Perth just arrived.'

48

Beth

Marc and Sophie came back from their moonlit walk, all bright-eyed, saying they'd seen the Min Min lights. They sat by the fire, really close, arms touching.

Lauren was taking it all in. She said: 'You bailed, huh?'

Sophie was like, 'Yeah, we heard you screaming from the bush.' She looked back at Marc like they were sharing a private joke.

After a few minutes Sophie went off to use the non-existent bathroom.

Lauren stood and walked over to Marc. Stood so her hips were level with his face. And she goes: 'So, you wanna see what you missed?' Before he answers, she drops her pants, so it's just her underwear and a whole bunch of waxed skin.

And then, she goes: 'You were out of the game. Forfeit. You need to kiss it better.' She grabbed Marc's big curly mop of hair and smooshed his face right into her crotch.

Mike

Can you imagine, if a bloke did that to a girl? He'd get himself arrested, I reckon.

This is the problem with women's lib and all that stuff. You act like you're in a porno, that's how guys are gonna treat you. And you can't complain, when a man goes too far, or whatever. 'Cause you've already given him the green light.

Lauren, she wanted it both ways. And, like my old mum says, that's a busy street.

Beth

Marc had this big dopey smile on his face like a man in a trance.

Sophie's face. If looks could kill. For a second it looked like she was going to slap Lauren. I kind of saw her point. Lauren had broken all the rules. And Marc was male, and therefore weak-willed and susceptible. So Lauren pulled Marc up with her, and was like: 'We're going to take a break from the game. Marc is going to keep watch whilst I go to the bathroom.'

She led him away. A moment later we heard a tent unzip.

I mean. Marc *obviously* liked Sophie. But Lauren won.

We all sat around in silence for a few seconds. I was likely the only one who saw the funny side. Although I wondered how the sleeping arrangements were going to work out now.

I did feel sorry for Sophie. Only Lauren was there first.

It seemed to me super unfair that Sophie was mad with Lauren, but really it was all Marc's fault. If you're not sure about a girl, you shouldn't go all googly-eyed at her, and take her number and write her poems and stuff. And basically get her to like you. Then ditch her because something better comes along. That's just toying with people.

All in all, I think Marc was a total jerk.

After a second we heard these noises from the tent, and Sophie got up fast, and was like, 'I'm tired. I'm going to bed.' She walked to the other tent, taking one of the two sleeping bags with her and zipped up the door.

Paul got up like he was going to say something, and then just stood there, swaying. He muttered something like, 'Fuck this,' and strode off into the dark.

So it was just me and Mike by the fire.

I'm not proud of this, but it occurred to me in that moment, that he had a sleeping bag he could share with me.

I don't remember a lot of what happened next, but at some point Mike came and sat next to me.

'Look, Beth,' he whispered. 'Do you see 'em? The Min Min lights.'

I was so drunk I couldn't see anything.

Mike

I'm an Aussie bloke. Not romantic or anything. But . . . the lights were dancing in the trees. One and then two, splitting apart and coming back together. It was magic. Beth snuggled in close, and she fitted perfect, right under my arm. Like the spot had been made for her especially. We had a bit of a kiss. Cosied up under the stars. I'm not the kind of guy to push anything, you know? Paul's like that, but I'm not that sort of bloke. I was happy just seeing those lights with her. Looking up into the night sky. Feeling her breathing, real gentle, as she fell asleep.

49

The Perth team remind me of a pack of grim-faced crows as they trickle out of the interview room. There are three. Two of them – a man with an ill-advised moustache, and a dark-haired woman – descend on our paperwork without so much as an introduction. The third is a large sandy-haired man, with freckles scattered over every inch of exposed skin. The wrong side of health and thirty to be good-looking, with the suggestion of a paunch and a bloodshot cast to his blue eyes.

'Just our luck,' mutters Anderson as he leads me out. 'We got Detective Theory-First-Evidence-Later Connolly. Done a module in criminal profiling and reckons he's a psychologist. I'll be in my office.' Anderson departs as Connolly sweeps towards me.

He's eyeing me up in that slightly edgy way men do, when they've put you in a definite box marked FEMALE.

'Harrison? Tara Harrison, is it?' He holds out a freckled hand. 'Loving the just-got-out-of-bed-hair.'

I pass a self-conscious hand over my tousled hair, which has worsened in the heat. Dead Tree Creek sun has added sun-bleached stripes which stick out at angles from my barely contained ponytail.

'I'm Detective Connolly.' I grip his soft palm, consciously

attempting to mirror the pressure he applies. His eyebrows rise. 'Strong handshake,' he observes. 'Good to see a girl down here. These boys could do worse than have a pretty face on the team. Just-got-out-of-bed hair, eh? I like it.'

'I'd rather be judged on my work, sir.'

His hands fly up, face contorted in pantomime shock. 'Whoa there! We've got a firecracker here! Didn't mean anything by it, Tara. Just an observation.'

Unexpectedly, Craig steps quietly to my side. Close enough I can smell his minty shower gel.

'Observations on a person's gender are considered inappropriate in the police force,' he says with quiet authority. 'Even out here.'

Connolly's expression changes, as though he's reassessing both of us.

'That so? Well, thank you for telling me the *law*, constable . . .?'

'Dooligan.' Craig looks quietly back at him, something steely in his green eyes. He looks a lot less like a boy-band member now. The gym physique has taken on a new meaning.

'Constable *Dooligan*.' Connolly fixes him with a hard stare. 'I'll remember you.'

'Appreciated, sir.' Craig replies with the same mild-mannered expression he always carries, but he doesn't break eye contact, and I notice Connolly looks away first.

Connolly slides past with an angry look.

'We got a lot of backwater policing out here,' he announces. 'Laundry list of bad practice. Contaminating the crime scene, failing to use gloves, inadmissible interviews.'

Craig goes to reply, but I reach out and touch his arm. When he turns to me in question, I make the smallest shake of my head.

Don't give him the satisfaction.

Craig closes his mouth again, annoyed. He folds his big arms across his chest.

'Heard you wanted us interrogating the girlfriend, April Dean?' says Connolly, looking at Craig.

'Not interrogate . . .' begins Craig. Connolly talks over him.

'You aren't trained in psychological theory,' says Connolly. 'But in the city, we take it seriously.'

I see Craig's jaw twitch.

'What we've got here,' says Connolly grandly, 'is a classic psychopath-narcissist pairing.' He clears his throat. 'One feeds off the other.'

'We're talking about Lauren and Beth, right?' I ask innocently. 'Not city cops versus us outbackers?'

Connolly frowns, trying to decide if I'm serious. I keep my expression politely quizzical. Craig catches my eye and looks away, fighting back laughter.

'Correct, Harrison,' says Connolly finally. 'Let me lay out the crime for you, as seen by the experts.' He strikes his chest to denote himself. 'Load of regulars, including Paul Hunter and his Aborigine girlfriend . . .'

I clear my throat. 'Aborigine is offensive, sir. Aboriginal or Indigenous is preferred nowadays. Or you could use her name. Tula.'

He shoots me a filthy look. 'Witness accounts say Paul and *Tula* mysteriously vanished around midnight. But no security footage shows them leaving the pub, right?'

'Right,' says Craig.

'The blokes drinking that night reckon the backpacker girls were absent for an undefined period at some point during the lock-in. Am I correct so far?'

'Yes.' Craig and I speak together.

'Lauren Davis, this little blonde here,' he taps a picture of

Lauren on Instagram, her shirt pulled up to expose her bra, a weird winking expression on her face, 'she's having a sexual relationship with Hunter. He shows up with another girl. A *Black* girl. How's blondie going to react to that?'

I feel my teeth gritting together.

'We got this other one here. Nerdy one. Beth. She's the dark horse. Excited by death. Two killers with opportunity and motive, and . . .' he flaps a stack of xeroxed images from the girls' diary, 'a menu of murderous fantasies, *including*, pushing dirt into a victim's throat.' He smiles in a predatory way. 'We've got an open-and-shut case. I've only got one question remaining.'

He waits for us to ask what it is. Neither of us do.

'Why aren't the girls already in jail?' he concludes, fixing us with a hard stare.

50

Mike

Good times never last, do they? One minute I was sat with Beth leaned up against me, looking out on those Min Min lights. I went off to find the last sleeping bag. When I came back, Beth was with Paul.

What could I do? I just walked away. Slept in Paul's car.

I was gutted, but all's fair in love and war, right? You can't let a girl come between mates.

Beth

Last thing I knew I was falling asleep on Mike. Then Paul was sitting next to me.

The rest comes in flashes. Like a movie missing some parts.

Paul started unbuttoning my shorts. It was so unexpected. Even though I was too drunk to see straight, I remember how strongly I felt that. There was no invitation, no warning.

I began to say something, and he put a palm over my mouth. 'Shh,' he said. 'They'll hear us.'

I was so drunk, I didn't feel his hand sliding into my underwear.

I had this sensation of having a big clumsy cloth body, useless and numb. Next – I remember this so clearly – it was like *this* part of me, under my clothes, somehow wasn't drunk. This part could feel everything as intrusively as if I was stone cold sober.

Then it was like I went out of myself. I have an abstract memory of a thought process. My mind said: *Something bad is going to happen, Beth. Better put yourself somewhere safe.* And my body did it, without checking in with me.

So . . . the main parts of what happened are not there. Only moments, you know? I remember the weight of him at one point, because a button was digging into my hip bone. I also have an image of a circular whorl in his blonde stubble, about the size of a dime and orange-hued in the firelight.

The next thing I knew, Paul said: 'Are you going to lie there with your pants down?'

It took a few seconds to realise he was talking to me.

'Here,' he threw a sleeping bag, 'you can have it.'

I took it. I think I even thanked him.

Paul sat there looking at the dying embers. He said: 'Don't tell anyone, OK? This was just a bit of fun.' He didn't look at me. 'Hey,' he said when I didn't answer. 'This was just a bit of fun, right? If you ruin my chances with Lauren, I'll fucking kill you.'

I got inside the sleeping bag and lay down. It seemed like the best thing to do. My body ached and I could feel a bruise at the back of my head, like I'd been lying on rock or something. After a few moments I heard grass rustling. I risked a glance up and Paul had gone.

I sat up, and stared out into the dark night for a long, long time. It was ironic that I now felt super sober. Exactly when I didn't want to be that way.

After a while, there they were. The Min Min lights. Billowing and folding in on themselves in the distance. They say you get a wish on the Min Min lights. And if my life has taught me anything, it's that wishes can come true. But sometimes you have to give them a helping hand.

51

Detective Connolly has called Anderson, Craig and I into our small meeting space. An unnaturally dark boxy room of unplastered cinder block, with an old projector mounted in the corner that no one has bothered to take down. There's a smell like it's been recently bug-bombed.

'Where's Connolly?' I ask, looking out through the open door.

'Engineering a big entrance, so he can dazzle us locals with his big-city genius,' observes Craig darkly.

'He's in with Lauren,' says Anderson crisply. 'And just our luck, Connolly's got Lauren in an upbeat mood. I reckon she'll tell 'im everything. Judging by the state of her.'

'That's . . . good, isn't it?' I venture.

'Yes, it's good, Tara, if you're a perfect professional such as yourself. As a flawed human being I can't help but notice it also makes us look like prize dickheads.' He pauses. 'Not to mention, I don't think it's right to decide on a suspect's guilt before you start.'

'You don't think the girls did it?' I ask, confused, since he brought the murder charge.

Anderson looks over his shoulder, to where the female member of Connolly's crew is diligently typing, then silently pads over and closes the door.

'I think everyone deserves a fair bloody trial, is what I think,' says Anderson, lowering his voice. 'Not a show trial in the newspapers, and a court case where Connolly and his cronies bring evidence to support their own bias.'

We're all silent. My eyes drift to the whiteboard Anderson filled in earlier. 'Harassment? Provocation? Broken lock, access to pub, journal', in jerky scarlet writing. They are circled, with arrows darting between to imply a connection.

'No mystery Holden?' I suggest.

'We've linked it to the dead girl, right? So we can assume she drove it there.'

'Yeah, but . . . the witness said there was a man sitting inside it.'

'Won't give a statement, though. Reckons he was too drunk to be sure.'

'What about the account from long grasses?' I say. 'Missing girls. Tula played a part in their disappearance. Could be relevant?'

'Bit of a weak link,' Anderson frowns, but I guess we're still at the ideas stage. He takes a pen and adds, 'Long grasses girls'.

'Has there already been a search for the missing Indigenous girls?' I press. 'A woman named Mary in the long grasses says she reported them to you weeks ago.'

Anderson's face creases like he's remembering. 'We didn't follow it up. I remember Mary coming in. Her and her mate were extremely agitated. Half of what they were saying wasn't even English.'

'This is her country, sir. Do you speak her language?'

'They were shouting about a whatshisname roaming around the long grasses,' continues Anderson. 'What was I supposed to do with that?'

The fight goes out of me a little. 'Do you mean a yara-ma-yha-who?'

He frowns. 'Maybe. Do you know what that is?'

'I'm not entirely sure, but I think a yara-ma-yha-who is, like . . . a blood-sucking monster that hides in trees.'

'Nice. Well, last I heard, vampire hunting isn't on the formal policing agenda.'

'Sir, Paul Hunter had a wallet full of cash and bragged to Trish at Magic Molly's about opening a brothel. Then his Indigenous girlfriend is involved in the disappearance of three girls. Surely that's a connection worth investigating?'

He rubs his forehead, looking pained. 'We'll check the hospital records. See if we've got anything that matches, alright? But often girls from the long grasses vanish, you know?' He heaves up a world-weary sigh. 'Take a glug of bad homebrew, and don't even realise they're dying until the symptoms kick in two days later.'

'Maybe if the government didn't ban Indigenous people from buying legal alcohol, they wouldn't brew up deadly grog,' I say quietly.

Anderson holds up his hands. 'I don't disagree. But I don't make the policies. Just manage the problems they create, OK?'

I nod, pacified.

'So, what's left,' says Anderson. 'Craig, you cover off all the alibis?'

'Yep. All the fellas in the pub check out.'

The door bangs suddenly, making me jump, and Connolly swaggers in with his team hot on his heels.

'What's all this then?' he asks. 'Mothers' meeting? Let me save you all the effort. You'll be pleased to know yours truly has got the goods on Lauren. Nothing further to be done than wrap it all up.'

Connolly's strong cologne fills the room as Craig, Anderson and I look at him wordlessly.

'So, people,' he says not discouraged by our silence, 'if we pull together, we can get these killers put away by tomorrow's happy hour, right?' He's eyeing Craig and I, nakedly suspecting us of the kind of indolence that sabotages half-price drinks.

Connolly puts his hands on his hips and makes a show of considering the whiteboard, before picking up the eraser and slowly rubbing out every last word.

'For those of you who don't know me,' says Connolly, 'I've got a formal qualification in criminal profiling.'

He dumps a bunch of pictures on the desk. Mainly of Lauren in various states of undress. I notice the ones showing the most skin are disproportionately near the top.

'OK, boys and girls, let's take a look at a classic psychopath-narcissist pairing.'

His eyes drift over pictures of Lauren.

'Here's our narcissist,' he declares, stabbing at an image of Lauren on a beach, her tanned ankle displaying a shell anklet. 'This here is the psychopath.' He slides out a shot of Beth, staring unwaveringly into the camera.

'Now, your psychopath recruits the narcissist, who is prepared to lie on her behalf, so long as she's getting her ego pumped. Beth's psychopathic fantasies grow until she is compelled to act them out. Suffocates a girl at college. Lauren covers for her. But the crime itself is unfulfilling. So the cycle begins again.'

'You think they killed the girl at college?' I say, struggling to keep up with his leaps of conjecture. 'They were acquitted.'

'Exactly,' says Connolly. 'They got away with it, so they're pumped to do it again.' Connolly takes a moment to sweep the room with his gaze, allowing his genius to sink in, then claps his hands together. 'That's who we're dealing with. Let's get as many locals in here as possible with dirt against those girls,' he says, looking at his own team. 'Get 'em to spill the beans. By the end of the day we should have enough material to refuse bail. In the meantime, let the nearest jail know they'll be on their way this evening. Anderson, I'll leave you to arrange that with your lot. On second thoughts . . .'

His eyes drift to Craig and I. 'Harrison and Dooligan. You'd better take a look at the recording of my interview with Lauren Davis before we go much further. Might learn a thing or two about technique.'

52

Beth

When we woke up the next morning, everyone was so hungover it wasn't funny. All of us except Lauren, who doesn't get hangovers because she's riding a wave of prescription painkillers. But *I* have never felt so bad in my life. Second thing, we were all in pain. Those waxing strips were painful when we were drunk, I woke up with these deep red patches, like sunburn.

Lauren was in a worse state than me, because I got a glimpse of her when we went to pee. She seemed surprised when I asked if it hurt, and shrugged it off. Like, I'm fine. No big deal. But I'm fairly sure she took a larger handful of pills than usual for the ride home.

Mike couldn't look me in the eye but it didn't matter, because at that point, I'd decided not to feel it. Not at all. Paul was completely different around Lauren. Like, *nasty*. The first thing he said to her, as she crawled out of the tent with her hair a mess, was, 'Fuck me dead, you stink.'

She did. It was true. Like fermenting fruit. But it was mean to say it. It wasn't like any of us had a shower that morning.

Lauren

Marc got up super early and went for a long walk in the bush. He was extremely in tune with nature in that way. Like he didn't want me with him, so he could, kind of, commune with the trees and stuff.

The whole campsite was a wreck. Bottles and tins, and the burned-out fire. And all these bloody waxing strips scattered all over. Beth I and got fits of giggles as we cleaned up.

Paul was in this totally black mood. Barely said two words to anyone, just drove us all back. We all slept in the car and that seemed to make him madder.

I remember it was around this time I decided I needed to double my dose. Of the good pills, I mean. The ones the doctors won't give you, but they sell over the counter in Thailand. Because things were hurting that I didn't want to hurt, and feelings were bubbling up that I wanted to squash. You know?

Looking back, I was having Sneaky Thoughts. In rehab my therapist always encouraged me to call them that. Not really part of you. Things you shouldn't listen to.

At that point it was hard to know which was the Sneaky Thought and which was the regular thought. I mean, on reflection, OK sure, maybe it was obvious. But at the time, the Sneaky Thoughts were coming up with some seemingly good ideas. And one of them was: if I cut out my medication *entirely*, I could take more of the other pills. Because technically you're not supposed to mix, so I was always holding off on the better kind of pills for the sake of avoiding liver failure. Which almost happened to me once, and was totally gross, but that's, like, a whole other story.

53

Craig and I are in a darkened cleaning cupboard, since it's the only spot in the now overcrowded police station to view recordings.

'Sorry.' Craig manoeuvres his large frame further into the corner, standing on my foot. I bump against him in the dark and hit solid muscle.

I open Connolly's battered laptop, which has an I HEART THE GOLD COAST sticker picked out in the Australian flag. The video file is labelled LAUREN GIVES UP THE GOODS.

'Professional.' I raise my eyebrows at Craig before leaning in and pressing play.

The interview room swims into focus, with a band of two static lines running across like tyre tracks.

We can see the back of Connolly's head with a bald spot he's tried to arrange his sandy hair over. Lauren is smiling brightly. Her fingers dance across the table.

'She's manic, right?' I say to Craig.

'Looks that way. Not that it's stopping Connolly.'

'What's that on the desk between them?' I peer closer at an array of brightly coloured objects. 'Bloody hell . . . It isn't?'

'Sex toys,' confirms Craig. 'They were found in Lauren's belongings.'

'Can you tell us about these?' Connolly's voice comes over the recording. He points accusingly towards a lurid pink clam-shaped object.

'Oh, that one is just . . .' Lauren holds up her hands, fingers splayed, palms out, 'The. Best. It's basically suction. For your clit. So, like, it's giving you a mini blowjob. Could not live without it. You should get your girlfriend to try it underwater. Oh my gosh.' She looks at him, her eyes dramatically wide. 'Or your boyfriend,' she adds. 'No judgement.'

Connolly's shoulders tighten. He clears his throat. 'The hand-cuffs found on Paul Hunter's body are the same colour, aren't they? Same shade of pink. They would appear to have been bought with this . . . device.'

'It's called the Womaniser,' Lauren explains happily. 'Almost $200 but worth every cent.'

'I wish we could see Connolly's face,' says Craig wistfully.

'You admit it belongs to you,' says Connolly. 'What about these?' He dangles the evidence bag of muddied fluffy handcuffs used to restrain Paul.

'Yes, those are mine.'

I roll my eyes. 'He could have just asked her that,' I tell Craig.

'Can you explain how they might have ended up on the body?' demands Connolly. 'Did you put them there?'

Lauren looks to the ceiling momentarily. 'No comment.'

Connolly leans in, and I picture his face darkening. 'Lauren, we have a body found in completely vile circumstances. A man we know you had a relationship with—'

'It wasn't a relationship.'

'But you were having sex with him?'

'Sure.'

'I'm gonna need a yes or no for the tape.'

'We were like fuck buddies, I guess. We explored each other's boundaries.' It's hard to be sure, but I think I detect a wave of sadness pass over Lauren's face.

Connolly pounces. 'You're saying it was rough?'

She considers this. 'Sex is all about pleasure for me. I like to see how far things can go in pursuit of that. Push limits. You know what I mean?'

She looks directly at Connolly. Beads of sweat shine on his bald patch.

'What sort of limits did you like to push?' His voice has taken on a throaty quality, I notice.

'Anything and everything,' replies Lauren. 'But I think, maybe Paul was more into like . . . I wanna say porno stuff? My interests are probably less mainstream. Like, psychological experimentation.' She flips her palms like she's weighing two items against one another.

'You have a big interest in extreme sex?' I can almost hear Connolly salivating. It occurs to me that Lauren has been thrown from one pack of wolves to another.

'And?' Lauren sits on her hands and bounces. 'Oh my gosh. This century is, like, the best time to be a woman. We are having orgasms, like, all night.'

'Surely a medic watching this tape would confirm she's manic, right?' I observe to Craig, looking at Lauren's twitching posture. Her glittering eyes. 'Think they'll let this one stand?'

'Connolly clearly thinks so.' Craig's pained eyes, under their dark brows, are reflected back in the laptop screen.

'You're saying it's usual to leave sex toys strewn around?' asks Connolly.

Lauren's eyes widen. 'Haven't you ever been to a sorority house? There's always at least one bathroom stall making a buzzing sound. It was even on one of our meeting agendas. Like,

"Could girls please use high-quality motors, because it's keeping people awake."'

Connolly doesn't have an answer.

Lauren brushes a strand of hair back from her face. 'Maybe my dad's generation would have been ashamed of female pleasure. But it's different nowadays. Guess the enlightened sex memo didn't get here, though,' she adds, looking incongruously delighted.

'Are you claiming you didn't use those handcuffs on Paul the night he died?'

'No comment.' Her eyes roll around in her head. 'I don't feel so good,' Lauren holds her stomach. 'Do you have any painkillers?'

'We'll end the interview there,' says Connolly, signalling to his colleague to cut the tape.

'What's he *doing*?' Craig is outraged. 'He could have got a load more out of her about the relationship. It sounded abusive maybe, right?'

'Guess that's not the story Connolly wants to tell,' I say, my eyes fixed on Lauren. She does look unwell.

Connolly turns to the camera and gives it a thumbs up.

'Ugh.' I turn to Craig. 'What do you make of it? Think she's guilty?'

'If she is, I don't think she's wholly responsible for her actions,' says Craig. 'Unfortunately, Connolly isn't a guy for mitigating circumstances.'

We stand and shuffle out of the broom cupboard. Craig glances over at me.

'You went to college, right?' There's a wistful edge to his voice. I nod.

'And the girls' bathrooms . . .'

'Not at my college,' I interrupt firmly.

'Right.' Craig adjusts his collar, looking crestfallen. 'Right.'

54

Lauren

I suffer from manic depression. Most of the time it's managed by medication. But, if I'm not taking care of my health, or whatever, it can get bad. I don't know exactly why, but I was super low after that camping trip. Like the hangover never went, you know?

Then on our first shift back, things got a lot worse at the bar. Somehow they had found out that Beth and I were volunteering at the reserve.

Beth

Paul told them. Obviously.

Lauren was already a mess, even without the extra stress. Marc had ghosted her after the trip. She would scroll through his old messages when she thought no one was looking. Like she couldn't believe he could change his mind so suddenly.

The main problem if Lauren gets low, is you know, right around the corner, she's going to get totally manic. That's when stuff happens.

Lauren

It got nasty. Every other sentence was about whether I liked to have sex with Black men or Black girls. Almost like they wanted me to deny it, or something. They also started switching the cooler off when we weren't looking, so Beth had to make more trips to the cellar.

Beth

Lauren began insisting on doing that cellar run, which I did not want at all. She would come up blank-eyed with her hands shaking.

We both started drinking on shift to get through it. Lauren wasn't herself. She looked kind of . . . run down. Like somehow, she suited the place now, when she didn't before.

Lauren

Beth's zoned-out episodes were becoming regular enough for the drinkers to notice. The guys would literally click fingers in her face, and she'd jerk like they'd slapped her. I tried to get her to sneak up to the apartment to decompress for a few minutes now and then, especially if she had just come from the cellar.

Beth

We were on a knife-edge. Sometimes the little apartment breaks were the only thing keeping my mind in my body, and this was terrifying in itself.

The journal was getting extreme now. Imagine, you've been psychologically abused, like fifty times, and you've had to suck it up. Like people have shown you the grossest dirty videos, and asked you what your favourite sex position is, and how old you were when you lost your virginity. And you've had to somehow field it all, without seeming like you're a bad sport, but obviously not encouraging it either. It was a thin tightrope to tread. Then all the men decided they hated us anyway. Dedicated each shift to making our lives difficult. That was when the journal began taking on a life of its own.

We were five days until the weekly bus out of town.

A lot can happen in five days.

55

It's a short drive from the police station to my rented house, but for some reason, I can't face going home. I pull the car onto the highway, and bump along, the red setting sun bright behind me.

On the opposite side, I see a family from the community trudging on the hard shoulder.

I'm slowing down to offer them a ride when a road train thunders by; five mammoth trucks coupled together.

I'm not fast enough rolling up my window. The huge vehicle barrels past me, blocking out the light, sending up a dust storm. My car is filled with flying sand and grit. I pull over covering my mouth, coughing.

As the debris settles inside my car, I'm a helpless spectator to the family caught in the dirt squall, throwing up their arms to shield themselves from the worst of it.

I put the car into gear and cruise down to them.

'Hey!' I shout, rolling down the window. 'You want a lift?'

They all shake their heads fast. I swallow, not expecting to feel so upset. For the first time it really hits home what a divide my uniform has created.

'No need for police,' says the woman defensively as though I've accused her of something bad. 'We haven't done anything wrong.'

'No. I know. I know you haven't.'

They're already backing away. I watch them go.

'Fuck.' I thump my steering wheel. *'Fuck.'*

I push sand from my hair. 'Nice going, Tara,' I mutter. 'You joined the force to help relations with Indigenous people. They'd rather walk six kilometres in a dust storm than get in your car.'

Angrily I pull into gear and bump my wheezing car back on the highway.

It's not exactly deliberate. But ten minutes later night is falling and my headlights flash on a blue-and-white government sign.

PRESCRIBED AREA: NO LIQUOR
PROHIBITED MATERIAL: PORNOGRAPHY

I've driven to the mission.

My eyes fix on the thick writing. Below each heavyset decree are the list of fines and prison sentences for being in possession of alcohol or pornography. Up to $78,000 and eighteen months in jail.

This was what Yindi was arrested for. Joining a protest against this sign.

I wasn't there, but I'm told it started peacefully. Then a woman whose son had died from a bad batch of homebrew had showed up screaming racist abuse.

It had absolutely nothing to do with what the protestors were objecting to. But things quickly turned ugly, and the peaceful protest became a riot.

It's dark now. The stars are coming out, millions of them, swirling against the blue-black night. I can hear singing and music from the other side of the fence. I could get out of the car and walk in. Tell Jarrah I want to pick up where we left off, before Yindi died. For a second I let myself picture being on the inside again before letting it evaporate in the imaginary fire smoke.

There's a tap at the window and I jump. I just have time to process a familiar face when the door opens, and a woman climbs into the dusty passenger seat.

'Hooroo, little sister,' she says in Moodjana. 'What you doing out here, feeling sorry for yourself?'

It's Mirri. One of Yindi's many aunties and the woman whose house I basically lived in as a kid. Despite the heat, she's wearing a tan polyester cardigan over her floral dress. Her black hair, caught in its bright scarf, has the same dramatic white streak, I remember. V-shaped, like a sugar-glider.

'Mirri!' I throw myself at her in an ungainly hug. She smells of incense and home cooking.

'You waiting for a formal invitation?' she asks, pulling me close.

'Nah. Came here to think. You still taking in waifs and strays?' I ask. 'Yindi and me didn't put you off?'

She smiles. 'I still got a houseful,' she says, watching my face. 'You alright?'

I give a half smile in reply. I sigh. 'I just . . . I miss her, you know? I miss all of you.'

There's a silence like she's understanding the words and everything around them too.

'Yeah,' she says finally. 'We all do. Why don't you come have a yarn at the fire? Jarrah would be pleased to see you.' Her eyes slide to mine mischievously. 'He stayed single, you know. Reckon he never got over you.'

'Nothing to get over.'

'He looks at police cars in a different way nowadays, is all I'll say on the matter.'

I should be happy to hear it, but I don't feel it. Mirri's probably just stirring the pot, anyway. Jarrah more likely thinks of me as a little sister. My thoughts flick to Craig. Solid, dependable, uncomplicated.

I shake my head, and Mirri considers my face for a long time. She pats my hand and gets out of the car.

'I'm always here if you change your mind about coming in,' she says, leaning through the open door. Her face clouds. 'If you're not, you should head home,' she says. 'This isn't a nice spot to park up alone. We've had trouble recently, you know? Whitefellas driving around in their shiny vans.'

This jolts me out of my self-pity. 'Why are whitefellas driving here?'

She shrugs again. 'Same reason they always do. Come to pick up young girls. Take care of yourself, Tara.' She slams the door.

'Wait!'

She's gone, vanished into the dark. For a few seconds I consider getting out and running after her. But I know Mirri well enough to know she'd never give a statement to the police. Not after what she's seen in her community.

With more force than necessary, I hit the accelerator, and pull out, heading at speed back to Dead Tree Creek.

56

Craig gave me a key for the firing range, so I spend a frustrating hour missing targets. I take my final shot before trudging out into the evening's slow heat, defeated, hand throbbing. I've improved fractionally. But I'm nowhere near to passing the firearms criteria.

Twenty minutes later, after a clothes drop at the launderette, I'm joining the line inside Goody's Take-Away, the greasy lino floor sliding under my police boots. The clientele is a mix of low-income Indigenous people and mine workers, choosing identical-looking fried-things that swelter on a stainless-steel hot plate behind oily glass.

A dark-skinned man with worn-out pants and the soles flapping on his sneakers nudges me. 'Better food in prison, eh?'

I smile uncertainly, wondering if he's ripping on me, or being friendly.

From Goody's, it's a short journey via the launderette to my rental property. Almost as soon as I close the door and flyscreen, the tiny house seems to loom at me.

Suddenly, I feel so alone I'm almost breathless with it.

My brain is bubbling away. I grab my chin-up bar and do a few chin-ups. It helps.

To distract myself, I open my laptop, and sit cross-legged on my spartan floor, pooling my thoughts.

White men driving around the mission at night. Three sex-trafficked girls escaping their captors. Yara-ma-yha-who. Tula betrayed them to yara-ma-yha-who. My mind floats to the pornography ban outside the mission. If Paul and Tula were involved in trafficking local girls, surely that gives another strong motive for violent murder?

I think for a moment, before typing 'yara-ma-yha-who' into the search engine. My description to Anderson was mostly right. Blood-sucking monster that feeds continually off its prey, swallowing and disgorging it until another yara-ma-yha-who is made.

Not much help. I drum my fingers. What if it was like . . . a nickname?

I put that into Google, and end up with a bunch of images of frog-like mythological creatures.

I rest my chin on my hands, staring at the screen.

Maybe . . . there's a local variant. Something specific to this region. I start with 'yara-ma-ya-who' and 'Dead Tree Creek'.

This time, one picture that doesn't fit.

I stop for a moment, wondering at what I'm seeing. It's a photo, in amongst the cartoons and monster illustrations. A digger, ploughing up red earth. I lean closer and make out a familiar livery on the side.

The Mining Corporation.

I sit back, piecing possibilities together. Maybe I had the nickname thing right. It would make sense for Moodjana people to refer to the Mining Corporation as yara-ma-yha-who. Blood-suckers who swallow living things and spit them out again.

If the Mining Corporation were known to locals as yara-ma-yha-who, that would mean . . . That was who came and took them in the night.

The possibility is both simple, and overwhelming. The Mining Corporation is huge. Powerful. What could they want with three Indigenous girls?

I click on the image of the Mining Corporation digger – and the result is totally unexpected.

Sexual abuse imagery is illegal. If you see sexually explicit imagery of abuse you must report it. If you need anonymous support to stop viewing this material, click here.

I look at the screen for a long time, my heart pounding a slow, steady beat. A Mining Corporation digger has been flagged by Google as sexually abusive. What does it mean? Resting my head on my temples, I try to pull together what I know.

Pornography. Brothel rumours. Missing girls. Sacred land.

Tired, I go to shower off the thick dust from my walk. My hips have deep bruising from the weight of my weapons belt. I tug on the T-shirt I sleep in, and lie on the thin mattress of my single bed staring at the wall. There's a gunshot arrangement of dry rot on the ceiling.

I close my eyes and the tune Tula was singing drifts through my thoughts. Precious lands, and orange rocks. I knew all the words once.

Something about the song jerks at my memory. As if I can sense answers, swirling in the dark. From the shadows, Yindi steps forward, eyes hard.

You can't follow me around anymore, Tara. It's different now.

I pop open my eyes. With a shaking hand I fish around for the TV remote, and click on a random channel.

Turning the volume all the way up, I close my eyes to sleep.

57

Beth

Lauren began acting more and more erratically. She wasn't sleeping. Like. Not at all. Out on the reserve, you could see she was losing what she'd built with the girls. She was totally hyper at least half the time.

Marc had stopped driving us. We got this friendly girl called Katie, whom Lauren would barely speak to. And all day, Lauren checked her phone for messages from Marc that never came.

One night she went out for a walk whilst I was sleeping. By herself, dressed in short-shorts and a tight shirt. In Dead Tree Creek, which in the early hours is filled with drunks and gnarly street walkers.

Lauren

I went out to see if I could get a phone signal. There was a spot of high ground at the edge of town. Like twenty blocks' walk. Got there, held my cell at the black sky. Nothing.

There were dark clouds covering the stars. A static humidity. I should have paid more attention, but I didn't.

Instead, I walked to the backpacker hostel where Marc was staying. At about 3 a.m. I think I figured if I appeared in person, he wouldn't be able resist me. Messed up, right?

When I got there, there was an English girl asleep in the lobby because the beds were full or something. Mousy hair, very pale, with terrible sunburn patches on her shoulders.

She was like, 'The guitar guy? Oh yeah, they left. They patched things up.'

And I'm like, 'You mean Marc and Sophie?'

She says yes. And a good thing, too, because the screaming in French kept her awake. Not to mention the guitar that he would pull out, unasked, at any social gathering.

'I didn't realise they were an item,' I said.

'They were sort of together, and then they had this big fight. Apparently, some big old ho-bag on a camping trip waved her snatch in Marc's face, or something. *Literally* in his face. And Marc went and fucked her.'

She lay back down on her yoga mat, and pulled the blanket higher.

'Hey,' I said. 'You want to go somewhere and get a drink?'

'Um.' She gave me that smile you give people, when you're basically saying: 'Weirdo!' 'No thanks. I was asleep.' She made a point of closing her eyes.

By the time I started walking back this crazy storm began. Like nothing I had ever seen before. About twenty tonnes of water seemed to dump right out of the clouds, and keep dumping. I was wearing denim cut-offs and a singlet. I had no idea what to do. I kind of cowered in this porch but I was soaked to the skin. It felt like . . . I don't know. Like my lowest point. Marc had ditched me. I felt absolutely, completely alone. I would have to go back to that damp room and . . . what? Drink one of the bar liqueurs that Pete doesn't notice going missing, with Beth being all weird and hostile? Try to sleep on the stinky mattress? This seemed so awful I pushed my palms flat against my eyes until I started seeing spots and stars.

It all felt so familiar. Like I was right back to before college. Before rehab, when they pulled me off the Colorado Street Bridge. This was my default. Relentless, fucking misery.

I wished the water would wash me away.

And then I saw something. Like a flash of white. A man, walking towards me in the downpour. He was muscular. Broad-shouldered. It was Paul.

Up until that moment I had never actually realised he was handsome. Like, I knew he was considered good-looking by the freaky women who lived in the town, but I had never properly noticed it before. He had that chiselled jaw, very blue eyes. The chip in his tooth could be seen as cute, as well as a flaw.

'Hey!' he shouted, above the crashing rain. 'Lauren? You alright?'

I looked up at him. My make-up was almost certainly running down my face.

'You're soaking wet.' He came right into the porch, and looked at me, like he really *cared*. Like he was honestly concerned, that I would get sick, or something. 'Do you need rescuing?' He said it very quietly, like he meant a lot more by it, than getting me out of the rain. I looked into his eyes, and it felt like time stood still for a moment. As if I was falling into him.

My teeth were chattering. 'I don't know,' I told him. 'Do I?'

He took a step forward, and wrapped his arms right around me. I stopped shivering completely.

It was one of those kisses where everything else melts away. Where it's the two of you. Me and him in the rain.

He lifted me up, right off the pavement, like I weighed nothing, and said: 'I'm taking you back home.'

He carried me all the way back to The Gold Rush, like he wanted to protect me from everything. Even the wet ground.

When we got in, Beth was passed out, snoring out back. Paul laid me down on the couch.

'Guess I'll see you tomorrow,' he said.

I pulled him towards me by his shirt.

It was crazy. Like, *so* intense. I have never known anything like it. My body had this electric buzz for hours.

Afterwards I fell asleep in his arms. When I woke up, Paul was gone and everything seemed different. My *brain* felt different. Like, this tight cluster of bad feelings had been exploded. I was standing in the aftershock, staring at all this new space.

I had this tingle every time I thought of him. It was like our souls had joined in that rainy porch.

Dillon

Apparently, she was waiting opposite his house, soaking wet, with her nipples showing. What did you expect him to do?

58

I'm deep asleep when my phone starts buzzing, lighting my gloomy room with a ghostly glow. I grab it. Craig is calling.

'Hello?'

'Tara? Did I wake you?'

'Mmmph.' Am I late? It feels like the middle of the night.

'Can you come to the station?'

I'm alert, sitting up in bed. 'What's happened?'

I hear a sigh, and he lowers his voice. 'A bloody hotshot lawyer from America arrived by light aircraft a few hours ago. No expense spared. Wants to meet with us, 8 a.m.'

I check my clock. Six a.m.

'Listen, it's probably nothing to worry about,' continues Craig, immediately setting my heart racing, 'but he's talking about wrongful arrest.'

'*What?*'

'Yeah. Might just be talk but . . . He saw your interview notes. Asked for you by name.'

'Is an American lawyer allowed to be involved in an Australian case?' I ask hopefully.

'Technically he has ninety days grace until he has to register. But this guy has already submitted his papers. He means business alright.'

A horrible feeling of being in deep trouble swirls around me. I'm pulling on my trousers. 'Give me ten minutes.'

I trip over a bag of laundry on my way out of the porch. I forgot they said they'd drop it back last night. Least I've got a clean shirt to face the music.

It takes me several attempts to start my car. As I round the corner to the road with the police station on it, I slow, staring.

The street is completely crammed with reporters and photographers. What the . . .? I swing the car around and park up at the back. But as I'm getting out of the driver's seat, a reporter catches sight of me. She runs towards me, microphone held out, as I desperately try to locate my key.

The door swings inwards, and Craig grabs my lapels and pulls me quickly over the threshold. He slams it shut.

Craig turns the lock.

'Fuck!' I exhale. Behind me fists begin hammering on the glass. 'Is it true that Lauren and Beth ran orgies at The Gold Rush?' shouts the reporter. 'Was this all a sex game gone wrong?'

'You OK, Tara?' Craig has circles under his green eyes, and his usually sculpted hair looks like he's styled it in a hurry.

'Yeah. I guess. Where did they all come from?' I move towards my desk and start putting things in file order.

'Connolly,' says Craig darkly. 'He's got the press digging for him. Tipped them off about one of Lauren's ex-booty calls who's ready to spill the dirt.'

I grimace. 'Whatever happened to unprejudiced evidence gathering?'

Anderson appears, looking grey. 'Thanks for coming in, Tara. You finally got hold of an iron, I see.' He looks my pressed shirt up and down.

'I found a launderette who do a service wash, sir.'

'Headed in the right direction, I suppose. Your desk is looking in better shape too,' he adds, glancing at my alphabetical files.

'I've been following an organisation coach on Pinterest.'

'Ri-ght. Each to their own, I guess.' If Anderson's being polite, I'm guessing something is badly wrong. 'Just had a long phone conversation with a Mr Gottlieb, Lauren's new legal representation,' he says.

'She called a lawyer?'

'Nope. Her family must have seen the headlines and taken matters into their own hands, and whoever they've hired wasn't cheap. Mr Gottlieb has never lost a case. He's already hit the ground running. Apparently, old Danno's toxicology report wasn't signed in the right box or something.' He shakes his head. 'As if we didn't have enough with Perth breathing down our necks.'

'Where is Connolly?'

'On his way.' Anderson sighs. 'This is going to make him all the more determined to wrap it all up fast.'

I take a breath and blurt out my suspicions. 'Sir, I know I'm only a probationer. But I think I might have found something. About yara-ma-yha-who.'

'Tara, is this the time to discuss monsters in the bush?' Anderson uses my first name like he's concerned for my mental health.

'I think it could be a local word for the Mining Corporation. Like, a nickname.'

Anderson is silent for a long moment, taking this in.

'You think, or you know?' he says finally.

'I think, but . . .'

'Come back when you know.'

'But, sir . . .'

He holds up a hand. 'No arguments, Harrison, we're talking about one of the most powerful companies in the country.' He checks his watch. 'And right now we need to defend ourselves from a grilling about our evidence gathering.'

'Sir, if I could just . . .'

'Not now, Harrison. This lawyer means business, and I wouldn't put it past Connolly to sacrifice a young probationer to save his own skin. Keep your energy for fighting your corner. I'll do my best to protect you, but there's only so much I can do, alright?' Anderson eyes me grimly. 'Doesn't matter what you find out about the Mining Corporation, if you don't have a job here.'

59

Beth

Lauren was like, *happy*. Humming a tune, pouring herself juice from the refrigerator.

I asked her why she slept on the couch, and she was like: 'Paul was here last night.' Said it with this little secret grin.

I had the worst feeling of total violation. Like, he hadn't just gotten me, he'd gotten her too. Checkmate. By *Paul*, who has probably never even read a book from beginning to end.

I stood there, waiting for Lauren to tell me she regretted it. She was drunk, or high, or whatever. Her phone beeped on the table. I picked it up, inadvertently reading the message as it was so short.

Checking you gave me the right number. Paul.

'He's not exactly a poet, is he?' I told her as I handed over the phone.

But she smiled and smiled. 'Might as well have a little fun.' She was already texting him back as I left the room.

Mike

Things definitely changed with Paul and Lauren. Like before, she had all the power, you know. But he got his own back, that's for sure.

Proves what I've said all along. Girls want blokes who treat 'em badly. Take Beth, for example. I would have treated her right. Taken good care of her. Nice guys finish last.

Beth

That night Lauren spent the whole shift making eyes at Paul. When I couldn't take it anymore, I took an apartment break, just to get myself together. I was standing near the broken microwave, when I heard footsteps behind me. It was Dillon.

He leaned right across me, brushing my arm with his tattooed hand. 'I can fix that for you, if you like.'

I took a step back. 'You can't be up here,' I told him.

He frowned, his little goatee sticking forward. 'No need to get shitty,' he said. 'Only trying to help. And from what I hear, Paul comes up here now.'

A horrible familiar fear was creeping through me. I could feel my mind fluttering around like a bird in a cage.

'Paul told us about the party up here last night,' continued Dillon. 'Didn't think you could get away with not inviting the rest of us blokes, did you?'

I had no idea what he was talking about. Had Lauren organised a party without telling me? Confusion and fear were washing through me. I pushed past him and more or less ran back downstairs.

That was it for me. I didn't even care about getting paid. The bus was leaving the next morning. I just had to persuade Lauren.

60

The American lawyer is an intimidating man in his mid-fifties, immaculately shaved and trimmed with dark hair and eyes. Despite the fact he must have flown overnight and be suffering major jetlag, there is no sign of tiredness on his features. His expensive suit is perfectly pressed, and his handmade shoes polished to a high shine. Even his face has a tidy tucked-in quality that speaks of the subtle work of a premium surgeon.

He stands and extends a hand as I enter the room, where Anderson is already waiting.

'Ms Harrison?'

'Pleased to meet you.' He doesn't smile.

'I'm Mr Gottlieb,' he says. 'Lauren's lawyer. I flew in from Los Angeles last night. This morning,' he corrects himself.

It strikes me as a little strange that he refers to her by name, and I wonder if he is a friend of the family. I'm struck by an intuition that he isn't who he claims to be.

He sits and nods. I do likewise. 'My client is being brought here?' He directs this to Anderson.

'She's on her way,' he confirms. 'Constable Dooligan is bringing her now.'

Gottlieb switches his attention back to me. 'You made the arrest?'

'The charges,' I clarify.

'But you're not a police constable yet. You're a probationer, isn't that right? So what were you doing bringing charges?'

Anderson clears his throat. 'Constable Harrison has the authority to make arrests and bring charges.'

'Maybe in your *locality*.' Gottlieb's mouth lifts and drops in a smile that doesn't meet his eyes. 'But according to international law my client must be arrested and charged by a *qualified* police constable. And your "officer" interviewed her illegally, in a distressed state.' He glares at me and I feel my stomach turn over. 'I've drawn up papers for Ms Davis to be repatriated to her own country, since you have failed to follow procedure.'

Anderson shakes his head. 'Nice try, Perry Mason,' he says. 'But it's a load of bull. Firstly, you'd have to clear that with an international court. They take into account the seriousness of the crime. Last time I checked, torturing two people to death is serious. So can your bloody bluster, mate. You're not taking the suspect. Today or ever. And if you keep wasting my time with stupid threats, I'll do you for obstructing the course of justice.'

The lawyer gives no indication Anderson's words have affected him. He simply shuffles papers and plucks one free.

'I'll be filing against the Dead Tree Creek police for unlawful arrest, false imprisonment, mental distress and malicious prosecution.' He eyeballs Anderson who steadily meets his gaze. 'I have the charges compiled by Detective Connolly. They make for entertaining reading. Your star detective appears to have diagnosed my client with a personality disorder based on his personal disapproval of female liberation.'

Anderson's mouth clamps shut. He's got no answer to that.

'My client wasn't given the opportunity to make a victim statement,' says Gottlieb.

'That's only standard with suspected domestic abuse victims,' says Anderson uneasily.

'But coercive control is a form of domestic violence, isn't it?'

'I don't follow.'

'Female staff in The Gold Rush live on the premises, depend on the pub for meals and are forced into late-night drinking in a sealed room with predatory men,' continues Gottlieb. 'They were required to wear tight-fitting T-shirts. Reports of harassment and intimidation are on file with the employment agency who hires for The Gold Rush.' Gottlieb takes a breath. 'My vulnerable client was subject to this, and the lock on her apartment was broken. No one thought she was a victim?'

Anderson coughs, avoiding my eyes.

'Then there's this.' Gottlieb slides forward a newspaper.

'Connolly's been feeding the media his deranged sexualised conjectures,' says Gottlieb. 'Miss Davis now has zero chance of a fair jury trial in this country. Which brings me to . . . The use of an illegally obtained journal.'

'The journal was taken as evidence . . .' begins Anderson.

'Not from a crime scene,' replies Gottlieb, moving his gaze to both of us, daring us to correct him. 'From a private residence without a warrant.'

'The girls—'

'To be clear, I am only referring to my client. Lauren Davis.'

'Ms Davis was no longer resident when the search was made, and we had the permission of the landlord,' says Anderson.

'My client was asked to vacate on the twelfth,' says Gottlieb, his eyes shark-like. 'No formal rental contract was signed, so a midday departure is implied. Your officer's notes state she entered at 10.52 a.m.'

'We'll get you any papers you need to prove we had a right to enter,' says Anderson calmly, but I'm pretty sure it's a bluff.

'With no journal, which trust me, will be stricken as evidence, you had no reason to charge my client with murder.'

'They were the only people on the premises at the time of death without an alibi,' says Anderson, tightly.

'This is the time of death as estimated by a hospital coroner, who moonlights in forensics? A man who didn't even complete a toxicology report?'

'The girls were previously involved in a fatality by suffocation,' counters Anderson.

Gottlieb scoffs audibly. 'Is that the best you can do? You didn't know that at the time of arrest. In any case that charge was dismissed and my client found innocent. I don't think even *Australia* allows their police to prejudice a jury with prior arrests.'

This time, Anderson flinches fractionally.

'Not to mention, you have no evidence the victims were force-fed anything,' says Gottlieb.

Anderson widens his eyes deliberately. 'Can you think of any other way they could have suffocated on mud?'

The lawyer leans forward, his eyes glittering. 'I've read the file, Detective. Many times over. Nothing in your notes suggests anyone leaped to that conclusion, *until* you found the unfortunate diary entries of these two girls. It was only then you put two and two together and made five. And you and I both know that journal is not making it into the evidence folder.'

He leans back. There's a tap at the door. Connolly enters, looking angry.

'Ms Davis is on her way,' he announces, before leaning over the table and shaking Gottlieb's hand like he doesn't want to. 'You flew a long way to defend a killer,' he says, without smiling. 'Bet you sleep well at night.'

'I'll sleep well once my client is released, and your department answers charges for malicious prosecution.'

Connolly sits and glances at the door. 'You've read the reports,' he says, 'but I'm going to level with you, bloke to bloke. There are nice girls and there are nasty ones, and Lauren is nasty. Simple as that.'

The door opens and Lauren is led in. She looks smaller and paler than I remember her. Less striking. Sick, I find myself thinking. She looks sick.

Her bloodshot eyes register Gottlieb, and widen.

'Daddy?' she whispers. 'What are you doing here?'

The colour drains from Connolly's face. 'This is your daughter?' His voice comes out as a squeak.

'She goes by her mother's surname.' Gottlieb's eyes don't move from Lauren. 'And before you ask, yes, lawyers are permitted to represent family members.'

There is an immeasurable sadness in his eyes.

'Don't worry, honey,' he says. 'I'm here now. I'm going to take you home.'

61

Lauren

I always bring out the worst in men. I swear. I can take the nicest
guy and turn him nasty. It's, like, my superpower, or something.
Since college, Beth has kind of been like my protector. But with
Paul, there was no helping me, *at all*. I'd axed my meds, doubled
my happy pills, and was sinking as low as I possibly could. All
aboard the burning train for self-destruct city.

That shift I remember Beth was trying to tell me something
about Dillon in the apartment, and leaving town, but all I could
think about was Paul, and I am so extremely ashamed to admit
that now.

Mike

Lauren did have an impact on Paul. I would say she did. In
the days before the last lock-in, Paul said some stuff about his
mum dying. I never heard him talk about that before. Think he
mentioned that maybe he should have spoken to someone, when
he was younger. 'Cause of how it all happened, you know?

Lauren

Those first few times Paul told me a lot about his childhood. I could relate, because my mom also died when I was young. But I was privileged enough to get therapy. So I felt like I had stuff to teach him. About coming to terms with grief.

Mike

If you ask me, Paul was fucked up long before his mum . . . did what she did. It was when his dad left that Paul started being a little shit. Not many people know this, but it turns out, Paul's dad had a whole family out in another town, someplace. God knows how he kept that going. Anyway, one day he just up and went. That's when Paul began acting out, fighting all the time. Gave me a bloody nose more than once, for sure. After his mum died, he . . . I dunno, went into himself for a while. The lights were on and no one home, if you know what I mean. But no bloke from round here is gonna sit in a therapist's chair, is he?

April

Paul never liked to talk about his mum. I only found out how she died a year ago. He was a strong man in that way. Left the past in the past.

Lauren

It got twisted with me and Paul right away. When my shift

ended, we had run upstairs to the bedroom. Couldn't keep our hands off each other.

I heard Paul say, '*Shit*,' and, like, flatten himself out against the wall. I had no clothes on, and Paul is, like, waving his hands – get away from the window! I mean, why should I care who sees me? Then I saw. Tula was standing in the street outside, looking up.

At first, I was totally confused. Last I heard she had left town, taking three other girls with her. Why was she here?

But the way Paul was acting, I had the nastiest feeling. I was like, 'You're not together, are you?' Paul gave me this thing about how they'd broken up and she was obsessed with him, and made her sound dangerous.

The worst thing was how much I wanted to believe it.

Paul said he'd go talk to Tula. I tried to stop him. Deep down I knew he was choosing her over me. I became totally vocal and dramatic. Hated the way I sounded. Even before he went outside, something felt broken between us.

Beth and I heard parts of their conversation from the apartment.

Tula didn't sound mad, or obsessed. In fact, I didn't hear my name mentioned once.

It's embarrassing to admit it, but it changed . . . Like this stupid fun thing became, like, I don't know . . . When he wanted Tula . . . I *wanted* him to want me. Pretty fucked-up, right?

Beth

Tula looked a complete emotional wreck. She had dark circles like she hadn't slept for days. Paul kept telling her to shut up, but she wouldn't keep her voice down.

Tula was saying, 'If I don't get the girls back, it's on both of us.' Then some other stuff, about eyes everywhere, and how there was nowhere to run.

After they went, I tried to talk to Lauren about how shady that sounded, like maybe even illegal. But Lauren was on another planet, figuring out how to get Paul back.

After Paul left, I spent a long time persuading Lauren to get on the bus the next morning. When she finally agreed . . . The relief at that point is hard to describe. I wish I could have bottled that relief.

Lauren

It was maybe 2 a.m. Beth was saying, skip town. I said I would because I wanted to sleep. I didn't know how I'd feel in the morning, but it didn't matter anyway. The alarm didn't go off. Beth got super shitty about it. Trying to blame me, or something.

Beth

I remembered setting the alarm. I suspected Lauren shut it off. I had this growing distrust of her after that. Either way, we overslept and the bus drove off without us. We had no money to pay for a ride. There was absolutely no question of hitchhiking with Lauren in her current state. That left seven more days.

62

Lauren crosses the police interview room and crumples into a seat, making no acknowledgement the rest of us are even here. Her head drops down towards the table, and then she props her temples on her fingers. When her face remerges, it's like she's regressed fifteen years.

'Daddy,' she whispers. 'I didn't do it. I swear I didn't do it.'

A twitch flickers at the corner of Gottlieb's eye. As though a torrent of relief has flowed through somewhere deeply hidden.

'I know.' He breathes out hard and now he can't stop a slight smile pulling at his lips. Lauren's father leans across and grabs her hands. 'I know, honey. Michael has already booked your flight out. You'll be back in LA by Wednesday.'

There's something so pathetically trusting in Lauren's face. A naked desperation to believe her dad can make all this go away.

'What about Beth?' she croaks.

His face darkens. 'That trailer girl has been taking advantage of you since you first met.'

'She's a good person, Daddy,' says Lauren quietly.

He frowns impatiently. 'Did she tell you her mother has four arrests for drunken violence?'

Lauren chews her lip miserably and raises her eyes to his. 'You investigated her?'

Her father ignores the question. 'It's like the last time you fell in with the wrong person.' He pats her hand with certainty. 'There are people in life who are out for what they can get, Lauren. Get you into bad situations. Beth . . . well, look where she led you. A shady bar in a dead-end town.'

Anderson clears his throat. Gottlieb pays no attention.

'I always told you, there's something not right about that girl,' he tells Lauren.

'She doesn't show much emotion, is all,' says Lauren. 'People misread it.'

'Honey, you always like to see the good in people. But sometimes,' he looks at her sadly, 'sometimes people are bad.' His face looks anguished. 'Don't worry. We can easily prove you weren't in your right mind. That the police had no right to search your property.'

'Wait.' Lauren's brow crumples. 'You're going to get their evidence thrown out?'

There's a loaded silence, and I can hear Connolly's excited breathing.

Gottlieb swallows. 'Remember what I always told you?' he says, lowering his voice as if it could somehow stop the rest of the room hearing. 'Life is strategy, honey, and winners pick the right games. Judges like hard evidence. You weren't taking your meds. You've a documented history of doing and saying . . . certain things when unmedicated, and police interviewed you in that state. You were charged by an unqualified individual. Your journal was obtained in an illegal search.'

He's good, I think. If he can make all that fly, he's toppled every part of our case.

'You want to win by changing the rules,' Lauren says darkly, 'like you always do.'

'Did your great-grandfather follow the rules?' There's a touch of anger to him now. 'Did he get on that train?'

'This isn't Nazi Poland, Daddy,' says Lauren quietly.

'I'm going to get you home.' He pronounces every word with such conviction that you can't help but believe him.

I glance at Anderson, who has a strained look to his features. His two sons must be about Lauren's age, I realise, thinking to the pictures on his desk.

'No,' says Lauren. All eyes swing to her. 'No.'

'Lauren . . .' says Gottlieb, a pleading note to his deep voice.

'We had a bad time in that bar,' she says. 'Like. A really bad time.' She lifts her eyes to stare at her father, and suddenly they're like steely mirrors of one another. 'We were trapped. There was only one bus a week. And those jokes weren't funny.'

Lauren's father opens his mouth to reply.

'Someone should do what's right,' says Lauren. 'Someone should explain to men like that, there's . . . mitigating circumstances, or *something*. There's a point where you're asking for it.'

Gottlieb's face is unreadable. He glances up at Connolly. 'I'd like some time alone with my client, please.' His voice is baritone, authoritative.

Lauren stands, shaking her head. 'Those men crossed the line. A bunch of times.'

Her father's expression couldn't be more pained than if she'd just knifed him in the heart.

'Honey . . .' he begins, switching his eyes to us, as if he wishes we couldn't hear. 'Courts acquit men for killing with provocation. Not women.' He shakes his head. 'They hold women to a higher standard. I can show the journal wasn't lawfully obtained . . .'

'That's not right.' Lauren looks at him steadily. 'We lived above that bar in an apartment with no goddamn lock.'

'You heard her,' says Connolly victoriously. 'She doesn't want your version of the truth, Mr Gottlieb.'

'Shut up, Connolly,' growls Anderson. He swings to Lauren. 'Ms Davis, you're due to be interviewed. I strongly advise you talk to your lawyer.'

We all stare at him in shock. Gottlieb glances at Anderson, a glimmer of gratitude in his eyes.

'I want to go back to the cell,' says Lauren. 'With Beth.'

Gottlieb looks afraid now. 'You're in together?'

'We've only got the one cell at the station,' explains Connolly. 'But please don't concern yourself, Mr Gottlieb. They'll be in prison by the end of the day.'

A frightening fury passes over Gottlieb's face. I have a feeling that if beating Connolly to death would save his daughter, he'd do it. But he's a measured man, ready to play a longer game.

Lauren stands. Anderson takes her arm to lead her out. Gottlieb watches her go, then turns to Connolly.

'Interviewing a girl on hard narcotics. Contaminating the crime scene. You boys are looking like an embarrassment. Bumbling sexist morons who try and pin a murder on two innocent young girls, because they happened to belong to the twenty-first century.' He smiles thinly. 'Two can play at feeding the media, and it's a fickle beast. Women-hating cops are big news.'

I can't help but admire how fast Gottlieb has discovered another avenue of attack. Connolly looks visibly ruffled. I'm guessing he doesn't like the idea of looking bad in the papers.

Despite the circumstances I get the feeling Gottlieb is in his element. 'Everything you have is circumstantial. You'll be releasing her by the end of the day.'

'That depends on whether Ms Davis accepts your representation,' says Connolly.

'She will.' Gottlieb stands, looking suddenly thick with exhaustion. 'She just needs time.'

63

Despite his bravado with Gottlieb, Connolly is noticeably agitated as we come out of the room. 'Onward and upwards,' he says, more to himself than any of us. 'What we need is a confession before Gottlieb gets his hands on her. Something on record that the press can't spin. Lauren practically admitted she was a psychopath, didn't she? Said Paul Hunter was asking for it.'

'Does a person have to be psychopathic to react violently to sustained harassment?' I ask. 'Isn't there a point where someone can only take so much? They're just . . . being a human being?'

I'm thinking of how our foster mum expected Yindi to swallow down racial abuse and ignore it. As if the responsibility for good behaviour was on her.

Connolly's eyes boggle. 'Yeah, a snaky lawyer might argue that. Us true blue coppers, we find a murderer, we lock 'em up. End of.' He gives me a disgusted glare. 'Sounds like you've got anger issues.'

I glare back. 'Funny how women expressing opinions are angry, but men are just being straight with you.'

'Sir,' Dooligan interrupts us, approaching Connolly, 'I made you the report from Paul's phone like you wanted.'

'Well, let's have it,' he demands.

Craig hands several sheets of paper over.

'Lots of texts.' Connolly holds the pages at a distance as though he thinks this could reduce their number.

'Plenty to Lauren,' says Craig. 'And to his mates, boasting about what he's been getting up to. But the last text was sent to his sometime-girlfriend, April at 2.13 a.m.'

Connolly straightens, skipping to the final message.

'*Lauren means nothing*,' reads Connolly. '*She's just a stupid little slut.*' He pauses for effect, raising his eyes to us. '*Wait up for me, possum.*'

We all absorb this.

'Hunter's phone was found smashed to bits, right?' says Connolly. 'Fingerprints?'

'Lauren's and Beth's fingerprints were all over it,' says Craig.

Connolly breathes out, his earlier concerns forgotten. 'What's the betting our stupid little slut read the message?'

Even I have to admit it doesn't look good for Lauren.

'Sir,' I try, 'I've got a working theory about Hunter starting up his own brothel. Maybe even trafficking girls . . .'

'Let me rein that rookie imagination in, nice and quick,' says Connolly. 'Hunter dropped out of high school, took an entry-level mining position and ten years later, hasn't graduated from loading drill rods. Does that sound like a businessman to you? If he's setting up a brothel, who's supplied the money and the know-how?'

Connolly raises an eyebrow. 'We'll stick to a theory with facts behind it, I reckon.' He slams his palms together in an unpleasantly jarring way. 'Paul's relationship with Lauren in texts. Hard evidence.' His eyes drift upwards as if reassuring himself, picturing Gottlieb's reaction. 'Hard evidence,' he repeats. 'Alright, let's get to work on Lauren. I think she might confess.'

His female colleague who has been guarding the cell crosses

the room and mutters something to Connolly in a low voice. I make out the words 'sick' and 'highly distressed'.

He frowns impatiently. 'She's hamming it up for attention,' he says. 'I need to interview her. Get the medic after that.'

The constable looks deeply concerned. 'Sir . . .' she begins, 'I think . . .'

'Are you stupid enough to fall for it?' barks Connolly. 'Give Miss Davis a cup of water and tell her she'll be right.'

He swings the flimsy operator's chair backwards, and sits with his legs splayed in a ridiculously masculine stance. 'Harrison, Dooligan,' he announces, 'job for you.'

We face him expectantly.

'Dooligan, you've been on at me to talk to the girlfriend. April Hunter.'

Craig nods hopefully.

'I'll allow it,' says Connolly. 'But I want you to stick to what she thought about Lauren, right? She'll have plenty to say about blondie.'

'She let slip she was having a relationship with Dillon,' I say. 'What if—?'

Connolly raises a warning finger. 'Don't go upsetting her, making her clam up.' He glances down at a print-out. 'Says here she lives out in . . . a dug-out?' He signals a question with his face.

'About half the houses in town are old mining homes,' Craig explains. 'They were blasted out of the rock back in the day. Keep a constant temperature, so they're still popular with . . .' he hesitates, 'with some people.'

'Bogans?' fills in Connolly. 'Trash?'

'I guess some people might put it that way,' says Craig, reddening. 'The homes are cheap to buy. And low cost to make 'em bigger, if you're not above breaking the law. You get a few

271

mates in at the weekend with some sticks of dynamite and make another bedroom, or whatever,' Craig elaborates, at Connolly's raised eyebrow.

'What a town, eh?' Connolly shakes his head. 'Off you go. I'll bet April has plenty to say about Beth and Lauren. Plus, the press have helpfully located a load of Lauren's old squeezes.' He looks delighted with himself. 'We'll have sworn statements she liked it every which way by the end of the day.'

64

Beth

The bus had gone without us. We were trapped in town for another seven days. Paul started trying to cool things off, and that's when Lauren got really into him. And he couldn't exactly let her go either. It was like watching two addicts. You could see the defeat in Paul's eyes, like he hated her for luring him against his will. I mean, *Lauren* versus the other women in that town? The ones who went to the five-and-dime nail bar, and shaved between their eyebrows? No contest.

And whilst I don't blame Paul for being attracted to Lauren, I do blame him for taking advantage.

Consent isn't a defence for hazing. You as an individual are responsible for not hurting another person. Even if they *ask* you to. The same doesn't apply for sexual consent, though. There's even a 'rough sex' legal defence for murder. Mainly used by men. Obviously.

So there's no law against Paul totally pushing Lauren into things she wasn't comfortable doing. I know he did, because neither of them bothered much with privacy. I've heard people use the word 'fucking', and never thought about it that much. But what they did really earned that word.

Lauren

It got dark. Maybe violent. I don't know what it was. Something about the whole situation brought that out in me. Like it was something I needed to explore in myself.

There were times when he took it too far. Like further than I wanted him to. Often, though, I'd let go and then it was good. Better than good.

And I always initiated it. That's on me.

Beth

The guys in this town have an attitude, that because Lauren agreed to sex with Paul, she also consented to whatever degree of violence he brought to it. But she didn't consent to that.

Lauren wanted affection. Drama, probably. But drama is different to pain.

Dillon

Let me get this clear. Lauren did not want or need love and affection. She could have got that. There were people, yeah, maybe me included, who would have given that to her. Lauren wanted one thing, and that was attention. She didn't care how she got it. Paul would tell us blokes some of the freaky shit she did. Total shock value. Like everything a guy has ever dreamed of doing to a girl, she would ask him to do to her. You're not gonna say no if a girl like Lauren asks, are you?

Beth

Lauren had agreed to leave town. But she had started avoiding the subject when I brought it up.

I was counting the days. Five more days. Four more days. I remember very clearly the night I went up to the apartment, made to lock the door, and found it had been busted. With a shaking finger I pushed the broken latch up back in position and watched it fall again. Then I heard a noise deep inside. Probably nothing. Maybe nothing. I turned and ran right back down to the bar, with this white noise in my brain that wouldn't stop.

It was three days until the bus out, at this point. Three more days.

Pete

They were always making a drama about something. Reckon the blokes broke their lock, and were stealing sex toys from the bedroom or something. I told 'em straight: 'What do you expect if you keep stuff like that on the premises? Blokes are gonna have a mess-around with you if you do things like that.'

65

'What has Lauren's sex life got to do with murder?' I steam as Craig and I exit the station and head for my car.

'Makes her look unstable, I guess,' he replies, looking at my battered vehicle for a long moment.

I'd forgotten about the road train. The entire car is coated with a deep layer of sandy dirt, with the barest arc of smeared glass visible on the windscreen where I've tried to run the wipers.

'Because she liked having sex?' I unlock the car.

'That and the pills. Reckless.' Craig hesitates before pulling the handle.

'Was Casanova reckless?'

'Who?'

'Never mind.' I climb in.

Craig stares at the filthy interior in shock. Dust has settled on every surface, forming deep pockets on the seats and in the footwells. He puts out a horrified finger and draws a line in the dirt of the inside passenger door.

'Lost a fight with a road train,' I admit, attempting to brush off the seat, and only succeeding in sending a cloud back up into the air.

Craig kicks at the lolly wrappers that sit deep enough to cover his feet in the footwell.

'Did the road train also eat five bags of strawberry clouds and toss them on your floor?'

'Ha ha. Don't open the window on that side,' I tell him as he reaches for the button. 'It doesn't shut again unless you push it up from the outside two-handed.'

I turn the key and nothing happens. 'Wait a sec,' I tell him. 'I forgot to connect the battery.'

'You disconnect the battery every time you park your car?' His voice registers flat disbelief.

'The light switch is broken,' I explain. 'Drains the power if I leave it connected.'

I pop the hood and fix the connection, trying to keep my fingers clear of the sparks. The lights glow on.

'We'll take my car,' says Craig determinedly.

'You sure? It's my turn to drive.'

'Oh, I'm sure.' Craig is already walking to his car.

'OK.' I pull free the battery cable, shut the hood, and head for where Craig holds the door open for me. My headlamps fade slowly, like they're sorry to see me go.

We both get into the freshly vacuumed and scented interior of Craig's car, and he pulls out smoothly. Before long we're on the main highway.

'How's the gun practice going?' asks Craig.

'Did you see my targets?'

'Ye-ah.' Craig looks at me sympathetically.

'That's how it's going.' I huff out air. 'I'm hoping Anderson will see how hard I work and let it pass. He's allowed to do that.'

'He won't.' Craig glances at me. 'Seriously, Tara. If that's what you're pinning passing through probationary on, don't. Anderson will go to his grave saying a police officer's first duty is to defend themselves and the public. Keep going. OK?'

'Thanks.' I decide to change the subject. 'What do you think about sneaking a few rogue questions to April Dean?'

His mouth twists. 'I don't think it's worth the risk.' He sighs. 'I'm not saying Connolly's theory is right. All the crap about them being serial killers. But . . . can you imagine a scenario where Lauren and Beth *weren't* involved?'

He's right, I realise. It would take an extraordinary leap of logistics and chance.

The daytime trade traffic of utes and battered cars trundle along.

Craig peers at the highway. A Jester's Pie Shop stands out brightly. 'You want to stop for a pie?'

'It's 10 a.m.'

He shrugs. 'We started early.'

'OK,' I agree, distracted.

Craig pulls the car off the road, and we slow, approaching the order box. He turns to me. 'What do you want?'

I scan the choices. 'I'll have the Stockman's,' I tell Craig.

'Double meat? I'm paying?'

'Regular is good, thanks.'

'Eat in?' suggests Craig.

'We'd better get them to go,' I decide, thinking of the hours sliding away.

Craig looks disappointed and pulls to a stop by the take-out window. 'Double cheeseburger pie and a Stockman, please,' he tells the bored-looking baseball-capped girl. 'And two ginger ninja juices.'

We park up to eat, watching the occasional traffic of the highway. Utes with various ratios of bull-bars and lights. Dilapidated cars likely headed for the mission.

Whitefellas in their shiny vans. That was what Mirri said. Not many shiny vans in Dead Tree Creek. The roads keep them bashed-up and dirty.

I take a bite of pie. Chew.

Jarrah said something about young girls, too, didn't he? It got pushed out of my mind, after I saw the corpse.

Paul Hunter was arranging parties with our girls. Young ones.

'Not bad, eh?' Craig demolishes half his pie in one bite, revealing layers of cheese and processed beef.

'Yeah,' I sigh, distractedly trying the catch my thoughts.

Young girls. Shiny vans.

Yara-ma-yha-who. Sacred land.

'So . . . what do you think?' Craig has been talking to me the whole time, I realise.

'Sorry, what?' I turn to him, half smiling.

'Would you like to go out for dinner with me sometime?'

My face must register shock, because he instantly backtracks.

'I just mean, with you new to town and everything. It's changed a lot since you were here last. There are some good places.'

I look at him, deciding whether to go with the long answer or the short one.

'Yeah, maybe in a few weeks after I've settled in,' I tell him.

'OK. Cool.' He looks hurt and I feel bad about the brush-off. But the last thing I need is complications with a colleague. We're both silent for a moment, looking out on the busy road.

'You still hoping to prove Connolly wrong?' asks Craig, fitting the straw to his outsized juice and taking a long pull.

'It's not about proving him wrong,' I say. 'I want to make sure those missing Indigenous girls get a fair look-in on the case.'

There's a long pause. Craig's gaze follows a truck along the highway. 'Don't get personal about this, Tara,' he says, not meeting my eye. 'After what happened to your sister, I wouldn't blame you—'

'It's got nothing to do with Yindi.' I say it too loud and too quick and regret it. 'I just . . . think it doesn't all add up,' I say, frowning.

Craig sighs. 'We've got a duty to follow procedure. That's part of being a police officer.'

A Mining Corporation van rolls by, liveried and gleaming black. It stands out. The only vehicle on the road not covered in dents and red dust. They take good care of their fleet.

Whitefellas in their shiny vans.

I remember what Anderson said, about needing a better lead on the Mining Corporation. Could this be it?

'Hey, Craig.' I say. 'Could you drop me off at the mission?'

'Alone? It's a dangerous place for a cop.'

My heart sinks, remembering his earlier health and safety warning about sticking with a buddy. 'It's important,' I tell him. 'I'm not taking a risk. They know me. Cover for me if Anderson checks in.'

Craig puffs out his cheeks. 'I don't know, Tara . . .'

'Please?'

He blows out air. 'OK.'

66

Lauren

Beth once told me she has this superpower she learned as a kid when her mom yelled at her. 'I realised I could exit my body and not feel anything,' she told me.

I remembered telling her I wish I could do that. I always thought it would be cool to have no regrets.

Because Tula . . . I do regret what we did to her. But I also think of what she did to me, at Wooloonga Ridge.

Beth

Now Dillon had been in the apartment it was like they were all entitled to. They would sneak up and come down with Lauren's vibrators. My underwear. Total violation. You never felt safe. Not anywhere. Even in bed at night.

Lauren was acting crazy. Completely crazy. She would talk and talk and talk. And at one point she was telling me how we should stay in town and open up a women's clothing boutique. Dead Tree Creek would be a nice place to settle down and have children. She was on another planet. In theory, we were all set to get on the next bus, a few days from now. But Lauren had total Stockholm syndrome. Spoke like her and Paul were in a relationship.

I think he figured out she would do anything to keep him around. Sexually, I mean.

That's why he took Lauren out to the sacred site.

Lauren

Beth would not stop about how we had to leave town. But . . . things between Paul and I were growing. It wasn't all about fucking. For example, one day Paul showed up in the daytime, wanting to drive to this place where we could dig up crystals. I thought that was totally cute.

We drove out of town, past the mine, which was completely incredible. I remember Paul being pleased at how impressed I was by it. It's like this crater in the ground like a meteor strike or something.

'Yeah, it gets its own tourist trade,' he told me proudly, pointing to a line of coaches peeling off to this spiralling bypass which ran next to the dusty work road. 'Maybe I'll take you in for a look one day,' he added, glancing across at me.

I was still taking in all the crazy infrastructure of looping asphalt tracks, huge steel girders and machinery. Totally insane. Like something out of *Mad Max*.

He reached across and closed my hand in his, driving with the other. Then his phone rang.

Ringing and ringing. Texts popping in.

'Want me to answer that?' The phone was on the dash.

'No!' He whipped his hand from mine, then pulled up on the edge of the dirt road.

Paul answered the phone. 'What?' he barked, frowning. His face switched to concentration, then shock. 'I'm with Lauren,' he said. 'Just passed the mine.' Paul looked at me. His jaw tightened. There was another pause. 'Fine. *Fine!*' he said angrily. 'I'll come now.'

When he hung up the phone there was this . . . energy to him. Like an excitement.

He turned to me and said: 'How would you like to see a real-life Aboriginal sacred site?'

67

Craig drops me outside the mission, right by the chain link fence.

I start walking the red dusty road, and this time when I pass the sign banning pornography and alcohol, something else strikes me.

Paul Hunter's phone. All that pornography. Was he distributing it? *Making* it?

I feel like I've peeled up an edge of something important, but I don't know enough to get underneath.

Filing the thought away for later consideration, I pick up the pace. Sweat prickles my hairline.

My phone beeps, and I take it out to see a message from Craig. **If you change your mind about dinner, the offer still stands.**

I smile. The first building I pass is the new school – a construction site when I left – now a glistening vision of glass and asphalt. I press on to where I'm hoping to find Jarrah, noticing some newer houses. Same design. Fibro, lowest possible cost.

As I hoped, Jarrah is at the community hall, barefoot, in jeans and a band T-shirt standing with a group of men – Elders – pointing at the roof. They seem to be discussing repairs. I recognise white-bearded Jimmy from the TV. He notices me and looks nervously at the others. They all stare at my uniform.

Jarrah sees me and my mouth smiles of its own accord.

'Tara?' Jarrah bounds over. 'You can't just show up in your police gear.'

'Thanks heaps.' I'm trying to disguise my hurt. This is going to be harder than I thought.

Jarrah takes my arm and leads me inside the community hall and into a small office area at the back.

There's a table loaded with files. It reminds me of my desk, pre-Anderson's influence. I notice Jarrah look at it a shade too long, then position himself nearest to the paperwork.

Jarrah looks at me intently. 'OK, Tara. Ask me what you want to ask me.'

I consider this. 'I spoke to Mirri,' I say. 'She said Indigenous girls are being picked up by whitefellas in vans. Do you know anything about it?'

He frowns. 'Um. Like I said before, there was a fight about Paul Hunter and some parties with the young girls around the time the backpackers started coming here. Grog showed up. I think there was a van that came late at night, yeah.'

'Could the van have been from the Mining Corporation?'

'It's possible. But we're not very friendly with the Mining Corporation round here after what they did to Wooloonga Ridge. Bashed it up so bad . . .' He stops.

'What?'

He looks at me for a moment, deliberating. 'Nothing,' he says finally. 'Only some of the women reckon it's haunted now.' He's examining my face, as if he's expecting me to laugh.

I frown. 'What makes them think that?'

'Ah, just, weird noises at night.'

'What kind of weird noises?'

He shrugs. 'No idea.'

We're silent.

'That all your official visit over?' asks Jarrah, a ghost of a smile on his face.

'Um. No.' I self-consciously adjust my police radio . 'Three of your girls went missing from the long grasses. I want to find them, if I can.'

There's a flicker in his eyes. Confusion. Something else.

'I don't know anything about missing girls,' he says.

'Keira, Medika and Charlee are their names.'

This time it's unmistakable. His gaze switches to the desk of papers and up to me again.

'They're not missing,' he says slowly.

Is he telling me the truth? Or trying to get rid of me? It's the first time I've ever doubted what Jarrah is saying.

His cell phone rings. 'Give me a sec.' He holds up his hand and answers. 'Yeah?' Jarrah glances across at me, then lowers his voice and walks away, out of the room, switching to rapid Moodjana.

My eyes drop to the papers. Making a check at the door, I step quickly towards the desk, and begin methodically sorting.

They're legal papers. Pages of numbered points that relate to the leasing of land to the Mining Corporation. I pick up a few. They're mainly about Wooloonga Ridge. I read some more. There's information about the site being for women's business. Which means . . . initiation?

Women's initiation.

A painful memory flashes up. Yindi wouldn't tell me what happens to the girls during initiation. It's a sacred secret known only to Moodjana women.

My eyes land on something else. A dog-eared note, handwritten, paperclipped to the information on Wooloonga Ridge.

My eyes widen. It's the song. The same song Tula was singing.

'*Let me take you to my precious land, where the rocks run orange red . . .*'

'Making yourself at home?' Jarrah's tone is icy. I whip round to see him in the doorway, phone in hand, and flush scarlet.

'I just . . .'

'You were just being a copper, I get it.' The disgust in his voice makes me flinch.

'You know something about the missing girls you aren't telling me,' I say.

Jarrah looks me in the eye. 'I was *about* to tell you when my phone rang. Keira, Medika and Charlee went bush for a few weeks. Drove out with their swags. Camping trip. They're grown-ups, don't need to check in.'

I'm remembering how he glanced towards the paperwork. 'Did they go out to Wooloonga Ridge?' I ask.

'You should leave.' The ice in his tone breaks my heart.

'If Wooloonga Ridge is a women's site, initiation is performed there, right? Girls become women.'

Jarrah grabs my arm to move me out of the office, I shake it free. 'Do that again, and I'll bloody arrest you.'

'So do it. Throw your weight around. Prove you're real police.'

We glare at one another. Jarrah's face flashes an unreadable expression, and he turns suddenly, and walks out, calling back a parting shot. 'You haven't changed, Tara. Always did start things you couldn't finish.'

I'm so angry I run out after him. 'Just admit it!' I shout from the doorway. 'You regretted it the moment you kissed me!' The group of Elders turn to look in our direction.

Jarrah swings around and strides back, moving in so close my heart starts thumping.

'I didn't regret it,' says Jarrah in a low voice, his eyes burning into mine. 'But I regret that you ignored all my calls. I regret that you ran away to the city. I regret . . .' he hesitates, shaking his head. 'Doesn't matter,' he mutters bitterly.

I swallow, struggling to keep a grip on my rapidly dissolving anger. 'My *sister* died, and you went to her wake without me,' I accuse.

Jarrah looks confused, and I feel the heat between us slip away. 'What did you expect, a gold-embossed invitation? We don't do things that way.'

This should give me pause, but I'm not in a mood to see reason. 'Stop pretending it could ever have worked with us,' I tell him angrily.

Jarrah's jaw tightens. 'You're so bloody stubborn, Tara,' he says, turning and walking away again.

Fury rises. 'You *never* understood!' I shout after him. 'You've got your big *amazing* extended family. A hundred brothers, a thousand cousins. I've got nothing. Nobody. Not even my own mother wanted me.'

It vaguely occurs to me I'm in police uniform, having a very undignified public row, but I'm too angry to care.

Jarrah stops a little distance away and turns his head with a frown. 'Must get pretty lonely up there on that cross,' he says in an infuriatingly calm tone. 'You got plenty of people who want you, if you ever bothered to notice.' He glances over at the Elders. 'I'm sure one of these fellas will give you a ride back to town,' he says. 'See you around.'

He strides off down one of the unmarked roads, his familiar bouncing step retreating into the distance.

I watch him go. It feels like there's something in my throat. I swallow hard.

When I take out my phone, Craig's text is still on the screen.

A million emotions are racing through me. Jarrah was another lifetime ago. Craig is a decent guy, and I need to stop living in the past.

With shaking fingers, I reply to Craig: **Dinner sounds good. Can you pick me up from the mission?**

68

Lauren

So I was in the car with Paul. Like, *miles* out into the outback or bush or whatever. I remember taking a few extra pills. Eventually, Paul pulled up at this huge rock formation. Like a cave. I am all about vibes, you know? And suddenly I was getting really, really bad vibes.

Paul told me he had some business to sort out. Shouldn't take long.

'Is this illegal?' I was totally confused, and a little afraid. Was Paul involved with gangsters or something?

'I wouldn't want the police finding us here, put it that way,' he said. 'Wait in the truck. I'll be right back.'

I just flat refused, getting out and following along after him like a puppy.

'It's forty degrees in the shade,' I told him, hating how whiny my voice sounded.

He glared at me for a second. 'Fine. Just do what you're told.'

I nodded. Paul led me up some rocks, turned on his phone-torch and took me right inside through these winding tunnels. There was this big cavern at the end. All lit up, but kind of grim, with cheap lighting. A generator whirring. Also, a crate of vodka bottles, and a stack of plastic cups, which struck me as strange.

Paul poured me a shot of neat vodka. I was trying not to freak out, wishing I'd just stayed in the car. I haven't drunk vodka since college. It's a taste that gives me bad memories. The whole feeling of being trapped in the gloom was reminding me in the worst way of that pledge night.

I gulped the drink which was strong enough to make my eyes water. Paul was like, 'Go easy on the grog, eh? It's a lot stronger than the stuff you get down the pub.' He looked deeper into the dark. 'Stay exactly in this spot, OK?' he told me. 'I'll be right back.'

'Where are you going?'

He tapped his nose. 'Ask me no questions I'll tell you no lies. Don't move. We clear, Lauren?' He gave me this long look, then vanished into an opening on the far side of the cavern. I stood there, not knowing what to do. There was nothing particularly special about where he'd left me. It was a cave with a bad smell and running damp.

He hadn't said when he was coming back, which made me extremely nervous. I refilled my cup, right to the brim and chugged. Vodka burned my empty stomach.

Suddenly, I heard the noises. Like inhuman, awful noises. Shrieking. Like shrieks of pain.

I had this total freak-out. Images were, like, popping into my brain. Girls in trouble. Scared girls. Dying girls. I needed to run, leave, right that second. Get my head straight so I could work out what to do. Only I couldn't remember which way we'd come in.

The vodka seemed to be hitting me fast. Maybe my pounding heart was pumping it round, I'm not sure. The whole place was spinning.

I shouted for Paul, like screamed for him. And ... Could

have been my voice echoed. But it *sounded* like girls' voices came back. Familiar voices. Calling for help. Exactly like at college.

My body just reacted, and I puked right on the floor. Basically, pure vodka and I watched it pool and run in clear rivulets over the cave.

I was in total blind panic, and I just staggered in the direction I thought Paul had taken. I didn't get far before I got caught in a wave of nausea. All I could do was wait for it to pass, resting my head against the damp wall. From that angle I could see up ahead a corner where there was a temporary light, slung on the dirt ground and some mattresses. Like three gross, dirty mattresses.

As I watched, two big boots walked up to the bedding. The tan safety boots all the mine workers wore. They moved out of sight, and I saw a pair of bare feet, girl's feet, kind of dragging on the ground.

The shrieking pain noises started up again. I put my hands over my ears and screwed up my eyes tight.

69

By the time I make it back to the station, it's approaching lunch-time and Connolly and his team have decamped for beer and sangers.

The first thing I do is plead my case to Anderson.

'There are so many things unexplained that could be a motive for murder,' I tell him. 'Three trafficked girls are missing. The Mining Corporation, whose employees drink at The Gold Rush, might be involved. Paul and Tula were up to something really shady, I'm sure of it.'

To my disappointment Anderson isn't convinced.

'I don't get how it's a direct link,' he says, looking apologetic. 'This is circumstantial to me. The girls haven't been reported missing by their families. All you've got on the Mining Corporation is the testimony of a woman with no fixed address. That doesn't look good in front of a judge.'

I feel a furious sense of powerlessness.

'Look, the system's not perfect,' continues Anderson. 'What do I never stop telling you, Harrison? Our job is to make it stick in court.' He sighs. 'What about Mirri as a witness? She saw girls getting into what could have been Mining Corporation vans, right?'

'She won't testify,' I say with certainty. 'But . . . maybe I could ask around the Moodjana people . . .'

'Come off it, Tara, if you can't even get Mirri, you're never going to get anyone else. I've tried a couple of times to get statements, stuff like that. Complete stonewall. Gave up asking in person with the Moodjana years ago as a fool's bloody errand, not to mention a long dusty drive.' Anderson looks weary. 'There's no motive for your theory, Harrison.'

'There *is* a motive,' I insist. 'The illegal sex trade got cleared out recently. York Street is dead. If the Mining Corporation brought trafficked sex workers in-house, they could make a lot of money.'

'More money than they make from twenty tonnes of gold per annum? Get off it, Harrison.'

'Retention then,' I say. 'Staff retention. Hundreds of men, right? Mostly single, some flown in from overseas. Bored, lonely.' Anderson's face says it all. 'We can't *get* hard evidence until someone goes and takes a look,' I say, exasperated.

'Welcome to the police force. Connolly's not going to authorise an investigation at Wooloonga Ridge unless there's some lesbian pornography featuring Lauren and Beth at the end of it. It's a nightmare for paperwork anyway. You'd have to get the Mining Corporation *and* the Aboriginal Elders to give permission, and that could take weeks.' He sighs. 'You're better off spending your time at the firing range. Your gun scores aren't anywhere near good enough. I can't pass you without three clear targets, no matter how tidy your desk is.'

I try not to let my hopelessness show.

'How about I ask around at the Mining Corporation? We don't need permission for that, right?'

'I already put the request in,' says Anderson. 'Bloke called Anton Becker – CEO or MD or whatever they call themselves – issued a strong statement. Not talking to police without reasonable cause stated, and we don't have one.'

'Isn't that suspicious in itself?'

'Maybe,' concedes Anderson.

'Sir,' I say desperately, 'if I'm right a brothel could still be operational, with those Indigenous girls forced to work. Held captive, even.'

'I think you're letting emotions get the better of you.'

'Is that a bad thing?'

He hesitates. 'No. But Connolly will have my balls in a carrier bag if I let you go.'

I wince at the image.

He looks at me steadily. 'Look, if you don't *ask* me, I can't say no. And if the Perth boys get on my case about it, well, you're a rookie, and we never had this conversation, right?'

'Right,' I agree slowly.

'Drive around the perimeter, and see if anything looks suspicious. Temporary accommodation. Access roads not leading anywhere. That kind of thing.'

I nod.

'Don't take any risks, and don't get out of your car, OK?'

'Yes, sir.'

'Well, bugger off, Harrison,' he says, spinning around in his chair to offer me a view of his back. 'I never saw you. Oh. And take the west road out,' he adds. 'Connolly's man might be sniffing around near the south exit, but you didn't hear it from me.'

70

Lauren

I can't tell you how long I sat on that cave floor. Everything was spinning. Eventually, I felt a hand on my shoulder and Paul was back. His sneakers were at the edge of my vision.

'I thought I told you to stay put.' He sounded angry.

I opened my mouth to reply, but I couldn't make my words.

'Too much grog and pills, eh?' said Paul. 'Shouldn't mix. Give it a moment to pass.'

'What were those noises?' I managed to get this part out. 'Like screaming or something.'

'What? Ah, just bats.'

But they hadn't sounded like bats.

He stood, and a pair of bare feet arrived next to him. I couldn't tell if they were the ones I'd seen before, or a different set.

I heard a female voice. I knew who it was, but my brain didn't want to be completely honest with me, at that point.

'The girls don't want to do the work,' she said.

'Tough,' said Paul. 'They agreed. They shouldn't have tried to run.'

'They never agreed to *this*.'

I had the strangest feeling of déjà vu. The pledge night. Didn't one of the older girls say something like that?

They never agreed to this. It was ringing around my head with some other sickening feelings that were too dark and awful to be with.

I hiccupped loudly and when I opened my eyes, Paul was standing near me again. So were the bare feet.

'She's out of it,' Paul told the owner of the feet. 'Keep her busy.'

Then Tula was there. It was like a dream or something. She was just as beautiful as I remembered. But I was frightened. I'd last seen her outside the apartment and I didn't know what she thought about me and Paul. I badly wanted her to like me. I don't know where that came from. I hate myself for it now.

Tula knelt and took my hands, and for a moment she reminded me of Beth. Like she'd come to fix everything up and get me out of there.

Instead, she leaned in and kissed me, very full on and unexpected. I broke away. My head was hurting, and my mouth must have tasted completely gross.

The next thing, Tula was gone, Paul was helping me out of the cave. Sunshine seemed to split my brain open.

'Where's Tula?' I asked Paul as we climbed into the car and pulled away.

'She's making her own way back,' said Paul, a little too quickly, looking straight ahead.

'I thought you said she was dangerous.'

He glanced over and caught my expression. 'Tula's cool now,' he said, looking shifty. 'She was having a moment, that time outside the pub.' His eyes were back on the road.

'What was the work that the girls didn't want to do?'

'What?' Paul jerked in his seat.

'I heard . . . I thought Tula said something about girls not wanting to do the work.'

'Fuck me dead, woman.' Paul's voice came out as a roar. 'You really are fucking crazy, aren't you?'

I felt my cheeks heat. My headache pulsed into something worse.

Paul glanced across. 'Few less of them pills, I reckon,' he said nastily. 'Or they'll put you in the nuthouse again.'

We drove back in silence. There were more questions I wanted to ask about him and Tula. But if I was imagining things again, I couldn't be sure about anything anymore. When we testified in court, after the pledge night, I got a lot of things wrong. *A vulnerable young woman whose trauma caused her to fill in blanks*, was what the defence said.

I totally would like to say the pain in my head stopped me asking certain things. And that is partially true. But what is also true, is I didn't want the answers.

I kept looking at Paul, wishing he would go back to being the man who'd rescued me from the storm. Reminding myself he *was* the man who rescued me.

Realistically I had two options. The first was to face up to reality.

I chose the second. Take more pills.

Beth

When Lauren got dropped off outside the apartment, something was badly wrong. It was scary. Like she wasn't there or something.

'Hey, Beth,' she said brightly, hopping out of the car. 'What's for dinner?'

She had the exact same expression I remember from pledge night. A crazed emptiness to her blue eyes. Glittering, but also dead, somehow. Her mouth was stretched up in a smile that was too wide, like a clown.

Without waiting for an answer, Lauren walked past me towards the door. As she opened it and passed inside, her weird smile stayed imprinted on my mind. Like an old-fashioned slide show, other old pictures began clicking through. And without warning, I was plunged into this totally bizarre memory. I mean, it felt *real*. I had this powerful, immediate image of myself, half-naked, tied to a chair in a row with a bunch of other sorority girls, our eyes wild and terrified. Lauren mashing chocolate brownie into my mouth. Me choking, my body bucking.

'She's had enough, Lauren,' I heard someone say. 'Stop. She can't breathe.'

There was a distant pounding which I was faintly aware of as my heartbeat, but it had a detached, rubbery quality, like it belonged to someone else. The image swung, like someone had turned a camera, and I was looking down at myself from the ceiling. Before I could make sense of it all, I was back standing outside The Gold Rush Hotel, the wrought-iron verandas glinting in the setting sun.

I looked at the apartment door, and realised I was frightened to follow Lauren inside. Some nameless walled-off part knew what she could do to me in there.

71

After a long drive, and a lot of unhealthy engine noises, my battered old car has made it to the Mining Corporation. It's so hot I'm worried my battery will overheat, and the exhaust keeps misfiring like it's angry with me.

The perimeter fence is topped with the shiniest razor wire I've ever seen, and warnings of deadly voltage for good measure. Guess they're serious about security. Or perhaps they're concerned about repercussions, since their 'mishap' on sacred land.

From here I can see the massive pit of the mine, a feat of negative space, with its concentric tiers gnawing deeper and deeper. A steady convoy of working vehicles drains down and around the internal circulating roads like flies down a plughole. Dust clouds the bottom, but I make out a few monstrous diggers turning circles at the base, miniaturised by the distance.

It takes me a good half hour to patrol the perimeter, but I don't see anything suspicious. I park up in the shadow of some giant trucks, clustered together like dinosaurs at a feed, and tap my hand on the wheel, thinking. Why doesn't this Anton Becker person want to speak with police?

'Hey!' I hear a man's voice through the fence, just audible over the roar of machinery. 'You can't pull up here.'

I flash my badge. 'I'm police,' I tell the man. 'Do you know where I can find Anton Becker?'

'The offices are on the west side.' He points to an unmarked track. 'But you need an appointment,' he adds as I nod my thanks and drive away. 'Not even staff get in without one.'

After several minutes I make out a chunky building of glass and steel, and a sign simply announcing OFFICE. There's a chevron barrier, demarcating a car park of domestic vehicles, a slot for ID cards, and a dirt-streaked intercom that looks as though it no longer works. I decide to try it anyway, reeling against the heat blast as I roll down the window. I press the intercom button, then retract my finger from the burning plastic. The grille has distorted over the years, drooping like a sad mouth.

'Hello?' I call. Nothing. I jab it enough times to be certain it's broken.

For a moment I look at the parking barrier. It's an old one. Pre-laser-cut key access. Can't see a camera either.

My air con whines pathetically. Making a decision, I pop the glove box, and a fountain of litter pours free. I delve around at the back, where a good few centimetres of loose crumbs live. Aha! My set of rusty Allen keys, right at the back.

Palming them, I slide out of the car and examine the plastic housing of the mechanism. I haven't done this since I hung with a bad crowd as a teenager, kicking out and jealous of Yindi's initiation into her tribe, but this is just like back then – a square hole, for a square key.

I unbolt the catch and the panel drops off, showing the spring and metal innards. Glancing around, I pull the manual override lever, and stand quickly, and lift the barrier by hand.

Sweat is running down the sides of my neck. Grinning to myself, I dive back into the relative cool of my old car, parking a little way from the office building.

Checking again for cameras, I unlock the trunk and heave out my spare car battery. I shake it. Still plenty of acid inside. It takes me a few minutes to pour some carefully into an emptied-out ketchup squirter that forms part of my emergency breakdown supplies.

I move to the front of my battered car and scroll a thin stream of acid over the beaten-up hood. It's not exact, but I manage to make the words 'SACRED LAND' legible. The letters are already bubbling up my paintwork in the hot sun as I draw on the CEO's surname, 'BECKER', and 'PIMP' in the remaining space.

That ought to raise some questions inside the Mining Corporation. Work complete, I toss the battery and ketchup bottle back and endure five minutes of forty-degree desert hospitality on foot before I reach the entrance.

From a distance the building looks ultra-modern, but close up it has a dated feel. The chunky smoked-glass door sticks as I push it. I'm met with damp cool air and a blandly veneered reception desk which puts me in mind of Magic Molly's.

The Gold Rush. The mine. Magic Molly's. It occurs to me they're three sides of the same triangle. Men who dig the earth, and the deadeners they need to do it.

It's a soulless sense of entitlement, I guess, raiding the land for what you can get. I wonder if that disconnection got walked into The Gold Rush, along with the red dirt on the miners' boots.

The reception area is overlarge with an eerily isolated feel, and a few neglected palms in large pots. It's staffed by a plain brunette with heavy make-up.

'Excuse me?' I begin, making an effort to sound stressed. The searing outside heat is working with my mediocre acting skills. The receptionist takes in my flushed face and uniform with alarm.

'We've been tracking a suspect of car theft, and it looks like someone has made a protest in your car park.'

She blinks at me. 'A protest?'

'There's an abandoned car, with the name "Becker" scrawled on it,' I tell her. 'And something about sacred land.'

Her face drops and she grabs for the phone. 'Give me one minute.' She holds up a manicured fingernail. 'Take a seat, if you like.' She directs me towards some extremely uncomfortable-looking black leather-and-chrome benches that suggest the company don't get many visitors.

'Mr Becker?' she breathes. 'There's a police officer here.' She waits, listening. 'Yes. No. They're not here about that,' she says. 'Apparently, they're looking for a car thief, and there's been some vandalism in the car park.' She listens some more. 'Yes,' she says lowering her voice. 'I think so. It's about Wooloonga Ridge.' She glances at me. 'It has your name on it.' There's another pause, and she hangs up.

'Mr Becker will be right down.'

72

Beth

Sometimes I feel like I am a flat piece of paper, with all these overlapping memories, you know? As though the same thing happens over and over and gets stickered over the top of the first.

So right now, for example, whilst I am in a police cell in Dead Tree Creek, part of me is remembering us sorority girls after the arrest. Shivering, half-dressed in American custody.

Also, I'm currently dragging Lauren across the cell floor and it reminds me of dragging Tula. Only she was a lot muddier. Obviously.

There are other major differences. Lauren is still warm, and moaning softly. Tula was . . . not exactly cold. But getting that way. Oh, and she smelled bad. Unwashed. At first of alcohol, and then, as I pulled her over the cellar floor, this rancid smell of old urine caught my nose. She was leaving a wet stinking trail that made me retch.

Lauren, I can't think of her smelling bad, even though she does.

I give this some thought as I get Lauren in the position I want her, laid out flat. Does this mean I'm obsessed with Lauren? Or perhaps in love with her?

I brush hair from her face, relieved to be nearly done. Tula wasn't *half* so easy. Because I had to get her down the mineshaft.

Looking down at Lauren now, I'm filled with a lot of the same thoughts as before. Wishing I could tunnel down into the blackness with her. Only there's nowhere to go, and the bus has left town. Lauren would never think of herself as a victim. But in my opinion, it's why she got with Paul. The relationship with him was a defence mechanism.

I grab Lauren's hands, with the chipped turquoise varnish, and roll her over to her side. Recovery position. Then I start hammering on the door.

It's a long time before the cop arrives. A woman who I've never spoken to.

'Alright, alright, I heard you the first time,' she grumbles. The door is clear toughened glass, so she can see right away Lauren is unconscious. 'Holy shit.' She fumbles with her keys.

'I don't know what happened,' I gabble. 'She must have smuggled some pills in somehow. I think she's overdosed on something.'

73

Anton Becker emerges through a door at the back of the reception area. He is average-looking in every way. Medium build, brown hair, clean shaven, tidy suit, rectangular thin-framed glasses. When he opens his mouth to speak, somehow I'm not surprised to hear a European accent. German, I think.

'I am Anton Becker,' he says, extending his hand curtly. 'My receptionist says you are here about some vandalism?' I shake it, noticing how cold his palm is.

'We've been tracking a car thief,' I say. 'And found the car abandoned here. Looks like whoever stole it isn't a fan of yours.'

He considers this for a long moment 'This thief is still in the area?'

'We have reason to suspect they could be.' This seems like the right response to justify my unauthorised access. But I'm not prepared for his reaction.

'Stephanie, call Mr Banks,' he says. Something about his tone suggests Mr Banks is not a nice man. 'He should get some of his men on the east road, and issue a Code 5. All exits.'

He turns to me. 'Could you describe the intruder?'

I take a breath, wondering what I've done. 'I'm going to ask that you leave things to the police,' I tell him, trying to sound authoritative. 'There's no need . . .'

Anton waves a hand impatiently. 'We have good security,' he says. 'Ex-military. Firearm licensed. Out here, fast action and correct force is necessary, with official law enforcement so far away.' He thinks some more. 'Stephanie, please also ask Mr Banks to view the recording of the car park.'

I swallow. The cameras must have been well hidden. How long does that give me before whoever Mr Banks is sees me vandalising my own car?

'I think the police will want to see the footage,' I try. 'Maybe better to wait . . .'

Anton's lips press together. 'If you would please show me this car,' he says, extending his arm rigidly in the direction he wants me to go.

'Sure.' I head through the doors, my heart pounding. The sun feels even hotter as we troop across to my car. I'm jumping at the possibility I left some incriminating evidence in plain view. But another part of me is excited. His reaction implies I might be on to something.

Anton strides behind me, giving no indication the hot sun causes him any discomfort.

'Your colleague is parked somewhere?' He glances around for a squad car.

'Just outside the car park.' I try to keep a casual tone, but something tells me he suspects.

'I thought police officers were supposed to stay in pairs.'

I make no answer.

'I never got your name and job title,' he adds meaningfully as we near my beat-up car.

'Constable Richardson,' I lie.

To my relief we've reached the car. He looks unhappy at the sight of his name in blistered paint.

'Any idea why someone might have done this?' I ask, on surer ground.

He blinks at me for a moment. I have a feeling he's been caught off balance, and that this is a rare thing for him.

'I imagine you saw on the news, about our recent . . . embarrassment,' he says finally. 'We wanted to put all this behind us. The incident at Wooloonga Ridge. Paul Hunter's death.'

'I wasn't aware the two things were connected.' I keep my voice even.

He closes his eyes slightly, to signal grief. 'Yes, certainly a lot of people might think so.'

'A lot of people might think so?' I repeat, deliberately mirroring his statement as suggested in my interview training.

'Correct.' Anton nods with certainty. 'Paul Hunter was the man who destroyed the sacred site, after all.'

74

Beth

After Lauren came back from the sacred site with Paul, she wasn't the same. You could tell she was losing it. She stopped going to the reserve, stopped insisting on visiting Bluey.

Our last visit to Bluey, he had asked us about the Indigenous community. Lauren told him about the Stolen Generation, and got very animated.

Bluey went quiet for a bit. Then he said:

'You know that's me, doncha, love? I'm one of the Stolen Generation. My dad was white. So government reckoned I'd be better off on account of my white skin.'

There was a long pause. Lauren's eyes filled with tears.

'Oh my God,' she whispered. 'Seriously?' She took his hands in hers. 'That is so *awful.*'

Bluey shrugged. 'I wouldn't feel sad for me, love. I've done alright for meself.'

I could see Lauren taking in the shit-heap of Bluey's one-room house. The sofa where he slept, more stuffing than cover. Dog poop on the porch.

'How old were you?' whispered Lauren.

'Aw. Five, I reckon. Five or six. No one knows. No birth

certificate, nothin' like that, you know? I was in an orphanage for about eight years. Taken away from me mum, me brothers, sisters, cousins. You girls don't want to know what goes on in those places. They worked us through the week and sold the pretty ones on the weekend, even the little boys. Bad luck for me, I was pretty back then. Not so much now, eh?' He croaked out a laugh.

Bluey considered for a moment, his hand with the Swan tin trembling. 'But I got out. Got work, mining. Got married.' He grins broadly. 'Fucked it all up, but I'm still smiling.' He glances around as if he's lost something, focuses on the beer in his hand and upends it jerkily into his mouth. 'I'm alright. No need to feel bad for old Bluey.'

Lauren

We'd forgotten our focus, you know? Helping people. And the pills . . . they were good for floating above it all. Not noticing the rocks beneath.

After Bluey told us what happened to him, part of me totally couldn't handle it. It was too sad, you know? All those children. All that *pain*. When you look at Bluey, he's like this great smelly dirty mess. You don't see a cute little boy missing his mom, you know? But underneath, it's what he is, and I . . . I couldn't bear it.

75

The sun beats down on the car park, relentless, as Anton stands looking at my graffitied car.

A sheen of sweat has risen on his upper lip, I notice.

'You think Paul Hunter was murdered, because he destroyed the sacred site?' I confirm.

My radio squeals on my chest.

'Harrison? Constable Harrison?' It's Connolly.

Anton's eyes narrow in suspicion.

I put in my earpiece and press the button, just in time to stop broadcasting the next words.

'What the hell do you think you're doing at the mine? Over,' growls Connolly.

Shit. Connolly must have checked my tracker. I turn the off switch.

'You told me your name was Richardson,' says Anton, his tone mild, his eyes steely.

'This radio picks up all kind of frequencies,' I say, trying to sound casual. 'Must be another officer in the locality. Tell me about Paul Hunter and Wooloonga Ridge.' I'm working to keep my voice calm.

He's looking at me differently now. 'Well, this is all public knowledge,' he says. 'Paul Hunter drove a large digger into the sacred site. Claimed he misread the map. Dug out a lot of material from the rocks, and made the caves there unstable.' His face darkens. 'It was a dreadful, dreadful mistake,' he says quietly. 'A stain on our reputation that will haunt us forever.'

Anton looks genuinely sad. 'We are in talks with the Moodjana people as to how to put matters right. We've buttressed the caves with temporary supports. But they're extremely dangerous.'

'You can't make them safe? Big company like you?'

He absorbs my biting tone. 'Yes, we could. The Mining Corporation secures tunnels over a thousand metres deep.' He can't help but smile briefly at the mention of his mighty organisation. 'But the Elders don't want steel beams used. So we are in deadlock, currently.' It's an unfortunate term but Anton doesn't appear to notice. 'I'm afraid there have been numerous threats made from the Moodjana camp.' His eyes glide to the car. 'The local tribe say any non-Moodjana who set foot on that sacred site are cursed. Doomed to die a terrible death. People are angry and . . . I can't help but think it's symbolic, how Paul Hunter died.'

I consider this, carefully phrasing my next question.

'Some young Aboriginal girls have gone missing,' I tell him. 'Local women think they escaped sex traffickers and were recaptured.'

It's a millisecond gesture, Anton's gaze switches over and back to the word 'PIMP' scarred in blistered paint on my car. There's a long pause and I don't fill it. Anton raises his gaze to the horizon surveying his red dirt empire.

'You're suggesting someone is trafficking girls on our land?'

'You tell me.'

Anton's eyes seem to shrink back in his head slightly, as though a veil has dropped over them. A muscle in his jaw twitches.

'Constable Richardson, we employ hundreds of men, and only

a handful of women. Many work long shifts. They often have plenty of money in their pockets, and not many places to spend it. I would be lying to you if I said bad behaviour didn't go with the territory. But we did everything in our power to aid the federal police in their recent crackdown on sex trafficking.'

Anton's statement sounds overly long and polished, like a press release. I wonder what he's hiding.

'The fly-in-fly-out Asian sex workers have gone,' he says. 'We took steps to ensure particular light aircraft did not have permission for this airspace, and we moved on any trailers we found parked on our land.' He manages a thin smile. 'But we have a lot of land.'

'You *lease* a lot of land,' I correct him. 'From the Indigenous people.'

Unprofessional, Tara.

'Yes, yes. Of course.' He faces me, waving a hand. 'I greatly admire the native people. All that hardship, and they retain their traditions against all the odds. We have a similar history of oppression in Germany as you must be aware. Perhaps humankind is simply doomed to repeat ourselves. The oppressors and the repressed.'

'How about pornography?' I suggest. 'Is that part of the culture here?'

Anton closes his eyes for so long I wonder if he's feeling unwell. When he opens them, it's accompanied by a deep sigh. 'We were naive,' he says, 'after the sex trade was removed, something of a locker-room mentality developed.' His mouth twists in distaste. 'Very unpleasant images and videos were being shared as some kind of joke. Banter. Myself, I don't see the funny side. Neither did the company.' His eyes track back to the car, and he avoids my eyes. 'We had to give a small group of men a formal warning a month or so ago.' He frowns at the memory.

I breathe out, processing this. Is Anton trying to put a spin on the facts?

'You're implying blame is with only a few of your employees,' I say. 'But Dead Tree Creek has a culture of fighting, heavy drinking, and sexual assault, and the culprits are mostly miners.'

Anton makes a strange little laugh. 'You're surely not suggesting the Mining Corporation is responsible for the town's social problems?'

I shrug. 'Maybe people working in bad conditions behave badly.'

Anton considers. 'Or perhaps the local police force are rather heavy-handed with young men letting off steam after a long week at work. Waving guns and so forth.'

I've got no answer, because he's right.

'From what I have observed, men without women tend to gravitate towards a leader,' continues Anton. 'If this leader is unprincipled, a man like Paul Hunter, perhaps . . .' He opens his hands as if no more need be said.

There's a buzzing sound. Anton's brow furrows and he puts a hand to his hip and retrieves an immaculate smart phone from the smooth lines of his pocket.

'Mr Banks,' he says. 'Tell me.' He listens intently, and the longer he does, the more uneasy I feel. Finally, Anton looks at me and hangs up, his mouth is set in a thin straight line.

'You have no authority to be here.' His pale eyes grow hard. 'I am giving you a single opportunity to leave without encountering my private security. And please be under no misunderstanding. These are not tolerant men. If you are found on Mining Corporation property again,' he concludes, almost spitting the words, 'you will be treated as a civilian and a trespasser of the highest threat.'

Red-faced, I climb into my car and pull out, under Anton's

tight-lipped and furious gaze. It's only when I'm a good kilometre clear of the mine I risk pulling over and switching my radio back on. Almost immediately, Connolly's voice blasts through.

'Harrison?' He sounds irate, even over static. 'What the hell have you been doing?'

'I . . .'

'You need to get over to the hospital right now. Lauren got some drugs in. She's overdosed. In a very bad way.'

'*What?*'

'As the only female constable, it was your responsibility to search her,' he continues. 'Congratulations, Harrison. If our lead suspect dies, it's on you.' He pauses to let the accusation sink in. 'In the meantime, Dooligan reckons Lauren has been asking for you. By name. Thinks she might want to confess.'

76

Beth

Things were not good between me and Lauren. The bus out of Dead Tree Creek had become like a ticking clock that got louder and louder. Lauren would dodge the subject whenever I brought it up. We only had another two weeks of work, and if we didn't skip town soon, we'd have to do another lock-in. The 'last night' lock-in. I broke out in a sweat just at the thought.

Then, the Thursday afternoon before the Saturday bus, I came into the bedroom, and Lauren was in this Marilyn Monroe act, like in a cute fluffy negligee. And she started directing. Like, 'Beth, take off your clothes. Not like that. Slowly. Turn around.'

I was kind of laughing, but also, I could tell she was totally manic. In that moment I had a choice, you know? I could have walked out. I think a part of me did want to understand the hold that Paul had over Lauren. Or maybe, more accurately, I wanted to break it. Like I thought if I could approach it the right way, Lauren might realise . . . Anyway. It was weird. I was jealous of Paul, is what I'm saying. Which is why I went along with it.

Lauren walked over to me, and we kissed. For less than a second, it was like we were back in Thailand again, but then it wasn't. I could smell the cheap liquor fermenting on her breath. And I could just tell. She wasn't *there*. Not really. It felt mechanical.

I pulled away and was like: 'Lauren, I don't think this is right.'

That's when I felt someone behind me. It took me by surprise, obviously, but standing so close, I recognised his cologne without turning around, and that in itself brought up this dark, horrible memory.

Paul.

He must have put Lauren up to it, and been watching out of sight or something, waiting for his big entrance. I don't know how he managed to hide out in the bedroom without me seeing. Maybe snuck past when I was in the shower or something.

About a million feelings shot through me at once, mostly rage. Like pure, pure rage.

Of course, Lauren didn't know what had happened between me and Paul. But somehow it felt like she was to blame.

It was as though my body was layered, like one of those old-fashioned ice creams.

At the bottom was this absolute freezing betrayal, sickening and painful, like a colourful swirling bruise inside my ribs. But it was overlaid by all kinds of frothy-thick fury.

I hated her.

I hated her.

I *hated* her.

Lauren

That morning I just woke up feeling like I wanted to crawl out of my own head. I just needed something to *happen*. Anything to make me feel different. I knew Paul wouldn't come without a good reason.

Then, I had this Sneaky Thought.

It said: *You know what would make him come running . . . ?*

It did too. He came right from work. But . . . turned out to be the worst mistake. Because I ended up upsetting Beth which is one of those things I will regret forever. At the time I thought I would ruin the moment if I told her in advance. I wanted it to be organic. Sort of spontaneous.

Anyway, Beth and I were making out, and Paul comes in. Beth freaked. She started yelling this stuff at Paul in a way I'd never heard before. Like a 'wrong side of the tracks' kind of voice. It came from nowhere. Almost like she was an actress playing a character, you know? 'Mad-as-hell trailer park bitch'.

She called him a dirty rapist, and a paedophile and told him she was going to stab him in both eyes, and other pretty gross stuff involving areas of his anatomy and a baseball bat. That was only the parts I can remember. It went on and on. Totally extreme. At the time I was mad at her. Like, yeah, sure. I made a bad judgement. You weren't into it. I get it. But there was no call for that reaction.

I didn't look at her in the same way after seeing that side to her. If I'm honest, I was a little afraid of her.

77

I speed towards the hospital, thoughts rolling around my head. Is it my fault Lauren has OD'd? I didn't strip search. But . . . I went through her bag, her clothes, seams, inside pockets. Could I have missed something? I wonder what this means for my future in the force, and it throws something into clear perspective. It's been hard, stressful and frustrating, but . . . this job. I can't imagine not doing it.

As the dirt road gives way to tarmac, I go over what I've just learned. What if Paul Hunter destroyed the sacred site on purpose, so he could use the caves there without being seen?

Eventually, I pass the primary-colour medley of signs directing me to the hospital, and the three departments available: emergency, main hospital and mortuary; crook, dying or dead.

As I park, I pick up my phone and call Craig. I've barely cut my engine when I see him striding out of the main doors, red hair easily visible against the white of the building.

I get out of the car. 'Craig?'

'Tara?' He almost runs at me, green eyes wide with alarm. 'Lauren was asking for you, but . . . she's in and out of consciousness. They're still trying to work out how to treat her, and the doctors won't let us interview.'

'Connolly said it was a drugs overdose. Blamed me for a bad search.'

Craig's freckled nose crinkles in disgust. 'Connolly's a bloody mongrel, Tara. Wants all the glory, but first chance of blame he pins it on everyone else.' He starts rapidly towards the hospital and I follow. 'They're testing her blood for drugs. But no one knows what she's taken yet. We're on guard duty by the bed, since Lauren's still under arrest,' he says. 'You're up after me. But we can switch now. Maybe she'll come round and decide to say something to you, eh?'

I nod. 'Could Beth be responsible?'

'Maybe, but she's gone full mute. Connolly wants her transferred to jail by tomorrow morning.'

We move through the rickety sliding doors into the waiting room, with its screw-down chairs, and handful of injured people.

Craig glances back, and lowers his voice. 'Connolly's properly in the shit over this. That's why he's trying to blame you. Lauren repeatedly complained of headache and chest pains, but Connolly wouldn't let her see a medic.'

This sounds so horrifically close to what happened to Yindi, my whole body feels numb.

Craig comes to a stop outside a door with a rectangle of safety glass. Lauren lies on the other side in a bed, hooked up to a variety of tubes and machinery. She looks very small and alone.

Craig opens the door for me. 'Four-hour shift, OK? No visitors. She's heavily sedated. Not going anywhere, so you can use the bathroom, just stay mostly here, right? Nurses come and go a lot. If she wakes up, doctor's orders are to get the medics in right away.'

'Righto.' I take a seat in the ageing hospital chair by the bed. My eyes land on Lauren's pale bluish wrist. There's a handcuff, securing it to the metal bed frame. Like a bad practical joke.

I sit there for a long time, the beeps of the vital signs machine a background percussion.

'Beth?' Lauren's voice comes as a croak. I jump to my feet. There's an emergency call button, so I press it.

'Lauren?' I swallow, unsure what to say. 'Can you tell me what you've taken?' She looks away, as if annoyed.

The call button is lit up and flashing, but I hit it a few more times for good measure, and look to the door.

'It's Constable Harrison,' I try. 'Tara Harrison. Did you want to tell me something?'

Her eyes are closed and her lips are parched and pale. They split into a slight smile.

'You can't tell anyone,' she whispers. 'OK?'

'OK,' I say. 'Tell me.'

'Beth . . . What we did to Paul and Tula. It wasn't her fault.'

Something pulses at my temples. Lauren's eyelids are fluttering and her face scrunched as if in pain.

'It was my idea,' she says. 'Beth just went along with it.'

'What was your idea?'

Lauren doesn't answer. She twists uncomfortably on the bed and starts muttering.

'Alpha Sigma Psi, keep our secrets or you die.'

I pause. 'Lauren,' I say quietly, glancing around and taking my chances. 'Do you know anything about three young Indigenous girls? Medika, Charlee and Keira.'

Suddenly, the machine begins beeping wildly. 'The cave,' mumbles Lauren. 'Girls in the cave.'

My heart speeds up. 'Which cave? Was it Wooloonga Ridge?'

Was that an incline of her head? The door bangs open and a woman in a doctor's coat races in, accompanied by two nurses.

'Lauren,' I say forcefully, 'was Paul there? Was Paul keeping girls in that cave?'

'Excuse me,' says the doctor. 'What the hell do you think you're doing?'

'I . . . She woke up,' I say lamely.

'This is *my* patient, and you have no authority to interrogate her.'

I turn back to Lauren. Her mouth is moving like she's trying to speak.

'Do you know which caves, Lauren?' I ask desperately.

'You need to leave,' says the doctor. 'Before I lodge a complaint of police brutality.'

With one last glance at Lauren I head for the door, shamefaced and frustrated. I hear the doctor's voice as I exit.

'Until we find out what she's taken, we can't hope to improve her condition and she's declining rapidly.'

I leave the room, thoughts clashing in my mind. My phone rings and I answer it, only half concentrating.

'Tara?' It's Craig. 'I'm coming to relieve you. Anderson asked you to come in.'

'Why?'

'Dunno.' Craig pauses. 'It didn't sound good.'

322

78

Pete

I fired Lauren and Beth after April came and told me what was going on. At the end of the day, we're a family pub. We can't have girls having affairs with the customers.

I told 'em, pack your bags. I'll settle up your pay. One last shift and that's it. You work Friday night then you're out.

Dillon

Friday night we let loose. Especially when we've been working earlies for a full month. Then Pete tells us he's sending the girls off this weekend. So there was gonna be a lock-in. Party.

Mike

When you're all crammed in underground together, load of stinking blokes, you get ... I wouldn't say close, but there's a loyalty there. Bit of a pack mentality. Even more so the barmaids do their last lock-in.

Beth

Pete came to the apartment, which he never did. I actually thought he'd finally come to fix the lock. Instead, as he started looking around what passed as a living room it was like he was totally disgusted with us.

He told us The Gold Rush was a family place and he'd been hearing complaints from locals, about the kind of things we were getting up to. The only families Pete attracted were the possums that raided the garbage at night.

A big part of me was relieved. Obviously. I was hoping this would convince Lauren to leave town. But I had never lost a job before. I always follow the rules and do what the boss tells me. I'd kept the cooler stocked, the cash register right, the food how it should be. Done everything he'd asked. I smiled and agreed with the men when they said stupid stuff. And still he was saying I failed. It was a sucker-punch.

Pete said the bus came the next morning, like he was doing us a favour. We found out later the guys in the bar already knew we'd been fired. That was when I started feeling really afraid. We were going to have to do the lock-in.

Lauren

Pete came right out with it. 'This is your last shift.' I couldn't have cared less. No prizes for guessing who had complained. I remember telling Beth I was going to check out other jobs in the town. The place had grown on me. Crazy, right? I had a feeling April had picked her moment. Right before the Friday night.

Beth

Lauren was super mad with April.
  Super.
  Mad.

79

I park outside the station, and march straight into Anderson's office.

'Come right on in, Tara,' says Anderson dryly. 'Thanks for knocking. Shut the door behind you. So,' he looks serious, 'bad news, I'm afraid. You haven't made it as probationary constable this time around.'

It's so unexpected that shock reverberates through me.

'Someone high up has complained about you,' says Anderson. 'Trespass on mining land, the whole lot.' He eyeballs me. 'I thought I told you not to get out of the car?'

'Sir,' I say, talking fast, 'I had a hunch and I was right. It was Paul Hunter who damaged the sacred site. At the hospital, Lauren said something about girls inside a cave. Wooloonga Ridge is a cave network.'

'I don't want to hear it,' Anderson growls. 'Complaint aside, you put yourself in danger. First rule of policing. Protect yourself. Protect your colleagues.' His expression turns kind. 'It's a setback, OK, Tara? Come back in six months, try again.'

Embarrassingly, tears spring to my eyes. I blink them back. 'Give me another chance,' I say. 'I stuffed up. I know that. It won't happen again.' I swallow, gaining control of myself.

Anderson sighs. 'It's not just the health and safety,' he says. 'Your firearms isn't up to scratch for this beat.'

'It's at your discretion,' I say, trying to stay calm.

'It is, and what sort of superior officer sends an unarmed constable out into a town of aggro blokes? You need a gun for this job. I've told the fellas in Perth, this isn't a suitable position for everyone who passes the exam. Go back to the city. Wait out your six months. I'm sure they'll place you somewhere better next time.'

Anger takes over. 'You're dead wrong,' I tell him. 'The last thing you want is more gun-slingers down here. Your bloody beat is one of the toughest because you treat the community like the enemy, and police wade in waving pistols around and shouting. What you need is to stop squaring up to the miners and start communicating better with the locals.'

'If you've quite finished telling me my job, Harrison, I've got a murder inquiry to wrap up, and two suspects in custody who planned it all out in a journal.'

Desperation takes hold. 'Sir, even if you won't progress me to constable, hear me out. I think I could be onto something.' Anderson doesn't interrupt so I keep talking. 'Paul Hunter boasted about starting a brothel. If he was running it from the sacred caves, it would link everything together.'

'You've got to do better than that, Harrison. That's not even a working theory. And you didn't find any evidence of missing girls out at the mine, am I right?'

'No, I didn't, but—'

'And why the hell would you run an illegal brothel from a sacred cave and draw all that attention to yourself? I can think of a thousand better places. Locations with hot running water for a start. It doesn't make any sense.'

'True, but—'

'Good police officers take evidence impartially. You had a look around the mine, found nothing. That's the end of it.'

'If these were missing white girls, the whole force would be combing the area,' I protest. 'Indigenous women make up a fraction of the population, but nearly a quarter of all unfound missing persons.'

'Don't college lecture me, Harrison, fresh out of the bloody exam hall. I was working this beat when you were a snaggle-toothed urchin, and I used to bleat out statistics, just like you're doing. What you come to realise, painful as that may be, is there's only so many resources. And whether you like it or not, a lot more people from the Aboriginal community wander off without telling anyone where they're going. It's the plain bloody truth of it.'

I take a breath. 'When Yindi died, you cared about justice. What happened to you?'

He hesitates. 'I got old enough to know the difference between justice and revenge. We're investigating a murder, not missing persons, and we don't have the manpower to do both.'

'But you haven't got all the evidence. You need to send some-one out to the sacred site.'

'It's Connolly's call, not mine.'

I'm gripped with helpless rage. 'I think you're a bloody coward, sir.'

Anderson's face darkens. 'I'll pretend I didn't hear that, Harrison,' he says. 'Get out. You're lucky I don't permanently disqualify you for unacceptable language and behaviour.'

I pull off my badge and slam it on his desk. 'I'm going to Wooloonga Ridge. Try and stop me.'

Several expressions dance across Anderson's face at once.

'You step on sacred land, I'll bloody arrest you. We have enough trouble with Indigenous relations as it is. You've got the makings of a good copper. A real good copper. Don't throw it away.'

'You don't know the first thing about me, sir.' I instantly regret it. Anderson's expression is one of deep paternal hurt.

'Getting kicked off the force won't bring your sister back, Tara,' he says quietly.

I want to say something back. Something smart and cutting. But there's nothing to say. I march out, slamming the door behind me.

80

Lauren

Beth totally lost it after Pete fired us. I was feeling on edge anyway, and it was the last thing I needed. She said it was all my fault the guys in the bar were out of line with us. Because I shouldn't have been open about my bisexuality. I mean, *seriously*?

That wasn't even what we got fired for.

Beth

It should have been obvious to Lauren that you don't walk into a room full of very basic guys and tell them all about your colourful sexual history.

'What did you expect?' I demanded. 'You went right ahead and told them. "Oh, I was in a relationship with a girl. But I like guys too." What did you expect?'

Lauren blinked fast and hard. 'Oh, I'm *sorry*.' She was using a tone I'd never heard before. 'I should be ashamed, right? Cover it up, to be more acceptable.'

'You have no idea the privilege of asking that question. I spend my whole life apologising for who I am and you're bitching because in one small part of the world, where you don't even live, you can't shake your titties in public.'

'Titties? That is, like, *so* trailer park. And I'm not bitching. You don't get to trump my right to be a human being because you've suffered worse. Everyone deserves to be the best version of themselves. Enlightened.'

'Some of us don't get to be *enlightened*, OK? Most of us just get to survive.'

'I spent a year in "rehab",' she quoted with her fingers, 'because of people like *you*. It took me that long to realise I wasn't some freak. You're the freak, because you can't accept people who are different to you.'

'Oh. Wait.' I'm suddenly disgusted with her. 'Like because you have mental health problems, you're excused from behaving in a socially decent way, and we all have to suck it up, because otherwise you might get sad and kill yourself? You *knew* those guys were already creaming their pants to see you working in their bar and you couldn't resist dialling it up a level. You were rubbing it in their faces.'

She was quiet for a moment. 'You sound like my dad,' she said, finally. 'He says, "I got no problem with gays. So long as they don't rub it in my face."'

'It would have made everyone's lives easier.' It was true, but she flinched like I'd hit her.

'You know those girls, out on the reserve?' she replied. 'And Bluey? And the little barefoot Indigenous kids I see you get all sad over when you think no one's looking? You think they should start fitting in too? Adopt white-person culture? You think that's how prejudice is overcome?'

'No, but . . .'

She gave this big juddery sigh, looking more sober than I'd seen her in a while. 'You know what, Beth? I already tried pretending to be someone I'm not. Been there, done that. And it didn't work out for me so good.' She picked up her little daypack from the decaying sofa. 'I'm going out for a walk.'

'No,' I told her. '*I'm* going out. You need to tidy this place up. We're getting the bus tomorrow, and I don't want to lose my key deposit because of all your shit everywhere.'

'Fine.'

'*Fine.*'

FYI. She didn't clean up. Obviously.

81

I march out, determined to drive to Wooloonga Ridge. And the first thing that happens is my car won't start.

Shit. I left the battery connected in my hurry to get to Anderson. And the contents of my spare are all over the hood. I stand for a moment, feeling the heat of the day.

My eyes move to Connolly's shiny car, parked with the keys inside.

An hour later, I'm realising that Connolly's car isn't suitable for desert driving. I try not to imagine his furious face when he learns I've taken his car on a road trip without permission.

The rock formation sparkles on the horizon. Story goes, its shape is the final resting place of two giant snakes, who made vast underground tunnels of glittering snake-scale mineral deposits from here to the coast during Dreamtime. When they finally came up for air and intertwined, the world hardened, setting their huge bodies in stone.

To the east of the ridge, the mine site sits menacingly. To the west is the burning hot sun.

I'd been expecting some kind of obvious markers to lead me to the caves. A cordoned area. Warning signs. Machinery parked nearby. But there's nothing. Just a long few kilometres of towering stone.

My only option is to patrol its length in the car for the cave entrance. But the road is already degenerating into a stony track that Connolly's city vehicle isn't designed for. The car starts to judder and shake. I hit a rock at the wrong angle, and the steering wheel jerks to one side.

'Come on, car,' I plead, patting the dashboard. 'It's forty-five degrees out there.'

I wince as the car bottoms out on the uneven ground. The engine revs shrilly. I cut the power as the sulphurous smell of an overworked battery wafts into the interior. Better not risk killing the car, I decide. I'm in enough trouble as it is. Looks like I'm walking.

I try to gauge the distance. Half an hour hike, maybe. It'll feel longer in the heat.

Scouting around the interior supplies, I find a bush knife which Connolly keeps in the glove compartment. My own police gear includes a few basic navigation tools and my gun. I check the clip and holster it.

There's no phone signal, but my radio is picking up, at least for now. I strap it to my chest.

I get out of the car. A dripping sound from the undercarriage tells me the air con has been working overtime, dumping excess water.

Between me and the ridge, the red sand is a dappled covering of clumping spinifex grass, fluffy emu-tree bushes, low eucalyptus, saltbush and acacia trees. It won't be too far into the sparse bush before the car will vanish from view, disguised by foliage.

I take out my police-issue compass and get my bearings as a wave of dry heat slams me like a physical force. The last thing I want is to lose my ride.

'You've walked much further than this,' I tell myself, double checking north.

Sweat stings my eyes. Holstering the water bottle, I start walking.

82

Lauren

After the fight with Beth, I wandered around the apartment, lifting stuff up and dropping it. I called Paul. I knew he wouldn't be at work that day. He didn't answer for, like, the first five times. So I started messing around with different make-up, underwear looks, sending him pictures.

Beth

When I came back, not only had it not been tidied, but Paul was there.

It was so . . . Callous. So fucking insulting.

He didn't see me. Neither of them did. They were in the bedroom, making a tonne of noise as usual. I stood at the doorway watching them. It looked full on. I had no idea how Lauren wasn't in serious discomfort. But I guess she's always on those pills.

I would say my anger at Lauren vanished. But it didn't vanish. It switched teams back to Paul.

Then it doubled.

Lauren

Paul came over, and we were just *on it*. Like, it was some of the most intense sex of my whole life. I always felt I could loosen all my boundaries with Paul. There was nothing I couldn't do.

I had this crystal knife for aura cleansing, and somehow that got involved. I had a cut under my ear. At one point his chest was slamming against mine, and this spray of blood and sweat hit me in the eye. That was kind of cool. But in quite a narcissistic way, you know? Like, *Hey, look at us being badass!*

I even suggested we get Tula there, but Paul couldn't get hold of her.

Then just as quickly, this crazy high vanished. I felt a rush of cold air passing over me and suddenly I wanted Paul to leave. As he was getting dressed, something about the way he pulled white sports socks halfway up his hairy legs just grossed me out. Like the illusion had cracked. He was just some guy who worked in a mine.

After he went, I left the bedroom and there was Beth, looking super sad. And that was when it finally, finally clicked, and I woke up to my own stupid selfishness. Beth was my best friend, and she'd stuck by me this whole time. When I feel low, it's always her I can turn to. All this warmth in my heart surged out. I told Beth how sorry I was. For everything. Including not cleaning the shitty apartment. I was done with Paul. Didn't care if I never saw him again. Suddenly, she started crying. Said she was frightened about our last night. And she had something to tell me.

Beth

I told Lauren what happened on the camping trip. It was such a

337

relief. Her face went through this variety of emotions and it felt like she was feeling them for me. She kept asking me if I wanted to go to the police. I kept saying no. I'd driven out to the middle of nowhere with a bunch of guys. I had chosen to drink so much I could barely stand. Police don't have much sympathy in that situation. It wasn't like I could prove anything.

Lauren looked devastated. She said over and over she was sorry. That she'd seen her job as being friendly, and given the wrong impression. Put me in danger. Something snapped in me then. I was like, 'Lauren, *stop*. Listen to us. We're doing what women *always* do. We're blaming *ourselves*.'

Lauren

Beth was totally right. You can be friendly or drunk or wear a bikini in photographs or go to a party and not expect to be harassed and raped. We looked at one another.

I took her hands. 'Beth, you did absolutely nothing wrong. Was it *your* idea to play a drinking game with strong liquor? Those guys knew what they were doing. Don't you dare feel ashamed. *He* should feel ashamed.'

Beth said: 'Lauren, I don't see how that's going to happen. And I'm afraid. We're going to be locked in with those men tonight.'

I thought about stuff my dad told me. About winning. About strategy. I thought about our sorority house. How girls together have an advantage over the boys.

I told her. 'We're not going to be scared of those lowlifes, OK, Beth? They're going to be scared of *us*. And Paul *is* going to feel ashamed, because we're going to fucking *make* him feel ashamed.'

At the end of the day, Beth is my bestie. Always will be. And you don't let a pack of skeevy guys mess with your bestie. It was a rush. We were going to show *all* those fuckers what Alpha Sigma Psi girls are made of.

Beth

We made a plan. Get on the next bus together. Put all this stuff behind us. Right after a little payback.

83

Wooloonga Ridge is stretched out, the sun beating down on its curving features. What started as a walk quickly descended into a trudge. I've underestimated the distance by at least half. My lips are dry, and a slow headache is beginning, but I only took water for an hour-long hike and don't want to risk drinking any more. I can feel sunburn blazing on the back of my neck. The shade of the ridge is a long way off. No sign of a cave entrance.

In under twenty minutes the heat is utterly unbearable. I'm too thirsty to swallow down the lump in my throat and my failure grows on me in increments with every burning step.

I'm going to have to turn around, defeated. The dumb arrogance of coming out here is hitting me. How much could a lone officer even do, if they uncovered some shady brothel set-up?

I assess my situation. It's too hot to go any further. If heat exhaustion kicks in, your mind can play tricks. People have been found dead in the outback with a full bottle of water, a few hundred metres from their vehicles. Better to return to the car.

Beaten, I spin around. There's an emergency ten litres as well as food in the boot. I turn, keeping my direction steady, ready to retrace my steps.

But after an hour and a half walking in the blistering heat, my vehicle is nowhere in sight. Is my navigation wrong? I look at the ridge. Big concentrations of metal can throw off compasses, I'm right by a massive stack of mineral-rich mountains.

My first thought is I'm going to be a complete laughing stock. The policewoman who couldn't use a compass. But it's too late for pride. Better call for help before I become another heatstroke statistic.

Unsurprisingly, my mobile has no reception, so I pull free my police radio, praying it will be Craig receiving on the frequency. But when I buzz in, there's no static, or suggestion of a channel. Just a flat, quiet whine, like the radio's bored with my attempts.

I try for far longer than is necessary.

No signal. Guess not even police equipment works this far into the outback. Desperate, I swing around, hoping to catch a glimpse of the car amongst the low grass and trees. I hoist myself on the lower branch of a eucalyptus and scout around.

Nothing. No car. Only a thousand identical green bushes and shrubs that it could be hidden behind.

Panic arrives, thick and real. No one knows I'm here. I'm stranded miles from anywhere in the forty-five-degree heat.

There's no phone. No radio. Nothing but endless kilometres of searing hot road between me and the nearest civilisation. Even the mine buildings, domineering as they are on the landscape, are an impossible distance on foot.

It's then my eyes catch something low down on the sand. A tell-tale dark splatter where my car air con dripped water as I parked up.

Leading away are fresh tyre tracks. *My* tyre tracks.

A jangle of emotions jarring at my chest I head at a half jog towards them, hope clashing violently against what I already know. The tracks end, then veer off back where they came, in line with a broader, deeper set.

My car was here. Now it isn't.

I follow the tyre tracks with my eyes. They vanish in the direction of the mine.

Many possibilities turn through my overheated brain. I left the keys in the ignition. Was it driven away? Towed?

The heat is affecting my ability to rationalise. Thoughts, rather than connecting, are congealing like treacle. Did someone take my car to stop me investigating the ridge?

Currently only one thing for certain.

I've been left in the desert to die.

84

Lauren

Definitely I'm in a hospital. But . . . my dad is here, admitting he was wrong, which would never happen in real life.

'I know I haven't always done things right,' he says, holding my hand. 'After your mom . . . I was scared I would break down and you would have to see that too. I guess I turned to therapists because . . . well, we didn't have family. Only Grandpappy made it out of Poland.' He takes a shuddering breath. 'But I tried . . . I really fought against medication. It was only when your stepmom . . . She got it through to me kids don't grieve like that for seven years straight.'

I feel the pressure on my hand tighten. 'There are bad people out there, Lauren, and you are so trusting. I should never have let you go.' He releases my hand, and I hear him move away from the bedside. I want to call him back but my body isn't working like it should.

The girls on the reserve used to talk about Dreamtime. How time wasn't still, you know? It moved around. That's how I feel now. Like I've slipped into a time that isn't linear. Back to a childhood with my dad that never happened, but maybe should have. Pieces and fragments of things are floating around. All mixed up.

My stomach hurts so bad. As if electricity is pulsing through or something. And when I open my eyes, everything is tunnel vision.

The doctors are talking.

'The blood results haven't found any large doses of drugs in the system,' they're saying. 'But she has anion gap acidosis, which is consistent with poisoning.'

They start saying something about retinal nerve damage there.

'She's lost one eye already and is losing more vision by the hour,' I hear someone say. 'If we don't figure it out, she'll be permanently blind.'

Then come my Dad's low tones.

'Mr Gottlieb,' says a voice. 'We're doing the best we can. We're doing very extensive bloodwork now for drugs we don't usually test for. It's possible your daughter took a street drug cut with something toxic. But the most likely scenario is she deliberately ingested something a standard blood test wouldn't pick up. We're asking the police for a list of anything she might have feasibly gotten hold of. Photocopier fluid, industrial cleaning products . . .'

'No!' shouts my dad. 'She would *never* do that. Lauren would *never* do that!'

I try and fade it out.

As the shouting quietens off, my mind keeps floating back to the voices I heard in the cave. It's like they climbed out of the past. As though the girl who died on pledge night is haunting me. Trying to warn me that the other girls are dying too.

85

What started as a dull headache has grown to a jolting pain that hurts with every step. My lips are cracked and I can feel the wild throb of my burned neck and arms. Someone my size needs a cup of water every hour to stave off heat exhaustion, and that's not counting my heavy police-issue kit – the thick boots and bullet-proof utility vest. I lift the water bottle again, and find it already bone dry.

'Who drank my water?' I say it out loud, like a joke, and giggle. 'Keep it together, Tara,' I tell myself sternly, imitating Anderson's voice. 'Delusions are the first symptom of heat stroke.'

I'm trying to make it to the shade of the ridge, but it's too far, so I sit in the partial cover of a low shrub. Dizziness overwhelms me and I lay out flat, breathing hard. My body won't cool down. My feet, encased in thick police boots, feel like molten liquid; soft and boneless. My hands have a desiccated feel, like they're becoming part of the dry earth.

Tula's song on Paul's phone, has come into my head.

I'll take you to my precious land, where orange stones run red,
I'll take you to . . .'

I can't remember what comes next, which strikes me as funny. But I shouldn't be singing anyway. It's a waste of water.

I let my eyes close, the boiling noise of a headache growing until it's like a physical presence in my skull.

There's a twittering sound and I open my eyes to slits. Kookaburra, a few branches away. I try to focus on it, and give up. Even lifting my head feels impossible.

'If you're a sign, you're too late,' I tell it, closing my eyes. 'Tell Yindi she should have had a water bottle totem.' I grin at my own joke.

I look up to the cloudless sky, listening to the birdsong, the pain in my head ebbing and flowing. I'm dying, probably.

I hear Yindi's voice.

You gonna lie there whinging, bub?

'Go away, Yindi.' I close my eyes against the burning white sun. 'You left me like all the rest.'

There's a flutter of wings from the nearby bush.

I open my eyes and see Yindi's face, leaning over me, smiling her brilliant, dazzling smile. The sun lights her from behind like she's on fire.

'You're not dying, bub,' she says. 'Take your bloody boots off.'

86

Beth

A police officer has come to my cell, saying Lauren's father wants to talk with me. I consider refusing, but no one will tell me what's happening with Lauren. Is she dead? There's no way Lauren would have snitched. We both took the oath, and if she didn't break it last time a girl died, she's not breaking it now.

Mr Gottlieb is waiting for me in the tiny hot room where they did the interviews. The police leave us alone. He looks utterly broken. You can see the muscles and lines of his face slackening against whatever cosmetic procedures have tidied away his ageing. Like even his money is giving up on him.

To my great surprise, I feel a tug of something I haven't felt in a long while. I feel sorry for him.

He addresses me with a flash of energy, like he's pinning everything on one last push.

'OK,' he says. 'Here's the deal. I can get you anything you want. I'll get you out of here. You can have money. A house. A job, even. Name it. Just . . . tell me what's wrong with my daughter.'

She's still alive then.

'All I can tell you, is what the police already know,' I say. 'We were in a cell together, and I didn't see her take anything.'

A flash of anger shows on his face. 'What kind of person are you?'

'I took an oath,' I tell him steadily. 'I keep my word.'

'They're saying she tried to kill herself.' His face sags in on itself, and his shoulders slump.

'No,' I say automatically. 'Lauren would never do that.'

He lifts his eyes to mine, and something passes between us. Something about Lauren that connects us both.

'Do you know why she's sick?' The words come out loaded with super-human self-control.

I track back the events of the night, wondering whether admitting the truth would break my promise.

'I can't tell you,' I say. I'm always bad at this part. Tone. 'I'm sorry,' I add. Agitated feelings scratch at me. I want to disappear.

Mr Gottlieb considers for a moment, looking confused. Like he's perhaps seeing me differently.

'Your sorority oath?' he says. 'A load of play-pretend with a bunch of silly girls? Are you serious? That's why you're not talking?'

'You have no idea,' I tell him. 'The power behind these organisations. These people run America. They make the decisions. And when their kids mess up and kill someone, they make a few phone calls and everything gets forgotten.'

He pauses, his eyes tracking as though he's processing a lot of things at once.

'If you're scared, I can help you,' he says finally. 'You need to tell me . . .'

I shake my head firmly. 'No, you can't.' I tell him. 'You might be a really good lawyer. You might have great piles of money. But your family are second-generation immigrants. You can't protect me. And besides, it doesn't matter.' I frown. 'I made a promise to Lauren. She's my sister. I'm not going to betray her, even to you.'

87

My mind can no longer be trusted. I know this, because Yindi's face is dancing in front of my eyes, giving me unhelpful advice.

Take your boots off, bub, she repeats.

I blink, and she's gone, replaced by sunspots.

'Come back,' I croak, to the empty air. I close my eyes again, defeated.

It's too hot, and she's wrong anyway. Taking my boots off won't help. The silence of the desert is pressing down on me, like Yindi is waiting out my stubbornness.

'Fine, you win.' I jerk forward with supreme effort, and pull the laces of my right boot. I get the knot undone, but it leaves me dizzy. I take a moment to recover, my head throbbing.

'See?' I tell the blazing sky. 'I can't do it.'

No one answers. Panting, I somehow to get the boot off from the heel, and peel down my sweat-soaked sock. The exercise wipes me out. I lie back, temples pulsing, boot thrown aside.

My lower body is weighted, floppy and hot. Pain sparks through my eye sockets. I could just lay here and sleep, I decide.

'I told you, Yindi,' I mutter. 'I told you I was dying.'

The kookaburra twitters, like it's laughing at me. My bare foot lolls to one side, and the barest whisper of breeze rolls across the exposed skin, like someone has blown on it gently.

I ball my fists. Manage to hoist myself to sitting. Take off the other boot and sock, which is easier to do than the first. With a sweaty hand, I unzip my weighty combat vest and let it thud to the ground. I feel better. Light enough to float. I unbutton my shirt, so I'm dressed only in a T-shirt and police-issue pants.

My head still hurts. But walking doesn't seem as impossible now. I get to my feet, fighting the dizziness.

The kookaburra unhelpfully takes immediate flight and vanishes, as if to say: *I've given you all the help you're getting. You're on your own.*

Bloody Yindi.

My mouth and nostrils are so dry they burn. I struggle to remember something useful from my bushwalks as a kid, concentrating on what's around me. I notice a clump of noon flower not so far away. It's a desert succulent I'd forgotten about. There's moisture in the fat round leaves. Not much but it could stop a person dying of thirst.

I stagger towards it, wrench up a handful and chew. After an initial moist crunch, it's reduced to tough husk, but it helps. I chew more. With the meagre hydration comes a clarity of thought I didn't realise I had been missing. If someone took my car, I decide, someone is frightened of what I might find. And if they're frightened of what I might find . . .

There must be something here.

A single cloud passes over the sun, giving me a few moments of reprieve from the unbearable heat of the day. The realisation gives me new focus. Maybe I can make it to the ridge. It's just a case of putting one foot in front of the other.

Gritting my teeth, I begin the long trek for the rock face, one sweltering step at a time.

As I walk, the song creeps in again. The one Tula was singing in the video taken on Paul's phone.

'Let me take you to my precious land,
Where the rock runs orange red.'

I dismiss it in annoyance, trying to think clearly.

The red rocks stand before me, immovable. Implacable. Unforgiving. Like a closed door.

'Where the rock runs orange red.'

Something links in my mind. The song Mary sang in the long grasses, to make her way through the bush. What if . . . is it the same? A navigation song?

88

Beth

Our last night was a big deal. Everyone knew we'd be on the bus out of Dead Tree Creek the next morning. The strangest thing was, now Lauren had agreed to leave, part of me wanted to stay a little longer. Don't ask me why. Like, those crystal shops and Lucky's Convenience store got in your blood or something. Then there was Mike. He looked so cut up when I told him we were skipping town the next day. I owed him an explanation.

I managed to get him alone right before my shift in the pub. Tried to explain about Paul on the camping trip.

Mike's forehead did this cute thing, like he was thoughtful about it.

I got a little braver, and said I was basically passed out and Paul took advantage. I didn't say anything more than that, but I think maybe Mike got the idea.

Mike

Beth told me she didn't like Paul, and he'd cracked onto her when she was blind drunk. I thought . . . I don't know. I've never been good at reading between the lines. But maybe me and Beth had a chance, you know? Even though she was leaving in the morning. Pretty stupid, right?

Anyway, I told her. 'Beth, don't work so hard on your last shift. Drink all the old bastard's beer. A lock-in is supposed to be a laugh.' She smiled at that. Said her and Lauren had already planned it.

Lauren

We had kind of gone through this bizarre initiation with them, right? They made us feel dumb, and worthless, and made inappropriate comments. So it was our turn. And we had a lot more expertise than those guys gave us credit for. We set up all the sorority tricks, ready in the bar. A bottle of extra hot pepper sauce snuck in amongst normal ones. Loaded dice. And a big tray of mud pies.

Mike

The fellas arrived in the pub. Friday night. We're all having a good time, few drinks, feeling no pain. Lauren and Beth . . . well, they're not acting like barmaids anymore. But for once, Pete doesn't seem to mind. Maybe 'cause the girls got us paying to drink Pete's old bottles of liqueur. All the blackberry and creme de menthe and whatever other piss he keeps behind the bar.

Once we had all the shots lined up, they wanted us to play a game called Buffalo Club.

Beth

Buffalo Club can have a slow start. *Unless*, it transpires, you're a roughneck miner.

The idea is, you have to drink, using only your left hand. If you accidentally use your right hand, and someone sees you, they shout, 'Buffalo Club!' And you have to down your drink, and do a shot. That usually only happens when you're half an hour in, or whatever. But these guys spend all day mining. And it turns out your right hand is pretty important when you're operating the digger. So they had some kind of . . . I don't know. Like a mental block? I've never seen anything like it.

Lauren

It was so, so, so funny. It was like they couldn't help it, you know? We would be whispering, like, *'Mike, don't pick it up with that hand,'* and he still did it. We were literally crying with laughter.

Oh, and Beth and I totally cheated, of course. We had the pinky and thumb of our right hands stuck together with a tiny dab of superglue. Alpha Sigma Psi, boys. Alpha Sigma Psi.

Beth

There were times we were laughing so hard, we couldn't actually say 'Buffalo Club'. Like, barely. Lauren even started waving her glued fingers around. And they *still didn't figure it out*.

Dillon

I tell you what, I never liked that stupid game. I'd say that was around about the time those girls went from being fun, to being a pain the backside. Turns out women have some extra ability to use their left hand or something. The only person who could remember how he got home was Skinny Dave, and he's left-handed.

Lauren

Once we had them all good and drunk it was time for some good old-fashioned retribution. We were just waiting for the guest of honour.

Mike

Paul showed up, absolutely pissed. Most wasted I've ever seen him. With this blotto girl on his arm. Black girl. Stunner, but messy-drunk, you know? She had these big earrings that kept getting caught in her hair. Lauren's face was a picture.

You got the sense that Paul thought he was doing the Black girl a real favour, you know? Bringing her into the pub. But she didn't look too impressed. Didn't matter, 'cause now the tables had turned. The American girls were in charge, and they had all these dares and that.

Lot of the blokes were riled up now, like they had a point to prove. Salvage some male pride, you know?

Beth

Classically, hazing incidents gone wrong start with a line being crossed. But the interesting part, is how the group now gets invested. After one bad decision has been made, the group are more likely to make worse decisions. It's similar to gamblers, who bet to break a lucky streak. The group needs to justify the resources they've already expended, be they financial or emotional. That's when they'll start doing things that are actually dangerous. Lauren and I had them exactly where we wanted them.

89

I've hiked towards the rocks, trying to ignore the spinifex spiking at me. My savaged feet are numb.

The closer I get, the more sure I become. Tula was singing a navigation song. The same song that I found paper clipped to the Wooloonga Ridge documents in the office at the mission.

And as I take in the landscape, with its bent over eucalyptus trees and scruffy foliage, my childhood memories supply the rest of the words like magic.

'Let me take you to my precious land,
Where the rock runs orange red.
By the crippled trees beneath the emu's tail.
To the cave underground with the music and song.'

Immediately, I identify the first marker. Crippled trees. That must be . . . those eucalyptus trees. There's a line of them and I head for that part of the ridge. So far, so good. The success has given me an unexpected lease of energy. OK. Emu's tail. An emu bush? But they're on the ground. The song says the caves are beneath the emu's tail.

Perhaps if I get closer to the rock the puzzle might reveal itself.

In the twitter of bush birds, I hear another noise. The rumble of a far-off vehicle on the mine road, headed this way. My mind feels too dried-out to properly register this as a threat. Most likely, someone from the Mining Corporation took my car, and is returning to make sure I don't find anything.

The sun is moving down finally. I've got an hour or so of light, and the temperature is dropping to something manageable to walk in.

My eyes fall on something as I near the ridge. An old water bottle and a few empty packets of chips, sun-bleached and battered. Someone's been here. Someone who doesn't care about the land. Surely that means I'm on the right track? The plastic bottle has several centimetres of liquid sloshing inside.

I uncap the sandy top and sniff. It smells like sand and not much else. That's good right?

It's not like you have a choice, Tara.

I upend the bottle and sip. Tastes like water and burned plastic. I should be cautious. But the moment fluid hits my lips, some animal instinct kicks in and I gulp uncontrollably. It feels like a magic fountain flowing into my brain.

I drain the dregs, tilting my head back. Stars are beginning to peek through the rosy dusk sky. The outback sunset is putting on a full colour show of electric orange, soft pinks and deep violet. In under half hour the most incredible carpet of rainbow strata will map the inky night.

Yindi told me all the stories of the constellations, and how the first people of Australia used them to navigate. The wedge-tailed eagle, the big goanna, the flight of kookaburras.

I feel very close to her suddenly, like the stars might bridge the way to wherever she is.

'What do you think, Yindi?' I say, speaking aloud. 'Think your ancestors are alright with me finding that cave?'

No answer.

'Well, if you're in the area, put in a good word for me,' I tell her, trying to sound braver than I feel.

More stars are coming out now. A shape you can't see from the city. A long cluster of pinprick lights shaped like an emu in flight. Wait . . . beneath the emu's tail . . .

That's the last part of the navigation song. It's a constellation, I realise, giddy with the revelation. Could it be . . . Is that the answer, to how I find the cave entrance?

Looking up to the sky, I follow how the shape of the constellation appears to be flying up out from the ridge, the wide tail seeming almost to make contact.

There.

I track my eyes straight down, and magically, like an illusion revealing itself, I see it. Just visible by starlight in the striations of the rock. A dark entrance less than a hundred metres away. The cave. I've found it. Victory flushes through me.

It's not far. But now in the distance a flash of light makes me turn. Headlights on the main road. Close enough to see they're high off the ground like a van.

Whoever has driven here from the mine, they're closing in. I set off at a run.

90

Lauren

We hadn't expected Tula to show up. She was wasted and I wondered if Paul had spiked her drink. I could believe anything on him, since what Beth told me. We hadn't locked the doors yet.

Beth

Paul was so drunk, even *I* felt a little sorry for him. And that is saying something. He was basically drooling. Like, bits of saliva were flying out of his mouth when he spoke. He was with Tula. Only she wasn't so beautiful now. She was a wreck. A complete and utter wreck. They were staggering around, Paul with his arm around her waist in this ownership kind of way, that you got the feeling pissed her off, only she was too drunk to do much about it.

Paul was telling everyone his big business had fallen apart. He was slurring about how people always let you down. How he trusted this particular person, the same way he'd trusted his old man. And they'd both gone and done the dirty on him.

Mike

Paul kept saying, 'I'm too drunk. I'm too drunk.' I've never heard him say that before. Not even when he's wet his pants. And the girl he was with . . . man . . . She was *out of it*, you know? I mean, her eyes were rolling up in her head. At one point I saw her put her hand to her mouth, and vom squirted through her fingers, and she just wiped her hand on her shorts.

But something was wrong with Paul other than the grog, you know? He wasn't making a lot of sense, but he was talking about having to report something to the police in the morning. Like, something real bad. He wanted to get out of town. Paul looked scared.

He kind of shook it off and went back to the usual Paul, bragging and all that.

Reckoned he was gonna talk Lauren into a threesome, her last night and all. But it was pretty obvious he was in no fit state to do anything. Started talking the big I am, you know? How all the girls wanted him. Said he'd get Beth involved. Like she was his property.

I told him straight. I said: 'Beth doesn't want anything to do with you, mate. And if you go after her, you'll have me to deal with.'

Paul looked at me, all swaying about, and at one point I thought he might have a pop. Throw a punch or something. He sort of leered instead. Said something not very nice about Beth. I could have laid him out right then. Easy. To be honest, a little tap on his chest and he would have hit the deck. But you know what? That wouldn't have gotten me anywhere with Beth. She wouldn't have liked that at all. And I'm getting a bit old for fighting. It was good enough for me that Paul had shown his true colours. After all these years, I'd never faced off to his bullshit.

When I finally did, I realised he was nothing but hot air.
  We stood there. Me looking at him. Him looking at me.
  Then Beth rang the bell for last orders.

Beth

Pete left. We locked all the doors. That was when things got dialled up a notch.

Lauren

The lock-in had officially started. Beth and I were like: Bring. It. On.

91

Standing alone at the cave mouth, reality is dawning. It's almost fully night now. My radio doesn't work and my only weapon is a bush knife and a gun I can barely shoot. Whoever took my car, they're not messing around. But the dark entrance holds its own terrors. The stars twinkle above. A scatter of little kookaburras.

Swallowing hard, I recite the permission to enter I remember Yindi's uncles stating on sacred land, paying respects to Moodjana people as custodians, and ancestors past and present.

My request is met with silence. I stare into the black.

'I don't want to go in there alone, Yindi,' I whisper. 'I'm scared.'

I know, bub. But it's the only way. It's her voice, clear as if she was whispering in my ear. *You go fight for me in there.*

Then she's gone.

Approaching engine noise finishes the decision process. I turn to see the headlights bobbing in the middle distance. Quickly, I move forward into the cave.

Three steps in and the stars vanish leaving me in pitch darkness. There is a distinct change in the atmosphere. A muggy dampness too sudden to be natural. It's a smell with a physical presence. Like . . . I almost can't describe it. Something I've smelled recently and didn't like.

Sounds float towards me from the deep interior. It's occupied.

With shaking hands I take out my phone and turn on the flashlight, pointing it down to avoid alerting someone in the cave to my presence.

My heartbeat picks up as I step forward. I'm straining to hear, when a loud shrieking sound spills from deeper inside. I move back on instinct, heart racing, phone-torch spilling light sideways, hand fumbling for my gun. What the . . .?

It sounded like a woman. Screaming. Someone is being hurt down here.

I breathe out, raising my weapon one-handed into the dark and force my feet to walk forward.

I take in a bright new sign, announcing, DANGER OF FALL-ING ROCKS. And another that says: NO ENTRY. UNSTABLE CAVE STRUCTURE. They're official, and stamped with the Mine Corporation's logo.

You can see how digger damage has destabilised the rocky roof overhead. Wooden struts are crossed over, forming loose supports, but they have a very impermanent feel.

I move past the warnings into a narrower tunnel. My light throws up leering shadows and a path ahead.

Sounds come from deeper within. I stand still and black-out my phone. There's a sudden crashing of metal on metal, close, as if it's coming from right around the corner.

Did something give me away? The earlier screams have fallen to silence.

Keeping my light off, I put my hands out unsteadily and my bare feet feel out the rocks.

The familiar smell is getting stronger. Something long and hairlike drifts across my face, and I jump back, a scatter of stones falling on my head.

It's just tree roots growing down through the roof, I realise, as my hands close around a stringy clump, although my heartbeat won't seem to agree with what my mind is telling it. Putting out exploratory hands I find there are lots of them as I move through this part. Some feathery, hanging in drifts like curtains. Others thick as fingers. I pick my way through, feeling with my feet the scatter of loose rocks. The ceiling above is splitting apart where the Mining Corporation have damaged the caves, and roots are breaking through. The temporary supports aren't strong enough.

The tunnel widens and now there's a low light in the distance. Sweat breaks out on my forehead.

I have the worst feeling. Like I'm being watched. As if someone could spring out on me at any moment.

Paul and Tula's tortured remains flash in my memory. I tighten my grip on my gun, wishing I had better confidence in my shooting ability.

There's a disjointed clanging sound. Rhythmic. The unexpected noise makes me step back, accidentally shouldering into one of the wooden supports. I feel it nudge out of position followed by a weighty chunk of ceiling. I dodge the falling rock, and my ankle catches on a tree root. I trip and as I do, my gun goes flying.

The entrance behind me is collapsing freely now. A scatter of sand and pebbles rain, then larger debris explodes on the ground. My exit is rapidly filled, and my dropped gun buried with it.

I glance back helplessly. Whoever is in the cave must have heard me now. But the only way is forward. Abandoning any attempt at stealth I pound towards the sound and the light, hoping for a hiding place when I arrive.

92

Mike

We were all doing shots. Dares and that. Truth or dare. That's how I know that Lauren can drink a whole bottle of pepper sauce and Beth didn't lose her virginity until she was twenty.

Lauren

We had all the guys drinking pepper sauce, and naturally big alpha Paul wasn't going to turn down a dare. But . . . what we didn't tell him, was we'd totally rigged the bottles. Half were real deal, half were Bloody Mary mix, and one was our own Alpha Sigma Psi ghost-chilli brand. Paul Hunter was going to get a full dose of the sorority special.

Beth

Drunk as he was, Paul was smarter than we thought because he switched bottles with Dillon. Then took the bottle that was supposed to be for me. Dillon looked like he was going to die.

He was choking and sweating and his eyes were bulging, crying. He kept twitching his head like a dog or something. In front of all his buddies too. Paul's eyes were dead drunk, taking it all in. I knew then we couldn't get him. Like my mom says, you can't trick a trickster. Then Lauren had a good idea. Something Paul couldn't slide out of, 'cause everyone would have to do it.

Dillon

Lauren got us on this game called 'Look, No Hands'. Like a blowjob stripper thing on the bar with Pete's pink liqueur. It was like this dare we were all doing, only Lauren did it the best. I don't remember how it worked. Only somehow all of us ended up having to crawl across the bar on all fours, pick up a bottle with our teeth, then tip it up and down without using our hands.

Mike

Lauren did it better than anyone. She had this little sexy wiggle. It was like watching a show you'd pay for, only free, you know? Bloody *brilliant*.

There were some fluffy pink handcuff things involved, I think. Then they wanted us to play a game called 'Mud Pies'.

93

As I run from the collapsing roof, the tunnel curves, and I emerge in a cavern. Not vast, but sizeable.

A nearby central rock formation provides a little cover. I edge around the side of it, staying out of view.

From my vantage point, I can see a small generator rumbling away. It's joined to a string of industrial-looking lights, hooked untidily along the ceiling. The smell is much stronger and I recognise it now. Alcohol. It reminds me of The Gold Rush.

I wait, listening. Besides the generator are loud clanking sounds. No voices. No discernible footsteps.

I sweep the area for somewhere better to hide, creeping carefully out from behind the rock.

My attention is on the wider surroundings. Plastic barrels. A great metal vat, with tubes and pumps poking from the top. Another larger one behind it, all stainless steel. On the far wall is a crate of empty glass bottles. They are labelled, and I make out two familiar vodka brands.

Bootleg grog. *It's an illegal distillery.*

As I stand there, a shrieking sound emits from the large tank. I cover my ears. It's awful. Steam rushes out and the noise stops. My breathing slows a fraction. This was the tortured cry I heard before. It sounded so *human*, so female. I'd laugh if I wasn't paralysed with terror. The distillery is still operational. Someone very much alive is still running the place.

Are they here now? I keep very, very still. Nothing.

I arrange my thoughts based on the new information. Bootleggers are cooking up grog down here. A lot of grog.

That explains the cave location. Constant temperatures. Good humidity.

The steel vat is really big. Industrial size. I switch my attention to the bottles instead, which are arranged twelve per crate, and total around three hundred.

I don't know how much vodka sells for. But I'm guessing you could make at least $20 a bottle. And the government's 'banned drinkers' make the perfect client base, I think grimly. Plenty of people willing to pay retail price for an illegal supply, and never dob in the seller.

The mystery of the missing girls tugs at me. This isn't a brothel, that much is clear. My mind switches to whoever is driving along the mine road. They won't be able to get in where the ceiling collapsed. Is there another entrance? The cavern has several dark exits that could lead anywhere.

A static buzz at my chest jolts me out of my thinking. My radio. I adjust the dial with a shaking hand.

A fuzzy voice sounds. 'Tara? Tara? Do you copy?' It's Craig. My heart lifts. I can't believe it.

I put the radio to my mouth and whisper. 'Craig? Are you there?'

Nothing but jagged static. He's gone.

'Constable Harrison for Constable Dooligan,' I keep my voice low, but the sound will be like chum for a shark if anyone is hiding out deeper in the cave network.

No answer. I try again, loud as I dare, desperate. 'Craig? *Craig?* Do you copy?'

This time static comes back. I fiddle with the dial, tuning in.

'Tara! Are you OK?' Craig is on a steady signal. The concern in his familiar voice makes me unexpectedly emotional. For a few seconds I struggle to dislodge a tight lump in my throat.

'Yeah,' I cough. 'I'm in a cave at Wooloonga Ridge. How the hell are you receiving me?'

'I'm kind of in the area.'

'What?'

'Connolly's car was gone. Anderson was pacing round like a bear with a sore head. I put two and two together. Thought you could use some back-up. I drove in this direction. Kept turning the radio on and off until I picked up your signal.'

'I've found something in the caves,' I tell him. 'An illegal distillery.'

'Tara, get out of there, now,' he says. 'If it's operational, there'll be dangerous people around.'

'I don't know if I can,' I tell him. 'There was a rock fall the way I came in.'

'Did anyone see you go in?' He sounds desperate. 'Does anyone know you're in there alone, Tara?'

'Someone took Connolly's car,' I admit. 'And I saw a van headed this way on the mine road.'

'*Fuck.*' I can almost picture Craig's stricken face. 'OK, OK. Just . . . hide, right? I'm coming down. I'll be . . . I dunno, maybe fifteen minutes. Can you stay hidden that long?'

'I think so.' It's a creepy thought.

'You're not injured or anything?'

'No.'

'OK, I'm going to drive to the ridge and try to follow your tracks. Find another way in. Whatever you do, don't go looking around alone. Keep out of sight. Promise? Promise me, Tara?'

The signal cuts out. I switch the dial a few times, but it's gone.

I collect my thoughts. Time to act like a proper police officer. Map the scene. Identify hazards. I take out my notepad, and draw a rough sketch of my location as I understand it so far.

Temporary generator. If it gives out, no light. I look towards the entrance. Unstable rocks. Hanging tree roots. Could bring more of the ceiling down if you got tangled . . .

I make a sweep of the ground.

That's when I notice something on the floor. Empty Coke bottles are discarded all over. But one has rolled to the far edge of the cave, where it lays like a pointing finger.

In the artificial light, a distinctive shape is reflected inside the plastic.

A booted foot almost out of view. Someone is hiding in the shadows. Listening.

94

Mike

Lauren comes off as a bit of a hippy, doesn't she? Like a surfer chick. But I tell you what, there's a competitive streak there.

About an hour after the pub was locked up, all us guys had our shirts off, 'cause you got covered in grog from the game, you know? Paul could barely get up on the bar. His coordination was all shot.

The Black girl managed better than him. But you felt wrong watching her, you know? She was so out of it. The booze went all over her. Lauren took a picture, and I realised she must have been doing that the whole time.

To be honest, it made me think about how we'd acted towards the girls. Truth is, I would be embarrassed if those pictures of me got around. I'm pretty cuddly without a shirt on, and I can see the fellas down the mine ripping me for what I was doing to that bottle.

Anyway, all of a sudden, I look around, and *April* is in the pub. I don't know how, because it was a lock-in, right? But there she is. You could have cut the atmosphere with a knife.

Paul sees her. Has this shit-eating grin, like he knows he's been caught doing something he shouldn't. The Black girl is on the pokie machine, pushing in money and not even collecting her winnings. Just watching the numbers spin. April doesn't clock her. Only got eyes for Lauren, who is on the bar, giving this bottle a blowjob.

From nowhere, Beth walks across the pub. Tells April that the pub's closed, in this sharp little voice. You can tell she's nervous and she gets all polite about it, you know?

April lost it. Started throwing punches. Beth put her arms over her face and took it, like it this wasn't new for her. Reminded me of this rescue dog my dad got once, that had been kicked around. Used to lie there, rigid, waiting to get hit.

I have never wanted to save a girl more than I did in that moment.

Lauren was screaming at April. I got in the middle to break it up, but Beth was kind of . . . gone, you know? On another planet.

The rest of the blokes are sniggering, looking at Paul. He's standing up, ready to leave.

I got Beth sat down, and she's normal again. Like no harm done. She looked at Lauren, and something passed between them. Some girl thing.

Then Lauren gets up on the bar, and is doing this . . . like a striptease or something.

Obviously for Paul's benefit, but who's gonna complain?

She'd got as far as peeling her top off, when April starts screeching. Goes for Lauren. Couple of blokes basically hustled April out. I feel bad about that now. But we'd all had a few, and it looked like Lauren was about to get naked.

I think it was about that time that Paul and Tula left, but I couldn't tell you for sure.

We were all watching Lauren.

Dillon

The rest of the night . . . I dunno. It's all a bit of a blur. I went out after April. To check she was OK, you know? Lauren and Beth were gone for a while. I remember that 'cause there was this rumour that Lauren planned to do a gang-bang on the last night, and none of us wanted to miss it.

Beth was back in the bar looking proper crook. Lauren was kind of . . . buzzing, you know? Like she had this secret joke. They'd look at each other and say, 'Mud pies' and crack up laughing.

April

Dillon came out to see if I was alright. One thing led to another. I was just grateful, I guess. Afterwards, Dillon had to go back into the pub, 'cause he didn't want Paul finding out. As I walked away . . . yeah . . . it was a bit strange – there was a bashed-up car with a bloke sat inside. I caught a flash of a pair of mirrored sunnies under the streetlamp.

Beth

'Mud Pies' is essentially a team sport. You take your shirt off and are tied to a chair with duct tape, hands behind your back. Your teammate feeds you stale super-dry brownies. Winner is the group who finishes their food first. I had been setting up the brownies right before April arrived.

Looking back, I don't know what had gotten into us. 'Mud Pies' sounds like an innocent game, but once you get started, it can get intense. Especially if someone gets competitive, and we'd spent the last hour beating up on those guys' masculine pride. Drunk players can wind up almost suffocating a teammate, and they can't tell you, because their mouth is full. Both Lauren and I knew exactly how scary and dangerous that felt, because it had been done to us.

Lauren

We wanted to hurt those guys, I'm not going to lie. Neither of us was in a good place at the time. At the pledge night with Beth, I needed her to make a good show at the initiation, because I'd seen how girls who didn't got treated. I was doing it for her. But the men in the pub . . . that was war. It's like my dad says: *If you're going to hit someone, hit them so hard they don't get up. Otherwise, you'd better be a fast runner.* And we had nowhere to run.

95

I look at that boot for a long time. Whoever owns it must have heard everything over the radio. Moving as lightly as possible, I creep nearer, trying to get a better look around the corner. The light falls on the edge of a dirty mattress. Worn and stained with oily patches and raggedy brown-edged water marks. Littered around are empty food packages. Potato chip and lolly wrappers. Spent vodka bottles.

Fuck. Someone is living down here . . .

My heart is smashing about in my ribcage. I tread softly, my feet making no sound on the stony ground. The hidden boot slides into view with its attached bare leg.

It isn't moving.

The skin is mottled with broken veins. I catch the sob before it comes out, and force myself closer, visually connecting the limb, crooked at an angle, to a torso.

Leaned against the wall is a dead girl.

My eyes glide to mattresses.

Another lifeless girl is laid flat. Purpled skin like the first. Are these the missing girls? Keira, Medika and Charlee? I glance around for a third girl, but she isn't here.

Fuck. *Fuck.*

I'm too late. The enormity of it makes me want to sink to the ground and give up.

Anderson's voice floats into my mind. *Stay calm. Assess the scene. Say what you see.*

I gulp air. Speak aloud. 'Two bodies. Both female with dark hair and skin. Ethnicity appears to be Indigenous.' My voice catches, and I gasp, covering my mouth with my hand.

What's next? I can't remember.

You can do better than that, Harrison.

From a resistant part of my brain, I wrestle free the next step. *Wounds.*

'No visible injuries. No stab wounds, or spilled blood. No signs they were trying to escape or defend themselves.'

How did they die? I can't think of a single theory. I came here for answers, and only found more questions. I move closer. 'What happened to you?' I whisper, in Moodjana, to the body leaned against the wall.

I don't know why I say it. It's not like I'm expecting an answer from a dead girl.

So it's even more surprising, when she opens her eyes.

96

Lauren

From nowhere, it looked like Paul was totally about to dump both me and Tula. For *April*. Who has a face like a fake crocodile-skin purse. On my last night. And, yes, admittedly, I didn't have feelings for Paul at this point, but I was still like, *no way*.

I guess I got carried away with my performance on the bar, because Paul vanished, and no one knew where he was. Tula was also missing. Paul had left without playing any of the games. He'd gotten away with it. With what he did to Beth. To *me*. I felt mad enough to do something violent to Paul, and I don't feel bad admitting that. Most people would feel the same, in that situation.

That was when I noticed Beth was standing alone. She was looking at the photograph wall of all the previous barmaids. Only now there was a new photo.

Beth

I don't remember the picture being taken. It was us, only . . . it didn't look like us. We looked exactly like all the other girls.

Lauren

We were so completely drunk in that picture. Beth looked at me. She said: 'Is that me?' In this tiny little girl voice. 'No,' I said. 'It isn't you. It's what they want you to be.' Her shoulders were shaking, like her body was crying without her face taking part. I decided to take her up to the apartment to calm down. It never occurred to me that might be a bad idea. Anyone could follow us up there.

We opened the door with the broken lock, and there was a boozy smell in the air. Like, worse than usual. Beth flipped on the lights. And there they were. Paul and Tula. Sitting on the sofa, but totally crashed out. They were kind of leaning into one another, like they'd fallen unconscious in separate spheres and their bodies had converged without meaning to.

Their heads were touching. There was a cheap bottle of vodka lying between them, clutched in Tula's hand, like some messed-up family snapshot; Mom, Dad, and baby-booze.

Beth

It was dark inside, and the windows were rattling. Bluey had parked his road train right outside the window with the engine running. Again.

Paul was snoring so loud, it was like, how can he not wake himself up? You could hear it over the truck noise. I suspected drugs, because they looked a lot like the passed-out heroin addicts I used to see when I worked an early shift at the convenience store.

Paul's phone was continually flashing through the check material of his shirt pocket. It would stop for a few seconds then start over. Like someone was repeatedly calling him on speed dial.

Lauren had this look on her face. If I was to summarise, I would call it a look of final reckoning.

She stalked across the room, and slid out his phone. Lauren stood there for a minute, scrolling, with this bizarre smile on her face. Right at that moment, like perfectly timed, Bluey finally cuts the engine. So there's this eerie silence, overlaid by Paul's guttural snoring.

Then Lauren starts laughing, but it's a horrible sound. It went on and on. Like she was evil or something. Her reaction reminded me of the sorority night.

Lauren

Firstly. Yes. I am dumb enough to fall for a guy who uses six zeros as his pin code.

Second. Oh my gosh. His phone? There was all this sketchy stuff. Like he was obviously messaging a lot of women, which wasn't as big a shock as it might have been.

There were messages from Tula. Not assigned to any named contact. But I knew it was her. She said some mean things about me. How I wasn't a good kisser.

There was also a thread from his work colleagues. It was this list of orders from the other men, basically. Like sexual ones. And videos. Of me and him.

I breathed out. It's a rehab trick, like when you're feeling completely overwhelmed. It was so much information and I was *so* drunk. Now I was looking at Paul in a new way, and all muddled in with that was a grief too. Because the betrayal was so deep, and I could never, never *un*-see him that way.

I felt the exact same when I found out how my mom died.

Beth says, 'Check the dates.'

They all matched with the times I met up with Paul. From what I can remember, we did a lot of that stuff too.

Paul had been taking requests like I was his little toy or something, to be passed around.

For a second I feel cold all over. Then I'm like, *so what?* There's a bunch of guys jerking off over me. It makes me feel almost powerful, in actual fact. Like maybe I should be a porn star.

Beth is staring at me with this weird expression, and I'm humming all over. Buzzing, almost, you know? Beth's like, Lauren, don't do anything stupid. And I'm like, why would I? I don't care? We're out of here tomorrow and we'll never see any of these guys again.

But as I'm speaking, another message pops through.

97

The cave doesn't feel so dark and cold anymore. The dead girl is alive.

Her brown eyes are on mine, not focused, but open. I drop down and rest two fingers to the artery at her neck.

'It's OK,' I tell her. 'I'm going to get you out. What's your name?'

'M . . . Med . . .' She's not in a good way. I can barely make vital signs.

'Medika? You're Medika?' It's her. I've found her.

Her eyes track to where the second girl lays on the mattress. I move quickly over. Her pulse is so weak I hardly feel it. But it's there. A slow, limping flutter in the veins. The relief is indescribable. They're both alive. I just need to keep them that way.

'Can you hear me?' She's completely unconscious. I get her into recovery position before switching back to Medika, whose eyelids are flickering.

'No . . . police,' she croaks. Her breathing grows noticeable. Laboured. Frightened.

I take her hands. 'We're not all bad guys. I'm here to help. I swear.' Her breath calms slightly. 'Were there three of you down here?' I ask. 'Is there another girl?'

She moves her head down in a nod, eyes drooping with the

effort. 'Char . . . lee,' she manages. 'With him.'

'Someone took her? Who?'

Her eyes start to close.

'Do you know what made you sick?' My eyes drift to both girls' strange mottled skin. Broken veins.

'Medika, Medika! Stay with me. Did you take anything? Drugs?'

I'm looking round the cave for drug paraphernalia. Evidence she might have OD'd. Other possibilities track through. Hypothermia? It's not so cold, but if she's been down here for days . . .

I fiddle with my radio. 'Craig? Do you copy?' He's out of range again. I switch to the emergency frequency.

'This is Tara Harrison of Dead Tree Creek police,' I say. 'If anyone can hear me, I've found two very sick girls, a possible third still missing, and an illegal vodka distillery out in the caves at Wooloonga Ridge. I need urgent medical assistance, over.'

Nothing. Then I hear a whispering sound from where Medika is laying.

She's trying to say something. I strain to hear. It sounds like . . .

'Gr . . . Gr . . . o . . . g.'

'Grog? Medika, did you say "grog"?' I notice there's an empty vodka bottle a half metre away from her. Like it's rolled out of her hand. Does she have alcohol poisoning?

'Need . . . grog.' She huffs it out all at once, like a supreme effort, closes her eyes and breathes heavily.

She wants grog?

'Medika, you're sick. I don't think grog is a good idea. But I'll get you a medic, and . . .'

In answer, Medika's eyelids drop shut.

Shit. *Think, Tara. Think.*

Lauren. She's sick too. And she warned me about the cave, didn't she? Several pictures forge together in my brain. The warning posters I grew up seeing on the mission.

HOMEBREW CAN BE DEADLY! METHO THE SILENT KILLER.

The illegal distillery. That's homebrew grog, isn't it? On a large scale but even so . . . Backstreet distillers sometimes muck up, or contaminate a batch with methanol, don't they?

My mind buzzes back to the lock-in.

Two nights ago.

Methanol can take up to three days for symptoms to appear.

Meth poisoning. I'm suddenly sure of it. Lauren has meth poisoning.

Medika's eyes open again, tracking in my direction. Something's wrong with her focus, I realise.

'You have to go,' she croaks. 'He's coming. He's coming back to kill us.'

'Who?'

Her eyes are sliding shut. She shakes her head.

'Medika. Who's coming?'

Before she can answer, I hear a man's voice.

98

Beth

Beth

Lauren was staring at the message from April. It was just some shit about picking up milk or something. But Lauren starts scrolling up. And there's one from Paul to April. Basically saying Lauren is a dumb ho-bag. And this gooey stuff calling April his 'possum'.

Lauren had this expression . . . I'll never forget it. Like she'd been sleeping the whole time and only just then had woken up.

One by one all the little muscles in Lauren's face contract. It was actually fascinating to watch. A hundred little lifts, culminating in extreme rage. She hurled the phone across the room and it smashed in the corner. For a moment she stared in the direction she threw it, breathing through her nose like an angry bull. She turned back to Paul, passed out and drooling on the sofa.

Lauren

All his messages to her were the exact same things he sent to me. He even called her 'possum'.

I snapped. Definitely. I mean, how much bad treatment can you take?

It was like reality dawned. This shitty guy, who I'd let fuck me every which way, was passing me over for nasty little April. And then decides to break into my apartment, for one last spin with Tula. Like, *what the actual fuck?*

I remember getting madder, and madder and madder.

Can't recall the exact words I said to Beth. But I had an idea.

Beth

Lauren's eyes had this dangerous glitter to them. Like right before she's about to do something stupid. And she was like, *Beth*. Shall we get our own back?

It was just bad timing that Bluey's truck was at that moment pulled up outside, right under our window.

We'd asked him not to park there, because it disturbed our sleep. Sometimes he did, sometimes he didn't. Dumb luck that on that particular night, he'd forgotten to be considerate.

Lauren

It seemed like serendipity, you know? Like it had happened for a reason. Where the truck parked you could more or less step out on the top of the tarpaulin. Assuming it would take your weight, and it looked like it would.

Beth

Lauren was snickering. Like, 'I have this great idea.' And I'm like, 'What?' And she raises her finger to her lips, and whispers – and she's giggling so hard it's difficult to understand her at first. She says: 'Let's take Paul's clothes off, and load him on Bluey's truck.'

I looked at her. 'Well,' I said, 'that would be worse than "Mud Pies".' We just started laughing.

Lauren

It was such a funny idea at the time. We knew that Bluey's first stop was at the Aboriginal reserve, on the highway out of town. Paul would find himself stranded, stark naked, with a group of virtual strangers staring at him. It was like, *the best* revenge. Worse than the 'Mud Pies' game. That's what we kept saying to one another. *Worse than 'Mud Pies'.*

He was so heavy. I was absolutely sure he would wake up. When we got him to the window, I noticed I still had the pink handcuffs attached to my wrists, so I put those on him too. We were hysterical with laughter at that point. Completely hysterical.

Beth

Then we look at Tula. And it seemed, like, *what do we do with her?*

We figured if we loaded her on, too, she'd get a free ride back to the reserve. There was some messed-up logic at play, and probably an element of fuck-you-too, since she'd played us. But it wasn't like we were stripping her naked or anything.

It all seemed unreal, you know? It didn't seem dangerous, or stupid. Just like we were letting loose, and we didn't want to stop. We didn't want to go back to being those girls behind the bar, saying 'ha ha ha,' out loud.

We didn't think about what would happen when Paul got to the reserve. Or if he and Tula woke up and came back for us before we got the bus the next morning. We didn't think about anything like that.

We laid Tula carefully on top of the truck. Put a blanket over her.

Lauren got her brightest lipstick, and scrawled 'Alpha Sigma Psi' on the wall. It seemed funny at the time.

We went back down to the lock-in. When we came back a few hours later, Bluey had driven away.

We crashed out. Fell asleep. Truth be told, I don't think Lauren even remembered we'd done it.

99

Medika and I are both listening to the male voice, echoing through the cave.

I'm crouched low, her eyes are wide with terror.

'Tara?' It sounds familiar now, coming, bizarrely, from above my head. For a second I look at my silent radio, confused. I look up to see rocky ceiling.

'Tara? It's Craig!'

The relief is indescribable.

'Craig?' I'm shouting. 'I'll be right back,' I tell Medika. I walk in search of the voice.

'Up here,' he shouts. 'I don't think you can see me. I saw a vent pipe sticking out of the rock, came to take a look. I'm at a shaft on the roof. Hold tight, Tara, I'm going to get you out.'

I angle my head towards the top of the cavern, tracking where the distillation equipment vents out. There's a long, dark shaft leading up.

'Up there?' I tilt my head.

'Yep. I can see you even if you can't see me,' calls Craig, much clearer now. 'It's really narrow where I'm looking down.'

Everything hits me all at once and unexpectedly, tears flood my eyes. For a second, I can't talk, I'm so happy to hear his voice.

I take a breath. 'There's two really sick girls down here,' I say. 'The ones from the long grasses.'

'Fuck. What's wrong with them?'

I glance back. 'Meth posing, I think they've got meth poisoning. From the illegal distillery. I think that's why Lauren is sick too.'

'OK, I'll radio for the air ambulance and get a message out that Lauren has meth poisoning. Just a moment.' I hear him call it in, then he's back.

'I told the air ambulance two girls, a possible third,' he says. 'It was three girls went missing, right? You don't see her down there?'

'No.'

Craig hesitates. 'OK. We need to get you out. Give me a sec. I've got stuff to winch you up.'

'You travel with a rope-winch and harness?'

'Standard issue out in the bush,' he calls down. 'I bring it wherever there's rocks.'

'I can't leave the girls down here,' I tell him.

Craig pauses. 'Is there another way out?'

'Not that I know of,' I say. 'The main entrance is blocked.'

'Then we wait for the medics. Can't risk moving them up this shaft.'

'I'll stay with them.'

'You want me to abandon you down there?' Craig's voice rises an octave. 'No fucking way. Tara, please. Come out, OK? You've done all you can. You've taken all the risks, proved you're better than all of them. Work with me, for once.'

'It's not about proving myself.'

'Bullshit,' says Craig angrily. 'Police procedure is to put you and your colleagues first, alright? If you think I'm leaving you here in some bloody . . . criminal's lair.'

I hear a strap being ratcheted, a slap of rope hitting wall, and the gentle buzz of it being lowered.

The harness lands on my feet in a spray of dust, the line settling in a coil on top.

'I can't leave them alone.'

There's a loaded pause, and when Craig speaks, his voice is strained.

'OK, I didn't want to tell you. But a Mining Corporation van pulled up at the bottom of the ridge a few minutes ago. Five blokes with guns. They haven't seen me yet, but they will if I stay up here. And I'm not leaving without you.'

Fuck.

'Tara,' Craig sounds calm and clear, 'you can't help those girls by dying with them. The pair of us, we can hide out at a distance. Guard this vent until reinforcements come.'

I breathe out. 'Alright,' I say finally. 'Alright, you win. I'll come up.'

100

Beth

I woke up and couldn't see Lauren anywhere.

Second thing was that the streetlight from the window was blocked. Took me a long moment to realise why. Bluey's truck had come back.

I wasn't exactly sober, but I was less drunk than when I'd fallen asleep.

The memories of what we'd done came flooding back, but with a new anxious edge. What if Paul came back before we left?

Sitting up in bed, my worst fears were immediately confirmed. Lauren was gone.

Our super-funny prank now took on a different perspective. Just like that I was afraid. Like *really* afraid.

Where was Lauren?

This bad thought took hold of me. I was sure Paul and Tula had come back and were hurting Lauren.

I got up, looked around the apartment. She wasn't there. I went down to check the bar, which we hadn't locked. Empty. Total mess. We hadn't bothered to clean up after our shift. *Ha. Screw you, Pete.* Only it wasn't so funny now. Obviously.

It was dark, and for some reason, I didn't want to put the

lights on. I think on some level maybe I thought that would make it real.

That's when I heard noises from below. From the cellar. And I just knew. I knew what I'd find, even before I started down the ladder.

It didn't occur to me to call the police or anything rational like that. I just knew I had to get down there and stop it happening.

I gave zero thought to how I would do that. Had I have been in a better state of mind – a more sober state of mind – it would all have been different. I wouldn't have done what I did.

Obviously.

But I went down there, and I saw . . . I saw what had happened. Paul and Tula hadn't hurt Lauren. She had hurt them. And I had no idea *how*. Because there were two of them, right?

Then I had this kind of flashback, almost. My own sorority night. I remembered the look on Lauren's face as she stuffed brownies in my mouth. It was like she wasn't there.

Now it looked as though Lauren had somehow done it again. Only this time, there hadn't been anyone to stop her.

101

I feel the rope tense on my harness, and I'm lifted with strong surety off the ground.

'Hang in there,' shouts Craig. 'I'm going as fast as I can, OK?'

'OK.' I try to mentally prepare myself, remembering the labourious process from training.

Slowly, Craig begins winding me up the shaft. He's right, he is quick. Craig must be attacking the crank like his life depends on it.

'How long is the ascent?' I can make out a few stars right at the top, a long way away.

'About fifteen metres. I reckon . . . Fifty per cent chance of surviving the drop if something snaps.'

'Thanks. Reassuring.'

'No worries. What do you reckon's been going on?' asks Craig, his voice tight with exertion.

'I'm hanging on a line in the dark, Craig, can we talk about it later?'

'Standard rescue procedure. Keep them talking,' he puffs out. 'Usually, I chat celebs or footie. But you don't strike me as a reality TV kind of girl.'

I manage a smile in the gloom.

'Are you gonna tell me, or what?' demands Craig, catching

his breath. "Cause it's a fair way up. OK. How about I start? If Lauren and those girls have methanol poisoning, why aren't they dead already? They would have drunk the grog, what, two days ago?'

'There's a one-to-three-day window for symptoms, and Lauren was drinking heavily. Alcohol neutralises meth. It would have delayed onset.' I turn my thoughts to the dying girls in the cave. 'Medika and her friends grew up on the reserve so they would have known strong grog is an antidote,' I say, remembering the empty vodka bottle near Medika. 'Maybe some of a good batch got left over and they shared it, bought some time.' I squint up at the opening as Craig makes my painfully slow ascent. 'Can you see the men from the Mining Corporation?'

'I'm supposed to be stopping you panicking, not the other way around. Tell me about the cave.'

Guess that means they're close.

I think for a moment. 'Whoever runs the distillery has been supplying the local reserve,' I say, remembering the mysterious presence of mining vans. 'But I think the distribution must be wider than that, to account for so much grog. Paul would have had access to Mining Corporation vehicles, but . . . someone else must have delivered further afield.' It's working, I realise. The talk is taking my mind off the rope. More facts are coming together.

'How do you reckon the girls got down here?' asks Craig.

My mind flashes to how Medika was dressed. Heavy boots. Not standard issue for teenagers.

'It's possible the girls were working,' I decide. 'Voluntarily, or coerced. Or maybe both,' I add. 'Maybe they agreed to the work, and something changed their minds and they ran away. That would explain why they hid out at the long grasses.'

The rope stops.

'Hang on a sec. Muscle spasm,' says Craig. 'Give me a minute.'
I hang, suspended in the dark.

'OK, better now,' he says through gritted teeth. I picture him extending his cramped arm.

The rope begins winding up again. I think some more. 'Someone is keeping it operational after Paul's death,' I tell him. 'I feel like . . . We're missing something.' As I say it, I can almost feel something skitter away from me. My thoughts return to Medika, alone in the cave, then it hits me.

A distillery puts the Mining Corporation in the clear, doesn't it? There's no way a multimillion-dollar company would mess around with a few thousand dollars of illegal grog. So who has arrived with guns?

102

Beth

What would you do? Your bestie has killed someone. It wasn't her fault – for complicated reasons only you and her will ever truly understand, but *you alone* have the chance to get her out of trouble. You'd do it, right?

I had some momentary ethical conflict. Then I remembered the sorority oath. Lauren was my sister, and I'd sworn to keep her secrets. I was, in fact, *obligated* to cover for her.

This was a relief, because I was remembering how Lauren barely made it through the pledge night court case. Her sanity was hanging by a thread. And there'd be no sorority to protect her from journalists this time. The press would paint her as this evil femme fatale or something. That wasn't her. She wasn't like that. We'd been through some fucking awful shit together and that changes you.

But for Lauren it would be like a nightmare that would never go away.

So . . . make it go away.

One of my strengths is staying logical in situations other people find emotional. I assessed the facts. Paul was last seen blind drunk. Tula was like me. No family to miss her. If I could hide the bodies, it would be a few days at least until anyone noticed them gone. I could get Lauren on a plane out of the country in that time. Just so long as we caught that bus, first thing in the morning.

I have always been a practical person. Unpleasant jobs don't usually bother me. But, the problem was, I knew I couldn't *actually* touch a dead body. The old mine shaft was less than six feet away, but it might as well have been a mile.

I found myself looking at Tula's beautiful face. It was all battered, and her mouth was full of dirt. I never saw the girl who died on pledge night, but maybe this is how she would have looked.

Then just like that, my body did that thing. *Something bad is happening, Beth. Go someplace else.*

So I did. And my body took care of what needed to be done, without checking in with my mind. Turned out I could move a corpse after all – or at least, some facet of myself could.

I have some scattered images of a person dragging Tula across the floor. The person's movements are shaky, like they're drunk and their body is not cooperating.

I have a clear image, viewed from above of a struggle to get Tula's long body through the shaft. Then it's like I jump in time and space, and Tula's dead face is inches from mine. Her jaw drops open with this weird death rattle. Like a burp gone wrong.

Something about the shock of that is removed, because I'm still out of my body, even though the perspective has altered.

The next second, she plunges from view, and that's when I realise I'm holding her hands and she's taking me with her. Jolting back into myself was this most horrible unwelcome feeling. Like I'd been shaken in the middle of a dream, but I wasn't fully awake.

I let go of Tula's hands just in time to stop from being pulled down. For a long minute, I felt as though I'd lost something so important down that shaft. I honestly considered going head-first after it.

My body started convulsing. Laughing, and sort of crying at the same time. All my physical sensations got shaken back in, but too quickly in a way that felt icky and intrusive. I could smell something bad and feel the cool air of the cellar on my skin.

I turned back to where Paul was lying. Still naked. From this angle you could see the dusty corpse had an erection. I'd read about that in history books about hanging executions, but I didn't think it could occur in modern times. It was so complete-ly grotesque. Like even in death he was taunting me with his disgusting machismo.

I knew I had already committed a crime by moving Tula. I should finish the job.

But I just . . . couldn't. I couldn't go near him. I was so tired. I was staggering with exhaustion. It was the early hours of the morning. Somehow, in my drunken thought process it was log-ical to come back later. Deal with it then. I swear at that point, this made complete and utter sense.

But, of course, it was too late.

Bluey

I must have been on the road a few hours, when I took a long corner and noticed something wasn't right about how the canvas hung on my trailer. Pulled over. Climbed up to take a look and . . . that's when I found 'em. Paul and this Black girl. Never get over that. Never get over it . . . I'm still choked up thinking about it.

Dead. Both of 'em. I could tell before I even got close.

They looked like dusty lumps of meat.

I figured they must have gone up there drunk, for a laugh. Fallen asleep or something. Most people don't understand how much dirt the road train kicks up. Once you're out on the open highway, and you're hitting 100 kmph or so . . . you create your own dust storm. We're talking a cloud thick enough to choke you. Flying stones and whatnot. That's why road trains don't take livestock. And there was a truckie who towed a broken-down car back in the Nineties, who accidentally suffocated the two passengers.

So these two poor bastards . . . Paul Hunter and the girl. They'd been lying up there the whole while I'd been driving. Breathing in this cloud of dust.

I sat in the cab for a long time, with the dead bodies still on top of that trailer. Smoked all me tabs, and turned it all over in my mind.

Truth was, the truck wasn't exactly fair dinkum. I'd been running a little delivery service off the books for a month or so. Bottles of grog out to a few Aboriginal places on the way to Port Hedland.

I found myself remembering back when I was Beth and Lauren's age. Really thinking about what happened. I hadn't done that sort of remembering for years. Decades. Don't like to, if I'm honest, 'cause it leads to bad places. Everything that went wrong with me wife and family was down to thinking about that stuff, I reckon. When she left, I made a point of knocking all that on the head, you know? Stay in the moment, put one foot in front of the other.

But . . . if I hadn't been jailed as a kid . . . Nowadays I'd probably have been given community service. Or an alcohol programme. I dunno. Things were tougher back then. They didn't take into account if you'd been taken away from your mum as a little boy.

I let myself imagine, for a second, going back to jail. You don't want to know what goes on in an outback prison. Bad as the orphanages and some. When I'd finished thinking, I turned the road train around and drove back to The Gold Rush.

103

Craig stops winching whilst I'm hanging a clear seven metres above ground.

'Sorry,' he puffs. 'I can't feel my arms. Nearly halfway, though.'

'Craig,' I say. 'The distillery. There's no reason for a huge corporation to make a bit of pocket change selling illegal grog. Maybe the men you saw park up are security guards or something. Checking no one is trespassing.'

There's a loaded pause.

'Yeah, so I wasn't entirely honest with you about that. The van I told you about isn't parked up yet. It's about five minutes away on the mine road.'

'You lied to me?' I ask, uncertainly.

'I'm sorry, alright? I didn't think you'd agree to come out,' says Craig. The rope begins winding again, and I'm pulled up, powerless to stop it.

'That was my choice to make,' I tell him.

'I care about you. Get angry all you want, but people do care about you, Tara. Whether you like it or not.'

But he doesn't sound caring. He sounds . . . dramatic. Like he's acting a part.

'You need to lower me back down,' I tell him.

'No way.' There's something different about his voice now. 'I'm not letting you risk your life, for some girls who drank too much bootleg vodka.'

Bootleg vodka . . .

The next words out of my mouth, I regret, even as I say them.

'How did you know it was vodka?' The suspicion. The false casual note. It's all there.

The rope stops.

'Ah, I guess . . . that's what people bootleg, isn't it?'

We both know it isn't. Rum is the hooch of choice in these parts.

There's an eerie silence.

'Craig?'

But I know. I already know.

After all, he somehow knew exactly where to find the vent shaft, didn't he? I was so relieved, I never questioned how he'd located the chimney so quickly. But he couldn't possibly have tracked my footprints there.

Other things jump up for my attention.

Medika, begging me not to bring the police. Craig provided homebrew for Paul and his crew at high school. Another disturbing fact punches me right in the gut. The radio-in Craig made . . . I heard his voice. But there was no buzz of static.

What if . . .? I'm trying not to all out panic. What if he never made that call? That would mean no help is coming at all. It's just me, alone, hanging in the dark.

'I'm truly sorry, Tara,' comes Craig's voice. 'I thought we had something. Business first, you know how it is.'

The rope winches faster. A green light flares at my hip. My radio. I must be high enough for signal. I unhook it with shaking hands, inadvertently shining the tell-tale beam upwards.

'No radios, Tara.'

'Craig!' I hate the pleading tone in my voice. 'We can talk . . .'
In reply, there's the sound of a ratchet loosening.
Then the rope goes into free fall.

104

Lauren

I didn't sleep that last night. Ended up getting up and going out for a long walk. I think part of me wanted it to happen again. Like it did before. With Paul. The storm.

When I came back the sun was coming up, Beth was awake. Her shirt was super dirty, and covered in mud. Blood on her leg.

'Are you OK?' I asked her.

'Cleaning up after you.' She sounded mad. I couldn't handle it. Beth being mad with me.

I felt this . . . despair. Like everything good had been sucked right out of me. I had been swept along by this wild version of myself, and now I had to face the fact that unmedicated Lauren was crazier than she was fun.

I reached in my pocket for a package of pills, and stuffed a whole handful right in my mouth. But even as I did it, I knew it wasn't going to work anymore. This was the down part. And no matter how many tacks I threw on the road, it was coming for me like a motherfucking freight truck.

Beth watched me with this peculiar expression on her face.

'Have you been taking your medication?' she asked.

'No,' I admitted.

She shook her head like she was totally disgusted with me.

'We need to get out of here,' Beth said. 'Now. Bus leaves in half an hour.'

The idea of buying a ticket and finding a seat was so overwhelming I couldn't deal with it. I needed Beth. How could I cope without her?

Bluey

The more I thought about it, the more it didn't seem like it was really my *fault*, eh? Not even a blind drunk man would have lain on that canvas and been pummelled with flying grit and dust clouds. He would have sat up, tried to climb off. *Something*. The way Paul and the girl were . . . it was like they'd just lain there and taken it.

I was thinking other things too. Lot of thoughts rollin' around the old head, you know?

The canvas that attached to the trailer was held in place with big clips. If you take the first eight off, it drops and anything caught slides off. I'd done it a hundred times to clean off dust and dirt after a long trip.

And The Gold Rush had a street-level chute down into the cellar, with a padded mat at the bottom to stop rolling barrels getting damaged.

If I unlocked the hatch and unclipped the canvas, the bodies would slip down the beer ramp. I reckoned, if they weren't found until mid-morning, I could be back on the road. No one would know.

In the end it was easy. They slid out and off like I thought they would. But . . . they got dragged over a fair bit of debris along the way, and all the stones and stuff that caught in the roof rained down on them too.

All I ever wanted to do was buy some time, you know? I'm an old man, I won't last long anyhow. I've not had the official diagnosis, but you can hear me lungs aren't right. Haven't been for a while. Years mining underground, you know? Plus, the smoking probably doesn't help. Yeah. Looking back, it wasn't such a good plan. I hadn't thought it through, truth be told.

But I would never have done it if I'd known Lauren and Beth would be accused. That's why I went and told everything, to the lawyer, Mr Gottlieb. Couldn't have it on my conscience.

105

As I plummet downwards, all my police training about falling flies from my mind. I grip tight to the rope. But it's all over before I know it's happening. My body is jerked painfully, expelling all the air from my lungs, and my head whiplashes backwards.

The radio jerks from my hand, and I hear it smash below.

It takes me a moment to realise I'm still suspended, turning in space, my knuckles white on the rope. I turn my head to look down. The cave floor is still a long way beneath me. How far did I drop? Two metres? Three?

'Tara?' Craig's voice. I'm too confused to reply. The fall has knocked all logical thought out of me.

My waist jolts in the harness, and I'm moving up again. What is going on?

'Tara?'

'I'm here.' I force the words out, scanning the shaft. Too far to make contact with any walls. I'm completely at his mercy, suspended in mid-air. 'What's going on, Craig?'

'I needed enough cash to make a new start in the city,' he says, with a sigh, and I know with a sinking jolt that any pretence is over. 'You want to get out of this town, like I do.'

I don't reply.

'You had it right,' he continues. 'Paul and I were running an

409

illegal distillery out here. The caves made perfect conditions for brewing.' There's a pause. 'I figured all it would take was a little accident with a digger. The local people hardly ever used the site, and they'd get to buy our grog . . . you know? Tula was right behind it. She wanted money to start her business and she didn't think the law should discriminate against Aboriginals,' he adds. 'It was Tula who found Keira, Charlee and Medika to work for us.'

'Tula is Moodjana,' I say in disbelief. 'I can believe she would help you to manufacture grog. But damaging her people's sacred cave?'

There's a long pause and I wonder if I should have kept my mouth shut. A strangled sob echoes through the tunnel.

'We didn't know,' says Craig. 'I swear, Tara. We didn't know what the place meant to them. The girls all freaked out when they saw where they'd be working. Did a runner at the roadhouse on a supply run. I thought that was the end of it. But Paul tracked them down somehow. Brought them here without me knowing.'

I don't believe him, and I'm wondering why he's trying to convince me.

'How did the girls get methanol poisoning?'

'No idea,' says Craig a little too quickly. 'Probably drank the grog before it was ready.' He sighs deeply. 'I'd never ask you to cover for me, Tara. I'm going to skip town. Once I get you out, you can direct the air ambulance to those girls.'

But there is no air ambulance. Craig never made the call. He doesn't realise I know that too.

Which puts a far darker cast to his motives for winching me out. Only one reason. Craig is going to kill me.

The rope starts winding again, quicker this time. A window of starlight at the top is taking on a very different meaning.

I think through my options. Craig can shoot me point blank before I get within a metre of him. My only weapon is Connolly's bush knife, tucked into my waistband.

Cut the rope.

It's both a terrible idea, and the only option. What did Craig say? At fifteen metres I had a fifty per cent chance of survival. Every second I delay, the fall gets longer.

No time for mucking about, Tara.

I hold the blade against the thick climber's rope. A few good slashes and I'll be through.

I close my eyes, pulling to mind all the things I didn't do on the first drop. Relax your limbs, pull your head in.

I draw the knife across. One of three strands snaps free and the line jolts fractionally downwards.

'Tara?' The winding speeds up. 'Did something happen to the harness?'

Keep him talking.

'What about Paul and Tula?' I ask. 'How did they die?'

My ascent slows fractionally. 'That was nothing to do with me,' says Craig, a little too quickly.

I risk another slash and a second strand pings apart. But now it has its own momentum. My weight alone is breaking the small threads of what's left. I tuck my head in, but my body is a coiled spring. I drop another inch, and begin turning fast as the last strands unravel.

The rope snaps and down I go.

106

Beth

Lauren's father has tricked me into talking with him. I kind of admire his determination. I've been steadily refusing to see him. Then the police told me the state had allocated me a free lawyer. When I go into the boxy little interview room, there he is, Mr Gottlieb.

'Lauren's dying,' he says shortly.

I swallow. 'I'd like to go . . .' I tell the police officer.

He interrupts. 'I spoke to a man named, Robert "Bluey" Williams.'

That brings me up short.

'I think you protected Lauren,' continues Mr Gottlieb. 'Even when you could have gotten yourself out of trouble. I respect that. It shows you keep your word. You're a decent person. Better than I gave you credit for, maybe.'

I absorb this steadily. The police officer is looking at me questioningly.

'I'll stay for a few minutes,' I tell her. She nods and leaves us both alone in the room.

'Please,' says Mr Gottlieb. 'Sit down. I need your help.'

He pushes a phone towards me.

'This came through on the emergency frequency,' he says pressing play on a recording. 'A message from the police constable who Lauren was talking to in the hospital. Something about a distillery and vodka. All garbled up. No one can make sense of it, or track where it came from.'

I listen to a bunch of static and some barely decipherable sounds.

'How did you get this?' I ask.

'Let's just say, I don't play by the rules. Same reason I took Bluey for a few strong drinks before interviewing him about the case. That's how I realised you thought you were covering for Lauren.'

He retracts the phone looking tired. 'Winning cases is all about telling the right story. Good lawyers assemble the right angles, so the jury pick the correct ending. We get information however we can. And sometimes we accidentally stumble on the truth.' He gives me a small lopsided smile that makes him look younger and then it vanishes.

'So what do you make of the message?' The hope on his face breaks my heart.

'Lauren doesn't usually drink vodka,' I say finally. 'Not since the pledge night.' I'm speaking slowly. 'The only time I saw her drink vodka was . . .'

I stop, because I don't think I can tell him any more. I can't tell him my memory of Lauren picking up the vodka bottle from Tula's unconscious body and taking a swig.

I swore on the oath.

'The night of the lock-in, right?' presses Gottlieb.

I don't reply because I'm concentrating on shuffling the events like cards in a pack. Carefully. Methodically. Putting things in the right order. Fanning out possibilities.

I picture the vodka bottle in Lauren's hand. We never carried that brand in the bar.

The answer slides into place with pleasing logic. Tula must have brought her own alcohol to the pub. And where did she get it from? I don't recall seeing it sold in any of the stores in town.

Why was someone trying to report an emergency about that vodka?

That's when I remember all the posters and campaign materials down at the reserve. Methanol poisoning. Don't drink homebrew.

I feel like everything is crashing in my brain and it's too much.

'Mr Gottlieb, give me your phone,' I say.

His eyes widen.

'Give me your phone,' I repeat. 'Please,' I add remembering that part is important.

Wordlessly he passes it over. I punch in the search term to Google and slide it back to him.

He picks it up. Looks at the results. 'Methanol poisoning?'

107

I fall, tight with panic, barely managing to stop my arms windmilling.

The narrow crumbly tunnel I'm tumbling down runs at an angle, rather than straight vertical, and my taut body slams against every sharp rock. I've underestimated the distance Craig had already winched me up.

I slam down feet first, and as my legs crumple, my hips hit the ground next and pain bursts along my right side. The floor is far softer than I expected. Bouncy almost.

Before I have time to focus on what this means, I hear gun blast in the shaft above me. I roll to dodge a chunk of falling rock.

Out of range now, I lie, completely winded, a swelling lump to my temple.

How am I not dead? I manage a tentative examination of my injuries. My hands feel out a wet patch of blood at my hairline. An immediate tightness around my eye that suggests the beginnings of a sizeable bruise. But nothing spongey or shattered.

For a moment, I have the elated feeling of surviving disaster unscathed. Judging from the view up to the surface, I must have fallen at least ten metres. Laying my palms flat, I push to sitting by torturous degrees. My ankle pulses. Then, as if waiting for the right moment, blooms into awful pain.

I'm aware I'm sat on something soft. My strangely bouncy landing has been explained with another mystery.

Heaped in a pile where I fell are three dirty mattresses.

Did Medika move them to break my fall? She was too sick to speak, barely.

No time to think about that now. I look for my knife and see it broken to the side of me, the blade snapped to a useless nub. I grab for it anyway. Using the hilt to prop myself, I try to stand, a gasp spinning involuntarily from my mouth.

The shadow at the top of the shaft moves. Craig's coming to get me.

I'm suddenly weak with fear. There's no way out. I can't run.

Desperately, I look around the dingy cave for something to take Craig unawares with.

Places to hide. Not many. A rocky outcrop that I'll be found behind in moments. The distillation equipment. I remember the hazards I wrote in my notepad earlier. Could I use them in reverse to defend myself?

A ratcheting sound tells me time has run out. I spin around to see two police-booted feet belaying down the same winch system I was being pulled up by.

Seconds later Craig is in the cave, unclipping himself, gun in hand.

108

Lauren

I'm totally tired of people pulling me around. I've been wheeled into, like, seven different rooms, and since I can't see a thing, it's hard to know what's going on.

I heard them telling my dad I needed an injection, but because we were so remote, a drug was being flown in and couldn't be administered for several hours.

My dad started roaring at them, like what kind of place was this, and he would pay for it to be helicoptered.

'Mr Gottlieb,' said the doctor. 'Australia isn't a Third World country. Your money can't bring a dose of fomepizole any faster than we can.' You could tell he was totally sick of my dad at this point. I must have missed the next part because the doctor said: 'An infusion of ethanol is extremely dangerous. We'll be attempting to administer alcohol orally whilst we wait for the medication, but we need your daughter's cooperation.'

Next thing, a nurse or somebody is pushing something boozy smelling against my mouth, telling me to drink it. I shoved it away fast. Like, get that stuff away from me.

Then my dad is there, and he's like, 'Drink it, drink it.' Honestly. Like a crazy dream or something. And I don't know if it's being without the pills or what. But suddenly I can't trust anyone. Not even my dad. Like, 'Who are you?' I was screaming at him to get away.

'Please.' My dad was sobbing. 'Please, honey. You'll die. If you don't drink it, you'll die.'

I was still covering my mouth whilst my dad was demanding the medics declare me incompetent, so they could force me to take whatever was in the cup.

That's when I knew. He was trying to medicate me into being a good little girl again. It was a moment of total clarity in the weird floaty dark world of shapes and lights.

'I'm of sound mind and body,' I announced. 'You have no right to make me take anything without my permission. I don't want to drink that. And I don't want my dad here either.'

I hear people saying Dad has to leave or they'll call the police, and I have a right to refuse treatment – according to the law they can't force me.

109

For a long few seconds Craig and I look at each other. He doesn't raise his gun, but runs his hands through his hair, thoughtful.

'I can't go to prison, Tara,' he says, matter-of-factly. 'You know what they do to cops in jail. Illegal supply on the reserve is up to an eighteen-year sentence.'

'I think you murdered Paul and Tula,' I tell him.

'That was those backpacker girls. Nothing to do with me. Tara, you don't have to make this difficult.'

'Tula threatened to report you, didn't she? After you and Paul damaged the sacred cave?'

'I . . . Yeah.' He slumps a little. 'She kept going on about a big angry snake or something.' He sounds different. More vindictive. More self-pitying. He takes a breath. 'Tula was a lot smarter than Paul.' Craig looks annoyed at the memory. 'She knew I wouldn't let those girls go after they'd seen me. Tula went to the long grasses to get them somewhere safer, but I was waiting for her at the roadhouse where she parked her car. Number plate recognition.' He flashes me a cold grin. 'Handy being a cop sometimes.'

'You've been abusing your position all along, haven't you?' I accuse.

Craig throws out his hands. 'What could I do? Everyone turned on me. Paul started talking about leaving town. That might have worked for him. But every cop's DNA is on the system. And you can't clean a fucking *cave*.' There's a bitterness to his voice. 'After I drove Tula and the girls here, Paul was already there. I said, "Why don't we all calm down and have a drink? Work out what to do." I pulled out a bottle of the finished grog. The safe stuff. Poured us all a measure. Convinced Paul and Tula we needed to wait until morning. Give me and the girls time to scrub away the evidence. Made everyone promise not to talk.' He hesitates, looking strangely pleased with himself. 'When they weren't paying attention, I switched bottles. Topped up their drinks from the unfinished batch. They all drank it down and never suspected a thing. I thought I'd pretty much solved the problem. No one was gonna ask too many questions about some bad grog. They'd figure Tula and her friends had a party. Invited Paul. It was perfect.'

'Then you waited in Tula's car outside The Gold Rush,' I say piecing it together. 'You wanted to be sure the methanol had worked.'

He nods. 'When all the blokes rolled out in the early hours, laughing, I knew something was wrong. I saw Bluey's road train come back and unload something into the cellar.' He shakes his head. 'Gloved up, got the hatch open and couldn't bloody believe it. Only Bluey had keys to that hatch and the stupid old fella would probably spill our whole operation in a police interview. Best I could do was come back later, damage limitation. When Anderson sent me in, I just had time to move Paul's body into the bar to throw everyone off the scent, but Tula had vanished. I figured she'd show up dead someplace in a day or so. At least that part would look legit.'

'The toxicology report,' I say. 'You tampered with it, didn't you? Made it look like our forensics were second rate. So no one would see that Paul and Tula had lethal levels of methanol in their system when they died.'

'There you go, clever Tara. You're right. It wasn't exactly an accident. But I didn't want it to be this way,' he adds, tapping the gun against his leg.

'You know you can't use that?' I tell him. 'The bullets will ricochet against the cave walls.'

Craig's face twitches. 'Not if you stand still,' he decides. 'At point blank it will be clean and easy.' He pauses for emphasis. 'Else . . . you could get wounded, and maybe I wouldn't risk two shots. Maybe I'd leave you here with the other girls.' Something flares on his face. I wonder if he's remembering Charlee, who wasn't found dying with her friends.

'Only one of us is leaving this cave,' I tell him. 'And it's not going to be you.' I shuffle back, stepping over the wires leading to the generator.

Craig spreads his hands. 'There's no way out. I'm sorry. Really I am.' He looks thoughtful. 'You have to admit, Anderson's not all wrong about women on the force,' he says. 'Seriously, what chance do you have? You've managed to lose the gun you can't shoot straight. I'm a lot stronger.' He grins. 'What does that come down to? Your conversation skills?'

'Comes down to what I've been telling you meatheads since I joined the force.' I aim a sideways kick at the power line connecting the generator, jerking it free. 'Brain over brawn.'

'What are you doing?' There's a note of true panic in Craig's voice as the lights flicker and die.

The cave is plunged into total inky darkness.

IIO

Beth

Lauren's father got me to her bedside. Obviously. Don't ask me how, but I'm guessing money, threats or probably both.

He had already told me about Bluey's big confessional torrent. Mr Gottlieb had barely asked anything before Bluey blurted out how they died, and then came to be in the cellar. It was a relief to know that Lauren wasn't capable of what I thought.

Lauren is only partially conscious when I get to her, propped up in bed. I don't think she can see the bottle of vodka in my hand.

'Hey, Lauren.'

Her eyes flutter but don't open.

'Beth,' she says. 'They're trying to poison me. My dad is in on it.'

'I'm here now,' I tell her.

She smiles a little.

'Lauren, I don't have time to explain this,' I tell her. 'Do you remember the Alpha Sigma Psi oath? A sister asks, you have to drink.'

She frowns. 'Sure. Why?'

'Just . . . trust me, OK?'

I pour straight vodka into the plastic hospital cup by her bed, filling it almost to the brim, and push it into her limp hand. Her nose wrinkles at the smell.

'I . . . quit.' She even pulls a smile, which falters. 'Am I dying?' she asks.

'Not if I can help it,' I tell her. I raise the cup in her hand. 'Alpha Sigma Psi.'

'Alpha Sigma Psi,' she intones, letting me press the cup to her lips and tip the contents in.

I don't think anyone else in the world would have done it. There's no one else I can imagine who would accept a strong drink whilst semi-conscious in a hospital bed with paranoia and giant pharmaceutical withdrawal. But Lauren. God bless her. She drank it all down. Of course she did. I knew she would. We're besties.

'Hey, Beth,' she manages, swallowing. 'Dad told me about Bluey. Did you try to cover it up to protect me?'

I smile at her. 'If I told you, I'd have to kill you.'

III

The moment the cave goes black, everything changes. My senses switch. I feel the sandy ground beneath my feet. Taste the damp on the air.

I hear Craig crash about, presumably trying to find the generator. Silently, I step away, sensing where the wall starts and laying my hands against it. Before the lights died, I logged a route to the way I came in. Now just a few metres of narrow tunnel blocked by fallen rock. It's harder than I thought to navigate in pitch black.

'You've pissed me off now, Tara.' I hear Craig's voice come as a snarl. 'I know your arm's bad, I saw it. Reckon you must have concussion at least. That fall.'

I can picture his stance, poised for an answer that will never come.

'I'm not planning on staying in this shit-hole town,' says Craig. I hear his boots crunch, and I get the sense he's talking to alleviate his fear of the dark. 'Gonna get out of here. Reinvent myself. Wife. Family, all that. Not going to throw all that away for an accident, Tara. A stupid accident.'

I step softly. There's a smell of rich earth, from where the ceiling recently caved in.

A slim white-light beams from the other side of the cave.

Craig's turned on his phone flashlight. I stay completely still as it sweeps towards me.

I hear a sound like plastic tapping on rock. Then buzzing as electricity flows through wiring.

Fuck.

A weak light emits from an emergency lightbulb on the floor, partially illuminating the furthest rock face.

Back-up lighting. Faint but it won't stay that way.

The filaments are heating up, taking the glow steadily brighter.

I scoop up a handful of pebbles from the ground and hurl them into the start of the fallen tunnel, ducking behind the large rock for cover.

The light bounces towards the noise, and I see Craig, illuminated by his phone, walking into the narrowing route out.

I move fast, running and shouldering all my weight into one of the temporary buttresses. With my injury I don't have enough strength. The wooden strut shifts a tiny amount then no more.

Deeper in the partly collapsed tunnel, Craig spins around, as crumbling stones from above scatter harmlessly on his hair. A smile of victory spreads over his face.

'Sorry, Tara,' he says, raising his gun. 'It was a good plan . . .'

His expression changes, and I feel someone pitch in behind me. A body slams into the thick wooden buttress and I turn to see an unfamiliar girl has appeared from nowhere. She's wearing the same workwear as Medika and Keira. Her face is muddy, lined with exhaustion and dehydration. But her eyes are determined as she barges the post again. It's Charlee.

Craig lunges for us, but he's too late. Charlee has dislodged the support, and it cannons towards him. He puts up his hands on instinct, and the heavy wooden upright knocks him to the ground. His gun goes off and I push Charlee away from the entrance. Pain erupts in my calf.

The roof above Craig collapses. His arms cross to protect his face, but the falling rubble smacks them instantly back, felling him and pinning him under rocks. We both lie there on the floor of the cave, waiting for any sound Craig is still a threat. There's only the patter of settling soil. After a moment I risk sitting up. Charlee raises herself too. Where Craig once stood is a heap of dirt. Charlee's eyes shine with the exact strange mixture of horror and victory she must see in mine. We stare for moment before hugging each other, in sheer shocked relief.

'You saved me,' I whisper. 'Thank you.' I can feel her body, thin under the work clothes after days underground.

She's shaking uncontrollably. 'I didn't think anyone was looking for us,' she says, teeth chattering.

'You didn't drink the grog?' I deduce.

'I pretended. My aunty always told me not to trust police.'

I smile at that. 'You can trust some of us.'

She looks at my leg. 'Yeah. Is he dead?' Charlee's voice trembles.

In answer, a silent flow of blood streams from beneath the rocks that crushed Craig, pooling in the lower ground.

I suddenly feel very, very tired. I sit, and lean against the wall.

Somehow, it's becoming impossible to tell the dreams from reality. Or maybe the dreams have been the reality all along.

I close my eyes and when I open them, Charlee is kneeling next to me wrapping my leg.

'It's not bad,' she says. But I can tell from her voice she isn't telling the truth.

I've no idea how we're getting out of this cave. And I'm growing colder as the floor gets wetter.

Everything is blurry.

I don't know how long I've been out for, but my calf aches like a sore tooth and the smell of damp earth is horribly familiar.

I hear mumbled conversation. My hearing isn't so good.

'We're over here!' I hear Charlee shout back towards the entrance. 'It's OK,' she says. 'They'll be here soon.'

'Who?' I'm surprised enough to sit up a bit.

'Tara!' It sounds like Anderson's voice. For a moment I think I'm imagining things. When it comes again, I know for sure. Anderson is here. Somewhere.

I black out and then he's next to me, helping me up.

'Medika and Keira . . .' I say.

'They've been taken out already,' says Anderson. 'We'll have to wait and see how they go, but . . . they'll live, I think.'

I digest this. 'How did you find the sacred cave?' I ask him.

Anderson hesitates. 'Bit after you left, I went up to the mission. Just to check if anyone had something to tell me.'

I cough. 'I thought asking for information in the Moodjana community was a fool's errand and a dusty road?'

'Yeah, well. I wasn't going to just hare off in the vague direction of Wooloonga Ridge, like a certain young policewoman I could mention. Wisdom of age and all that. Lucky for me, this time an Indigenous lady came forward. First time that's ever happened.'

'Which lady?'

In reply I hear a woman's voice. 'You alright, Tara?'

It's Mirri. I make out the contrast of her white-streaked hair in the dark. She must have helped Anderson find another way in.

'I'm OK,' I tell her weakly.

'She offered to take me where the sacred site was. And based on her information of illicit grog, I had Danno take another look at the toxicology report,' adds Anderson. 'He noticed it had been tampered with. Put a few things together. Thought I'd best get out here sharpish.'

He shines his torch around. The beam falls on Craig's unconscious form.

'I see your superior communication skills came in handy,' he deadpans.

'Is he dead?'

'Don't worry yourself about that.' Anderson's tone says it all. 'Let's get you out.'

I black out again and everything else comes in patches. At some point there's a stretcher. And Mirri taking my hand.

'Copper thought you were in trouble in the cave,' she says. 'Needed someone to show him where it was. I told him, "I'm coming with you,"' her hand folds around mine, '"that's our Tara down there."'

112

Lauren

I feel like I have been run over by a ten-tonne truck. Everything hurts. Mostly my head. It's like I have a solid steel band of pain between my skull and brain. Two months of hangovers catching up with me. Guess I got what I deserved.

'The strangest thing,' a doctor is saying in a suspicious tone, 'is somehow some strong alcohol got into her system. It probably saved her life. She was a few millilitres of formic acid away from total organ shutdown.'

There's a silence, then I hear my dad clear his throat. 'She'll be alright?'

I can hear a different voice. A woman talking in an Australian accent. 'There's extensive kidney damage,' she says. 'Most likely there'll be some brain injury, too, but we won't know how much for a while. She's blind in one eye, and it's probably too late for the other one. But she's going to live.' There's a pause. 'The mystery is how she might have ingested methanol. Not been a case in the five years I've been at this hospital.'

'Lauren.' My father's voice, strained. I feel two warm hands taking mine. 'It's going to be OK, honey.'

This is when I realise they are talking about me.

They've totally got some stuff wrong, because I'm not blind. Or brain damaged. Thoughts are . . . a little soupy, is all.

That's when I open my eyes to find I can't see. Just some lights and shapes.

'Hey there,' says the Australian woman's voice cheerily. 'Look who's decided to wake up.'

'Lauren?' My father sounds like a little boy.

'Hello, Daddy.' I press his hand. 'I can't see you,' I add, choking down a sob.

'I know, honey. I know. When we fly you home we'll get that looked at. Best doctors. OK?'

'You're flying me home?'

'Soon as we can.' He pats my hand. Doors bang and I get the sense the nurse has left us alone.

'Won't there be a court case?'

'I'll get you out of here. I promise.'

'I don't think . . .' It's not easy to find the words. 'I'm pretty sure you're not going to fix this with money, Daddy. I'm sorry,' I add. 'I let you down again. I just . . . get overexcited.'

There's a long pause.

'You know, you remind me a lot of your mother,' he says eventually.

I've never heard him say that. There was always a quiet understanding this would be a bad thing.

'She would get excitable too,' he continues. 'It was one of the things I loved about her most.' He has this soft tone in his voice that makes my heart break.

'Then why did you . . .' My voice catches. 'Why did you try *so hard* to stop me being like that?' Tears are falling down my cheeks.

He takes a shuddering breath. 'After your mom did what she did . . .'

'You can say it, Daddy. You can say suicide.'

'After your mom's suicide. Or. Right before. That's how she was. Glowing. Like a beautiful painting all lit up. Almost too bright to be real. I guess maybe that's why . . .' He chokes up. 'Maybe why she couldn't stay, you know? She was too good to last.' He sobs.

I pull his hands tighter into mine. He squeezes my fingers.

'Anyway,' he says, fighting to keep his voice steady. 'You can see why . . . When you acted that way. When you were like that. I was so frightened you would leave me too. Because if I had lost both of you, I would have gone out of my mind. I should have been stronger. You deserved better. I'm sorry. I'm so, so sorry.'

'It's OK, Daddy,' I tell him. 'You did the best you could. You didn't come from a perfect place, and Grandpappy came from worse.'

He's silent again. 'He never spoke about it,' he says quietly. 'Let everyone think he left before the worst things happened. But after he died, I saw the immigration dates on his green card.' He takes another breath.

It's like my thoughts and vision are overlapping. I have a strange shape that twists into a memory. If I focus, some shapes get clearer edges. At least I think they do.

Grandpappy in his exclusive country club. *My little paradise*, he called it. Heaven on earth. But he was always so on edge. Like someone might find him out.

I never thought about how that might have affected *my* dad, because he seemed invincible. But I guess at one time, he was soft too. Like in Dreamtime when time was fluid and the spirits left tracks. Someone left tracks on my dad, before he hardened up. And maybe some of those tracks were from people he'd never even met. Like, ancestors and stuff. Could be . . . they left tracks on me too.

113

Since the hospital is so small, I end up about three rooms down from Lauren. I'm on a ward, but with so few people, it's just me in here. Me and five empty beds. My leg is strapped up.

I'm trying to work out the TV when Anderson walks in with a bunch of flowers I recognise from the meagre hospice shop on the way in.

'Got you these,' he says, waving them vaguely, then striding over and depositing them at the side of the bed as if pleased to be rid of the task. 'I'm not the only one who brought you something, I see.'

My bedside table is layered with gifts. Mainly from well-wishers in the Moodjana community.

'Leg on the mend?' he asks.

'Not bad. How are the girls?'

'Good. Back home. No long-term problems. Craig left the girls in the cave to die, and when her friends got sick, clever Charlee worked out why. Spent the whole time giving little sips from two bottles that hadn't been shipped out. Stopped them getting as bad as Lauren, but she didn't have enough alcohol to hold it off forever. Brave girl that,' he adds, his eyes misting slightly. 'She could have left. Gone out into the desert, and probably survived long enough to get to safety. But Charlee wouldn't leave the other girls.'

'Her cousins would have done the same for her,' I tell him. 'How about Lauren? How's she going?'

'She's alright,' he says slowly. 'Regained vision in one of her eyes, which was unexpected.' He sits down.

'Just the one eye?' I try to sit upright.

'Yeah, she'll have depth-perception problems. But one is a lot better than none,' he says with unnecessary certainty. 'They'll have to wait and see for brain damage. Let's face it,' he lowers his voice and glances to the door, 'a girl like Lauren, it's not like you could tell either way, is it?'

I smile. Same old Anderson. 'She's sharper than you think,' I tell him.

He pulls up a chair, and clears his throat, his face becoming serious. 'Right then. Time to get down to it. You went against my specific orders, which is a disciplinary offence. The drill is I'd recommend you don't progress any further in the force. Ever.'

'Yes, sir,' I say miserably, thinking he could have saved it until I was healed at least.

'But, you made some good decisions, Tara, I'm proud of you. Charlee says you talked Craig out of a shoot-out, and your notepad shows sensible observations under exceptional stress. You kept going when other people would have admitted defeat. Courage, resilience. They're seen as old-fashioned by the smart folk who favour fast-track training. But *I* think they're worth a merit pass. Plus, you stole Connolly's car, which more or less wipes out any bad behaviour, in my book.' He winks. 'You should have seen him. I thought he was going to have a bloody heart attack.' Anderson's face lights in a brief, uncharacteristic grin.

'Did he get his car back?'

'Ah, yeah,' Anderson waves a dismissive hand. 'Superficial damage where Craig had driven it away over some rocky ground. You did good out there, Tara. Real good. And . . . it so happens we've got a job going locally for a constable, if you're interested. Turns out the last fella in that position was a bit of a mongrel.'

I consider this. 'You'd have to accept women have skills to bring, and policing is not all about how hard you can thump a bad guy.'

He nods. 'Noted. Might need some help from you there. Old dog, new tricks and all that. But I'm willing to learn. That work for you?'

'Yes, sir.' I think for a moment. 'One last thing.'

'I'm listening.'

'The internet page I found, with the Mining Corporation digger,' I say. 'It was blocked for sexual content and I can't figure out why.'

'For a young person you're not very tech savvy,' says Anderson. 'I took a look on the dark web. It was a blog, written by a young Moodjana fella, criticising the Mining Corporation. My guess is some PR whiz from the mine wanted it down quick. Reported it as sexually explicit. That's an automatic take-down while search engines investigate. And there's a long queue.'

'Is that illegal?' I ask hopefully.

'No law against being a dickhead, Harrison.'

I absorb this.

'You planning on visiting your Moodjana friends when you get out?' Anderson enquires casually.

I hesitate. 'No firm plans, sir.'

'Well, I suggest that's where you go as soon as you're discharged. No point staying in town if you don't see your fella, eh?'

'Which fella?' I try to sit up, but the cast stops me.

'The good-looking lad who was here. Dark skin.' Anderson clicks his fingers. 'Jarrah.'

'Jarrah? I didn't see him.' I can't hide my smile and Anderson beams unexpectedly. 'I'm sure he'll be back.' He lifts his arm like he might want to pat my hand but thinks better of it. 'Good,' he repeats. 'Well, I'll bugger off, Harrison. You get some rest.'

114

Maybe there is something in all this shared trauma stuff. Because Beth and I are closer than ever. What we went through has changed us in ways only we understand.

My dad, well, he can't help being my dad. He found a surgeon in LA willing to swear on a Bible that he's the only person on the whole planet offering progressive treatment for eyesight or something. Petitioned senators and everything to get me airlifted back to the States on some humanitarian clause in the Australian constitution.

From there, Dad planned to use every legal loophole to prevent extradition. He'd win, too. Always does.

I said no to all that. I think Dad is finally accepting it.

Being close to death . . . it's given me this bravery I never had before, you know? I know that sounds totally cliché, but it does change you. Nearly dying does change you.

First off, I want to go back and learn from those Moodjana girls. I am totally embarrassed to see now, how crazy I must have seemed. Coming from this miserable lonely place, telling those girls how great it was to be me. They've got a lot to teach me about family.

Before that, though, I want to face up to what I did. I feel as though I've got a second chance. The thing that happened at college . . . we were all completely traumatised. No one meant for that to happen. It truly was a terrible accident and no one was to *blame* exactly. The girl who died could only have had a few sips more of alcohol than everyone else. But why didn't any of us speak up? We never questioned what had always been done.

So, I want to be accountable here. Take responsibility for what happened and get the message out.

We got our own back on those guys in The Gold Rush. We humiliated them. We took pictures. And you know what? It didn't feel good. Unless you transform that trauma, it gets passed on and on.

Since putting them on the truck was my idea, not Beth's, she won't be charged with manslaughter. Though she will be in the frame for obstruction of justice. From what I understand, we'll most likely get some kind of community service. Diminished responsibility. Maybe a couple weeks' jail time, but they think the judge will probably have a lenient view of vulnerable young women.

Dad thought a good lawyer could totally get Beth off completely, but he wasn't the right man for the job. Conflict of interest. He wanted to represent Bluey.

Beth

My sorority sisters raised $40,000 dollars to cover my court costs. They got this incredible lawyer who was an expert on dissociative personality disorders and fugue state, and basically kept bringing out psychiatric studies until the defence collapsed.

I learned more about myself during that trial than I would have in ten years of therapy.

My lawyer explained how the combination of my violent upbringing and hazing PTSD had pushed me into an artificially constructed personality forged by my unique deep traumas. Now I know what was happening, I can start deconstructing and getting back in touch with feelings and stuff. I don't think I'll ever be exactly like other people. But that's cool too.

Lauren and I refused to testify against one another, which should have been bad for both of us. But for some reason the court took a dimmer view of her. Despite her lawyer delivering a boatload of social media showing how she'd been harassed and the provocation would easily cause a reasonable person to lose control, the townspeople of Dead Tree Creek had made up their minds. Guilty of manslaughter. She won on appeal, though, and was bailed in between times, so ultimately got thirty days in jail.

Between you and me, I think the sorority might have been involved in that conviction reversal. We're their golden girls currently, for keeping our oaths under exceptional circumstances. They're offering me internships in the Senate and Pentagon. But . . . High places have a lost their charm for me. My time with the Moodjana people has made me reconsider my priorities. I don't think a single one of the Indigenous girls would have done what we did on the pledge night. That feels important.

Lauren and I are looking for ways to learn from the women around here, whilst hopefully helping them too. Bridging the gap between the political system and the local people. There's too many voices not being heard. Besides, this place has grown on me. I might even go on a date with Mike.

To say Lauren is back to her happy self is an understatement. Only Lauren could see the loss of an eye as a positive thing. She talks about how old Norse gods gave an eye for wisdom and this to her is very symbolic. Accessorising different eyepatches is her new hobby, even though she doesn't really need one, and she's looking to start a business working with Indigenous fabrics and designers.

When it comes to Paul, though, she's philosophical and has elected to remember him fondly. A love affair that didn't last. I always admired that about Lauren. She makes her own reality.

Mike

No one starts out at the mine, thinking they'll be there for life. You leave school, figure it's good money whilst you work out what to do. A month becomes a year. You're spending a lot of your cash in the pub. Before you know it, you're in your thirties, laughing at the newbies who say they'll do a few weeks then go train for something better. But this whole thing with Paul, it's made me think there's more to life than digging gold out of the ground, you know? Few of the other blokes too. We're thinking about getting out. Doing something different. Growing stuff, instead of tearing it up.

Bluey

They told us in the orphanage that sometimes in life, you get angels. Never happened for me before. But Mr Gottlieb showed up and offered to take my case. Reckon he gave me the court hearing I should have got the first time around. I never saw myself as a victim before. Just thought I was a bad boy, you know? Mr Gottlieb talked for a long time about how the Stolen Generation was a holocaust and the country owed me a debt it could never repay. He had the whole jury in tears, no joke. At the end of it all, the judge stood and apologised to me for what the Australian government had done. Can you believe it? A judge apologising to old Bluey. Wig on and everything.

After they acquitted me, Mr Gottlieb set me up with a service called Link-Up. They're gonna see if they can find any relatives I might have, since Mr Gottlieb got hold of paperwork I thought was lost. He doesn't give up, that bloke, I'll tell you that. Doesn't give up. Must be in the blood or something. Mr Gottlieb found the adoption papers they'd told me never existed.

I welled up, reading that Certificate of State Adoption, I don't mind telling you. Hands were shaking everything. Someone had written 'fair-skinned child, removal from parents advantageous'.

Then just above. My name. My real name. The one me mum and dad gave me.

115

The community hall is full of familiar smiling faces. Despite my leg not being completely healed, I've managed to stand for a good hour, answering questions. The women and girls clap as I finish. I see Charlee, Medika and Keira smiling at the back. Jarrah comes to help me off stage.

'You look different,' he says, tilting his head. 'Did you change your hair?'

'Charlee did it,' I admit. 'She used some special oil you can't buy in shops. Takes the frizz out.'

'Oh.' He takes it in. 'Suits you. You match the uniform now, I reckon.'

'Is that a good thing?'

His mouth twists mischievously. 'I'm getting used to it.'

'Thanks heaps.'

'OK, OK, it's growing on me. Bossy police lady.' He smiles at me. 'You did great on stage, Tara,' he says. 'I know you were nervous.'

'I'd like to come regularly if you'll have me. Hopefully get people to see they can trust the police.'

We walk on towards the edge of the mission. A pack of kids hurtle past on bikes, followed by an excited dog.

Jarrah gives me a sly look. 'More of our young girls, probably

442

thinking about being police officers now.'

'Tell them the pay's bad and the uniform's bloody hot.'

He laughs.

'Seriously, though,' I say. 'Send anyone interested my way. It's not the easiest work. But I wouldn't do anything else.' I sigh. 'You think I can make a difference?'

I'm remembering tearing about with Yindi, completely free. Every year older felt like more doors shutting.

Jarrah considers. 'One of the Elders, Jimmy, tells a story about when he was a little kid. His mum used to cut the wings off the chicken before it went in the pot.' He mimes chopping with his hand. 'Jimmy asked, "Mum, why you wasting good meat?" His mum said, it was the way her mum did it. Must be the right way. So Jimmy goes, asks his grandma. She said, it was the way her mum had always done it. She learned it from her. So now Jimmy goes to his great-grandma. Real old lady. You know what she said?' He pauses for effect. 'She only had the one small pot.' He smiles. 'Some of us are lucky, eh? Some of us had a great-grandma with a bloody big pot.' He shrugs. 'And . . . Some of us didn't.' He looks at me. 'But we can all choose how to cut up our chicken.'

'Your metaphor just got weird.'

He laughs. 'You'll come back soon? Not gonna make me wait three years for you this time?'

We've reached the edge of the mission. Both of us stop walking.

'No,' I say, turning to him. 'I'm not going to make you wait three years.'

Jarrah leans to kiss me goodbye.

A car horn blasts. We spring apart, and I see Anderson, pulling up in his squad car.

'I know we're building relations with the Indigenous

community, Tara!' bellows Anderson, through his rolled down window. 'But remember you're in uniform.'

'Guess I'll catch you later,' says Jarrah. We grin at one another.

'Guess so.' I head for the idling car. 'Thanks for the lift,' I tell Anderson, sliding into the passenger seat. 'My car gets repaired next week.'

'You'd be better off sending that bloody wreck to the scrapyard. Buy yourself something decent,' grumbles Anderson. 'Oh,' he adds. 'On that note, I've got something for you.'

'For me?'

'Don't get too excited, it's a work thing.' He reaches into the backseat and hands me a heavy box.

I open it. 'A new gun?' I'm confused.

'Turns out you're not the only one to struggle with a standard issue firearm,' says Anderson. 'It's not well publicised, but it's permitted for officers who need it to use a 9mm instead of a 40 caliber. Connolly's got one,' he says. 'Should fix your recoil problem. Now all you got to do is shoot straight.'

'Thanks.' I fit it in my palm and my finger slides full round the trigger with ease. I put it back in the box, smiling. 'Choose a bigger pot,' I say.

'What?'

'Nothing, sir. Just something Jarrah said.'

'You two back on again, are you?'

I look at him in surprise.

'What makes you think we were on in the first place?'

'That young lad was the first to your hospital bed after you were admitted. He looks at you same way I look at my wife.' He grins. 'Why d'you think I sounded the car horn so loud? Keep him guessing, eh?' He winks.

'I never credited you with that much sensitivity, sir,' I say dryly.

Anderson laughs aloud in response. 'I have my moments, Harrison. I have my moments.'

I look in the rear-view mirror to see Jarrah, watching us, with a smile on his face. I hold up my hand to wave. Anderson puts his foot on the accelerator. We drive out in a cloud of red dust, the land enveloping us in a long goodbye.

Acknowledgements

I feel so lucky to be a writer, because I never stop learning. I also get the chance to work with amazing editors, Emad Akhtar, Celia Killen and Lucy Frederick, and of course, my amazing agent Piers Blofeld, who have made my writing immeasurably better.

For this book, my most significant acknowledgement goes to the First Nations people of Australia, who have left me awestruck, envious and humbled. Special thanks to the individuals whose expertise and wisdom helped shape this book. Aunty Munya Andrews for her fascinating insight into Dreamtime culture (mostly how vast, complex, and weighty this subject is – a lifelong study wouldn't barely scratch the surface), and her patient explanation of totem animals to the uninitiated. Also to Jackie Tapia at Evolves Australia – an incredible resource dedicated to spreading knowledge of all aspects of Aboriginal culture.

Blood Sisters has been a humbling journey coming to terms with my own privilege as a person born with white skin in a colonial country. This came up in many painful and, frankly, embarrassing ways whilst writing this book, and I'm indebted to my editors for helping me work this through. Also to the many research accounts and Indigenous authors who helped me begin to fill in the huge gaps in my knowledge of historical genocide and apartheid in Australia. It's awful to admit I had no idea there were many different Indigenous cultures and languages, and the barest appreciation of the First Nation's stoic commitment to their land and ecosystem in the face of relentless attack and disdain. A huge amount of research on this topic, interviews with native people, countless personal accounts of life as a First Nations person in Australia has only proved to me how little I know. My favourite resources were the beautiful poetic books of Alexis Wright and the works of Archie Weller. Deborah Bird Rose's anthological study *Dingo Makes Us Human*, provided an in-depth explanation of the skin system, which proved too complex to make it into the final cut, but many other insights did. Thanks to Coral Edwards and Peter Read, who compiled the heart-breaking *Lost Children*, documenting the experiences of thirteen First Nations children who were stolen from their families, and their struggles and triumphs in reconnecting. Jane Harrison's *Stolen* was also a poignant look at the same topic for which I thank her. In contrast, *Growing Up Aboriginal in Australia* by Anita Heiss, collates glowing accounts of happy kids with joyful networks of cousins, which informed my book, and made me realise what my children are missing. Thank you for making me try harder to cement an extended family, and I live in the hope of improving on my nuclear upbringing and passing the baton for my children to do better than me. 'What does it profit a man to gain the world but lose his soul?' really couldn't be a more fitting description of colonialism.

Additionally, I am indebted to Australian linguist, Professor Peter Austin, who fascinated me by sharing a small portion of his expertise on the lost languages of his native country. He was extremely kind in innovating the fictional names of the languages and communities mentioned in this book, and I am in awe of his knowledge.

In policing aspects, several important people helped me with key details. Senior Constable Adam Winter, who polices a vast district with one other officer from the small town of Jeramungup several hundred kilometres west of Perth, with a population of 253. Thanks so much Adam for your fascinating stories of life Down Under.

Enormous thanks to Jade Sorin, Intelligence Coordinator for the Engagement and Hate Crime Unit in NSW, who runs a police team dedicated to making the world a better place. Her insights into relations with First Nations communities have been invaluable, as were the personal accounts of being a woman on the force, from the heavy gun belts to the experiences engaging with minorities.

I'd also like to pay homage to the documentary makers of 'Hotel Coolgardie'. This incredible real-life fly-on-the-wall of two backpackers and their time in an Outback pub was one of my first inspirations for the book. I recommend everyone to watch this controversial depiction of a not-so-typical Aussie bar.

Thank you as always to my incredible partner Simon Avery, who is always my last reader, and my sister Susannah Quinn, who also happens to be my favourite author. To my parents for all their love and support, and my amazing children Ben and Natalie.

Oh, and one last thank you to our battered old Audi on which Tara's car is based. All the loveable flaws are true to life. We still see the old girl being driven round town by our friend Andy, who kindly loans it back to us occasionally, so thanks to him too.

Credits

Cate Quinn and Orion Fiction would like to thank everyone at Orion who worked on the publication of *Blood Sisters*.

Editorial
Emad Akhtar
Celia Killen
Lucy Frederick

Copy-editor
Jon Appleton

Proofreader
Linda Joyce

Editorial Management
Jane Hughes
Charlie Panayiotou
Tamara Morriss
Claire Boyle

Publicity
Leanne Oliver

Audio
Paul Stark
Jake Alderson
Georgina Cutler

Contracts
Anne Goddard
Ellie Bowker
Humayra Ahmed

Design
Nick Shah
Nick May
Joanna Ridley
Helen Ewing

Production
Ruth Sharvell
Fiona McIntosh

Sales

Jen Wilson
Victoria Laws
Esther Waters
Frances Doyle
Ben Goddard
Jack Hallam
Anna Egelstaff
Inês Figueira
Barbara Ronan
Andrew Hally
Dominic Smith
Deborah Deyong
Lauren Buck
Maggy Park
Linda McGregor
Sinead White
Jemimah James
Rachael Jones
Jack Dennison
Nigel Andrews
Ian Williamson
Julia Benson
Declan Kyle
Robert Mackenzie
Megan Smith
Charlotte Clay
Rebecca Cobbold

Finance

Nick Gibson
Jasdip Nandra
Elizabeth Beaumont
Ibukun Ademefun
Afeera Ahmed
Sue Baker
Tom Costello

Inventory

Jo Jacobs
Dan Stevens

Marketing

Katie Moss

Operations

Sharon Willis

Rights

Susan Howe
Krystyna Kujawinska
Jessica Purdue
Ayesha Kinley
Louise Henderson